Advance praise for Claudia Gray's

The Late Mrs. Willoughby

"What a terrific concept—to take a cadre of beloved literary characters, wrap them up in a murder, and extract a wonderful investigative duo from the bunch! Claudia Gray's *The Late Mrs. Willoughby* is a clever, delightful treat for Jane Austen lovers. Ms. Austen would be thrilled!"

—Colleen Cambridge, author of
Mastering the Art of French Murder

"Absolutely delightful! Fans of Jane Austen and historical mysteries will fall in love with this series. Gray remains true to Austen's style and intent for her beloved characters while still adding her own spin on them and their progeny—one that is both refreshing and absorbing. I'm already looking forward to the next installment."

—Anna Lee Huber, *USA Today* bestselling author

"Delightful. Claudia Gray is systematically taking out all the unpleasant characters in Jane Austen's novels, and I am here for it." —Juneau Black,
author of the Shady Hollow Mystery series

Praise for Claudia Gray's

The Murder of Mr. Wickham

"A well-done pastiche that balances menace with wit, recrimination with reconciliation, sin with redemption and justice with mercy." —*The Wall Street Journal*

"Had Jane Austen sat down to write a country house murder mystery, this is exactly the book she would have written. Devotees of Austen's timeless novels will get the greatest possible pleasure from this wonderful book. Immense fun and beautifully observed. Delicious!"
—Alexander McCall Smith

"What a splendid conceit! . . . There's so much fun to be had in this reimagined Austen world—and the mystery is so strong—that one can only hope, dear reader, that more books will follow." —*Booklist* (starred review)

"An astonishingly convincing and tremendously entertaining pastiche. . . . Written elegantly, with a keen eye for Regency detail as well as a deep knowledge and affection for Ms. Austen's oeuvre, this is an entirely plausible continuation of the Austen canon that stands as a worthwhile read in its own right." —Criminal Element

"Who would *not* want to read a book in which one [of] literature's most notorious rakes meets his final demise? . . . A delightful Agatha-Christie-meets-Jane-Austen romp."
—Laurel Ann Nattress, Austenprose

Claudia Gray

The Late Mrs. Willoughby

Claudia Gray is the pseudonym of Amy Vincent. She is the author of *The Murder of Mr. Wickham* and the writer of multiple young adult novels, including the Evernight series, the Firebird trilogy, and the Constellation trilogy. In addition, she's written several Star Wars novels, such as *Lost Stars* and *Bloodline*, and is one of the story architects of the High Republic series. She makes her home in New Orleans with her husband, Paul, and assorted small dogs.

claudiagray.com

THE LATE MRS. WILLOUGHBY

The Late Mrs. Willoughby

Claudia Gray

VINTAGE BOOKS
A DIVISION OF PENGUIN RANDOM HOUSE LLC
NEW YORK

Library of Congress Cataloging-in-Publication Data
Name: Gray, Claudia, author.
Title: The late Mrs. Willoughby / by Claudia Gray.
Description: First edition. | New York : Vintage Books, [2023].
Identifiers: LCCN 2022038311 (print) | LCCN 2022038312 (ebook)
Classification: LCC PS3607.R38886 L38 2023 (print) |
LCC PS3607.R38886 (ebook) | DDC 813/.6—dc23
LC record available at https://lccn.loc.gov/2022038311
LC ebook record available at https://lccn.loc.gov/2022038312

Vintage Books Trade Paperback ISBN: 978-0-593-31383-1
eBook ISBN: 978-0-593-31384-8

Book design by Steve Walker

vintagebooks.com

Printed in the United States of America
1st Printing

For my family

THE LATE MRS. WILLOUGHBY

October 1820

Mr. Jonathan Darcy of Pemberley had, to his parents' delight, been invited to visit some highly suitable friends in Devonshire. The friends in question had been deemed by them "highly suitable," a judgment that would have been shared by nearly all of society. They were young men of good breeding and fortune, all of whom had known Jonathan at school, gathering at the recently inherited estate of the eldest among them.

To Jonathan, they were not suitable in the slightest. He was not certain that the young men even fulfilled any proper definition of friendship. But the invitation had so pleased his mother and father—who had, for so long, been deeply concerned about his social connections, or rather by their nonexistence—that Jonathan had not had the heart to refuse it. Thus to Devonshire he must go.

"How good it is that you are able to see more of the country," enthused his mother, Elizabeth, who was looking over the clothing the valet had set out for packing. "There is life in England beyond Hertfordshire, Derbyshire, and London, loath though Londoners are to admit it. First Surrey, then Devonshire."

"I hardly think the Surrey trip should be counted," said Jonathan's father, Fitzwilliam, who stood in the doorway of his son's room. "Given the unfortunate event that transpired there, the entire journey would be as well forgotten."

"I cannot agree," Jonathan ventured. "Regardless of what happened, I *did* see Surrey."

Father did not quite smile, but he came close. "Quite so. I stand corrected."

In truth, Jonathan would have argued with the entirety of his father's statement; he had no wish to forget that trip, given how interesting it had proved, and the true friendship he had forged there with one Miss Juliet Tilney. But young men could not speak of friendship with young women without exciting parental thoughts of matrimony, and he had no desire to either enthrall his mother or dismay his father by making such a premature suggestion.

And the "unfortunate event" in question had been the murder of Jonathan's uncle George Wickham. Although Jonathan felt no strong grief for his uncle—a man both dishonest and discourteous—it would be extremely improper to admit as such, even to his mother and father, who had yet stronger reasons for disliking Mr. Wickham. A great deal of propriety seemed to be rooted in not admitting things everyone knew to be true.

The great pleasure of his journey to Surrey had been investigating the murder alongside Miss Tilney. Learning more about the other houseguests—their suspects—had sometimes been difficult, and perhaps impolite, but it had been undeniably fascinating. Furthermore, their investigation had prevented a great injustice from being done. It was both the most interesting and, to Jonathan's mind, worthwhile experience of his life.

Unfortunately, his parents had insisted it would be improper for him ever to speak of it.

"You will need more than this, surely." Mother frowned as she counted his coats yet again. "Will you not stay the month? You were invited for that duration."

"I had thought to return after two weeks or so," Jonathan

said. He had privately calculated that one week and four days could be honestly described as *two weeks or so.* "There is no cause for me to stay so long."

"Nor any cause for you to return so early." Father shook his head. "One cannot cut one's visit short without a worthy excuse, and you have none."

Never before had Jonathan had cause to regret matriculating at Oxford early. Had he not done so, he would be returning to his college at this time of year. There, he could avoid most social situations by holing up at the Bodleian. But earning his degree had cost him that sanctuary.

His mother, more sensitive to Jonathan's character, gave him a reassuring smile. "If you absolutely despise it there, you may write us to that effect, and we will invent an excuse so impeccable even your father could not object." Father looked as though he wished to object immediately, but he kept his peace as Mother continued, "Yet I dare to hope that you will find it more pleasurable than you now fear."

Jonathan knew full well that he would not, but he had no socially valid reasons for refusal. If this trip had to be endured, so be it.

Miss Juliet Tilney of Gloucestershire had, to her parents' dismay, been invited to visit a highly unsuitable friend in Devonshire.

Her father, Henry Tilney, shook his head as his daughter held up that gown and this, choosing favorites to take on the journey. "I mean no disrespect to Mrs. Brandon, but it must be acknowledged that the woman is a murderess."

"You cannot be afraid for me," Juliet protested, frowning

at the pale green dress she had liked so much more just days before. "It is not as though Marianne Brandon goes about slaughtering people wherever she may wander."

"Do not be impertinent." Henry Tilney was in fact quite fond of impertinence—both his own and that of others, if phrased with enough justice and wit—but was stricter with his daughter in this regard. "No, I have no fear for your person. Your reputation, however, could be in greater danger."

This won him a censorious look from Juliet's mother, Catherine. As an authoress, she could be more imaginative than most and could put herself in the place of another more easily. "Society should not punish Mrs. Brandon for her action. She only did what she was forced to in order to escape"—she paused, searching for phrasing that could be spoken aloud in front of her daughter—"an act of terrible brutality. The law found her behavior to be fully justified."

"Rightly so," her father concurred. "However, one cannot expect society to be equally generous."

"Society *should* be." Her mother put her hands on her hips. "Just as we should pattern our actions on what we know to be right and just, not on what the small-minded among us may say."

To anyone who did not know him well, Juliet's father's expression would have appeared very stern indeed. "Which one of us is the clergyman?"

"Based on our words alone, I am sure nobody would know." Her mother had begun to smile.

Juliet liked that her parents teased each other so often and so gently. Whereas some husbands and wives she had observed used such jokes to disconcert or even discredit their spouses, her parents employed wit where others stooped to anger. Despite Juliet's youth and inexperience, she had seen enough of life to be glad that she came from such a happy home.

Not everyone had the luxury of such happiness, which was exactly why it was so important that she make this journey.

"Marianne Brandon is gravely distressed by her circumstances," Juliet said. "This is when she needs friendship the most. Had she not invited me there, I would have asked to invite her here."

"I see I am quite outclassed in Christian charity by the women of the household." Her father shook his head, more exasperated with himself than with Juliet or Catherine. "Very well, then, go and visit your friend. But this time—should there be any hint of trouble—you will write us immediately, *without* addressing the letter so poorly that it takes three weeks to arrive."

Juliet's cheeks pinked at the memory of her stratagem. Rather than admit to it, she simply said, "I promise."

Juliet's mother laughed as she patted her husband's arm. "Really, Henry, you are so devoted to imagining trouble where none will be. If I am to take up the pulpit, you can become the novelist of the household."

Marianne Brandon had been heartily glad to leave Surrey. Who could not wish to depart from a place with such terrible memories? Kind as Mr. and Mrs. Knightley had been throughout her stay, she would be grateful if she never saw their house again. All she had wanted at the time was to return home, where she would be able to put the terrible event out of mind.

She had been home now for seven weeks, long enough to know that a murder is not so easily left behind.

At night she had dreams in which Mr. Wickham again menaced her: sometimes at Donwell Abbey, sometimes in her home at Delaford, once even at the great house where she had spent her childhood. Nightmares, ghastly as they were, Marianne could accept as the price of what she had done.

Yet memory and menace did not only haunt her slumber; they claimed her waking hours as well, and in a fashion she could neither govern nor understand. If one of the servants appeared unexpectedly in a hallway, in that first instant of motion—before the person and his purpose had been recognized—Marianne was thunderstruck with terror, so much so that she paled and grew dizzy. Any sudden loud noise could make her cower or even shriek. The same symptoms happened at other moments, too, in response to anything, everything, she knew not what. She might go days without a single instance, and believe herself improving; then the next day would fell her two, three, four times, sometimes even more.

Worst of all were the moments where her vision went almost black and Marianne believed herself—for but an instant—to be back at Donwell Abbey. The fear that gripped her then was every bit as piercing as it had been at the moment of extremity; it could take several minutes for sense and truth to again penetrate her thoughts.

Marianne wondered at times if she was going mad. Her husband and family all assured her she was not, but she could tell that they spoke to comfort her, not from a thorough consideration of her condition. They *hoped* for her improvement, and so she was determined to have hope as well.

Her husband of less than one year, Colonel Christopher Brandon, was on that morning readying himself for a journey into the village of Barton. Marianne knew he wished for her to join him but would not urge her to do so before she felt ready. He was taking unusually long with his preparations, to give her time to summon her courage. She would need more time than this.

I must go into Barton eventually, she thought. *No one could hide within Delaford forever.* (Marianne had considered this seriously enough to have determined its utter impossibility.)

Thus far, she had kept to her home, or to the parsonage inhabited by her sister Elinor and her husband, Edward Ferrars, or to Barton Cottage, where her mother and younger sister, Margaret, dwelled. Marianne had entertained visits from their neighbor, Sir John Middleton, and his lively mother-in-law, Mrs. Jennings . . . but had only once been invited to their home; and when she had mustered the courage to accept, had been welcomed by Sir John's wife, Lady Middleton, with the bare minimum of civility. If that was the reception she could expect among friends, what could she anticipate from the rest of the village?

Beyond all that—what if one of her spells came upon her in public, when all could observe her? The townspeople would certainly consider her a madwoman forever after, and Marianne could not swear they would be wrong.

Brandon finally spoke. "I shall not be long. Miss Williams has not entirely settled into her new establishment; she will not wish to entertain guests."

How long Marianne had wished to be introduced to Beth! It now seemed likely that introduction might never take place. Beth Williams had long been Brandon's ward, and popular supposition in the neighborhood held that she was Brandon's illegitimate child. Marianne knew the truth of the matter. Beth's mother was, indeed, Brandon's long-dead, long-lost love, Eliza. However, he was not her father; he had undertaken Beth's care as the natural extension of his love for Eliza, the fulfillment of the promise he had made to her upon her deathbed. He had done all except give Beth the family name, which, had he done so, would have given strength to the few scurrilous rumors that claimed her to be his natural child. Instead, he had bestowed upon the little girl her mother's maiden name—one more way in which he could honor the late Eliza.

No, Beth's father had been revealed as the late George Wickham—the man Marianne had murdered.

She thought, *Etiquette has nothing to say about such an introduction as that, I should imagine.*

On the other side of the village, at Barton Cottage, that murder, and the fate of she who had committed it, was indeed being discussed—but with more compassion than Marianne had granted herself. No less could be expected from her mother and sisters.

"Wicked!" Mrs. Dashwood insisted as she stabbed at her embroidery such that her needle seemed a weapon. "It is nothing short of wickedness to condemn a woman for defending her virtue against such a man."

Elinor Dashwood Ferrars sat with some discomfort on the settee nearest her mother. This was no judgment upon the settee; Elinor expected to become a mother within but a few weeks, and this condition could not be made comfortable by any seat in Christendom. "No one *has* condemned Marianne, Mama. People are curious, and though their curiosity is undeniably morbid, it is also understandable."

"If people are unkind to her, I do not know how Marianne shall bear it," Mrs. Dashwood insisted. "She endures so much already. How the memory pains her!"

"Marianne never used to care what anybody thought," said the youngest Dashwood sister, Margaret, who was struggling to knit a tiny shoe for her niece- or nephew-to-be. "She said small minds were worth no notice."

"Indeed they are not," Elinor said, "but none of us can entirely divorce ourselves from the society in which we live. One cannot let one's actions be dictated by the cruelest and most foolish among us, but one must equally accept that our reputations precede us, whether just or unjust."

Mrs. Dashwood shook her head in wonder. "Your rationality sometimes takes you beyond normal feeling, Elinor."

"Not so, Mama. I feel Marianne's plight most keenly. Yet what any of us feels will not change the realities of the situation."

"Then how are we to help her?" Margaret asked. "We must do *something*."

"We will speak the truth to all who will hear," said Mrs. Dashwood.

Elinor privately thought that a great many would wish to hear, though their interest would be more a matter of gossip than justice. But if the former could serve the latter, so be it.

The village of Barton had been Marianne's home for less than three years. She had spent all her earlier life at Norland Park, the great house in Sussex where she and her sisters had been born. In accordance with law and custom, they had been forced to leave after their father's death in order to make way for John—their elder brother, product of her father's first marriage—and his wife, Fanny. John and Fanny had been wealthy even before the laws of inheritance, which so favored sons above daughters, delivered Norland into their keeping.

Would it have been easier, facing people I had known all my life? Marianne wondered as she stood at the window of her sitting room, which looked out upon the grounds and, at the very distance, the turnpike road. *People who had more experience to judge me by, rather than only these past few years—most of which I spent making a fool of myself for the sake of John Willoughby.*

Willoughby had swept into her life the very image of a romantic hero, courting her with all the spirit and emotion a young woman of sensibility could have wished. Everyone had assumed the two of them to be destined for the altar, to the point that Marianne had already begun daydreaming about the furnishings she would buy for Allenham, the greater of the two houses Willoughby would own.

Then he had left her with almost no explanation. His vagueness spurred her hopes more than her caution, for Marianne's trust in Willoughby had been complete. So it had been all the crueler when she discovered that he had abandoned her to marry a Miss Sophia Grey, who had a dowry of fifty thousand pounds.

Worst of all: he had felt compelled to do so because his aunt had threatened to disinherit him after learning that he had dallied with a young girl of the village and left her expecting his child.

That girl was none other than Beth Williams. Brandon had taken the insult to his ward gravely. There was no telling which of the three of them wanted to see Willoughby the least.

But Miss Tilney would arrive in three days' time. Then Marianne would have the consolation of friendship, and with someone who had been at Donwell and truly understood. Until then, she would have to endure.

Yet fate rarely contents itself with giving us but one burden to bear at any given moment. Usually, it is far more generous. So it was with Marianne, for as she watched the turnpike road, she glimpsed a carriage she recognized—a fine one, finer than any other in the village of Barton. Once it had belonged to Mrs. Smith, Willoughby's aunt and the owner of the Allenham estate not so very far away.

Five weeks ago, not long after the Brandons' return from Surrey, Mrs. Smith had passed away. All that she had ever owned now belonged to John Willoughby.

He and his wife have come to claim the estate, Marianne thought, her heart sinking further. *Willoughby has returned.*

The village of Barton was filled with its usual clatter-clamor— rattling carriage wheels, clopping hooves, the squeak and splash of a water pump, a fiddle's tune floating down from the rooms above a woodworker's shop. Colonel Brandon noted that all the persons he passed met his eye, acknowledged his presence, even smiled as they generally did . . . but a sense of distance marked every interaction. It would take more time yet for the villagers to accept the truth of what his wife had been forced to do.

His destination was a small but well-appointed house not far from the village square. As Colonel Brandon approached on horseback, one of the new-hired servants emerged, a widow of the parish who had an excellent reputation as a nursemaid. This was fortunate, as many respectable servants might have declined work in a household that was not quite respectable itself.

In her arms was a little boy, not yet two years old, whose fair wispy hair ruffled in the breeze as he blinked up at Brandon.

"He's having a lovely day today," the nursemaid confirmed as Brandon dismounted. "Our mouser had kittens a few weeks ago, and how our little Georgie loves to watch them. Soon they'll be able to play with him, though I don't like to think what will happen if he gets scratched."

Brandon smiled down at the boy, who smiled back. "He will learn to take care. How is Miss Williams?"

The nursemaid's enthusiasm dimmed very slightly. "She's in one of her moods. Keeping to her tasks, mind you, and spending time with her wee baby, but . . . well, you'll see for yourself."

Beth was so like her mother, Eliza, in both good ways and bad. When Brandon entered the house, he found her sitting not in the parlor but in the kitchen, wearing an old calico dress appropriate only for working in the home. She leaned upon the broad table with floury hands, staring at what appeared to be a bowlful of dough, covered with cloth, in hopes that it would rise.

Although she did not stand to meet him, her mouth quirked in what was almost a smile. "Did you come to warn me, Colonel? Or to console me after I heard the crushing news?"

"I know not to what you refer."

"Why, Mr. John Willoughby of Allenham has returned to Barton at last—quite some time since he promised he would return, and, as it happens, he returns with his new wife. She is reported to be lovely and elegant, and very unlikely to be found baking bread in a kitchen."

Her humor would have reassured most. Brandon knew Beth well enough to understand that, for her, wit was often a way to conceal feelings she did not wish to express. Yet to press her further upon the subject would only put an end to the wit while deepening the concealment. "Has your cook left you? I can recommend another, or the bakery across town—"

"You mean, I should be sitting on a refined chair, doing some refined embroidery, thinking only of refined things, as I have become a young woman of property. Society claims that gaining respectability is more than a matter of wealth, but it appears that wealth assists greatly in the endeavor." Beth was, indeed, in one of her moods—but it appeared her future troubled her as much as her past. "When I lived in a farmhouse, I wished to be a fashionable creature who lived in a town and had little to do. I have realized these ambitions, and what do I find I actually wish to do? I wish to bake bread."

"You are an excellent baker." Brandon had enjoyed her rolls, pies, and the like since she first began baking as a child. How often she had delighted in making treats for him on his visits! The role of ward had ever had its complications, but when Beth had been smaller, the task had been easier—and, in truth, one of the great joys of his life. Since her misadventure with Mr. Willoughby, all had become less forthright, more fraught.

She said, "That explains it, then. I like baking because it is a skill I have acquired. I do not like dressing up in my finery and being elegant because those are skills I have not yet so much as begun to acquire."

"It will come to you in time." He had arrived at the point of his errand, and as surely as he believed he was doing something for the benefit of both those involved, he found it difficult to speak the words. "I have long intended to ask you—would you welcome an introduction to my wife? She would be an excellent model in all such things, and Mrs. Brandon has been very eager to make your acquaintance."

Brandon hoped such an introduction would distract Marianne and engage her interest. He was proud of his wife's fair-minded nature, and while friendship between the two women would be impossible, given their different spheres, he knew neither Beth's own illegitimacy nor that of her child would be held against her by Marianne, even though most women in polite society shunned Beth.

But she did not respond with eagerness; instead, she immediately acquired a far greater interest in cleaning the floury table. "I would not think of imposing."

"It is no imposition."

"It would be, and she cannot be properly entertained here. No, it is impossible at present."

Her tone of voice told him that he should not ask why.

Beth did not wish to meet Marianne. Did she blame his wife for what she had been forced to do to Mr. Wickham? As incomprehensible as Brandon found this, Beth was clearly in no mood to be argued with, and—for the moment—her refusal must be accepted.

Pemberley had horses and carriages enough for each member of the family to travel independently. Jonathan was grateful for that, as traveling by post coach would involve extra hours, all of which would be spent in close proximity to strangers, and the opportunity for any number of unforeseen situations. Jonathan liked order and predictability; he did not care for strangers, particularly ones who tried to look him in the eye.

But even strangers seemed preferable to the acquaintances he would encounter at the end of his journey.

Three of them had been invited. Jonathan himself—chosen for reasons he could scarcely guess, given how little liked he had been by his schoolmates.

Next came Ralph Bamber, of a wealthy family in Dorset, one year Jonathan's elder. His ginger hair and freckles had made him a victim of teasing nearly as vicious as that faced by

Jonathan himself. They also came in at the top of their classes in marks together; that ought to have made them allies. When they were alone, in fact, Bamber was always fair, even cordial. Yet when others tormented and ridiculed Jonathan, Bamber never failed to laugh.

Then there was Laurence Follett, a proud Londoner a couple of years older than Bamber. His family was not as wealthy as many of those whose sons attended the school, but the deficiency was not enough to hold him back socially, given his dark good looks and ready wit. This wit had often been employed in finding creative new insults to hurl at Jonathan, and once or twice, when they were younger, the punishments had been physical as well as verbal. No one had thought the less of Follett for it; if anything, mocking Jonathan had further enhanced Follett's standing.

Follett, however, had not been the worst of those who bullied Jonathan. That distinguisher belonged to the eldest of the four men coming together for this party, their host, who said he wished for them to help him celebrate the new house he had just inherited, a fine estate in Devonshire known as Allenham.

Jonathan could not help wondering yet again: *What can John Willoughby want with me?*

Chapter Two

In his letter of invitation, Willoughby had told Jonathan Darcy only that his aunt had very recently died, leaving him a great house named Allenham; the gathering of old school friends was to celebrate this inheritance. To Jonathan this seemed remarkably like celebrating his aunt's death, which went against both propriety and Christian feeling. Usually, when individuals behaved in ways that seemed to defy society's rules, Jonathan attempted to puzzle out why. In this case, however, he could not wonder at it. Willoughby had lacked all proper feeling as a boy, so it was hardly surprising that this remained true in his adulthood.

"Almost there, sir!" the driver called. Jonathan thumped on the carriage door to indicate that he had heard and understood. He looked at the view beyond the window, mildly curious to see Allenham itself, but as yet the carriage was still traveling through gentle, rolling countryside. The road was unusually rough, and Jonathan felt a moment's gratitude that he was able to make the journey in his family's own comfortable carriage. How wretched the trip would be by post coach, he could only guess.

"Ow!" Juliet Tilney winced as her head knocked against the door. "Will they not go any slower?"

One of her fellow passengers in the stagecoach—a woman

carrying two clucking hens within a crate—chuckled at her. "'Twould only put them even further behind than they already are."

Juliet's stomach turned over treacherously. She had been jostled from one side to another, back and forth and up and down, for many hours at this point. The small watch she wore pinned to her pelisse suggested that she still had at least an hour to go before reaching Delaford. If they ran into another muddy stretch or a flock of obstinate sheep, salvation and stillness might be even further away.

Her father said that prayer should be a testament to devotion, not mere begging. But Juliet could not help the inward voice that said, *Please, O Lord, let the coach arrive as soon as possible.*

The stagecoach bumped again, to the groans of the passengers and the cackling of the hens. Musty brown feathers fluttered though the air, and one caught on Juliet's skirt.

And please help me to arrive before I look to have been tarred and feathered.

Delaford, like some other great estates of such considerable age, was enclosed by a wall; between wall and house had been planted a multitude of trees to provide ample shade, fruits and nuts in season, and a sort of respite between the tumult of the outer world and the occasional tumult of the inner. Brandon had always been glad of this place, and from boyhood had been drawn to it whenever his spirits were troubled—as they could not fail to be, upon his learning of Willoughby's return.

Brandon and Willoughby had last met on a dueling field. Both men emerged with their lives, but Brandon had passionately hoped never to see the man again. This desire was held both for the sake of the woman for whose honor he had fought—the unfortunate Miss Williams—and for the woman whom he and Willoughby both loved.

Whom Brandon had married, whom Willoughby might love still.

During the tumultuous days at Donwell Abbey—when Brandon had all but known of his wife's guilt, and it had seemed as though a noose were being drawn tight around them both—he had accidentally found a letter from Willoughby among Marianne's things. Although he did not stoop to reading its entire contents, the mere existence of such a letter indicated Willoughby's claim of an enduring passion for Marianne, as well as his strong desire to be alone with her once again.

Brandon had left the letter where it was and had never mentioned it to Marianne. They had been bearing far heavier burdens at that time, and there had been no point in increasing them through such a discussion. Besides, he knew his wife's character well enough to be assured that she had never so much as contemplated writing a reply.

What he did not know was how she would react once she and Willoughby were reunited.

What I believed *Willoughby to be,* you *truly are,* Marianne had said to him, professing her love for her husband in warmer, more heartfelt words than he had ever dreamed he might hear. Yet who could say how being with Willoughby again would influence her? Even if she had come to love Brandon—did it necessarily follow that she could not still love Willoughby as well? Brandon carried in his heart both his true affection for Marianne and the embers of feeling for his long-dead Eliza, so he knew better than most that the spirit can contain more than one passion and that those passions could contradict without ever overcoming each other.

Demanding answers of Marianne would do no good, as he suspected her confusion in the matter rivaled his own. There was nothing to be done upon Willoughby's return but to wait, and watch, and see.

Allenham was an imposing house, one of the largest in the vicinity, handsomely situated atop a hill. Most observers were greatly struck with its size and beauty; some were intimidated, as evidence of wealth introduces an element of fear into human relationships—one which is difficult to acknowledge, and speaks well neither of wealth nor humanity, but cannot be denied.

This did not affect Jonathan Darcy, who, as a lifelong resident of Pemberley, was unlikely to be overawed by any structure save for a palace. His sanguine appraisal of the house did little to assuage his fears of the visit to follow. Nor did the appearance of John Willoughby striding across the lawn to greet Jonathan, with both Ralph Bamber and Laurence Follett behind him. The smiles on their faces were too familiar for the wrong reasons.

"Thumps! Here you are at last!" Willoughby slapped Jonathan's shoulder by way of greeting, and only with great difficulty did Jonathan manage not to cringe from the unexpected, unwelcome touch or from the nickname he so disliked. "About time you arrived."

"This is the hour I indicated in my letter," Jonathan pointed out.

The three men all laughed; he had been funny without meaning to be, again. Jonathan despised this circumstance, which was unfortunate, as he found himself in it quite often. "Still trying to pin everyone down to the minute!" Follett said. "You haven't changed a bit, Thumps. Yes, it's a good thing you're here. It's been dull as tombs so far, and we need some amusement."

"And poor Follett arrived a day early, so he's had twice as long to be bored." A note in Willoughby's voice hinted that he did not appreciate his company being considered dull.

Jonathan felt foolish for not having realized from the beginning that he had been invited as entertainment. He had always known that teasing would be a part of his visit to Allenham. He had not understood that it was, in fact, the entire point.

Meanwhile, not very far away, the weary Juliet had been picked up in her hosts' carriage, then taken to Delaford, where she was greeted with far greater sincerity.

"I am so very glad to see you." Marianne clasped Juliet's hands with great feeling. "To have another person by my side who understands how it was at Donwell Abbey!" This phrase, apparently, was to be the euphemism for Mr. Wickham's murder.

"Has it been very bad?" Juliet asked as Marianne led her through the entry hall. Behind them, Brandon told the servants where to take Juliet's things. "Have people been cruel to you?"

"In truth, I have scarcely dared to face them—only friends, and even they have stared." Marianne plucked a stray chicken feather from Juliet's bonnet, which would have been mortifying had her hostess's attention not so obviously been elsewhere. "How good it is to have a true friend one can speak to openly, from the heart, without any pretense or slavish devotion to unnecessary propriety! With anyone else—even my dear sister Elinor—I should have to ask after their journey, remark upon the weather, and speak of any number of things besides what either of us really wished to speak of!"

"I agree completely," Juliet said. There were few topics she would less wish to discuss than her time in the stage-coach, which she hoped never to think upon again. "From the moment of our introduction I wished we would become friends, and though I may regret the circumstances that brought it to pass, I am so glad my hopes were fulfilled."

Marianne brightened, more cheerful than Juliet had seen her since before the murder . . . since before Donwell Abbey. "Oh, it is very good indeed that you are here, Miss Tilney. Just in time for all of us to take tea!"

Juliet felt queasily unsettled after her bumpy ride in the post coach, but this was not an ailment that could be discussed in polite company. At first she tried to think of a suitable excuse to delay tea. But that unpleasant sensation comes in two types: one which rejects food in all its forms, and another which food alone can cure. Juliet realized that hers was of the second variety. "Tea sounds delightful."

Jonathan had earned his nickname the very first week he spent at school.

He had been studying in a corner of the library. Jonathan had loathed school on its own merits from the very beginning: it was filled with people he did not know, most of whom were very loud; the familiar tempo of his life at Pemberley had been entirely upended and replaced with a schedule as demanding as it was strange; and he had almost no chance to be alone.

Thus studying came as a relief to him, and he became deeply absorbed in his Latin grammar. Ancient Latin, at least, had not changed since his lessons at home with the tutor; the language felt firm and solid, and thus reassuring.

When Jonathan became very much absorbed in his own thoughts, however, one of his peculiar habits often came to the fore—his habit of rocking back and forth, back and forth. This always soothed him, particularly when he hugged his arms against his chest. So engrossed was he in both this practice and his Latin that it took him a very long time to hear the counting.

"Forty-*seven*." It was the gleeful whispering not of one boy but of many—dozens, perhaps, all in unison. "Forty-*eight*."

Jonathan realized that he had been rocking, something his parents had impressed upon him was never to be done in public. Dismay broke his rhythm, and he let his chair fall forward one last time, its front legs striking the floor with a heavy thud.

"*Forty-nine!*" The shout rang through the library, followed by yelps of laughter. Jonathan's face reddened as the librarian rushed to restore quiet, his academic gown fluttering behind him.

Although the librarian's best efforts restored a semblance of order, stifled snickering continued to percolate. Jonathan attempted to resume reading, but he could not concentrate for the laughter and because of the many boys who found excuses for collecting books in locations close enough that they might whisper to Jonathan, "*Thump!*"

By day's end, the story had become the favorite anecdote of the entire student body. It was at dinner that someone had referred to Jonathan as "Thumps" for the first time. Upon reflection, he thought that no one besides the schoolmasters had ever again used his surname, and of course nobody had spoken his Christian name at all. One of the best things about leaving school had been his conviction that he would never have to hear that nickname ever again.

Instead, here was John Willoughby smirking at him amid wreaths of cigar smoke. "What's the matter, Thumps? Never developed a taste for cigars?"

Jonathan shook his head. "No. They are very bitter."

"Ever manly, our Thumps." Follett clapped Jonathan on the shoulder in a manner apparently meant as good-natured. "Always reading and playing the pianoforte. I suppose he means to leave the cigars and the shooting for the ladies."

"Pemberley will be quite a sight once he inherits." Willoughby laughed. "Imagine a flock of ladies in their muslins carrying rifles!"

Jonathan did not see why a lady might not handle a rifle as well as a man of similar build, but the mere idea made the others laugh so loudly that it took all his self-control not to flinch.

Then a silky female voice said, "My husband is merely jealous. Compared to Pemberley, Allenham might as well be a thatched hut."

Willoughby stiffened before managing a too-polite smile. "Thumps, let me introduce you to my wife. Mrs. Willoughby, this is Thumps, whom you obviously already know to be Jonathan Darcy."

Mrs. Willoughby, wearing a silk dress the color of moonlight, walked deeper into the room. Everything about her seemed to glitter: her expensive jewelry, the metallic braid on her dress, her brilliant blue eyes. She moved slowly, which Jonathan realized was done so that she might attract greater attention. This he would have thought unnecessary. Everyone in the room had turned to gaze upon her—Willoughby with annoyance, Bamber with politeness, and Follett with an expression Jonathan could not read.

Should he compliment Allenham? The house was almost the size of Rosings Park, which belonged to his elderly and formidable great-aunt, Lady Catherine de Bourgh. His cousin Mr. Collins often likened furnishings to those at Rosings, intending it as praise, but Jonathan had observed that it was not always received as such. He decided against making any mention.

Instead, he ventured, "I am pleased to make your acquaintance, Mrs. Willoughby. But—have you been to Pemberley before? If so, I must apologize, for I do not recall our meeting."

"My family toured the house and grounds one summer, when your family was away from home and I was very young. But I never forgot its incredible beauty. *That* is a true estate, one worthy of the name. Please share my compliments with your parents."

From most people, Mrs. Willoughby's statement would have sounded polite, even pleasant. Yet her tone was strange, and the way she glanced over at her husband made Jonathan doubt he was the person she most wanted to hear her words—that she wished Willoughby to feel the difference between a house such as Allenham and a house such as Pemberley. Her compliments were not meant to please Jonathan, only to wound her husband. Having no idea how to navigate such a strange situation, Jonathan simply bowed his head in what he hoped was gracious acknowledgment.

"What is this, then?" Willoughby came to his wife's side, smiling too broadly for the occasion. "Are you wishing you'd married Thumps instead? You'd have made a very bad bargain there."

Bamber said, "Never underestimate the charms of a

house, Willoughby. Much less one that is often compared to *Chatsworth*."

Jonathan would have had to admit that Pemberley was rather compelling matrimonial temptation. His marriage-ability as a person seemed beneath reckoning. On the balance he was merely relieved to be as little a part of this conversation as possible.

Follett said, "Many do marry for fortune—it cannot be denied. I doubt whether they are always happy with the bargain they have struck."

"I suspect they are not," said Mrs. Willoughby. "Nor do they deserve to be. Those who marry for purely material considerations, with no thought of love, or even concern for the person they marry—I say, there is no punishment too great for them."

"No doubt their marriages are punishment enough." Willoughby said it as though it were a joke. Why did Jonathan sense that it was not?

"Have you no particular guests of your own for this celebration, Mrs. Willoughby?" Bamber civilly asked. "I do pity you, forced to share your home and husband with three young ruffians such as ourselves."

"I do not require your pity, Mr. Bamber." Mrs. Willoughby smiled directly at her husband. "We have only just settled at Allenham. Calls will be made, which we will need to repay in turn. My dear Willoughby already has many friends here, whom I expect to befriend in return. Why, a whole host of new acquaintance awaits me. I do not think it shall be very long before I have met many ladies with whom I shall no doubt have much to discuss."

This all sounded entirely ordinary, and to be a good thing for Mrs. Willoughby, so Jonathan could not understand why Willoughby himself had gone so very pale.

At this point in our narrative, it is only just that we should consider the case of Mrs. Willoughby as she herself might have seen it.

Not so very long ago, she had been Miss Sophia Grey, an heiress with a dowry of fifty thousand pounds and London society at her feet. Although she was not particularly handsome, neither was she plain, with no blemishes that the glow of her considerable fortune would not conceal. She was of age, fashionable, reasonably clever, known to all the right people: Is it any wonder that she believed those about her to be dazzled by more than her money? It is a mistake frequently made by those with greater fortune and fewer merits than she.

Many young men sought her notice, and a select handful of them received it. John Willoughby had been among these—charming, handsome, affable, everything a young man should be. While his wealth was no match for hers, he was already in possession of one fine house and would inherit an even greater one, both of which his future wife could expect to reign over as mistress. The combination of his future estates and his exceedingly attractive person distinguished him from most other suitors and marked him for Miss Grey's particular attention.

But he was only one of the young men about her, and while he might be the most attractive among them, he was not singularly devoted to her, nor she to him. When he left London for a time, Miss Grey had bid him farewell with only a slight sense of loss and devoted her attention to her other suitors. One of them had seemed very near making an offer. Although he was far from the most eligible man courting Miss Grey, he was the most ardent. His feeling for her ran more deeply, she sensed, and although his inheritance was not impressive, it was substantive enough. Her heart began to be more truly touched than the usual whirl of high society courtship would allow, and she had given this other young man hints that a proposal would meet with a favorable response.

Then John Willoughby suddenly returned to London, seemingly afire with love for her.

How often he called! How hopeful he appeared! He would have danced every dance with her if propriety permitted it; as it was, he spent as much time with her as could possibly be allowed. Willoughby charmed, spoke, flirted as never before, dazzling her beyond anything she had felt for him prior. Her other suitor might have striven harder for her affections—but he had quitted the field of battle almost immediately, he as cowed as she was delighted by the ardor of Willoughby's courtship. When Willoughby proposed, Miss Grey had accepted without hesitation.

Yet hesitations did arrive, the first of which came before the wedding, when all might yet have been changed. Willoughby's erstwhile flirtation with a poor country girl of no dowry whatsoever—Miss Marianne Dashwood—had apparently confused the girl's wits to the point that she actually believed a man of wealth and property had intended to marry her. After an unfortunate incident at a London ball, Miss Grey knew something had to be done. Willoughby must put an end to Marianne's delusions immediately by writing her a firm letter and returning everything she had sent to him. It was the most decent course of action, and in truth the kindest.

But when Miss Grey saw how many letters Marianne had sent to Willoughby, she knew—the girl might have been imprudent, but she must have had the most sincere belief in an engagement to take the step of writing at all. When she further saw the lock of hair Willoughby put into the envelope, Miss Gray knew that Marianne Dashwood had in fact come very close to that proposal, too close for any subsequent lady's comfort.

Yet Willoughby wrote the letter (with Miss Grey's help, or else he would have been too vague), and he had come to the altar unfettered. She had become Mrs. Willoughby and stepped into her brilliant future . . .

Only to discover that Willoughby had, in fact, been under threat of disinheritance when he proposed to her, and therefore penniless. Only to learn that he lived at the very limit of his income, always, and her greater fortune simply pushed the limit further, suggesting that their old age might not be spent in equal comfort to their youth. Only to see him react with petulance to the fact that some part of her fortune had been put into a trust, ensuring she had a reserve of money that even her husband could not claim as his own. Only to find him more and more eager to spend his time with the men of his set, shooting and gambling and drinking port, than he was to be at home with his bride. Only to realize that, in Willoughby's eyes, his wife would never be quite as lovely or perfect as poor little Miss Marianne Dashwood.

When Mrs. Willoughby had subsequently learned of his premarital dalliance with a farm girl of the parish—a Miss Williams, who had borne him an illegitimate child—the last link of the chain broke, and she was bound to illusion no longer. She knew at last that her husband had married her for money, not love; that he was not the kind of man to be faithful and devoted; and that the other young man—the poorer one, the one who had been so close to making an offer—was the one for whom she should have waited. Instead, she was bound to Willoughby until death did part them.

Can she be blamed for coldness? For anger? For impolitic words? They might not represent the wisest or best responses, but there can be no doubt that her situation was a pitiable one. Mrs. Willoughby had no experience in being pitied. She found she did not care for it.

However sorely tried Marianne Brandon or the former Miss Sophia Grey felt herself to have been by Willoughby, there was another in Barton with even greater reasons for grievance.

Miss Beth Williams was not blameless in the matter—she had believed too much upon too little evidence, and her passionate nature had overcome good sense—but Willoughby had marked her life forever. She had, until recently, believed him to have ruined it entirely. She loved her little son, George, but had believed that the entire misadventure had spoiled whatever chance she had ever possessed of marrying a respectable man or taking a position as a lady's companion or a governess. Beth would continue as she always had—dependent upon Colonel Brandon, now with a son by her side. All Beth's fondness for the colonel could not make her dependence and lack of freedom less irksome. As a mother, Beth regretted bitterly that she could provide only the same shadowy upbringing she had had herself.

Then had come the word that her father had been identified as Mr. George Wickham, who had been very corrupt, very wealthy, and by then very dead. The wealth passed on to Beth as his only known heir. She had struggled mightily within herself before resolving to return Wickham's ill-gotten gains to those he had defrauded—but the struggle had been easier once the accountants had informed her that a large amount of money would be left over at the end. Thus Beth found herself a woman of considerable property.

She remained an unwed woman with a child. She still owed a duty to Colonel Brandon. Her future would not look like her past, but Beth could not imagine it. Nor could anyone else around her. Her position was unique.

Beth had longed for some hint that would help her resolve the matter, and on that morning it seemed the hint had come, for in the post was a letter from Allenham.

I will not hope, she resolved as she held the unopened missive in her hands. *I will not hope.* Like most such resolutions, it could not be kept.

Chapter Three

Jonathan arose early on his first morning at Allenham. As a more informal meal, breakfast could be taken whenever it was wished, with whoever happened to be in the breakfast room at that time. It was Jonathan's fervent hope that no one else would be there at all.

These hopes were disappointed, for as soon as he reached the landing, he saw Follett standing near the bottom of the staircase, apparently in conversation with Mrs. Willoughby. They spoke in low tones—perhaps of something they did not wish the servants to hear. Jonathan had no intention of eavesdropping, but he caught a word that excited his interest. Was it truly possible that Follett and Mrs. Willoughby were speaking of the Oracle of Delphi?

"Good morning," Jonathan called in good cheer, hoping to be made part of the conversation.

Once again, he found but disappointment, because Mrs. Willoughby gave him no more than the briefest civil greeting before returning upstairs. Follett, who appeared irritated, said only, "You never fail to appear at the wrong time, Thumps."

Jonathan frowned. "It is surely the hour for breakfast, is it not?"

"Of course it is." That was Bamber, who had stepped from the breakfast room to greet them. "So come and have your meal, will you? I'm in need of pleasant company—but you two will have to do."

Follett laughed, assuming Bamber's comment to be a joke.

Was he correct? Jonathan was uncertain. Although his careful study of social niceties had added to his comprehension, in the company of his old schoolfellows, he felt as awkward and unsure as he ever had. Thus he remained silent at the meal's beginning, leaving all talk to Follett and Bamber.

Indeed, Bamber seemed to be in a mood to tease, but for once his attention was focused more on Mr. Follett. "I can see bringing a sketchbook along to Allenham, all right, but canvas, brushes, and all your paints? Are you turning into an *artiste?*"

"I have begun receiving commissions," Follett said. "Many in society prefer a portrait-painter of good family, rather than someone come up from the working classes. Why, Baron Wenlock wishes me to paint his wife's portrait next month, should I accept the commission."

Jonathan had little imagined that Follett might possess an iota of artistic sentiment, though as he thought upon it, he recalled Follett's many satirical cartoons of teachers and fellow students, in particular several of Jonathan himself. These were circulated among the schoolboys to general delight. Cruel and mocking though the drawings had been, they *had* been executed with great technical proficiency.

"Well, then, I suppose you must practice," Bamber said. "But it will be deuced peculiar, seeing you sitting out in the gardens with an easel and smock."

The previous evening's conversation came to Jonathan's mind and made him frown. "You found it peculiar that I should wish to play the pianoforte or read, because you consider those to be feminine pursuits. But are not drawing and painting also encouraged for young women?"

He meant the question in earnest, which made it both surprising and dismaying when Follett scowled and Bamber laughed aloud. "He's got you there, Follett!"

"It's not the same sort of thing at all," Follett insisted. "Those are mere *hobbies*. Did you not hear me say I am receiving proper commissions?"

Jonathan did not see how to both escape the awkwardness and attain clarity. As awkwardness would be ever present in these gentlemen's company, he chose clarity. "So it is acceptable to undertake feminine pursuits as long as one is paid for them?"

Follett's face flushed red. Before he could reply in anger, though, Bamber clapped him amicably on the shoulder. "Oh, admit it, Follett, Darcy's made a fair point. Now, tell me more about this baroness you'll be painting. Formidable old dowager or fetching young thing?"

"Dowager, I'm afraid." With that, Follett had to laugh, and the dangerous moment had passed.

Jonathan could not be sure, but he thought Bamber had actually interceded on his behalf. This was so entirely contrary to his expectation that he could not wholly credit it—nor could he deny that Bamber had called him Darcy rather than Thumps.

Elinor Ferrars resembled her sister Marianne Brandon in few respects. Where Marianne was fiery, Elinor was cool; where Marianne rejected rules, Elinor cited them. Despite their differences, or perhaps in part because of those differences, they remained close after their marriages—closer in some ways than they had been before. This was not the only reason Elinor greatly anticipated a trip to Delaford later that day, but it added to her happiness.

When Elinor remarked as much to her husband, Edward, that morning, he said, "I should say that I envy you your greater closeness with your sister, but I must confess that I do not know how Robert and I ever should have shared such feeling, even before my estrangement from my family."

"Nor can I imagine him as one of our closest acquaintances." Elinor had met Robert Ferrars on a few occasions before her marriage, but this had been sufficient to impress her with the man's vanity and frivolity. "Whenever there is a rift within a family, however, one cannot help but wish to amend the breach."

Edward did not take the hint. "Such a breach as this? Robert, given the whole of my inheritance because I committed the crime of proposing to Lucy Steele—and then forgiven by my mother after he marries Lucy instead? I defy all England to provide a better reason for a break within a family."

"Very true." Elinor would have delved deeper into the topic had she not felt sensations within that reminded her of the child she would soon bear. When she placed one hand over the spot, her husband noticed with joy.

"We will be a family together very soon." Edward beamed with pleasure. "When my father was alive, Elinor, my family was a better one than it became without him. It has always been my opinion that my siblings would have been far more amiable if they remembered him better, if they had had more chance to learn from his good principles. With our child—our family—all will be as it should have been."

No one could guarantee the future. Even at such a warm moment, this was a truth Elinor was unlikely to forget. But she was a wise enough wife not to say so. Let clouds come later, if they would. For the time being, happiness shone down and was to be embraced.

Some women took confinement to extremes, scarcely being seen by anyone beyond their own household from months before the birth until months after. Others disregarded their condition until very nearly the last possible moment—their friend Mrs. Palmer had been among these. As Elinor did in most things, she had taken the middle path in this: not out in society but still willing to visit or be visited by her family and nearest friends.

Marianne and the colonel were now hosting her sister's young friend Miss Tilney. Elinor would have shied from most new acquaintances during this period, but Miss Tilney must be the exception. Were it not for this young woman, either of the Brandons might have gone to the gallows. Yes, this was one acquaintance she intended to make.

Delaford, too, saw a bright and happy morning. Juliet came down to find Marianne with a cup of coffee, gazing out at the garden. This house's breakfast room, unlike those in many other great homes, had a broad window that looked out on an expanse of greenery, in which Marianne appeared to take great delight.

"What a charming view," said Juliet as she took up her plate. "Did Colonel Brandon plant all this for you?"

"Not for me." Marianne smiled with pleasure. "Ever since he inherited the house, he has maintained and improved the gardens. We share a fervent love of nature's beauty, and the view from this vantage point is incomparable."

"Delightful." How wonderful it must be, where husband and wife took joy in so many of the same things. Juliet settled in to enjoy her morning coffee with a bit of sugar—slightly more than she usually took. This was a holiday, after all.

A rap at the front door caused Marianne to startle, which in turn confused Juliet. Why should she be so astonished by a small, ordinary noise? Then again, no visitors would normally be expected quite so early, and any tradesman would have gone to the back entry. From the hall came the murmuring sound of the butler's voice, as well as a higher-pitched one, apparently in polite but stiff disagreement. Gathering herself once more, Marianne rose to investigate.

Juliet hesitated for a moment—was it more polite to accompany her hostess or to pretend she had heard nothing amiss? Curiosity more than logic led her to prefer the former, and so she hurried along in Marianne's wake.

In the entry hall stood a young woman, only a year or two older than Juliet herself, with cornsilk hair, wearing a very fine day dress, so crisp and perfect that it had to have been sewn new very recently. "If you could fetch him from the grounds—"

"When the colonel goes riding, he does not wish to be disturbed save in case of emergency," the butler insisted.

Brightly Marianne said, "Miss Williams, is it?"

The girl—Miss Williams—stared at Marianne as though she had not expected to find her present, which to Juliet's mind was an extraordinary expectation. "Yes."

"I am Mrs. Brandon, and you are very welcome to Delaford." Marianne gestured toward Juliet. "We already have one guest, you see, Miss Juliet Tilney. Miss Tilney, this is Miss Beth Williams."

"A pleasure to meet you," Juliet swiftly said, but Miss Williams seemed to have no interest in returning the greeting in kind.

"Forgive me for disturbing you." Miss Williams stepped back from the door. "I had wished to speak to the colonel. Please tell him I called—"

"You may wait for him, if you wish." Marianne took a step forward, welcoming in every sense of body and manner.

Miss Williams only stepped farther back again. To Juliet

it seemed as though the woman wished passionately to avoid Marianne's company—rather strange, given that she had come to Marianne's door.

"I do not wish," said Miss Williams. "Just tell him. That is all."

After the butler had closed the door, Juliet ventured, "How peculiar. Who was that?"

"That was"—Marianne breathed out heavily—"a very long story. The beginning of it you learned at Donwell Abbey, and the rest I must reveal to you now. At least we will begin upon it early in the day!"

After finishing breakfast quickly enough to avoid both Willoughbys altogether, Jonathan felt free to take a short morning walk upon the grounds. Why should he subject himself to his disagreeable hosts any earlier than necessary? He had little expected anyone else to wish for the same liberty. Thus it came as a surprise to find Ralph Bamber near the fishpond.

Even more surprising was the state in which he found Bamber: crouched down low like a child, half surrounded by the reeds. Jonathan, not knowing what to make of this, decided to err on the side of caution. "Bamber? Are you unwell?"

"Right as rain, Darcy." Bamber's good cheer was evident from his voice, and was confirmed by his smile when he stood up, a bundle of greenery in his hand. "Just collecting samples."

"Samples?"

"I wish to analyze them. We can do amazing things with chemistry now, you know—it is by far my favorite element of natural philosophy." Bamber shook his head ruefully. "I believe I study more now than I did at school. What would old Willoughby say to that?"

"He would have little respect for any such endeavor," Jonathan said.

This made Bamber laugh. "You don't mince words, do you, Darcy? I have always liked that about you."

Jonathan could make no sense of this. "I never thought you liked me."

"I liked you well enough," Bamber said amiably as they fell into step side by side. "You *are* a bit of a prig—but you know that, don't you?—and there are worse things to be. Certainly I should rather spend time with you than with bloody Willoughby."

The oath made Jonathan's cheeks flush; he hoped it was not very noticeable. "But you accepted his invitation to Allenham."

Bamber raised an eyebrow. "As did you, and you had even more reason to despise Willoughby than I. What courtesy demands, we cannot avoid."

Despise Willoughby? Had not Bamber and Willoughby always been friends? He ventured to say, "I believed you to enjoy Willoughby's—humor."

"You mean being beastly to younger boys at school? I would not call that humor." Bamber stopped along the gravel path, facing Jonathan with a remorseful expression. "Yes, sometimes I laughed along with the others. When I did not, he would turn his cruelty on to me, too—as indeed he always did, before you came. It all seems craven of me, now that I look back upon it, but at the time it seemed no more than—"

"Survival." Jonathan finished the sentence. What would he have done if someone else had taken his place as Willoughby's chief target? Although he would have liked to imagine himself bravely defending any others so cruelly mocked and berated . . . he realized he would have been at least as likely to shrink back into the shadows, to be grateful he no longer suffered the worst of it. It was not impossible that he even would have laughed, only as a matter of vanishing into the crowd.

"Exactly," Bamber said. "My anger at Willoughby's behavior became only relief when that behavior no longer punished me most. I wish that it had become something better, but . . . here we are. It was wretched for you, I know, and I am heartily sorry to have played any part in it. I most humbly beg your pardon."

"Then you have it." Jonathan was surprised to see the true relief in Bamber's answering smile.

After due consideration, Beth felt glad that she had been unable to confer with Colonel Brandon. He would wish to be consulted before any meeting with Willoughby, but such consultation would undoubtedly have ended with his insistence that she refuse the meeting entirely. Having gone to Delaford in search of him, Beth had done her duty, and could now do as she wished—two actions that do not always combine.

If only she could have avoided meeting Marianne Brandon! Still, it was done, and perhaps the invitations to Delaford would cease, as the new Mrs. Brandon's curiosity was now satisfied.

Yet in the absence of any guidance, Beth felt uncertain how best to receive Mr. Willoughby. Etiquette's rules, though plentiful and precise, had failed to describe her exact predicament: how to welcome without disgrace the visit of a man with whom disgrace had already been done.

The servants had been given tasks to busy themselves in the kitchen; little Georgie, with an obliging timeliness uncommon in infants, had settled down for a nap. Thus Beth could sit alone, at liberty, with a book of poetry in her hands.

The words stared up at her unread as the hour came for Willoughby's visit, went several minutes past, then many more. When at last the rap on the door came, it jarred her so that the book nearly fell from her hands.

Do not be cowardly, she scolded herself as she went to her door. (The servants knew she wished to answer this call herself.) *The best and worst has already passed between you, has it not?*

How many times she had scolded her heart for its fondness of memory, and how little it availed it! When Willoughby smiled at her—as charmingly, and regretfully, as she had always imagined—Beth felt her cheeks grow warm and did not know where to look.

"Miss Williams," he said. "It is good of you to receive me."

Should she thank him for coming? Was it not the least he could do? No, the least he could do was nothing, and this he had already accomplished. "Please come in."

"Quite a snug little cottage you have here." Willoughby walked into her parlor as easily as though he had visited many times before.

"I have yet to accustom myself to it," Beth confessed. "I keep waiting for the lady of the house to arrive, before recalling that I am she."

His laugh warmed her through. "All will come in good time. But have you purchased it outright?"

What a strange question. "For now I have only taken the property for a year, but the owner wishes to sell, so I expect to buy." Not all of the funds she would inherit from her late father had been made instantly available to her.

But surely Willoughby had not come merely to discuss accounts and ledgers.

Then again, she had no notion of what he *had* come to discuss. Beth had but one expectation of this visit: Willoughby could not have come without a desire to see his child. It would mean taking him from the public areas of the house to the private, but how could it be wrong to allow a man to meet his son? "Little George—he is asleep, but we could go to his room—"

"Let him sleep. I would not wish to disturb the child."

Perhaps he meant to remain in her house until George awakened. If so, that meant he wished for a longer visit. For true conversation. Hope betrayed Beth, yet she could not but hold it close. Why did she long for the love of a man who had so wronged her? Perhaps because such wounds seem as though they will never heal until those who have hurt us are sorry for their sins—but waiting for such medicine is often worse than the injury itself.

Willoughby paced toward the window, staring at her sliver of a view as he continued, "I am heartily glad that you are both now persons of property."

Five pounds he had sent her—a token payment shortly after the duel. What a flighty, irresponsible thing he must have thought her, to believe that a sum for a brief spree in London would distract her from the costs—monetary and otherwise—of raising an illegitimate child alone. The edge of that memory sharpened her tongue. "We will not end a burden upon the parish, no."

"Far beyond that, from what I hear." Willoughby turned to face her, so earnest, so eager, that Beth's hope flickered back into flame—until he added, "Enough money to allow you to resettle anywhere you should desire."

What could he mean? Did he perhaps have a house he meant to offer for his son's upbringing—a cottage on the estate of Combe Magna? "Though our stay here has been of short duration thus far, I believe this house will suit our purposes very well."

Willoughby's expression darkened. "What purposes might those be?"

"I do not understand you."

"Why here, by G-d? Why in Barton, not a mile from my home? Do you intend to shame me? To degrade me in front of all my family and friends?" Willoughby's outburst struck Beth as hard as any blow. "If you think this behavior will induce me to alter my own, you are sorely mistaken."

This, then, is my child's father. This petulant, arrogant boy wearing a man's boots.

Beth drew herself upright. "*You* are mistaken, sir, if you believe that my choice of domicile was in any sense predicated on my sentiments toward you. I sought only a fit house in the town nearest my good guardian, who provides your child with the attention you seem ill-disposed to give."

"To be near Brandon? You claim this is your reason? You ought to choose your lies with more care."

Indeed, she *was* lying. Beth had hoped Willoughby would take some measure of interest in little Georgie. More than that, she had thought not that they might be together—as he had married and that path was forever barred to them—but that he might show her, through his attentions to their child, enough warmth and kindness that she could console herself on her past impropriety. She would have liked to be able to say to herself that George's father was a good man, and one who had at least cared about them to some degree. What a fool she still was for him.

"I ought to have known you would have nothing to offer us," she said. "Certainly you offered me nothing when we parted, and from that I should have learned my lesson."

Willoughby lifted his chin. "Will you again claim that I left you with no word of my whereabouts? I tell you, I believed I had given you the address where I was to be found."

"You believed wrongly." The weeks, months, she had waited, terror creeping up around her like thorny vines, more every day, as her delicate state became undeniable, then undisguisable: had Beth possessed any hint whatsoever where Willoughby might be, no power could have prevented her from going to him. "If you believed it at all, which I doubt."

He dared to act himself affronted. "I tell you, my advice was kindly meant. You should leave this village, this county, altogether. It would be better for you and for the child. Think on this and you will see the wisdom of my words."

"Wisdom? Is that what you offer me now? You gave me only lies before."

"There was never any understanding between us," Willoughby said, as though they had no natural son together. "You were far from unwilling."

This, then, was too much to bear. Beth's temper, already sorely tested, finally burst beyond the limits of propriety. "If I had known then who you truly are—what you would do to me—I would not be what I am now, all but outcast, shamed for life. Nor would you be where you stand, for, I swear to you, you would lie in your grave!"

As Beth's anger had heated, Willoughby's countenance had grown cold. "I see I have outstayed my welcome. I will not trouble you again. Perhaps I should see myself out."

She wanted to throw him out, bodily. She wanted to hurl something else at his head, something heavier than a book this time. She wanted to weep. She wanted him to come back, to say he was wrong, to say he loved the child they had together created. To say—even now, even after all this—that he loved Beth.

Yet when had fate ever delivered what she wanted? Beth could only watch him go.

✑

Juliet worried that it might be unseemly to take such a great interest in the history of Colonel Brandon, the late Eliza Williams, and Miss Beth Williams, particularly as it intersected with the story of the late Mr. Wickham. Fortunately, Marianne was so much caught up in her subject that she did not seem to notice any undue enthusiasm on her guest's part.

"So, you see, she and I are oddly twined together," said Marianne, "but in ways we can never speak of, and thus it is difficult to know how our acquaintance should begin, if indeed it should. My mother thinks it unwise, but . . . Beth is very dear to my husband."

"I admit I have no experience of any such," Juliet answered, "but to me, yours seems the correct path. The colonel is a wise, good man. If there were aught of imprudence in your wishing to know Miss Williams, I daresay he would know it better than any other."

"That is just my thinking." Marianne smiled. "And my opinion is the stronger for your encouragement."

Juliet felt rather worldly, speaking of such serious, even secret, concerns. "How strong your love is for the colonel! Many women, I think, would not be so sanguine upon encountering the evidence of a husband's former attachment. But you are above such petty concerns."

Marianne's expression clouded, and Juliet thought perhaps she had gone too far—once license to speak of the forbidden was given, it was so difficult to determine how far such license allowed! All worry of awkwardness was, however, put to rest that very moment, for then arrived an older woman of the parish who bustled past the Delaford butler into the morning room as though she were very used to doing so. "Well, well, and here's a to-do. Dear Marianne, I hope you shall forgive me when I tell you all!" The older woman's eyes lit upon Juliet then. "But your young visitor has arrived, I see."

Although clearly curious about whatever news had been brought, Marianne did not neglect the courtesies. "Miss Tilney, this is our good neighbor Mrs. Jennings. Mrs. Jennings, this is Miss Juliet Tilney, who was of such assistance during the . . . unpleasantness in Surrey."

Juliet wished to make a polite reply but was given no chance by Mrs. Jennings. "You are very welcome to Barton, Miss Tilney. I am sure I speak for all Mrs. Brandon's friends when I say so. What a lovely young girl! No doubt you have left many beaux behind you in—"

Quietly, Marianne supplied, "Gloucestershire."

"Oh, I—no, ma'am," Juliet said. For a moment she thought of Jonathan Darcy. "I am very pleased to make your acquaintance, Mrs. Jennings."

She was answered with a chuckle. "No beau, eh? Indeed I am much surprised. Never fear, we'll soon see to *that*!"

Juliet had not been much in the greater world beyond her home, but she knew enough to realize that she had just fallen into the clutches of a veteran matchmaker—and, to judge by the gleam in Mrs. Jennings's eyes, an irrepressible one.

Marianne said, "But what am I to forgive you for, Mrs. Jennings?"

The old woman's cheer was immediately overtaken by exasperation. "My elder daughter can be most obstinate, though I say it myself, and Sir John—he is such a good man, but such an obliging one, and not all whims should be obliged!" It took some time for the rest of the story to emerge, and for Juliet—only half acquainted with the persons and events in question—the matter seemed somewhat confusing. Still, she was able to gather the following:

Sir John Middleton and Mrs. Jennings had formerly suffered one of their rare disagreements on the matter of Mr. and Mrs. Willoughby. Mrs. Jennings considered Willoughby a good-for-nothing, felt that he had treated Marianne abominably, and did not wish to associate with him or his rich, haughty bride. In these opinions, Sir John largely concurred, but he was a man of easy temper with a socially ambitious wife. Lady Middleton had left her card with Mrs. Willoughby at the first opportunity, and once she had taken up the acquaintance, Sir John could not shirk it without confronting his wife—a task he undertook seldom.

Thus it was that, when Sir John mentioned that he was to hold another of his large dinner parties on the night following, Lady Middleton had promptly invited Mr. and Mrs. Willoughby and their houseguests. Were they not the new master and mistress of Allenham? Had they not long planned to honor the couple in a most particular way, upon the claiming of this inheritance, toasting the house with a fine aged port? Even the genial Sir John had blanched upon this news, for while he was very fond of the port ritual and the attention it won him, he had specially intended this particular dinner party to welcome Miss Tilney. This meant of course that the Brandons had also been invited!

By any standard of hospitality, this was wholly unacceptable. Yet an invitation, once made, cannot be withdrawn for any but the most serious offenses. Thus Mrs. Jennings had been dispatched to inform the Brandons and give them the opportunity to gracefully decline. "You can always tell them your sister needs your help, and near as she is, none will argue it," Mrs. Jennings suggested.

To Juliet this seemed to be the obvious course of action. Yet Marianne sat quietly for some moments, considering carefully, before she said, "No. We will attend as planned."

Juliet could not but stare, and Mrs. Jennings showed even less restraint. "What? You mean to be in the company of that odious man and his odious wife?"

"I would avoid it forever if I but could, Mrs. Jennings." Marianne had taken on a resolve that made her seem older than her years. "Yet I cannot. The Willoughbys are come to Allenham to live; they will be our neighbors for perhaps the rest of our lives. Although I will never consider them friends, I must learn to endure them. So perhaps it is best to have this first meeting, to get past it and have it done with."

"Well, well," said Mrs. Jennings, her smile returning to her face. "I had thought to skip the evening entire rather than meet the Willoughbys. Instead, I see I shall attend in order to watch what may result."

Marianne said firmly, "There will be no scenes, Mrs. Jennings. Please assure Sir John and Lady Middleton on that point."

Mrs. Jennings paid this no mind. "Yes, yes, it will be something to see Willoughby set down as he deserves. Tomorrow night will indeed be an occasion to remember!"

Chapter Four

Jonathan noted with some relief the arrival of an invitation at Allenham. Such invitations often came when guests were known to be present and in need of amusement; he assumed the plan would be announced to them shortly. His emotions were mixed. This was yet another disruption—he had not yet settled into a pattern at Allenham—and there was the chance that Willoughby and Follett would see it as an opportunity to tease him before a new audience. Jonathan's occasional peculiarity of manners meant he did not always make a good first impression. Luckily, the mention of Pemberley generally overcame this to some degree, but he did not wish to be liked only for the house he would someday inherit.

However, a dinner might provide fresh amusement for Willoughby, distracting him from Jonathan entirely, and furthermore might lessen the tension that seemed to accompany Mrs. Willoughby from room to room like an oversolicitous servant. As some engagement with the local community beyond Allenham was inevitable, perhaps Jonathan was foolish to wish it might be delayed. Dinner parties were governed by habit and etiquette, so at least the evening would be free from surprises . . . or so Jonathan thought. The first hint he had that the evening would not proceed as expected came when Willoughby looked at the note sent and laughed. "So it is Allenham's turn to be toasted."

"'Toasted'?" Follett said, looking up from his newspaper. "What do you mean?"

"It is a silly, affected ritual much beloved by Sir John Middleton," Willoughby explained. "The new owners of a house are to drink a toast to their own home, just after dining. His servants set out glasses of port all evening long, merely to increase his sense of ceremony. Would you believe, he does this not only upon inheritance, but also upon purchase? Any newcomer is treated with the same deference as the scions of the families. I ought to have expected it. At least you will meet a few persons of the town . . ." His voice trailed off.

"What is it?" said Mrs. Willoughby, who had just then entered the morning room. She seemed to avoid looking at Jonathan—or was it Follett? They sat too near each other for Jonathan to be certain. He must be the one somehow in error, as Mrs. Willoughby had been willing to speak with Follett earlier in the day. Had he spilled something upon his shirt?

As Jonathan surreptitiously checked his attire, Willoughby gave his wife a strange look. "They have invited *all* the nearest households. No doubt you will wish to absent yourself."

"You would leave your wife at home alone while you go forth and make merry?" Bamber shook his head and chuckled. "Not very gallant of you, Willoughby."

"Then I shall be gallant for us both." Follett folded the newspaper as though he meant to take it with him. "I will of course be happy to stay behind."

Mrs. Willoughby's smile was small and tight. "I declare, Willoughby will scarcely notice our absence. He wishes only to speak to a certain former correspondent, a great favorite of his."

"Is she not a respectable married woman of the parish?" Willoughby's enthusiasm only brightened as his wife's displeasure became clearer. "Will her husband not be in attendance? Though *that* may be difficult to determine—so dull a fellow, one can forget him even when he stands in plain sight.

Besides, were you not eager to make a broader acquaintance in Barton?"

Mrs. Willoughby became even paler than before. "I would of course have invited guests to Allenham . . . and trust that I shall, regardless of the Middletons' party."

Bamber, who sat near Jonathan, made no secret of his interest in the argument unfolding before them. Impolite, surely, but if the Willoughbys made a spectacle of their disagreement, Jonathan could not wonder that others chose to watch. Under his breath, Bamber muttered, "We shall have to see who this mysterious figure is tonight, eh?"

No power on earth could have induced Jonathan to reply. His attention was reserved for Mrs. Willoughby, for if she and Follett were able to decline this invitation, their example might show Jonathan how to avoid Willoughby's company in future.

Willoughby finally turned back to his wife, his expression quite blank. "If you will meet everyone in the end, might as well stay home tonight . . . don't you think?"

Mrs. Willoughby could not decide how to answer.

She did not particularly want to go anywhere with her husband. But Willoughby's presence had to be borne, and she might as well accustom herself to bearing it in company.

What Sophia Willoughby most wished was for a good long look at the famous Marianne Brandon. What she least wished was for Willoughby to see his Marianne ever again.

Given the proximity of Delaford to Allenham, it was unlikely that the two could be kept apart forever. Although the two women had once been at the same dance, Mrs. Willoughby had then but a glimpse of Mrs. Brandon—and she had not then known any reason to look as closely as she now wished she had. Mrs. Willoughby had intended for their next meeting to take place in her own home, at her own convenience, where she would be able to govern the time and the extent of their interaction.

Yet she had recently learned that Colonel Brandon's wealth was even greater than her husband's (whose wealth was, in turn, mostly her own). It would not have done to have Marianne Brandon walk into Allenham and find it wanting in comparison to her own home! So perhaps it was best to seize this opportunity to meet Marianne Brandon, to dislike her dresses and find fault in her person. To blunt her conversation, to outshine her, to remind Mrs. Brandon that she had lost the race to be Mrs. Willoughby. (Sophia did not know whether she could say that she had won that race—it was not a contest that admitted of a winner—but Mrs. Brandon had definitely lost.)

Was it too much, even, to hope that Willoughby might find his memories of Marianne Brandon fairer than the woman herself? That, upon seeing the woman's country fashions and dull husband, he might remember that a far more sophisticated creature sat by his side, wore his ring upon her hand?

Mrs. Willoughby was not even certain she still loved her husband. All the same, she wished for one more proof that he loved her. A moment of Willoughby's adoration might not bring them closer, but it would make Mrs. Willoughby feel less like a fool.

"The Middletons mean to honor us both upon the inheritance of Allenham," she finally said. "It would be most uncivil for me to decline the invitation. No, my husband, I will be by your side all night long."

Willoughby looked disappointed, as she had anticipated. So, too, did Follett, but his disappointments were to be considered at a later time.

Much to Marianne's relief, the next caller was even more welcome than Mrs. Jennings, and far more likely to soothe her jangling nerves. She lit up as the butler announced, "Mrs. Edward Ferrars."

How was it possible that Elinor should be even greater in size than she had been when last they saw each other, only days before? *Her time,* Marianne thought, *must be very near indeed.*

Elinor's thoughts, however, were only for her sister. "I hope I have not called too late," she said, "but I thought you should rather have me late than not at all, nor would I wish to go so long without meeting your friend."

"Dearest Elinor," Marianne said, "how good of you to come, and at the very moment I need as many good listeners as I can find. Though of course a very fine one is here already—may I introduce Miss Tilney?"

Juliet practically shone with good humor and hope of friendship. "I am very happy to meet your sister at last. How do you do, Mrs. Ferrars?"

"Quite well, and I am the happier to meet you, Miss Tilney. You did my sister a great service, ensuring that a difficult truth was known at the right time, and in the right way." Wise as ever, Elinor did not delve into the matter any more deeply. "For that alone, I will be forever in your debt, but I am confident we will find many other sources of friendship."

"I hope so, very much indeed." Juliet's freshness and eagerness to please put Marianne somewhat in mind of their youngest sister, Margaret. No, Juliet Tilney was no longer a child, but she was not so far from childhood that its last traces could not be glimpsed in her face.

"Thank you for sending the carriage, Marianne," Elinor said as the three women were again seated. "Generally I prefer to walk, but today, I felt I could not, and to ride—why, that could prove not only dangerous to me but also punitive toward the horse. Now, what is it you need me to hear?"

"Give me strength," Marianne said, "for tonight I will again see Willoughby."

Elinor's evident dismay was a balm to Marianne's spirit. Her mother would have exclaimed and wept and raged. As this was her mother's response to many lesser travails, however, it signified little. Even a small gasp from Elinor spoke more of genuine feeling and shock.

Marianne poured out the full story as tea was served, summoning her courage for not only her sister's sake but also her own. "You see, I have learned from your example, Elinor. Instead of thinking overmuch upon the Willoughbys—I look forward to seeing Sir John and Mrs. Jennings and enjoying their better company. I am also happy to have more for Miss Tilney to do than to simply console me for the calumnies of the village. Perhaps it is vain of me, but I am even anticipating wearing my favorite dress."

"It is not vanity to distract oneself from that which is upsetting," Elinor replied, "and I feel for you most keenly. My hope is that Willoughby comprehends the difficulty of this moment sharply enough for prudence to govern his behavior. He must know that the only proper course of action is for the two of you to acknowledge each other as little as dinner party manners allow."

Marianne hesitated—even to Elinor, she had not admitted this much, but it would be better for someone to know, and who else could be told? Miss Tilney, listening quietly by their sides, could be trusted with such matters; that much had been proved at Donwell. "Willoughby wrote to me several weeks ago, when I was at Donwell. He said he hoped we could speak alone, as friends. Of course I did not reply. That should suffice, should it not?"

Miss Tilney's eyes had gone wide, reinforcing Marianne's conviction that such a letter should never have been sent. Elinor took it more calmly, but she shook her head. "It is impudence to assume that anything not expressly forbidden is allowed," Elinor said, "but Willoughby is an impudent man. Yet your propriety may have had good effect. The lack of response would have told any true gentlemen that his attentions were no longer desired."

"Wretched man! Will I never be free of him?"

Elinor smiled. "Not if Margaret has anything to say of it. Our younger sister would happily forgive Willoughby anything." Margaret, still but a girl, had been unable to understand the complexities of the situation, and remained too young and innocent to have the worst of it explained. To her, Willoughby remained dashing, honorable, beloved. "If Mama and Margaret come to visit this evening, I shall not mention the dinner at Barton Park, for otherwise Margaret will be mad to go and will arrive here at dawn to ask for details of all the pretty dresses."

Marianne sighed. "No doubt they will hear it from Mrs. Jennings, if they have not already. I should imagine that by this time half of Devonshire has been so informed."

Miss Tilney ventured, "Marianne, if at any point in the evening you require—shall we say, an escape, ask me any question, and I shall answer it at such a length as could scarcely be believed."

"How clever you are." Marianne had rarely been so happy in a friend as she was of Juliet Tilney.

"And prudent," Elinor added, for such was her most prized virtue. "Keep in mind, however, that Willoughby apparently has some guests staying at Allenham, who will also be in attendance. Some of them may provide more sources of amusement, or at least distraction."

Marianne could not muster much enthusiasm for Willoughby's friends. "It depends, I should say, on who they prove to be."

As it turned out, Bamber's evening hat had been badly crushed during his trip into Devonshire, and thus he proposed a general journey into Barton, where he might purchase a new one at the haberdasher's. Mrs. Willoughby had already sent a servant into town to procure new shoe-roses, so she declined; this, in turn, meant there was no need to call the carriage. Thus the four men walked together along the road that led into Barton village.

"Good of you to come along with me," Bamber said. "Or do you have errands as well? Don't tell me all evening hats were lost to the calamity of bumpy roads."

Follett replied, "I wish to purchase a copy of the *Times*, if one is to be had in this village. Really, Willoughby, you ought to take a paper or two besides the *Country Journal*."

Willoughby did not take kindly to the impugning of his taste in such matters. "Whatever can you need to know that the *Journal* does not tell you?"

"Business matters—shipping and the like," Follett said shortly. Jonathan could not imagine what need an artist had of such information. Did painters send their work to patrons far away, sight unseen? Or perhaps Follett awaited the arrival of some ship arriving from the Indies with rare and valuable pigments. He would have asked about this, as the subject seemed potentially quite interesting, had Follett not spoken first. "Whatever calls you into town, Willoughby?"

"Allenham has been neglected the past few years. I must see to its restoration in ways both grand and plain. Besides, I am ever glad of reasons not to remain at home."

His tone of voice as he spoke lacked conviction. Jonathan suspected Willoughby's thoughts were elsewhere, though he could not guess where that might be.

Follett's mood seemed to be lifting. "What of you, Thumps? Will you go in search of another volume of your precious Gibbon?"

All of them laughed then, even Bamber. Jonathan's extreme interest in Gibbon's *The History of the Decline and Fall of the Roman Empire* had served as yet another point of hilarity at school. They would ask him questions as though they were interested, and when Jonathan took pleasure in answering at length, they would fall into mockery. It remained difficult not to take such easy bait . . . yet Jonathan did enjoy talking about it so much. Someday, someone would find the book just as interesting as he did; of that, he felt certain. He already knew that this individual was not a part of the present company, however. So he remained silent, even resisting the urge to point out that he had, of course, read every volume of Gibbon already, and more than once.

Both Follett's and Willoughby's errands took them in the opposite direction from the haberdasher's, so the party split into two shortly after they entered the village. This left Jonathan and Bamber to make their way alone toward the haberdasher's shop. Jonathan began, "Why should Willoughby be especially glad of going to the Middletons' tonight?"

"Apparently it is for the sake of one of the young wives who will be present. He courted her before choosing another bride—and but for the present Mrs. Willoughby's dowry, I suspect this first woman would have been his choice."

"That explains why Mrs. Willoughby does not wish to attend," Jonathan said. "It would be very disagreeable to be chosen only for one's money." His father had made it very clear that Jonathan would have to be cautious to avoid this same fate.

Bamber smiled ruefully. "True—but even more disagreeable not to be chosen for one's lack of money! Ask Follett if you don't believe me."

"Follett?"

"Did you not know? Then again, you have never been in London for the season—you would not have heard." Bamber leaned closer as though he were about to whisper secrets in the back of the schoolroom, though no one else walked along their path. "Before the sudden, ardent courtship of Mr. Willoughby, our hostess was very near becoming Mrs. Laurence Follett."

Jonathan's surprise was great but short-lived. Upon reflection, he recalled many meaningful looks between Follett and Mrs. Willoughby—the coldness between Willoughby and his wife—and perhaps even their teasing of Jonathan was so pointed precisely because it was a safe subject, not likely to cause further friction between two friends with a grievance already. As for the conversation he had interrupted between Follett and Mrs. Willoughby that very morning . . . it would be best not to dwell on it, as their words had assuredly *not* related to the Oracle of Delphi. He said only, "Then Mrs. Willoughby has my sympathy."

After a pause, Bamber said, "You are a kinder spirit than you are generally credited to be, Darcy," and for the first time, Jonathan genuinely liked the man.

Colonel Brandon might have been considered the person most in need of a calm afternoon in which to prepare for enduring Willoughby's company yet again. Instead, he was obliged to reckon with the man's wrongdoings anew. As impossible as Brandon would once have believed this, apparently Willoughby had found a new means of hurting Beth.

Beth Williams had never lacked for food, clothing, or shelter. She had been brought up with a farm family that was fond of her, sent to school to acquire a few minor refinements and no more education than was decorative, which happened to be as much as Beth had any interest in learning. Beyond this, the colonel had always given her his warm affection and interest, and he had ever been willing to hear her nearest concerns.

On this occasion, however, his advice had come too late.

"He wanted me to leave the county." Beth sat in her chair, her posture correct, but every line of her body betrayed the anger she struggled to contain. "He had no interest in George. He only . . . wished our son gone."

"You refused him, as you ought," Brandon said. He attempted to pitch his voice to soothe and give comfort, much as one might speak to a shying horse.

Her expression suggested he had only irritated her further. "You think I did wrong to see him at all, don't you?"

Brandon took a few moments to reply. "It was a mistake, but an entirely understandable one."

"It is a mistake I will continue to make, because he cannot be avoided. He will always be in Barton, where I must always be. Oh, why did he ever have to come back to Allenham?"

"The wound will heal, given time," Brandon said.

Beth shook her head. "Some wounds do not heal. Some wrongs cannot be borne."

The note of anger in her voice worried him greatly, but this was not the time to exacerbate her sense of injury. He simply needed to listen and console, giving all his understanding to her, while simultaneously dreading facing Willoughby once more.

Barton Park was not an especially imposing house, not even as much so as Allenham. Nor was this to be a grand affair; only one carriage had preceded them, it appeared, and they had been told to expect a small dinner rather than anything more lavish. Yet Jonathan felt himself uneasy as soon as the Willoughbys' carriage arrived at the steps.

This was too much: too much novelty, too much uncertainty, too much noise and light, too many people. Under normal circumstances, Jonathan would be equal to a dinner party, even one involving strangers, but after only two days of feeling uncertain and unvalued, with no friendlier face near him than Bamber, with none of his familiar things around him—it seemed more than could be endured. How was he to get through a full month of this? Or, at minimum, one week and four days?

As the party departed the carriage, Jonathan said, "If you will excuse me, I require a few moments of fresh air." This was one of the formulae his parents had taught him for escaping an overwhelming situation before he was entirely undone. Most people accepted this as appropriate (and, most likely, assumed it was a euphemism for requiring the privy).

Willoughby, of course, did not. "Whatever is the matter, Thumps? Are you *still* scared of new places?"

"After all this time?" Follett laughed, but without any real mirth. His attention was directed toward Mrs. Willoughby, who had sat between him and Willoughby in the carriage. Jonathan would have attributed this fascination to Mrs. Willoughby's abundant and overlarge jewelry, had Bamber not told him of the connection between the two.

For her part, Mrs. Willoughby was steadfastly ignoring Follett or successfully pretending to. Regardless, she was not in the least inclined to laugh. "You must be introduced, Mr. Darcy. You will embarrass us if you fail to appear."

I will embarrass you more if I am overcome, Jonathan thought. He said only, "I beg your pardon, Mrs. Willoughby, but I was introduced to Sir John when he delivered our invitation, and I will be more fit to meet the ladies after a few moments' delay."

To Jonathan's enormous relief, he faced no further protest and was allowed to walk into the garden. Framed with tall topiary as it was, he felt almost as though he had escaped into a room with a closed door. He took a deep breath, then another. Instead of focusing on the sound of chatter from within the house, he observed the smaller, softer noises that surrounded him: the wind rustling through the trees, the distant lowing of a cow, and . . . footsteps.

Jonathan peered between the topiary shrubs, seeking the source. There, near the back of Barton Park, his attention was drawn by a figure darting away, hurrying toward the fields beyond. Anyone at the back of the house could usually be assumed to be a servant, but in this case, the person wore a long, elegant, hooded cape in a pale shade of blue—certainly the garment of a gentlewoman.

He could draw no further conclusions. Nor did it matter. This person had left the house and was therefore one fewer individual with whom he would be forced to interact. Jonathan walked toward the door, bracing himself for the night to come.

✑

That evening, Juliet had elected not to wear her finest gown. Normally one wished to make the best possible impression from the beginning—particularly on wider acquaintance—but she expected it would hardly have mattered had she worn sackcloth and ashes. All attention would be on the reunion of Willoughby and Marianne.

Besides, Marianne had chosen to wear *her* finest dress as a statement of courage. It would not do to outshine her friend under such circumstances or, what is worse, appear to have tried to outshine her and failed to do so. So Juliet donned the pale green dress she considered second-best and went down for the short carriage ride to Barton Park.

As soon as they arrived, Marianne groaned. "The Willoughbys' carriage is already here," she said. "I would so rather have had a chance to place myself first."

"Were they not here," Brandon replied, "I suspect we would have disliked the suspense and wished them here already. There is in such situations no pleasing alternative."

"You are right, of course." Marianne gave the colonel a look of such fondness that Juliet felt somewhat abashed to be in the same carriage with them.

Juliet was of course last in precedence, so she had to wait for her turn to be announced. Though expected, this was somewhat irritating, because this meant she likely would not witness the moment when the Brandons first faced the Willoughbys.

It is a very unworthy impulse, this desire to snoop, she told herself, before continuing more honestly, *and besides, the night will provide ample chances for you to observe everyone involved.*

The butler intoned, "Miss Juliet Tilney," and she stepped into Barton Park's drawing room at last.

"Good evening, Miss Tilney!" Sir John's ruddy countenance wore a broad smile. "How lovely your young friend is, Mrs. Brandon. We have many young men in attendance tonight, so she is sure to break many hearts!"

"Some are already broken," said a man standing nearby, his eyes fixed on Marianne, and Juliet had not one doubt but that this was Mr. Willoughby.

Her first impression was that John Willoughby looked exactly like the sort of man who could make one lose one's head. He was dashingly handsome, tall, dark haired. For an instant his eyes flickered from Marianne to Juliet herself, and his gaze met hers with such warmth that she felt, for an instant, as though she were the only one in the room.

No doubt Mrs. Brandon had felt that way once, before he betrayed her.

After Mrs. Jennings had greeted Juliet with good cheer, more introductions unfolded: First, Lady Middleton, who seemed more interested in evaluating Juliet's dress and earrings than in forming any genuine acquaintance. Then came Mrs. Willoughby. She was not beautiful, but it took Juliet some time to recognize as much, for Mrs. Willoughby's hair was so perfectly coiffed, her dress so elegant and sumptuous, and her jewelry so resplendent that it was almost impossible not to impute as much grace to the woman within it. "Miss Tilney," she said, her voice correct but cold. "How good of you to accompany Mrs. Brandon. Under the circumstances, I am sure she is glad of *one* friend."

The allusion to the murder, though disguised, could not be plainer. Juliet simply curtsied and moved along, pretending not to hear.

Where should she now turn? Usually, after the first introductions, formality faded a bit, and conversations began, but here an awkward silence had begun to settle over all. Marianne steadfastly gripped Colonel Brandon's arm.

Silence could not long reign when Mrs. Jennings was near.

She came to Juliet's side and began guiding her within. "I declare, Mr. Willoughby, you have forgot all your manners, for you have come with three other gentlemen but have not introduced Miss Tilney to a one of 'em!"

Willoughby collected himself as Mrs. Jennings led Juliet deeper into the drawing room, where two young men— perhaps slightly younger than he, both handsome and apparently well-mannered—stood chatting to each other. "Ah, of course," Willoughby said, "Miss Tilney, allow me to present my friends, Ralph Bamber and Laurence Follett. Bamber, Follett, this is a Miss Tilney of Gloucestershire. I have a third friend—is he still not back yet?—ah, there he is. Thumps, come and be introduced."

A third man was indeed entering the room, emerging from shadow in the hall. "In this case," said a familiar male voice, "no introductions are necessary."

Juliet stared in surprise, then delight. Marianne said, "Mr. Darcy! Is it really you?"

"How very fortunate that we should meet again." Jonathan Darcy appeared as stiff and elegantly dressed as ever, his eyes darting away from Juliet's, but she knew him well enough to see how truly pleased he was. One might almost have said his expression was one of purest wonder.

Nor were they the only two in the room made happy by the circumstance. Marianne's smile brightened, and Colonel Brandon hurried forward to shake his hand. "Mr. Darcy, how good to see you. But what has brought you here?"

"Thumps is an old friend of mine from school," said Willoughby. Mr. Darcy winced slightly—Juliet suspected the nickname was not a kind one, and disliked Willoughby more than she already had—but he kept his composure. "Really, Mrs. Brandon, you astonish me. However did you two form an acquaintance?"

It was Colonel Brandon who answered. "Mr. Darcy, like Miss Tilney, was of invaluable assistance to us both during our stay in Surrey."

A silence fell, one long enough to tell Juliet that the entire company knew that this referred to the death of Mr. Wickham.

Mr. Darcy broke the hush by saying, "I am very glad to have found friends here in Devonshire."

"Do you not count us, Thumps?" Willoughby asked, and Juliet was pleased when Mr. Darcy did not supply this with the dignity of a reply.

Chapter Five

Like any other proper young man of his class, Jonathan Darcy had spent considerable time in church. Unlike the majority of them, he had listened to the sermons and read long sections of the Bible purely out of interest. His cousin Mr. Collins, on one of his very rare visits to Pemberley, had interpreted this as evidence of Jonathan's wish to become a clergyman and sometimes sent lengthy, conspicuously pious letters encouraging him in this vocation, apparently believing it so desirable that Jonathan might abandon Pemberley to one of his younger brothers for the honor of the cloth.

In Jonathan's case, however, what was taken for piety was merely avid curiosity. The Bible provided so much guidance for society, and yet so much else besides! Contradictory advice, stories of shocking depravity—even, in early books of the Old Testament, what appeared to be clear references to other deities, which the later books of the Bible went to great lengths to deny. (Strangely, Mr. Collins never wished to discuss any of these when Jonathan attempted to raise the subject.)

Thus Jonathan was familiar with the rejoicing of David as he danced before the ark, and the year of jubilee. As for the pagans, *The History of the Decline and Fall of the Roman Empire* and other classical histories had provided vivid portrayals of many an imperial triumph. But nowhere in all holy Scripture or the volumes of Gibbon could he find an appropriate analogy to the happiness he felt upon finding Miss Tilney and the Brandons here in Devonshire.

He would not, after all, spend an entire month trapped with only Willoughby, Follett, and Bamber for company. Instead, he would also be able to spend many hours with real friends—people who valued him, who *liked* him, who did not call him "Thumps."

Best of all was seeing Miss Tilney again. To judge by the sparkle in her eyes, she shared his enthusiasm.

"Did you find the journey to Devonshire long, Miss Tilney?" Jonathan offered. To his great gratitude, they had been seated near to each other, making conversation as easy for them as it would be difficult for anyone from Allenham to overhear.

"Very much so, I'm afraid. The stagecoach is not the most comfortable means of transport." Miss Tilney leaned a little closer and whispered, "Remind me to tell you about the chickens."

"Chickens?"

"Later, I will reveal all." She put her hand over her mouth to conceal amusement perhaps too broad for general company. "We may be served poultry with the next course, and it seems ghoulish to discuss the living before the dead."

Even Jonathan got that joke, and he did not bother hiding his answering grin.

As the soup was taken away, Mrs. Willoughby—seated between Jonathan and their host, Sir John—spoke loudly enough to be heard across the table, where Marianne Brandon sat. "We have not yet had your card at Allenham, Mrs. Brandon."

This seemed provocative to Jonathan, but either he was wrong or Mrs. Brandon was not easily shaken. "Nor we yours at Delaford, Mrs. Willoughby. There is so much to do at a new house, is there not?"

"So many things! And yet, visitors do come. As a new

bride, I am accustomed to receiving congratulations," said Mrs. Willoughby. "You must be receiving the same, even if not so many."

Mrs. Brandon's smile did not seem entirely sincere. "The heartfelt joy of my family and friends is wealth enough for me."

"We cannot congratulate each other, though." Mrs. Willoughby's eyes studied Marianne intently, almost hungrily. "Or, rather, I will not expect *you* to congratulate *me*. I am quite pleased with your choice of husband, and so I can most heartily wish you many years together."

From the corner of his eye, Jonathan saw Juliet staring, somewhat agog. Only the lively conversation throughout the rest of the table prevented this from being what he could call "a scene." Jonathan knew that good manners sometimes required one to ignore an insult, but there was only so much even the most genteel individual could be expected to endure.

Yet Mrs. Brandon smiled wider. "You are correct, Mrs. Willoughby. I cannot congratulate you upon your marriage. You do, however, have my heartfelt sympathy."

Juliet coughed, more likely choking on laughter than her food, but Jonathan knew he should assume the latter. He gestured for a servant to bring her water, availing himself of this excellent opportunity to look away from such an unnerving interaction.

Sir John, who had heard it all, either understood none or refused to acknowledge that he did. "Nothing better for the village than new young blood!"

Astonishing though the conversation to her right was, Juliet could not help overhearing much of interest to her left as well.

"Beautiful countryside here," said the red-haired Mr. Bamber, who was directly next to her at the table. "Tell me, Colonel Brandon, has your family resided in this part of Devonshire long?"

"I am the fourth generation to live at Delaford," replied the colonel, "and it stands upon the grounds of our family's former home, which apparently perished in a fire."

Mr. Willoughby, who sat closer to the end of the table, next to Lady Middleton, spoke loudly enough for his voice to carry to them. "Ablaze with excitement, no doubt."

The silence that followed this rudeness was appalling, and soon followed by Mr. Follett rising from his seat. He made no comment upon his exit, and so no one gave any hint of having noticed. When Juliet was small, she had not understood why it was so important to pretend that no one ever required the privy, but time and her parents' determination had rendered her more genteel. Yet the timing of Mr. Follett's departure—surely he realized it would only make the pained silence worse?

But as Juliet was learning, no silence could long endure once Mrs. Jennings opposed it. "Pray, Mr. Bamber, are you the eldest son of your family?"

"The only son, ma'am," Mr. Bamber replied. "My uncle has no children, and so he has endeavored to teach me much about the running of an estate."

"Excellent." Mrs. Jennings's eyes twinkled as she looked directly at Juliet. "How very, very excellent indeed!"

Mortified, Juliet would happily have departed for the privy herself, had Colonel Brandon not at that moment done so. Surely it would be easier to be a fox at a hunt than to be an unmarried girl too near Mrs. Jennings!

After dinner ended, the mood of the party might have drifted in any number of directions—some of them most undesirable.

Juliet was much relieved when Sir John Middleton immediately drew the company's attention. "Gather 'round, gather 'round! In five minutes' time, a toast is to be drunk!"

Murmurings and rearrangings occurred as everyone took their place in the great hall. Colonel Brandon had just returned, but Mr. Follett had not. "Where the devil has Follett got to?" Mr. Bamber said in good humor. "Let me search him out."

As Bamber departed, Juliet looked for Mr. Darcy, only to find Marianne Brandon by his side. "I hope you will join us at Delaford tomorrow, Mr. Darcy. Perhaps for tea?"

"I shall be happy to come to tea," he replied. "If you invite me to any other meals of the day, I will attend those as well, most gratefully."

Marianne laughed, thinking it a joke. But Juliet wondered if it truly was. Her suspicion was that Jonathan Darcy very much wished to be anyplace besides Allenham.

Mr. Bamber returned, Mr. Follett just after him. As they came in, walking toward Mr. Willoughby, a servant entered from another door, bearing a silver tray with two glasses of port. There was some sort of upset—Juliet could not entirely see what had occurred, but Willoughby seemed to blame Follett, while Follett blamed Willoughby, and the servant hastened to the antechamber to pour another glass before blame could find him in turn. This did not take long, however, so it was but another minute before their host clapped his hands, assembling them all.

Sir John began, "The late Mr. Smith—Willoughby's uncle—welcomed me when I took possession of Barton Park so many years ago. 'Twas he who introduced me to the idea that while we drink to our friends on many great occasions, we ought once to drink to our houses, which shelter our generations and entertain our friends, in the hopes that they will continue to do so for some time to come."

He spoke in the tone of one who plans to talk at length. Juliet felt grateful. She need pay little attention to any of this, which left her mind free to work out exactly how to be Jonathan Darcy's friend without Mrs. Jennings marching them to the altar this very week.

"Thus it is my duty to welcome you, too, Mr. and Mrs. Willoughby." Sir John gestured to his butler, who came forward bearing the recently reset silver tray laden with two glasses and an opened bottle of port. Both Willoughbys came toward Sir John, though they never once looked at each other. "This port is from the year 1795, when, as I understand it, Mrs. Willoughby was born. How better to welcome the two of you into the neighborhood, eh? And how better to begin your lives here than by drinking a toast to Allenham?"

Surely Mrs. Willoughby would not drink port after dinner. During a meal a woman could perhaps take one glass of port, but after? No—that was a strictly masculine pleasure. *She will simply raise her glass,* Juliet decided, before turning her attention back on the matter of Mrs. Jennings's matchmaking. Could no one repress her? It was such a degradation to a girl!

"Now, now, take up your glasses," Sir John said to the Willoughbys. Mr. Willoughby took one glass and handed his wife the other. Their eyes never met. Sir John continued, "For the new owners of Allenham are to toast their house and all the good fortune we hope it shall bring them."

"To Allenham!" Mr. Willoughby said.

"To Allenham," echoed Mrs. Willoughby, and to Juliet's surprise, she drank as deeply as her husband. A few others appeared nearly as astonished by this as Juliet, but most seemed to accept a woman's drinking port after dinner in this singular circumstance. All said, "Hear, hear," and the like. Willoughby grinned, as he was intended to, but Mrs. Willoughby grimaced, as though port did not agree with her.

"Am I to give a speech now?" Willoughby said, obviously willing to do so, as he did not wait for an answer. "Thank you, Sir John, for your hospitality. Combe Magna was the first of my homes, but not the most beloved. No other place could have such command upon my heart than Allenham; no village could be so precious to me as Barton. These hills, these houses, have contained the happiest hours of my life."

From the corner of her eye, Juliet saw Marianne turn her head, as though refusing to witness. Mrs. Willoughby took a step to the side. Her expression was one of dismay. Was this port truly so strong? Had only one sip overwhelmed her? Surely not. But no . . . she must be reacting to her husband's allusions to the happiness he had experienced with another.

Willoughby continued, "I intend to long remain in Barton, close to my dearest companions. We were parted once before—but I promise you, never again."

Those who did not understand Willoughby murmured their approval. Juliet, like her hosts, remained silent.

Afterward, the party became conventional once more. As ever, the ladies retreated to the drawing room for whatever secret enjoyments awaited them there. Jonathan, like all the other gentlemen, went to Sir John's study in order to smoke cigars and drink yet more port. "Not the Willoughbys' bottle!" Sir John announced with good cheer. "No, sir, that shall return with them to Allenham and help to make that great house also their happy home."

That, Jonathan thought, would have to be extraordinary port indeed. After he received a glass of another—still excellent—port, Jonathan soon found himself with Willoughby on one side and Bamber on the other. "You never told us you were courting a young lady." Bamber appeared rather impressed. "Well done, sir. She is quite lovely."

"It appears that the dullest fellows have the finest luck," said Willoughby, whose gaze was directed toward Colonel Brandon—which led Jonathan to belatedly realize that Marianne Brandon must be the woman Willoughby originally intended to marry. This would have been a choice so wise and discerning that Jonathan had difficulty crediting Willoughby for it, even with the evidence clear before him.

Bamber was not so easily distracted. "Are you already halfway to the altar? Or do the rest of us still stand a chance?"

"There is no understanding between myself and Miss Tilney," Jonathan said. This was the truth, but why did he so dislike admitting it?

"Too bad, Thumps," said Willoughby. "Your heart is not so easily broken, it seems. Not everyone is so fortunate."

"Indeed not," added Mr. Follett as he joined their circle. Bamber raised his eyebrows, but spoke only of a horse race to be held soon, one on which everyone assayed an opinion, if only to silence Willoughby and Follett on any other topic.

Meanwhile, among the women, Juliet had been reclaimed by Mrs. Jennings, whose zeal for matchmaking had risen from a glowing candle to the Guy Fawkes bonfire. "What a slyboots you are, Miss Tilney! You tell me you leave no beau behind, and yet here we find Mr. Jonathan Darcy, the heir to Pemberley itself. All attentive to you, all kindness, all courtesy, his interest clear for everyone to see!"

"Mr. Darcy is not my beau, Mrs. Jennings." Juliet had wondered once, at Donwell Abbey, whether he might declare himself—but he had not. "We became well acquainted in Surrey."

"What is that, if not the first step to amour?" Mrs. Jennings chuckled, too pleased with her own conclusions to be dampened by any protestations. "Ah, you have set your cap well, Miss Tilney. There is scarcely an estate in England to match Pemberley, they say. I have heard that even dukes look upon it with envy."

Did Mrs. Jennings think her a fortune hunter? The mere suggestion horrified Juliet. She resolved immediately not to pay too much attention to Mr. Darcy . . . at least, not when Mrs. Jennings was present. "Please do not think I wished to speak only to Mr. Darcy tonight."

Yet this statement was not one to quiet Mrs. Jennings's speculation. "Oh ho, another has caught your eye, has he? Perhaps it is the dark-haired fellow, the *artiste?*"

"Mr. Follett, you mean?"

"So *he* is the lucky one." Mrs. Jennings chuckled merrily. Juliet considered correcting her, but would that not be the same as declaring herself for Mr. Darcy? Her mortification knew no bounds as Mrs. Jennings continued, "Laurence Follett is eligible, too, from what I hear of him, and if he has no house to equal Pemberley, well, not half a dozen young men in England do."

Casting about for any potential subject other than their current one, Juliet noted that Lady Middleton, with something almost approaching energy, was engaging Mrs. Willoughby in conversation—or attempting to do so, as Mrs. Willoughby's attention appeared to be turned entirely inward. Indeed, she appeared somewhat agitated, her cheeks flushed and her breaths coming rather quickly. Was she embarrassed by the display her husband had just made during that unseemly speech?

"Oh dear," Juliet murmured, "I do not think Mrs. Willoughby is at all well."

Mrs. Jennings observed all. "After seeing how her husband attends to Mrs. Brandon, it is no wonder that she should be displeased."

Juliet shook her head. "It is more than that."

Mrs. Willoughby was in a state of inelegance, dampness upon her forehead and at the neck of her gown—this despite the fact that she stood very far from the fire. Her steps were halting and uneven as she made her way toward a settee. As Juliet watched, Mrs. Willoughby visibly held back her gorge—a sight so improper, so unexpected, that Juliet had difficulty not feeling sick herself. From a corner of the room, Marianne could not but stare.

"I believe you are right, Miss Tilney." Mrs. Jennings's voice had softened. "The woman is unwell, and it appears she has not one friend here to come to her aid. I shall do it."

"I will accompany you," Juliet said.

Illness was the equalizer of their society, the force that could render all etiquette and custom moot in an instant. In extremis, a stranger might aid another in almost unthinkable intimacies when they had not even been introduced. Sickness was of course most properly kept hidden, but it did not always comply with propriety, and at its worst, not all the self-possession of the Stoics would allow it to be contained.

Juliet wondered whether Mrs. Brandon would consider it a betrayal—this assistance to Mrs. Willoughby—but on the whole thought not. Marianne might have no affection for her erstwhile rival, but she would never deny succor to one in such evident distress.

"There, there," Juliet began as Mrs. Jennings guided Mrs. Willoughby to her seat. "Is there nothing we can fetch you to relieve your distress?"

"A glass of wine, perhaps?" Mrs. Jennings added.

This struck Juliet as the last thing Mrs. Willoughby needed. Perhaps Mrs. Willoughby agreed, for she made no reply. Instead, she stared into the middle distance, as though something stood just behind the firelight.

"Mrs. Willoughby?" Juliet ventured. "Should we help you from the room? I am certain the Middletons have a bedroom where you might find more repose."

"The fox," Mrs. Willoughby said. "I must catch the fox."

Did she think herself at a hunt? If so, she was in even worse straits than Juliet had suspected. "No—no, there is no need to do anything but rest—"

"It is untrue." Mrs. Willoughby was not replying to Juliet; there was no saying whom she spoke to, but Juliet felt convinced it was no being of flesh and blood. "I must go, I will not be pitied, I must go—which is the way? Where is this place?"

"You are at Barton Park," Mrs. Jennings said, more gently than before. "The house of Sir John and Lady Middleton. You are not yourself, my dear. Rally your strength, and we shall get you to a carriage to take you back to Allenham. I am sure there is no place you would rather be than your own home."

Yet Mrs. Willoughby could not rally. Her face had gone pale and shiny; her hands were cold. Juliet could not imagine the mortification of being struck ill in the middle of a gathering. Yes, Mrs. Willoughby would have to be taken to her house, where at least she would have servants to see to her. Ought Juliet to accompany her there, or leave that to Mrs. Jennings, or—

At this moment Mrs. Willoughby finally lost control and vomited.

Small cries of dismay rippled through the company. This breach had gone past what could be disregarded; the crisis was now clear to all.

"Dear me." Lady Middleton, who valued elegance above compassion, wished her new friend had had manners enough to excuse herself from the room first. "We must ring for the servants."

Then Mrs. Willoughby vomited again and collapsed upon the floor.

Juliet instantly knelt by her side, as did Mrs. Jennings. All kind words of condolence and assistance went unspoken when Juliet saw Mrs. Willoughby's face. Her complexion had gone sallow, her body trembled, and her eyes were wide with terror. Marianne, fully beholding Mrs. Willoughby's distress for the first time, cried out in dismay. This had the effect of summoning the men from Sir John's study, though surely they were as helpless in this matter as any lady.

" 'Pon my word, the young lady needs help," said Sir John. "Yes, yes, my dear, ring for the servants. We'll get a maid here to see to her."

Mrs. Willoughby's eyes searched the room, apparently in vain. She seemed to be seeking a face among them—was it her husband's? He held himself coolly aloof from his wife's distress. Perhaps she sought Follett, who stared at the scene quite as though he had forgotten everyone else in the room. The reactions from the others varied from mere embarrassment (Lady Middleton) to outright shock (Mr. Darcy). Marianne Brandon held her hand in front of her mouth, as though afraid the same horror might soon be visited upon her.

Is this about to happen to everyone present? Is this some foul, noxious air making us ill? Yet Juliet felt no illness at all.

As the servants rushed in, Mrs. Willoughby again lost control of herself in a far more humiliating manner. Stench filled the room, faces turned away, and Juliet felt the greatest pity for the poor woman.

Mrs. Jennings tried to be consoling. "All will be well, my

dear. Look, the maids are come to put you to rights. You may rest in one of the rooms upstairs until you are yourself once more, and I am sure Sir John will send for a physician." Under her breath she added, "'Tis dysentery, no doubt. It can come over one powerful fast."

"Dysentery!" Juliet found this alarming indeed. "Has there been an outbreak here?"

"Not that I have yet heard, but someone must always fall ill first, eh?" Mrs. Jennings patted Mrs. Willoughby's hand as the maids set about laying a blanket atop the fallen woman. This disguised the sight of her indignity, at least, though the odor was inescapable.

Yes, yes, surely they have sent for a doctor, Juliet thought. *A doctor will know what to do, for I surely do not.* She squeezed Mrs. Willoughby's hand in hopes of providing comfort; this was all that lay within Juliet's power. Yet the clammy hand in hers had gone slack. Mrs. Willoughby trembled once more, gasped, and then—

Juliet had seen this before, when her granny passed away. This dying of the light in the eyes, this sudden sure knowledge that the soul had left the body behind. Yet she could not bring herself to speak the words.

Mrs. Jennings did so instead. "I believe she has died."

A horrified silence filled the room for a long moment, until their host spoke and made the horror infinitely worse.

"By poison," said Sir John. "She has died by poison."

Chapter Six

Not an hour later, one of the constables asked, "How can you be so certain it was poison, Sir John?"

Jonathan had been wondering about this himself. It seemed an outlandish proposition, but Sir John remained resolute. "After you have seen poison at work once, you never forget what it looks like. We witnessed it many years ago, in the Indies—I know you recall it as well as I, Brandon."

Colonel Brandon's countenance grew even more grave than usual. "Yes, of course. A junior officer wanted revenge on his superior, and this he had."

"Probably only meant to sicken him, but he killed the man dead, and was hanged for it." Sir John shook his head. "To have such as this happen on such a glad occasion! To a woman so young, still a bride!"

The entire company had been moved into the library, leaving the late Mrs. Willoughby unattended except by the two constables. At present only the one called Hubbard remained with her; Constable Baxter had come to talk to them, and he seemed far from convinced that any crime had occurred. "Surely it is more likely that she was taken ill," he said. "Dysentery can have such effects, can it not?"

This only increased Sir John's opprobrium. "But to kill within one hour of first taking ill? That cannot be!"

Jonathan had no experience of dysentery, for which he was grateful. Others, however, were nodding their agreement—

most particularly Colonel Brandon, who as a soldier would have seen this ailment at work in the camps.

Baxter had to admit the justice of Sir John's point, but he was far from assuming any criminality. "Well, if it is poisoning at work, food poisoning is surely all there is to the matter."

Lady Middleton had previously shown no emotion more noteworthy than displeasure that her dinner party had ended in such a ghastly way. Now, however, she drew herself up, rigid with disapproval. "Our kitchens are well-kept, and our cook and servants well-trained in what they do. I hardly think such an error likely in *this* house."

"Now, now, miss. I mean, madam. I mean, my lady." Baxter sputtered. "I mean no disrespect, I assure you. It can happen in the best of places."

"I still think dysentery far more likely," Lady Middleton snapped. "Why are we discussing this with the constables? Should not the local magistrate take charge?"

"Normally, ma'am," Baxter said, "but there is no magistrate at present."

"You must remember," interjected Sir John, "Wallingford passed away just three weeks ago, and no replacement has yet been named. The constables will have to do their best for the time being. But mark my words, Baxter—do not be slack only because no one is here to supervise you. This was poison, and I am sure that if you look, a culprit will be revealed."

And so, for a brief time, the room was sunk in silence, as each person considered what these events might mean.

Jonathan could claim no great fondness for Mrs. Willoughby, whom he had known but briefly, during which she had little seemed to wish a deeper acquaintance. Yet he could not but feel compassion for the suffering of any living creature and—should her death prove unjust—anger at the arrogance that must underlie any deliberate murder.

Mrs. Jennings was not likely to be long disturbed by any tragedy that did not directly affect a person she cared for, and she had not cared one whit for Mrs. Willoughby. However, she felt great sorrow on behalf of another in the room. Poor Marianne Brandon! Already the entire village knew the role she had played in one man's death. They also knew of the attachment between Willoughby and Marianne not so long ago. How the people would talk! How suspicion would fly!

Willoughby stood, utterly silent, at the far edge of the room, staring through the window at nothing but the blackness of night. Often he had wished to be rid of his wife, but never had he wished to be rid of her fortune. Now he had lost the first and gained the last.

Laurence Follett sat in a chair, elbows on his legs, a posture that had nothing to do with decorum. He thought of a night he and Miss Sophia Grey had danced together, a night he had thought could be but the first of a lifetime's worth they might spend side by side. Willoughby had returned to town the very next day. Had Sophia hesitated to transfer her affections? Or had her heart been so untouched that she could not imagine the suffering she had caused? She would do no more dancing, ever again.

Colonel Brandon kept his wife's arm in his, as though at any moment he might escort her from the room, from the house, from Barton altogether. He thought such a thing might ultimately prove necessary. Yet at present they must show themselves honest and stalwart, so he did not move.

Ralph Bamber could hardly get over the shock of it. In his studies, he had learned much of the workings of poison on the human body—but there was a very great difference between reading dry lines in a text and seeing actual human suffering, brought about for no reason at all.

Juliet Tilney, deeply shaken, sat on a divan. She had found the dead body of Mr. Wickham during the unpleasantness at Donwell Abbey, but it was one thing to come upon a person already dead, quite another to watch one die. Her grandmother's passing had been as gentle as such could be, the old woman's breathing going slower and shallower until it vanished into nothingness; it had been her time. But Mrs. Willoughby had been not so very much older than Juliet herself, and her death might well prove to be unnatural. No, there could be nothing more horrible than witnessing that. But Juliet corrected herself immediately: *One thing only can be worse—to be the one dying by such terrible means.*

Sir John alone knew precisely what to do. "I have already sent a lad to fetch the doctor. Mark my words—Hitchcock will be able to tell us much."

Juliet's shock was at last punctured when she realized how pale Marianne Brandon had become. Most, observing Colonel Brandon in this moment, would have thought him largely unmoved, but Juliet had known him through circumstances that had taught her how to tell when he was troubled. Her duty in this moment was toward her hosts, and so she went to join them.

"Oh, Juliet." Marianne took her hand. "Is it not terrible? There was a time when I wished ill upon that lady, but it is long past, and even then I should never have wished for anything so wicked as *this*."

"It is terrible indeed." Already Juliet was dreading writing to her parents. They had been upset enough to learn of the first murder in their daughter's general proximity; there would be no bounds to their displeasure upon learning of a second. "Perhaps Sir John is incorrect. Mrs. Willoughby's death is of course grievous regardless of the cause, but an accidental death would not be nearly so ghastly as a murder."

Merely hearing the word made Marianne flinch. "They will all think it was me."

"They will not think it," Colonel Brandon said, with what Juliet considered more feeling than sense. "Everyone who knows of Mr. Wickham's fate also knows the circumstances that brought it about." This meant Wickham's wicked attack on Marianne late at night, a circumstance that made Juliet blush to think of it. Never before had it occurred to her how horrid it would be for Marianne, who had to allow public knowledge of such an upsetting moment in order not to be thought a cold-blooded killer.

"Some do not excuse me even knowing the truth." Marianne wiped her eyes. "How I repent of my lack of discretion with Willoughby! Had I conducted myself properly, if I had not made such a spectacle of our courtship, then the people of Barton would not be so quick to draw such conclusions."

"Perhaps they will not be as quick as you fear," Juliet said. "Yes, some will assume terrible things, but there is always *someone* willing to think the worst. It is work for which volunteers are never lacking. Wiser minds will consider the subject more rationally, and wiser voices may prevail."

Marianne was not consoled. "If only I could believe so. Wiser voices are sometimes the least listened to. Certainly I took long enough to heed them."

"Do not judge yourself for the trust and naturalness of youth," Brandon said.

"Others will," Marianne insisted. Juliet wished she did not agree.

Another guest realized he had a duty to his host, but his situation was even more distressing than Miss Tilney's.

Jonathan had arrived at a house presided over by a master and mistress, but Allenham had a mistress no more. Had this happened in a home where Jonathan felt warmth and kinship toward the newly bereaved, he could have offered true sympathy. Had it happened in a house where he was almost a stranger, he would have left as soon as decorum allowed, most likely directly after the funeral service. Instead, the circumstance had befallen him in a house where Jonathan was openly spoken of as a friend of the widower but actually had no liking for him whatsoever. Willoughby did not appear to need much consolation for his wife's death but could scarcely say so. Thus the forms had to be obeyed, though Jonathan felt they would be purely a matter of pantomime. (He had often felt that way toward other irrational social niceties, but the contrast had never struck him so sharply as it did at present.)

So it was with trepidation that he went to Willoughby's side. As though Jonathan's motion had been a cue, Follett and Bamber both went with him.

"You have our deepest condolences, Willoughby," said Bamber. "Such a fate should never have befallen her." Follett made a sound deep in his throat, the nature of which Jonathan could not determine.

Willoughby, by contrast, was distracted, disturbed. "What does Sir John think the doctor can tell us that we do not already know? My wife is dead. No doctor can change that."

"The doctor will be able, perhaps, to determine the cause of her death," Jonathan explained helpfully. "Then the truth or falsity of Sir John's accusation can be known."

"Sir John!" Willoughby scoffed. "Who has ever listened to such a fool? He thinks of nothing but filling his table with lively young people on every occasion, so he and Lady Middleton are never suffered to spend time with only each other for company."

This was very rude, particularly given the graciousness with which Sir John had honored the couple earlier that night. Rudeness from Willoughby, however, rarely came as a surprise to Jonathan—and, as Mrs. Willoughby's death had taken place at Barton Park, it was understandable that Willoughby might feel some irrational anger toward the host. If it was an accidental poisoning she had succumbed to, then her death was ultimately the host's responsibility.

But Jonathan agreed with Sir John. He had seen a cat poisoned once—a despicable act. The memory of the poor suffering creature he had seen years before kept coming back to him, and the similarity between its final throes and Mrs. Willoughby's was too great to easily dismiss.

If poison was at work, Jonathan thought, *I do not believe Dr. Hitchcock will find it to be accidental.*

The entire company anxiously awaited the arrival of Dr. Hitchcock, either because they very much wanted answers about what had truly taken place that night or simply because only after the doctor's consultation would anyone be able to go home with decorum—otherwise, a departure would look too much like a flight from potential responsibility. (Lady Middleton felt this point most keenly. The maids could hardly get to work cleaning up the mess until no guests remained to observe their more strenuous efforts.)

So it was that the next knock on the door led to many sighs of relief. However, Juliet felt certain she was not the only one whose relief dissipated somewhat upon first glimpsing Dr. Hitchcock. He was an elderly man, bony and angular, who dressed in attire that had been fashionable forty years prior. Several older gentlemen still wore powdered wigs, but Juliet had rarely seen one so yellowed, nor one worn so lopsided that it seemed likely to topple from its owner's head at any moment. His voice creaked as he said, "Where's the dead lady?"

His uncouth tone led to blushes, but Sir John was not easily discomfited. "She breathed her last in the drawing room, I fear. Good thing you've come, Hitchcock. I tell you, something dark was done to the girl."

"Poison, your messenger said." Dr. Hitchcock peered at Sir John then, and Juliet realized that—however fusty and negligent the doctor's appearance might be—his intelligence remained acute. "You have told the scullery to wash none of the dishes yet? To leave all pots and pans alone?"

"Yes, and the glasses, too," Sir John replied.

"Only this lady fell ill?" Hitchcock frowned. "Did she eat or drink aught that others did not?"

Sir John said, "No, every dish was shared by all. She drank a glass of port from a bottle shared only with her husband, but as you see, he remains well."

Hitchcock's sharp gaze swept over Willoughby, who appeared shaken but—to Juliet's eyes—not nearly as bereft as a new-made widower should be. "Port is usually decanted and let to breathe. Was this done here?"

"My servants know how port is best served," snapped Lady Middleton, whose housekeeping had never before been under such grievous assault. "It is decanted before the glasses are poured, and then the glasses are allowed additional time to breathe, so the port will be taken at its best."

"So the late Mrs. Willoughby's glass of port sat apart for a time?" Hitchcock shared a look with the constables, who, despite their lack of medical knowledge, could spy the importance of this fact. "Was it observed throughout that time?"

"It would rarely have been left alone!" Sir John protested. But comprehension became evident upon his features. "Yet I cannot swear that there was no moment at which the glasses were unattended."

The implications were now clear to all, but Juliet could feel the general reluctance to admit such a terrible truth. "Might it not be a case of dysentery?" Mrs. Jennings said. "Though there have been no other cases reported yet, others may be soon to come. One person must always fall ill first, surely?"

"Not even the most violent case of dysentery kills so quickly as this." Hitchcock shook his head and sighed. "The answers are always within the body, in the end. After the autopsy, much will be revealed."

Juliet frowned at the unfamiliar word, and she was not the only one puzzled. She was grateful when Mr. Darcy asked, "What is an *autopsy*?"

Hitchcock replied, "The dissection of a dead body in order to determine the cause of death."

At the mention of dissection, Juliet's stomach turned over. Marianne very nearly swooned against her husband. Lady Middleton winced as though in pain. Truth be told, most of the men appeared equally sickened. Such a thing could hardly be spoken of in polite society—only such a circumstance as this could bring it about, and it was a circumstance bitterly regretted by all.

Follett took several steps forward, confronting the physician. "You will not subject the woman to such barbarity!"

"I cannot see the need for it, either," said Willoughby. "We know she died of some form of poison, do we not? What else can the autopsy tell us?"

Hitchcock squinted at him. "You do not wish anyone to know how she really died? Is there any particular reason why you would feel that way?"

"I will defend myself against any accusation," Willoughby said in a fury, "but I will not have it said that I did my wife a wrong only because I would not see her . . . torn to shreds." At this last phrase, Follett closed his eyes, as if overcome.

Lady Middleton could bear no more and hurried from the room, Mrs. Jennings just behind. Juliet wished she could join them, but that would mean ceasing to listen—something she had no intention of doing.

Marianne, however, had recollected herself. "She is beyond any further harm now, Willoughby," she said, her voice steady and gentle. "The truth should be known."

Colonel Brandon stared at his wife, obviously surprised she had spoken. Perhaps Willoughby was astonished, too, for he could think of no more arguments against Hitchcock's plan. "Very well, then," he said, "if there is no other way, then there is nothing for it. But I am greatly shocked and grieved that such should be necessary."

Juliet thought this should compare little to the shock and grief a husband ought to feel upon his wife's sudden demise. It was as though the autopsy troubled him more than the death.

The next day was the Sabbath, on which no work could be done, even in the matter of determining the cause of Mrs. Willoughby's death. Thus all who had been present at

Barton Park that night were left with a long, silent day to con-
template what they had seen.

Although a widower might be expected to require greater
aid and comfort from his religion, there was at Allenham no
talk of attending church. Jonathan's breakfast was brought in
on a tray by a servant who informed him that this procedure
would be followed at both midday and evening. Delivered
with the tray was a black mourning band, which some seam-
stress must have been obliged to stitch in the wee hours of
the morning. Under any other circumstances, he might have
been grateful for the chance to hide in his room rather than
spend time with his former schoolfellows. As it was, however,
he found solitude an uneasy companion.

As the day drew on, Jonathan's unease deepened. The
uncanny silence of Allenham did not lend itself to anything
but reflection and recollection, all of which centered upon
the ghastly events of the evening prior. No matter how
many ways Jonathan attempted to consider the matter, his
thoughts all led him back to one conclusion: he must investigate yet another murder, once again with Miss Tilney at his
side. Would she see it the same way? Although he could not be
certain, he strongly suspected she would.

But what did this say of his character? Could it be wholly
Christian of him to take such an interest in an act so sinful?
Worse yet, Jonathan could not deny a certain feeling of anticipation at the prospect. It appeared that his stay in Surrey,
and the fate of his uncle, had had an enduring effect on his
character. Was it mere morbid curiosity, or was it a greater
interest in seeing justice done?

Finally, in the early evening hours, Jonathan dressed (complete with mourning band) and ventured into the rest of the
house. The servants must have been working hard through-

out the day, for already Allenham had been made appropriate for mourning. He wished only to spend some short time in the library, which, he thought, would allow for some leavening of the oppressive mood. It did not, however, for as he walked in, he saw Willoughby seated at the writing-desk.

"Forgive me, Willoughby," Jonathan said, preparing to depart. Should he give his condolences again? He had done so the night before, of course, but not in the usual formal manner.

"Thumps." For once, Willoughby pronounced the nickname with no particular scorn. He was pale, as though he had not slept, at which Jonathan could scarcely wonder. "You see me for once a man of business."

". . . I should imagine there is much necessary correspondence you must write, to inform relatives and the like."

"Sophia had little family—a few cousins here and there, an uncle and aunt who wanted no more to do with her. They have what they wished for, I suppose." Willoughby stared down at the paper, at the inkwell and sawdust, at the pen still in his hand. "Most of my letters must be written to various lawyers, most particularly the trustees who oversee her independent fortune. During our marriage, you see, that money was so unreachable for me that it might as well have been on the moon. Now, however—all is changed."

This struck Jonathan as an extraordinary statement for Willoughby to make, given that it suggested a very powerful motivation for the murder of his wife. Was his host indeed so innocent of the crime that he had not even considered whether he would be blamed?

Or was he merely confident that he would get away with it?

"I do not know the rule for this situation," Jonathan said, "whether it is considered more correct for me to end my visit to Allenham immediately, or at least immediately after the funeral, or whether I should stay." He wished very much to remain, the better to investigate. If Willoughby asked him to go—perhaps the Brandons might invite him—

But there would be no need. "By all means stay," Willoughby said. "I should not wish to endure the calls of every sympathetic neighbor entirely on my own. Besides, you must help me to conceal the truth."

Was this an admission of murder? Jonathan managed not to reveal his astonishment. "What do you mean?"

Willoughby at last looked up from his writing paper. "That Sophia took her own life."

This struck Jonathan as not at all plausible. "By poisoning her own glass of port?"

"Who else could have done it but she? Furthermore . . . our marriage was not a happy one. You had seen that much for yourself, at least. She must have realized that she did not have my heart and never would—and wished to spite me by doing herself harm in front of all my friends, before the whole neighborhood, and most particularly to be seen by—" Willoughby paused. Was he struggling for control? If so, it would be the first time he had needed to do so in this conversation. "To be seen by one whose hold upon my heart can never be conquered."

Jonathan said, "Mrs. Brandon, you mean."

Although Willoughby appeared startled, he rallied swiftly. "You came to know her at Surrey, of course. You must know how completely she could bewitch a man's heart."

Jonathan thought this a most improper time for Willoughby to wax poetical upon the virtues of a woman not his wife. He said only, "I will stay, then."

Willoughby nodded, then turned back to the letters that would enrich him so greatly.

After this, Jonathan was all too willing to return to his room, for he had much to consider. On the stairs, he came across Bamber, who appeared nearly as stricken as Willoughby. "A terrible tragedy, this," he said. "Not only for her husband. Follett's bedchamber is next to mine, and I heard him pacing all through the night, and today, too. Not that I could sleep well myself."

Was Follett's pacing due to grief? Or might it rise from other sentiments, such as guilt? Jonathan did not allow himself to speculate further. "It is shocking indeed."

"I would not have thought my excuse to leave Allenham would come so swiftly, nor that I would wish it never to have taken place," Bamber said.

"Willoughby wishes for us to stay," replied Jonathan. "He says that we must help him conceal the truth—that his wife did away with herself, to revenge herself upon him for the unhappiness of their marriage."

Bamber's astonishment could not be wondered at. "He has no small opinion of himself, if he thinks his wife would not have found life worth living without him."

"That is one possibility," Jonathan said. This next he had meant to reserve for the hearing of Miss Tilney, but how could any person present the night before not have similar thoughts? "Another is that he has come up with this story to disguise his own role in Mrs. Willoughby's death."

"Good G-d! Do you really believe—" Then Bamber paused. "But now that you say it, I can see . . . let me say only that I see it could be *possible*."

"Further than that, I would not wish to go," Jonathan quickly added. "I would not wish to be Willoughby's accuser with no proof at all."

❧

Jonathan's forbearance was not widely emulated in the village of Barton.

Some would say that the center of a village is its church; others, its town square. Those less literal might say that a village's heart is the cooperation and good feeling among its citizens. Those not given to such charitable feeling—or those from less congenial communities—would instead say that every village is centered upon one constant, irrepressible force: gossip.

Decried as it is by moralists and from pulpits, gossip is not entirely malevolent. Contained within it is much news that people are happy to hear, share, and have shared—loves, births, journeys, and dances. Sadder information, of sickness or death or broken friendships, is often heard with proper concern rather than petty glee. Yet this defense would not go so far as to claim that gossip *never* takes a malicious turn.

Certainly it had taken that turn in the village of Barton on the day after Mrs. Willoughby's death, the news swirling through every conversation held before and after Sunday services (and, thanks to a few whisperers, during).

Discussion of Marianne Brandon's role in the death of a man at Donwell Abbey had been plentiful and not always sympathetic. Yet most in town thought a young woman unlikely to even attempt violence against a former soldier unless sorely tested. They trusted the law in such matters. Also, the late Mr. Wickham had been unknown to any in Barton—he was a stranger, a cipher, no loss to any person there. So although public opinion had been very much shocked by Marianne's actions, and could not settle on how she was to be considered socially, it had not wholly turned against her.

The death of Mrs. Willoughby was a far different matter. Everyone remembered how, not so very long in the past, Marianne had adored Willoughby, how openly she had shown her great preference for him, how often the two of them had flouted convention to be together as much as possible. Poison was a woman's weapon, was it not? Certainly it was far easier to imagine Marianne Brandon with a poison bottle than to imagine her taking up arms.

The haughty Mrs. Willoughby had not been much beloved in Barton, but even this turned to Marianne's disadvantage: How could Marianne not have been tempted to lash out at such a prideful person? Especially if that person's death freed Willoughby to, perhaps, illicitly resume their formerly public amour?

No one was so bold or so hostile as to carry such rumors to Marianne's own ears, but this was unnecessary. She had predicted them herself with terrible accuracy.

"They will have me arrested by dusk," she whispered. "The constables might very well be on their way!"

"Do not torment yourself so." Colonel Brandon put a gentle hand on his wife's forearm. "The constables are not directed by gossip. Without a magistrate's authority, they will not act absent proof, and as we both know, there is no proof to be had, for you are innocent."

Juliet Tilney, who sat on Marianne's other side, joined in. "There is no resemblance between the crimes, so why should one connect you to the other?"

"It is a murder and a murder, and so they are the same!" Marianne insisted. "Who could not connect them? I would do so myself, if I heard it of another."

"You would not condemn without proof," Brandon said. "Neither will any of those who truly know and value you. The others are of no consequence."

Marianne could not be so sanguine, so she made no reply.

Meanwhile, Juliet had momentarily become lost in thought. To her it seemed natural that an individual who had killed once would be most likely to kill another in a similar manner as before. Very different crimes suggested different perpetrators—or did they? She wished there were someone to ask.

Brandon said, "I am to go into town today, on my usual business. When I am seen to behave as if all is well, others will come closer to believing it."

Marianne would not be so easily consoled. "Would that it were true!"

Chapter Seven

Juliet did not know how best to console Marianne for the horrible shock, but as soon as Monday morning came, the task no longer fell to her alone. Marianne's family arrived even before calling hours had begun.

Mrs. Dashwood, Marianne's mother, arrived first, along with Marianne's younger sister, Margaret. No time was wasted on false greetings; instead, Mrs. Dashwood clasped Marianne to her as soon as she had entered Delaford. "Dear child! Why did you not summon us at once? We stayed home from church—poor Margaret was sneezing a fit—and so we did not learn of it until this morning."

"I did not tell you because then I would have had to write it down," Marianne admitted. "To write it down—to see the words in ink upon the page . . . somehow it seemed too much."

"How very terrible for you," said Mrs. Dashwood, rubbing her older daughter's hands as though Marianne had just come in from a winter storm. "So soon after one shock, to be visited with another!"

Marianne nodded. "Yes, terrible—it can be called nothing less. Though I am not to be pitied nearly so much as she who perished."

"I don't see that it's so terrible," said Margaret. "Nobody liked Mrs. Willoughby, not even Mr. Willoughby. Why do we have to pretend to be sad?"

"Margaret!" Mrs. Dashwood turned on her youngest with motherly strictness. "A person has died young in wretched circumstances. That must cause us to feel some Christian sympathy."

The expression on Margaret's face was unchristian indeed, but the rebuke sufficed to silence her.

Elinor Ferrars arrived next, cloak scarcely sufficient to cover her in her present state. How much it spoke of her love for her sister, this willingness to venture out despite being in the tenderest days of her confinement! Elinor went to her sister and took her hands as though bracing her. "You must be steady, Marianne. You must show yourself to be free of guilt if you wish to be free of suspicion."

Marianne scoffed. "*That* is not so easily accomplished."

"Do not allow them to speculate upon your distress." Elinor was so composed, so steady, that Juliet half thought this speech was one she had planned. "Do not display your feelings to the undeserving. All that is most important—most true—keep this safe. Keep this within."

Certainly Elinor Ferrars understood how to do that, but Juliet was not so sure that Marianne would be able to learn the lesson.

The first news given to Beth Williams had come, hesitantly, from her lady's maid, not long before the midday meal on Monday. "You have heard, haven't you, ma'am? About Mrs. Willoughby?"

Willoughby was a widower. Willoughby was free.

Beth went to her son, George, and took him into her arms. So mothers do when they wish to comfort a child, but also when they wish to be comforted by one. Beth's heart beat fast against the heavy warmth snuggled next to her. "Shhh, now," she said, to herself and George both. "Shhh, all is well. All will be well."

Nothing could stop Willoughby any longer from doing what was right by Beth, if he wished to do it. If he did not come, then she would finally be sure, beyond any doubt, that he had no use for her any longer—not even the wicked, selfish uses he had put her to before.

After their disagreement days earlier, Beth could not be entirely certain that she wished Willoughby to return to her side. Yet she wanted *him* to wish for it. The contradiction made no sense, and she did not attempt to mold the feeling into any rational form. Was it so impossible that he might have wished for Beth's absence, and George's, only to placate the wife who no longer drew breath?

He had Mrs. Willoughby's fortune now, or would soon. He no longer had to fear his dead aunt's disapproval and disinheritance. For the first time, Willoughby was truly free.

Beth had always wondered what he would do if he were granted such liberty. Would it have been better never to find out? Perhaps. Yet one way or another, the truth would soon come; it could no longer be stopped. As she had long understood, this knowledge alone could free her heart.

Juliet understood that Marianne might be best consoled by her family without any other person present. Her friendship with Marianne was true and deep—yet new. There are intimacies shared between sisters, mothers, and daughters which few friendships of any duration can ever fully replicate.

So it was that Juliet set out for a walk into Barton, which was not even a mile from Delaford. She had no particular business in the village, but her parents had given her a bit of money, so she might purchase a few needful items (and, perhaps, a few that were less needful but highly pleasing). Of course, she could have delayed her walk until after she had written to her parents about Saturday night's terrible events, but Juliet could not yet bear to do it. This was only reasonable, she decided, for she could not yet say *how* Mrs. Willoughby had died—whether it was accident or worse—and surely it would be better to wait and tell the full truth rather than a partial one? (Reason too often responds to our wishes with an astonishing agility, as it did with Juliet that morning.)

On her own, Juliet drew little notice. Suspicion of her hostess had not increased to include the guest as well. What a relief, she found, to think of mundane matters for a few minutes—whether these buttons or those would be better for a frock, or which fabric might make the loveliest ball gown.

This last question proved tempting enough to draw Juliet into the shop, in order to better investigate a lovely pink cloth. To her surprise, she knew someone inside, and this someone was saying the words Juliet would least have expected to hear: "Certainly poison—in my kitchen, never!—Mrs. Brandon so peculiar lately, with her seclusions and her frights—would not be at all surprised to find Mrs. Brandon at the bottom of it all." This from Lady Middleton, Marianne's hostess and supposedly a friend.

Juliet mostly kept close watch over her temper, but not even the most careful vigilance can be perfect. "I beg your pardon, ma'am," she said, walking toward Lady Middleton and her listeners, "but there is not the slightest chance that Mrs. Brandon is involved. If there is wickedness afoot, she is not the source."

Lady Middleton appeared much displeased to have been

caught in the act, but was not the sort to become flustered. "I do not presume to know the truth, as *some* do."

"Certainly there are some things that should never be said if they are *not* known to be true." Juliet had no more interest in shopping for fabric, and turned to leave the store . . . only to find Colonel Brandon in the doorway.

He would have to have heard all. Lady Middleton turned an unbecoming shade of red and pretended to neither see nor be seen. The colonel simply escorted Juliet out.

"I will not speak to my wife of this," he began, "as it would greatly trouble her. The only regret I shall have in such an action is that Marianne will not know how true a friend she has in you."

Juliet's temper still blazed hot. "I only regret that she has no other such friends in this village. What sort of a place is Barton that such things are whispered of between neighbors?"

"You forget, Miss Tilney, that you know from experience much that others have only learned secondhand." Colonel Brandon's calm was not sanguine, Juliet thought, but a matter of will and habit. "You met Mr. Wickham. You saw for yourself his insolence, his cruelty. Given this, you are more readily able to comprehend what the man was capable of. This knowledge is what the others lack, and their ignorance gives rise to their suspicion."

"It is still wretched of them to speak so," Juliet insisted. However, it was clear that the colonel did not wish to dwell upon the subject. "Have you finished your business in town, sir?"

He looked toward one of the smaller yet fashionable homes near the square, and Juliet thought him likely to admit to one more errand. Instead, he said, "Not yet, Miss Tilney. I pray you will excuse me."

Lady Middleton, of course, had no thought of addressing Marianne Brandon personally upon this matter. Yet another person present that night proved eager to speak to her.

Once her mother and sisters had fully consoled her, then returned to their homes, Marianne took refuge in her bedchamber. As much as she had needed comfort, she found she also needed some moments of solitude to reflect upon what had occurred.

To think I was so frightened of merely seeing Willoughby! Marianne mused as she idly examined the necklace she had worn that night. Every item she had donned for the dinner at Barton Park would now forever be rendered strange to her. Perhaps she should have the stones reset, the gown remade. *How important it seemed to look my best in front of Mrs. Willoughby. How little it all signified in the end.*

She picked up the reticule she had carried that night with similar thoughts—then frowned. Saturday evening, she had departed for Barton Park with nothing inside the reticule save for a linen handkerchief. Now, however, something crisp seemed to be within. Marianne pulled it out and gasped. It was a note—from Willoughby.

> *You never answered my last letter to you. If I believed that was only because you did not so wish, a fine rebuke it would be. But I do not believe it. I know you better than that, do I not?*

He had to have slipped this into her reticule before Mrs. Willoughby's death—of that, Marianne was certain—but the note's presence horrified her all the same. She threw it into the fire to burn, resolving to think no more of it, and hoping—rather than believing—that Willoughby's grief would put the matter from his mind altogether.

Colonel Brandon had paused in his duty to Miss Williams when he'd glimpsed Miss Tilney in the fabric shop, but his responsibility toward his ward could not be long shirked.

Little did he wish to linger in the village, understanding the calumnies already being whispered far and wide about his wife. Yet Brandon had been born in the same house he lived in; his family had dwelled near Barton for generations. Thus he had more trust that this, too, would pass.

He was not as certain about what he would find at Miss Williams's home.

However, when he arrived there, all seemed to be proceeding very much as normal. The nursemaid set little George down to toddle to him, a smile on his tiny face. Strange, Brandon thought, that he had no children of his own, but this boy would likely fill much the same role as a grandchild.

(No children *yet*. He knew Marianne hoped for children, a wish he fervently shared.)

Beth came into the drawing room shortly after his arrival. To his surprise she was wearing her nicest day dress and appeared to be in excellent spirits—though his visit must have come as a surprise to her, for it took her moments to collect herself. "Dear Colonel. What brings you here?"

"I wished to inquire after you, given the disquieting news that has so unsettled the entirety of Barton."

Beth's countenance did not change in the slightest. Only then did it occur to Brandon that some of her good cheer was more performance than truth. "All is well here, you see. I suppose I should inquire after your wife. She, no doubt, is very much troubled."

"One could scarce be otherwise after witnessing so unspeakable an event." Colonel Brandon paused. It seemed to him that Beth was not showing appropriate sympathy for Marianne; also, while anything affecting Willoughby must have touched Beth as well, she gave no hint of it, and she was not one to hide her moods. However, he felt that prying further on the topic was likely to increase the disquiet she so evidently wished to conceal, so he mentioned another subject—also difficult, but less shockingly so. "You may not know that among Mr. Willoughby's guests at Allenham is a young man named Jonathan Darcy."

"No, I know nothing of his guests. Why do you mention him?" Beth folded her arms. "I have no need of matchmaking, if that is what you have in mind."

"Indeed not." It was impossible that a young man of Mr. Darcy's wealth and status would even begin to consider a young woman in Beth's situation, but this was beside the point.

Then, at last, Beth's expression altered, revealing both doubt and recognition. "But—the name *Darcy*—surely it is not the same family?"

"Indeed it is. Mr. Darcy's late uncle was Mr. Wickham, your father. Before departing from Donwell Abbey, both Darcy's parents expressed to me their wish to meet you someday, as you know. Wickham's legitimate daughter, Susannah—the young girl who died—was very much beloved by them, and as you are her half sister, they would welcome the acquaintance. Thus I believe the younger Mr. Darcy would also be glad of an introduction. It would begin to create the bridge between you and that family, and they are well worth knowing."

Some of this story had been told to Beth before, but as it had come when she was also being informed that her father had been both identified and murdered, and that she had inherited more than five thousand pounds, Brandon felt no great surprise that she had not remembered every detail. "Oh. I—I had not thought. What brought young Mr. Darcy here? *Willoughby?*"

"Apparently they were together at school." The friendship struck Brandon as unlikely, but it was not his to question.

"Let me think upon it." Beth shook her head as though the answer had already been decided in the negative. "At this time—for the present—oh, I do not know whether to welcome him or not. Everything is in such tumult and confusion!"

Was this not exaggeration? Horrible as Mrs. Willoughby's death was, Brandon did not see how it could much affect Beth. These thoughts he kept to himself.

She said, "Have you asked *him* whether he wishes the introduction? His parents wish it, but that does not mean he shares in their sentiments."

"There has scarcely been any chance." Saturday's party had only just begun when Mrs. Willoughby had succumbed to her illness—or worse. "Yet I will speak to him upon it very soon. Consider your own feelings in the matter, for you must give an answer promptly. I believe Mr. Darcy will be with us in Barton for a while longer—but not forever."

Only two days before, Mrs. Willoughby had bathed in her fashionable porcelain tub filled with bucketfuls of hot water brought upstairs by sweaty, puffing servant girls. She had risen to be patted dry with towels of linen, been laced into her stays, and held still as her gossamer muslin dress was draped around her. As she sat at her dressing table, her maid adeptly scooped her pale curls into the most fashionable style, fastened a handsome golden chain around her neck. So Mrs. Willoughby had got dressed on so many days, and had expected to do so for many more to come.

Instead, she lay on a cold slab. Her body had recently been washed of its befouled state, but in cold water, and with no more ceremony than would have attended cleaning an inanimate object. Her hair hung limp and loose, and she was clothed only in her skin. Even this small dignity was to be removed from her, as Dr. Hitchcock grimly took up his scalpel and began work.

He worked with no sure confidence of success. Poisoning could rarely be proved. However, certain signs in the body could indicate much. He found this deep within her vital organs, the corroded irritation that suggested exposure to a high level of poison. This was not what was seen in cases of bad eggs or fish.

Hitchcock had already suspected the worst, simply because food poisoning or other natural infections did not generally make their vile assault on life so swiftly and dramatically. Yet when he saw the proof, it still filled him with the gravest concern.

He would have to report that this was a case of deliberate poisoning. Beyond any question—Mrs. Willoughby had been murdered.

The word was brought to Allenham by Constable Hubbard and was delivered to Mr. Willoughby in the presence of his friends.

What are the chances that I should be in the presence of murder twice in my life? Jonathan wondered. Though he was excellent at probabilities—had, in fact, quit playing cards entirely due to the unfair advantage this skill gave him—he could not begin to fathom this particular likelihood. *Not only twice in my life, but twice this very year!*

"We shall have to speak to all present that evening," said Constable Hubbard, "including you four gentlemen, and of course we will question everyone at Barton Park, from Sir John himself to the lowest scullery maid."

"Have you the authority to act without a magistrate?" Willoughby seemed wholly unsurprised by the information that his wife had been murdered.

"I imagine one will be appointed shortly, seeing as how there is urgent need. Until then, never you fear, I am on the case." If Jonathan was reading Hubbard's tone correctly, the man was almost pleased to be working without oversight.

Willoughby had absorbed this information with a blankness that suggested either shock or nonchalance. Say what he might of Willoughby, Jonathan had always known him to be an active sort of person—forever talkative, seeking new diversions and interests, given to high emotion. Yet now he had gone silent and still. Perhaps he feared being criticized for conduct unbecoming a widower. Perhaps he had possessed some affection for his wife after all, not to the extent a husband should, but enough to feel pained by her wretched death. Or perhaps he truly did believe her death to be a suicide, which would be reason for the gravest reflection.

Or perhaps Willoughby's emotions were not all he strove to hide.

Hubbard seemed determined to act as though he were dealing with a grief-stricken, appropriately mystified widower. His tone was both grave and courteous as he assured Willoughby, "I shall get to the bottom of this."

Jonathan had no reason to doubt the perspicacity of Constables Hubbard and Baxter, and while Dr. Hitchcock came across a doddering character, he had not lacked the will to investigate, and certainly he had experience.

Jonathan had experience, too. He had gotten to the truth behind one murder—could he not do so again?

Not, he thought, without help.

Only a short time later, a different visitor to a similarly struck household was received with far more joy.

"How good of you to come!" Marianne said as Mr. Darcy entered Delaford's drawing room. "You are always welcome, never so much as in times like these, when one learns who one's friends truly are. You have only just missed my family— I would very much wish to introduce you to them while you remain in Barton."

Juliet felt certain she was even happier to see Mr. Darcy than Marianne was. But how was she to discuss the murder with Jonathan with her hostess present to potentially over-hear? She reminded herself that an answer could be found; in Surrey, she and Mr. Darcy had become quite adept at finding ways to communicate that others would not see.

If only we were staying in the same house! Juliet thought. Meeting late at night in the Donwell Abbey billiard room might have been improper, but it had unquestionably been convenient.

But would Mr. Darcy think her forward, proposing such a thing? Circumstance had brought them together before— that, their undeniable innocence in the matter, and their shared desire not to see injustice done. Here there was no sign of a hasty or improper investigation, and circumstance was no longer their friend. Shared innocence alone (for how could either of them have any reason to do Mrs. Willoughby a harm?) might be thought insufficient reason. And more than one person had taken exception to their efforts to solve the murder of Mr. Wickham, considering them presumptuous.

Which they had been. But had those efforts not helped to reveal the truth?

Her worries proved to be ill-founded, for as soon as Marianne had begun to show Mr. Bamber some of her sister Elinor's drawings, Mr. Darcy found the opportunity to lean over Juliet's shoulder as if to learn which book she had been reading. "Do you not think that—" he began uncertainly. "In the absence of any magistrate—Miss Tilney, given our experience—"

Juliet managed not to smile. "I understand you completely. It does seem as though we might play some useful role, do you not think?"

Mr. Darcy considered this. "We might be useful, but we shall most certainly be improper. My father takes a dim view of such activities."

"As does mine." Juliet's hopes dwindled. It seemed he had sought her out not to encourage her looking further into Mrs. Willoughby's murder but to banish the thought from their heads.

Yet she had read him wrongly, for he next said, "However, if we conduct ourselves prudently, we may be able to avoid our previous errors while still proving helpful to the course of justice."

The most invigorating and interesting experience of Juliet's life was to be repeated! She would have to pray for forgiveness, taking such delight in circumstances that had proved tragic to another. "I quite agree, Mr. Darcy," Juliet said. "Let us investigate."

Chapter Eight

The prospect of investigating another murder cheered Jonathan far more than was genteel, he felt certain, but no one else need ever know of it—save perhaps Miss Tilney, who seemed to share his sentiments.

Then again, was it so very wicked? Jonathan had found himself in a difficult situation with nothing of consequence to do. Surely there was not much harm in taking up a genuinely useful activity.

"I noticed some lovely trees at the edge of your orchard, Mrs. Brandon," Jonathan said, not adding that he had been studying them with express purpose. How much more at ease he felt at Delaford than at Allenham! "The one closest to the house has a very large knothole—do owls nest there, perhaps?"

Mrs. Brandon smiled, though her complexion remained wan. "The owls make their domestic arrangements without reference to me, Mr. Darcy. But I have never seen them there."

Just as Jonathan remembered, Miss Tilney was quick with a hint. "So the local children must use it as a hiding place for their treasures. Or couples seeking to exchange billets-doux."

Jonathan shared a meaningful glance with Juliet. They had identified a place to meet, and perhaps to leave and receive messages; once they could communicate freely, and secretly, all else would be made far simpler.

Colonel Brandon returned home not long afterward, and he graciously welcomed his gentleman visitor. Jonathan suspected he had received a warmer reception by leaving Willoughby at home. As it happened, however, the colonel had a particular reason to be glad of Jonathan's presence, and it was not long before he had drawn Jonathan aside.

"There is a matter of the greatest delicacy I had wished to discuss with you," Brandon said so intently that Jonathan wondered whether he was about to be *asked* to investigate the murder. Thus he was much surprised when the colonel continued, "You recall my ward, Beth Williams? The daughter of your late uncle Wickham?"

"Oh. Yes. Yes, of course." This connection had absented Jonathan's thoughts altogether since Mrs. Willoughby's death.

"I visited her this morning, told her of you, and asked whether she would accept an introduction. Though she is as yet uncertain—any reminders of the father who abandoned her must be painful—I feel certain she will wish to meet you, if that is welcome to you as well?"

Jonathan knew that his parents very much longed to meet Miss Williams. His feelings in the matter were far more complicated . . . but not for discussion with Colonel Brandon. He must do what politeness required. "Of course, I should welcome the introduction. Mother and Father will be very glad to know that I have made the acquaintance."

Gladness was the furthest thing from his heart.

As much as Elinor wished to be of comfort and use to Marianne during this time, she awoke heavy and weary on the following morning. In the end she sent her sister a note, apologizing for her absence, and inviting Marianne to the parsonage.

Her husband, Edward, heartily approved. "A change of scene may be the best thing for Marianne," he said when

Elinor informed him of her decision to remain at home. He had just returned from his morning walk into Barton, bearing the post in one hand and a basket of eggs with the other. "To leave the village entirely at this time would appear very wrong, so a smaller change—spending some time here, with family who love her—that may be the best means of refreshing her mind."

"It may also improve opinions of her, if it is seen that her clergyman brother believes her innocent." Elinor then caught sight of a small pear among the eggs—a little treat Edward had brought for her, one she took up with a smile. Absently she asked, "Has anything of interest come in the post?"

"A letter from Fanny."

"Your sister? What does she write?" Elinor had all but forgotten the pear. "Has someone died?"

"No, mercifully. Though that is the only kindness this letter grants us." Edward handed the pages to Elinor, who immediately recognized Fanny's sharply slanted writing. She read aloud:

> *"Dear Edward,*
> *Two years have passed since your break with your*
> *family. You have reaped the consequences of your*
> *actions and dwell in poverty and obscurity—"*

Elinor glanced around their parsonage. Small it was, and to Fanny such a residence would no doubt be punishment. Yet the parsonage was comfortable, well-appointed, within an easy walk of town and Elinor's family, and therefore all that could be asked of a home. She could pity Fanny, who believed it better to live in a mansion without love than in a cottage with it.

"And these conditions shall never change. It is the fate you have chosen, and the breach between us can never be entirely erased."

"Why did she write at all, then?" Elinor asked. Edward gestured to the pages. "Read on."

"Yet my husband informs me that we are soon to have another member of the family. Our affectionate mother feels it keenly that she should have a grandchild completely unknown to her."

"So affectionate she disinherited you," said Elinor. "Indeed."

"Therefore, Edward, I have been given permission to write and inform you that, if you were to apologize properly to our mother for your disobedience, your stubbornness, and your failure to uphold the standards of the family, she is willing to forgive you so far as to receive you and your wife, and to consider the grandchild a member of the family like any other."

Elinor's expression must have betrayed her astonishment, for Edward laughed. "Yes, that is Christian charity, is it not? If I ask for *her* forgiveness, then she will deign to see us and then spend the rest of her life attempting to influence our child's fate just as she wished to influence mine. Such an invitation will receive the reply it deserves, which is none."

Obviously he expected Elinor to instantly agree. She watched his face change as he realized she did not. "Your family wronged you cruelly," she said. "I do not blame you for not wishing them close. However, our child deserves to have some family connections beyond my sisters and mother and Colonel Brandon."

"Yes, that is what is deserved," Edward said. "We are not the ones who have denied those connections. My family did so, and if they dislike it . . . as Fanny says, they have reaped the consequences."

Elinor shook her head. "It is not like you to be so unforgiving."

"Nor is it like you to compromise principle for the sake of appearances," said Edward, who began walking toward his small study. "We need not quarrel, Elinor, for the point is moot. My family's desire for reconciliation is not deep, and my lack of response, I surmise, will end it completely."

Elinor was not convinced of this, but she said nothing further, for Edward's sentiments regarding the letter of reconciliation were still at a boil. Best to let them cool.

That morning, as both the colonel and Marianne were occupied by household matters, Juliet set out for a solitary walk. "It is such refreshing exercise," she said to her hosts as she tied her bonnet ribbons.

"How I love these paths and hills," agreed Marianne. "I believe it is the pleasantest place to walk in all the world." However, she made no motion toward her own bonnet or boots. "Perhaps I am partial, but best of all I like the walk toward Barton Cottage. If you should go that way, you know that you are welcome to call on Mama and Margaret. I am certain they are more congenial company than I can be at present."

Juliet nodded and smiled but promised nothing, and as soon as she had left the Delaford path, she headed in the opposite direction from Barton Cottage—toward the orchard, and the tree with the knothole. In her pocket was a list of names she had carefully labeled *Persons with Whom We Should Speak*.

We know far too little to call anyone suspect, she reasoned as she walked along the path. The roads were dry but not dusty, which was a mercy, for the wind blew strong. Autumn was beginning to make itself known.

When she reached the orchard, another figure could be glimpsed among the trees. How satisfying it was to realize that this was none other than Jonathan Darcy, no doubt carrying a list of his own.

Again! Juliet thought joyfully as she waved and he strode toward her. *We have a chance of investigating again. How fortunate for us—though surely it is wrong of me to think so. I would not have people murdered only so that Mr. Darcy and I may investigate. But if murders take place regardless of my wishes, can it be wrong to seek answers? And if it is right to seek answers, then it cannot be entirely wrong to take some pleasure in doing so.*

She suspected her father would have some theological arguments against her current course of reasoning, but she had no intention of discussing this with him in the near, or perhaps any, future.

"Miss Tilney," Mr. Darcy said, noticing her. "We are of the same mind, I see. If we are lucky, we may both be free at this time each day."

"Let us hope. When that fails, then this tree's knothole will oblige. Here, let me show you what I had meant to leave there for you to find."

Mr. Darcy took the note she handed him:

Willoughby
Mrs. Brandon
Mr. Follett

Colonel Brandon
Sir John Middleton
Mrs. Jennings
Lady Middleton
Mr. Bamber
The butler at Barton Park
Other servants at Barton Park
Each other

"Some of these people may have wished to see Mrs. Willoughby dead," Juliet said. "Others I do not think at all likely to have committed the act, but they may well have noticed details of that night which could lead us to the truth."

"Your list is very thorough, Miss Tilney. Incidentally, the butler at Barton Park is called Montgomery." Mr. Darcy appeared much caught up in thought. "Of those named here, the likeliest suspects seem to me to be Mr. Follett and Willoughby himself. Willoughby does not much grieve his wife, and he has inherited a great fortune."

"Furthermore, his enduring interest in Mrs. Brandon . . . let us say only that it could be construed as improper," Juliet continued. "But why Mr. Follett? I did note that he seemed to take particular interest in Mrs. Willoughby, but I detected no malice."

"It seems he courted her before she chose Mr. Willoughby," Mr. Darcy explained. "As we are both staying at Allenham for some time, I will endeavor to speak with Follett about it. He may have resented her desertion, thought her fickle. This seems to me poor reason to kill, but most reasons given for killing strike me as inadequate. Anything short of defense of one's person, or another, or of one's nation . . . no, that cannot be excused."

"Is Follett a very great friend of yours?" It had not struck

Juliet so, but their one evening together had not admitted of much chance for observation. "Such a conversation is not easily begun unless friends are indeed very intimate."

"Though I have known him since my earliest schooldays, Follett has never been a friend," Mr. Darcy said. He spoke without venom. It was, in truth, the very ordinariness of the statement that struck Juliet the most . . . as though Mr. Darcy did not expect to find friendship anywhere. "However, he knows well that I am sometimes—that I say things I ought not, ask questions that I should not. If I begin the conversation, Follett will think only that I am blundering again. There is some chance he will answer."

Juliet was well acquainted enough with Mr. Darcy's peculiarities to not find them very peculiar at all, and she considered the oddities of his conversation more refreshing than blundering. However, she assumed he spoke as he expected Mr. Follett to find. "Then both Mr. Willoughby and Mr. Follett had motive to commit the murder. Do you think one suspects the other of the crime?"

"That I could not say—Follett has thus far mostly kept to his room, so I have had no occasion to see them speaking together, or refusing to do the same—but I shall observe closely henceforth." He tapped the second name on Juliet's list as the autumn wind ruffled the page. "I think it wholly unlikely that Mrs. Brandon should take this step. She does not appear to welcome Mr. Willoughby's company, and even if she disliked Mrs. Willoughby, that would not be inducement enough to murder. We further witnessed her horror after the death of Mr. Wickham, though she was but defending herself."

"We are in complete accord," Juliet said. "Besides, Mrs. Brandon is a woman of strong feeling and changeable moods. It was not so very strange that she should strike out at Mr. Wickham in anger and fear, not in such extremity. But poison . . . it is a very *cold* weapon, is it not, Mr. Darcy? One who uses it must plan ahead, must harbor murderous thoughts for days at least, perhaps far longer! That is no accurate description of Mrs. Brandon's character."

"Very cold indeed," said a third voice, and Juliet and Mr. Darcy both startled. When they looked up, they found Mr. Bamber standing among the trees, studying them quizzically. "What on *earth* are you two doing?"

Jonathan allowed Miss Tilney to do most of the explaining. His own chagrin at having so easily betrayed their secret efforts caught his tongue; besides, in this manner, Miss Tilney could prevaricate or not as she chose. Somewhat to his surprise, she chose not to. She instead explained fully what they had done at Donwell Abbey—how they had helped to identify the murderer—and what they hoped to accomplish here. Jonathan feared Bamber's response; surely he would call them officious, imprudent, even ridiculous.

Instead, Bamber listened with the greatest interest, and at the end he turned to Jonathan and said, "Darcy, I did not know you had it in you."

"Well. The occasion called for such attention." Jonathan hoped he was fulfilling his mother's dictates about modesty, but in truth, he was proud of what he and Miss Tilney had accomplished . . . and prouder still that one of his old schoolfellows should know all. "It appears the occasion calls for our help yet again."

Miss Tilney, still somewhat apologetic, looked up beseechingly at Bamber. "With no magistrate in place—the local constables—"

"They do not inspire strong confidence, do they? More concerned about how they appear to their betters than in what those betters have actually done." Bamber pointed at the list. "I have gone as long as I can without asking why my name is written there."

"It is not that we suspected you!" Miss Tilney blushed rosy pink.

Jonathan quickly added, "Obviously you had no reason to wish harm upon Mrs. Willoughby. Nor had others upon our list, such as Colonel Brandon and Lady Middleton. Like them, you were present that night, Bamber, and something you might recall could be what leads us to the truth."

"Fair enough, I suppose." Bamber appeared to be already searching his memory for any details that might be pertinent. "Whatever has the butler to do with anything?"

"The poison must have been in the port," Miss Tilney explained. "It could have been placed in no other food or drink without someone else at the table being affected as well. The butler will recall where and when the port was decanted and let to breathe, and with that knowledge, we can determine whom among us had opportunity to tamper with her drink."

Only then did something occur to Jonathan, something so plain he could not imagine why he had not considered it before. "Can we determine which poison was used? That will help us in learning which persons had sources of the poison available."

"Anyone can buy poison," Bamber pointed out. "It is sold in shops to keep out the rats—as indeed Mr. Willoughby bought some just the other day."

"Willoughby? Purchase rat poison?" Jonathan was taken aback. "He would have sent a servant, surely."

Bamber raised an eyebrow. "One would think. And yet, do you not recall our trip into town? When he was so clandestine about his errand? I was curious enough to ask the house-keeper, and the good woman told me of it herself. This was before the dinner at Barton Park—I wonder what she would have said to me after?"

"Like as not, she would not have dared say a word then! Yes, determining the poison might prove useful." Miss Tilney turned to Bamber. "Particularly if it *is* the same one purchased by Mr. Willoughby. Are there tests for such things?"

"You are clever, Miss Tilney. Many are attempting to develop tests that could provide proof positive of poisoning for use in courts. The tests for arsenic that exist are not very sensitive, and they do not provide lasting proof that can be shown to a judge and jury, or so I understand it." By this time Bamber was nodding his head slowly. "But perhaps a discovery has been lately made—so we should discover whether Dr. Hitchcock knows of such."

Jonathan thought it showed a bit of cheek, Bamber inviting himself along. But as one who had studied chemistry, he might be able to help them understand the finer points of such tests.

Then Jonathan noticed how Mr. Bamber was smiling at Miss Tilney and realized his friend's interest might not relate so much to the investigation, but to the young lady engaged in pursuing it.

The local constabulary was not so intimidated or uncertain as Miss Tilney and Mr. Darcy believed. Although criminal acts were rare in the vicinity, Hubbard and Baxter had gained some experience through the years. Had they not apprehended the miscreant who had stolen Mrs. Leacock's cow?

Most would not consider this work sufficient as preparation for a murder investigation. Yet it is ever true that where cleverness is in short supply, confidence can be most abundant, and neither Hubbard nor Baxter was known for powerful intellect. To them, the case appeared to be one with an obvious solution.

Why should anyone wonder who had committed a murder during a gathering at which a known murderess was present?

Questioning Mrs. Brandon—this was a large step, one they were not yet willing to take. Colonel Brandon's position in town was one of great respect. As Baxter said, "'Tis a pity such a man should have chosen a wife so poorly."

"He may choose better next time." Hubbard felt sure there would be a next time, after the colonel was widowed by the gallows. A hanging, he thought, would soon follow the trial; the trial would soon follow Mrs. Brandon's arrest; the arrest would soon follow their questioning. With such speed to come, what harm could there be in tarrying now? If they acted too soon, without any magistrate, there would be those who said they were acting above their station.

Best to wait for the magistrate. Besides, the constables were not pitiless. Mrs. Brandon, however wicked, was yet but young—let her have her last few weeks of freedom, of life.

Juliet had thought Mr. Darcy might object to Mr. Bamber's accompanying them to Dr. Hitchcock's, but he did not. At this she felt some dismay. She had become accustomed to discussing matters with Mr. Darcy that were sometimes . . . indelicate. Unladylike. Whatever would Mr. Bamber think of her?

If Mr. Bamber is so easily shocked, she decided, *then he will soon leave us to our efforts.*

Hitchcock's house was a small one with a thatched roof wedged between others very near the town square. On the bottom floor was housed a millinery shop. Juliet, not wanting to be thought frivolous, refused to so much as glance at any of the hats for sale.

Although Hitchcock's manservant seemed much surprised at his master having visitors, he brought them up the narrow staircase into a small sitting room, very old-fashioned, with thick wooden beams holding the ceiling aloft. Hitchcock himself sat by the fire, a heavy book still in his lap. He was quite an elderly man—at least in his seventieth year, in Juliet's estimation—with a bald pate save for the very back of his head, where wispy white hair fell inches past his collar. His yellowed, ancient powdered wig sat atop a dusty marble bust of Shakespeare on a shelf near the door. The round lenses of the doctor's spectacles reflected the firelight.

Hitchcock appeared eager to return to his book. "If one of you is ill, it would have been far more useful to send a servant to fetch me."

"We are all quite well, are we not?" Mr. Darcy glanced at the others, as if uncertain whether he ought to speak for them. His concerns were rather dear sometimes, Juliet thought. "No, we have come to speak with you about Mrs. Willoughby."

"You know something?" Hitchcock squinted uncertainly at them. "Then you would do better to inform the constable."

Many older men are charmed by the freshness and vitality of a young girl. Juliet knew this and intended to turn it to their advantage. "We know nothing, Dr. Hitchcock," she said earnestly. "In fact, we hoped to learn from you. We were curious about poison, you see. What poison might have been used to kill Mrs. Willoughby, and how it might have been given to her. Given your position, and your great wealth of learning, we thought you likeliest of anyone to have the answers."

Mr. Darcy apparently had not recognized her stratagem, for he interjected, "I feel certain that if poison was at work, it was in the port."

Although Hitchcock did not seem to have been charmed by Juliet, he nonetheless proved willing to speak. "The port it certainly was. There was sediment in the bottom of the glass—grainier than one would expect in a port, and far more than is found in port that has been decanted, as it was that night. Furthermore, the grains were pale rather than dark, strongly suggestive of arsenic that had not fully dissolved." He smiled thinly as he added, "I have sent word of this to Barton Park, that they may not fear to eat off their dishes any longer."

Juliet frowned. "If the arsenic had not dissolved, how could it kill her?"

"Enough *had* dissolved to do the trick. Whoever did the evil thing must have put at least a teaspoon in, maybe more. That was so high a dose of arsenic that she would have begun experiencing symptoms within minutes."

"How can you know that? The dosage?" Bamber asked, before catching himself. "Forgive my forwardness. It is only that I am interested in the sciences myself, sir. If someone has developed a more precise test for arsenic, then I would be very glad of the chance to learn."

Hitchcock gestured to his chairs. Juliet could tell that he lived here alone, but the ample books on the shelves and the violin in one corner suggested that he considered his thoughts good enough company most of the time. Yet those who have not been given the chance to speak often will usually, given that chance, speak more than anyone else. She hoped this would prove true with Hitchcock.

"It is impossible to determine whether a person has died of arsenic poisoning *unless* the correct steps are taken immediately after death," Hitchcock began. "This opportunity presents itself but rarely, as most poisonings are more gradual—more questionable—than the one that took place at Barton Park. I had that opportunity here, as I could perform the autopsy almost immediately."

Mr. Darcy asked, "How did the poison show itself through the autopsy, sir?"

"Is the young lady willing to hear this? Never mind, never mind. If she swoons to the floor, I will know to stop." Hitchcock cackled at his own joke. Juliet decided immediately that no power under heaven would make her swoon. "Forgive the indelicacies, but how else can the matter be discussed? I used Rose's technique—do you know of it?" Mr. Bamber shook his head, and Hitchcock continued, "I removed Mrs. Willoughby's stomach postmortem and examined the lining."

Stomach. He had spoken the word *stomach*. This was hardly an unmentionable word within a family, but to hear a part of the inner body spoken of so blithely by a near stranger—that was new to Juliet, and shocking. However, she had braced herself, and her composure remained intact as Hitchcock continued.

"Its lividity—that means 'redness,' Miss Tilney—was so pronounced, so severe, that I knew it had come into contact with poison."

Removing the stomach from the body. Indelicate—somewhat disgusting—but Juliet retained full control of herself. She noticed that Jonathan Darcy appeared somewhat queasy as well.

Hitchcock began making illustrative hand motions just at the moment Juliet would have wished him not to. "I cut her stomach into small pieces and boiled them in distilled water. Then I took the resulting—one would have to call it 'soup,' would not one?—took that soup and filtered it"—Mr. Darcy had turned a definite shade of green; Juliet felt she was managing her reaction well, but she also did not think she would want soup again very soon—"and removed all traces of organic matter with nitric acid. That produced a precipitate, which I tested with Metzger's method. You, Mr. Bamber, you must be familiar with that, hmm?"

"Indeed I am, sir," Mr. Bamber said. "This is *fascinating*."

Juliet did not inquire further about whatever this method of a Mr. Metzger was. Hitchcock's thorough explanation, and Mr. Bamber's concordance, would suffice for their purposes, and she did not want to take even the slightest risk of hearing about such "soup" ever again.

"So we know that Mrs. Willoughby ingested arsenic. I have not a doubt that this was the poison that killed her. But can I prove this, for the purposes of the law?" Hitchcock asked. "I cannot."

Mr. Darcy expressed the astonishment Juliet felt. "What do you mean, sir? How is this not proof?"

"The test is not sensitive enough," the doctor explained. "We all come into contact with amounts of arsenic—it is used in cosmetics and paints. Metzger's test does not provide sufficient exactitude. A barrister would argue in court that we do not know whether the results indicate that Mrs. Willoughby was killed, or whether the results were affected by her wallpaper—for yes, that often contains arsenic, too."

"Would not the judge and jury reject that argument?" Juliet asked. She knew little of either, only that juries were meant to be fair and judges to be wise.

"They would not, and they would be correct in doing so," Hitchcock said. "The lividity of the stomach lining suggests to me that a considerable dose was ingested, but other phenomena could potentially account for it. Courts do not want the obscure theories of natural philosophy. They want fact."

"A considerable dose, you say?" Juliet clung to that fact, in the hopes it might provide illumination.

"Indeed," said Hitchcock. "What surprises me is that she did not vomit the stuff up immediately. So large a dose must have induced nausea within minutes."

The word *vomit* would have horrified Juliet had it been spoken before the discussion of the autopsy. After *that*, she could not be so easily discombobulated. "I saw that she—that she felt very ill. I believe that she would have been sick, had she not strongly fought the urge to do so."

Hitchcock shook his head. "Poor child. If her manners had been worse, she might still be alive."

Mr. Darcy moved to the half-opened window, perhaps in need of some fresh air. In truth, the breeze felt welcome to Juliet as well. It stimulated thought as well, because it seemed to her that there was something very important about the inquiry that they had not yet hit upon, a vital element that might be missing from their consideration . . .

Then Mr. Darcy startled and stared out so intently that she rose to join him. (Fortunately Mr. Bamber and Dr. Hitchcock were engrossed in a conversation about the uses of various acids.)

"Mr. Darcy, you seem unwell. Is there anything that would give you relief?"

"I am not ill," he said, "only very much surprised. You said any detail from the night of Mrs. Willoughby's death might be important—and I recall now that I saw a figure in a pale blue cloak, a woman's cloak I feel sure, on the grounds of Barton Park very shortly after our carriage had arrived there. I took a moment in the gardens to collect myself, and there I saw her darting among the greenery. The cloak she wore looked very much like that one."

He pointed at the precise person he meant. Upon his gesture, Juliet stifled a gasp. "Is that the woman you saw that night?"

"I cannot be sure," Mr. Darcy replied. "I saw her from behind only, and the hood of the cloak was drawn up. Whether or not the woman is the same, the cloak is extremely similar."

The woman in question was walking quickly through the square, her countenance showing some measure of distress.

"But, Mr. Darcy, that is Miss Williams," said Juliet. "Colonel Brandon's ward. Mr. Wickham's daughter."

No other words passed between them; none were necessary. They knew from all that had been revealed at Donwell Abbey that Miss Williams had once been in love with Willoughby and had borne him a child, one for which he had refused to take any responsibility.

Was it possible that Miss Williams might have thought all would change, if only Willoughby were once again free?

Chapter Nine

Marianne set out for the parsonage alone the next morning, saying to her friend only, "I wish to talk with my sister about her wishes for her lying-in."

"That is a matter for family, of course," said Juliet Tilney. "I shall walk on my own, perhaps in the orchard, but I hope we will see each other by teatime."

How fortunate I am to have a friend gracious enough to permit me silence and solace, Marianne thought. Sometimes it was easier to lay aside her many concerns in solitude.

The thought of facing all of Barton still overwhelmed her, but how good it was to go walking for pleasure again! The strange, overwhelming fits of memory that she had suffered had never yet struck her when she was outdoors, and if she was overcome at the parsonage, she trusted those who lived there to care for her well.

Indeed, the walk itself much restored her spirits; Marianne was rarely so glad as she was when surrounded by nature in all its wild beauty, and the incipient autumn had begun painting the trees in every shade of flame. True enjoyment was beyond her that day, burdened as she was by suspicion, but the weight of it felt less heavy for a time.

At the parsonage she found Elinor quite alone, her feet up and knitting in her hand. "What, have they all left you here?" Marianne set aside her things, hanging her gray cloak next to Elinor's blue one, the better to hurry to her sister's side. "Even the housemaid? Even Edward?"

"The housemaid is bringing back meat from the market, an errand I am not currently fit to undertake—or, rather, to be seen undertaking," Elinor said in good humor. "Edward is christening an infant at the church, an errand I *could* not undertake even if I wished it."

"But with your time so near! What if you were in need of help, and unable even to walk—"

"I am entirely capable of walking," Elinor protested. "It is hardly an enjoyable exercise at present, but it is far from impossible. Were I to feel that help must be summoned, I should be able to summon it, and I would not allow the modesty of confinement to overrule good sense."

"Still, it would be better to have someone with you, or at the very least, to ensure that a person visits the house every few hours." Marianne silently resolved to raise this subject with her mother and Margaret, who would undoubtedly agree.

Elinor, ever rational, did not argue. Her concern, as was the case so often, was entirely for others. "These have been very trying days for you, Marianne. How are you faring?"

"Not very well, I fear." Marianne took her seat in the chair opposite Elinor's divan. "I hope that Mrs. Willoughby's killer will be caught soon so that I can go about again with my head held high. Guilt clings to me like a shadow."

"It is hardly rational to feel guilt for something one did not do," Elinor pointed out.

"And yet how often we feel such guilt! Can you wonder at the feeling being especially strong for me, given the circumstances? Oh, Elinor, I envy you, for you have no problem more urgent than finding some comfort amid your confinement." Elinor hesitated before replying, a pause long enough to make Marianne realize she had erred. "But I am wrong to think so. What troubles you?"

Elinor did not seem to know whether or not to speak.

Finally she said, "Edward's family wishes a reconciliation with him, but he is against it."

"He is as well off without them." Marianne had no very good opinion of the rest of the Ferrars family. "I do not blame him for refusing to forgive them."

"They continue to insist that he is the one who requires forgiveness," Elinor said. "The difference is that they are now willing to grant it."

"Insufferable! What presumption!" Marianne could have boxed all their ears. "Tell Edward I am entirely loyal to him in this matter."

"I am certain he has no doubt of your support, but in truth, I wish he would reconcile with them insofar as possible."

Marianne knew that Elinor looked at matters in a far different way than she did herself, but she had never fathomed they could disagree so fundamentally as this. "You cannot think Edward has wronged them! Nor that they have *not* wronged him—"

"They have wronged him terribly, and for this they will never apologize," Elinor said. "Yet I think Edward might in sincerity express regret for having become engaged to Lucy without his family's permission. It was a foolish, childish decision, one that might well have ruined his life, and a failure of his filial duty. *That* was in error, a point with which I am certain Edward agrees."

"His error was hardly as egregious as theirs have been toward him," Marianne insisted. "Surely being engaged to Lucy was in time its own punishment!"

"This is not a matter of justice," Elinor said. "We must consider what is practical. We may have no need of his family's wealth and position, but this child someday may." She held up the knitting in her hands, which was taking the shape of a very small sock. "Consider, Marianne. What if we are granted a daughter? She will need a dowry eventually, and even if we practice strict economy, we will never be able to set aside much for that purpose. Even if we are granted a son, he will inherit only a very modest fortune. For that matter, this is but our first child. What if I have many? Our dear mama can do nothing for them. Edward's family alone will be in a position to secure their fortunes."

"Do you forget me entirely? Or my dear husband? You cannot think we would fail to dower your daughters, or care for your sons!"

"Of course you will do whatever you can. But in time, you, too, will have children, Marianne. If you have a son, he will inherit the Delaford estate in such a way that will not allow you to give away much else. If you have a daughter, then that is the first dowry the colonel will have to provide."

This silenced Marianne. Colonel Brandon was a man of property, but his wealth did not compare to that of the Ferrars family. Her promises could too easily go further than the Delaford estate's resources.

"So that is the question—how to convince Edward that this apology, however unjust, is what is best for our child?" Elinor sighed. "We do much for our family's sake that we would never do for own."

Marianne was not the only person to set out upon a walk that morning. Jonathan took the opportunity to escape Allenham's funereal gloom.

Yet the bleak mood permeated the entire estate. The few servants Jonathan spotted on his walk up the path wore black, bowed their heads, and said nothing. The hunting dogs lazed near the stables, as a day's shooting would be unseemly for a man only days into mourning for his wife. (This last was a profound relief to Jonathan, who could not abide killing without purpose—the furthest thing, in his mind, from that which could properly be called "sport.") As he approached the house, however, he saw one spot of color and activity in the garden due east from the house: Follett, wearing shabby and stained clothing, at his easel, painting something that blazed with red and gold. He had finally emerged from his rooms, seemingly older than he had been before—worn rough with either grief or guilt.

Jonathan approached silently, but Follett must not have been so caught up in his efforts that he would fail to hear footsteps upon the grass. "A sunset," he said. "Not today's, of course, as that is many hours yet to come. The one I saw the evening that . . . the evening of the Middletons' dinner, before we set out for Barton Park."

The last sunset Mrs. Willoughby ever saw, Jonathan thought. "If you are not painting this sky as you now see it, why have you assembled your easel here?"

"For the landscape. The trees, the hills." Follett dipped his brush in a daub of deep carnelian. "To spend more time outside Allenham's halls."

Jonathan knew the answer to this but asked it regardless: "Do you wish to give Willoughby time to mourn in solitude?"

Follett's laugh was bitter. "He has had all the time he needed for that, if he needed any, which I daresay he did not." He stabbed at the canvas with his brush; the resulting stroke seemed to Jonathan too bright, too fervent, against an otherwise soft sky. "I would wager that but for our presence in his home, he would already have set out for London, to enjoy all the diversions of the city—and to set his eye upon another young lady with another fine fortune."

"Bamber said you courted Mrs. Willoughby as well." If it

was gauche to speak of it, then Follett would think this but another example of Jonathan's many social blunders. "That she had to choose between you and Willoughby."

"She chose poorly." Follett's brush squiggled violently against the red streak he had just made. Jonathan would have thought this would mar the painting entirely, but instead, the color gentled, found its place among the painted clouds. "I say that as though I gave her the choice—but I did not. Had I but dared to ask her, what would have been my fate, or hers? Instead, I dawdled and dallied, fearing my lack of fortune would lead her aunt and uncle to advise against me. Before I found my tongue, Willoughby had found his nerve, and she found her husband."

How candidly he spoke . . . but Jonathan sensed that Follett was paying very little attention to his listener. He had been given an excuse to speak aloud that which he thought, and the audience of one was entirely beside the point. Also, Follett showed no awareness that others might suspect him of the crime—that, or he was well able to conceal it. Jonathan said only, "You remained very fond of her."

The painting seemed to require much more concentration than it had before. Leaning much closer to the canvas, speaking as though absent-mindedly, Follett replied, "She did not remain very fond of me, it seems, and thus the rest is of no consequence." He looked at his painting with far less satisfaction than its execution seemed to Jonathan to warrant. "This cannot occupy me, and I must have some occupation of mind. Otherwise this house will become unbearable to me long before I can quit it. I must find a superior subject."

His candor on the subject of Mrs. Willoughby had ended; thinking upon her had caused agitation, more than he wished to reveal. Jonathan could not determine whether this disquiet arose from affection, in which case Follett could not have been motivated to murder—or from anger, from resentment, for having been spurned. Novels and poems had informed Jonathan that such sentiments could lead to foul deeds.

A servant on horseback approached Allenham, then stopped. "Begging your pardon, sir, but is one of you Mr. Jonathan Darcy?"

"I am," Jonathan said.

"Message for you, sir!"

Glad of the excuse to leave Follett (a feeling he supposed mutual), Jonathan walked toward the man and his horse. He hoped for an invitation to take tea or dine at Delaford. His spirits brightened as he saw the seal upon the note, a bold *B* pressed into blue wax.

Indeed the missive came from Colonel Brandon, and it was an invitation to tea. But Jonathan was not to be entertained at Delaford yet.

Instead, it appeared that the following day was when he would fulfill his parents' wishes and meet Miss Williams.

As that afternoon was now to be dedicated to Miss Williams, Jonathan Darcy resolved the next morning to devote the first half of the day to the investigation.

His original intent was to slip out for a morning walk, the better to meet with Miss Tilney at their tree. Yet Bamber caught up with him at the stair, greeting him with "I say, just as well to leave breakfast behind and get a bit of the real work done, don't you think?"

Jonathan felt somewhat annoyed, then wondered why he should be so. Had he not always hoped for friends who shared his interests? Perhaps he was being selfish. (This was a criticism he had often endured both at home and at school, when he did not share with his brothers or fellow students. As a general rule, Jonathan felt he was simply too engaged with the item in question to permit any interlopers, but he had matured enough to realize both these possibilities could exist together.) So he said only, "You have anticipated me, Bamber. Let us go now."

As they went toward the door, however, they were met by Mr. Follett. "I go to Delaford this afternoon, gentlemen, if you wish to join me there at that time."

"What business have you there?" Bamber asked, relieving Jonathan of the need to do so. "I thought the Brandons no special acquaintance of yours."

"Indeed they are not. But that young lady staying with them—Miss Tilney, is it? She would make an excellent subject for a portrait." Follett seemed as grimly intent upon painting as soldiers were said to be in battle. "Daughter of a clergyman in Gloucestershire, they said, and that is precisely correct. Miss Tilney is not born so high that she will have been painted already, or to expect that her parents would have too much delicacy to allow the endeavor. Yet she is not born so low that anyone will mistake her for a mere hired model."

Jonathan asked, "Do you intend to sell the portrait to her family?" He did not know whether a clergyman could afford a fine portrait in oils. This was not his main source of concern, however; he very much disliked the idea of Miss Tilney spending so many hours in the company of a man who might be a murderer.

"I would rather exhibit it as a 'portrait of a girl,' a work that can hang in museums and galleries without my having to beg permission from a father or a husband of delicate sensibilities. Her coloring is excellent, and she is fresh and unspoiled, a condition rare to find in the streets of London. I daresay the girl will be flattered by the request."

When Jonathan and Bamber related this to her shortly afterward, as they all met in the orchard, Miss Tilney did not appear to prize the compliment so highly as Follett anticipated—but she immediately grasped the use to which it could be put. "This will give me such opportunities to study his character," Miss Tilney said. "Though my asking direct questions about Mrs. Willoughby would put him on guard, his conversation may reveal much about his state of mind."

"I believe you are right," said Jonathan. "If you keep us apprised of his planned comings and goings, those hours will also provide us with chances to speak to Willoughby on his own." They all understood, of course, that the sittings would take place at Delaford, under the watchful eyes of the Brandons; anything else would be highly improper.

"Did not Hitchcock say that arsenic was to be found in paints?" Miss Tilney asked. "Would it be in the sort of paints Follett uses?"

Jonathan looked at Bamber, who shrugged. "I would not think so, but I cannot be certain."

As Mr. Follett seemed unlikely to give an unbiased answer— at least, if he were Mrs. Willoughby's murderer—the party elected to go into Barton. Although such paints were probably not to be bought in such a small village, some merchant or other would be able to order them, and thus might possess information about the paints' contents. Jonathan decided it was as well to walk to the village now, as he would then be near the home of Miss Williams. Even thinking of the afternoon's appointment made him uneasy, so he was grateful that Miss Tilney and Mr. Bamber conversed together, largely about whether or not her family would wish to buy a portrait.

(She thought not, but Bamber gallantly insisted they would not be able to help themselves from purchasing a painting sure to be so lovely.)

As the cottages and houses came closer together and the murmur of the village square grew louder, Jonathan caught a glimpse of pale blue in a small pathway. A few more steps forward, and he could see Miss Williams standing there, pale blue cloak about her shoulders . . . speaking to Mr. Willoughby.

How had Willoughby left Allenham without informing any of his guests—perhaps even not his servants? Why, at this of all times, should he be seen not only out and about but also with a young woman with whom he had a shameful history?

But Willoughby clearly did not mean to be seen long. He turned immediately and disappeared down a side path, one that led to his pasturage, a place where none would remark on his presence. Miss Williams lingered a moment longer, her expression unreadable, before she turned and walked in the opposite direction, toward her home.

It had all transpired so quickly that Jonathan had not even time to draw Miss Tilney's attention to the event before it was over, but he did so immediately thereafter. They all stopped where they stood to consider the matter.

"Would you judge their countenances to be angry?" Miss Tilney asked. "Or might they have been—it is but conjecture—could they have been conspiring?"

"Sometimes I am well able to comprehend the feelings of others," Jonathan said, "but at other times, they seem wholly mysterious to me. This moment is among the latter. They both seemed somewhat furtive, but I imagine any meeting between them, out of doors, would look so, even if both are wholly innocent."

"And yet she could have been there that night," said Miss

Tilney. "If she had been, she could have slipped into Barton Park and have—have had access to the glasses . . ." Miss Tilney seemed to lose her place in the conversation altogether.

Jonathan's curiosity was awakened. "Miss Tilney?" he asked.

"Oh!" Miss Tilney exclaimed. "We have been fools—blundering fools—how could we have been so simple? I have just hit upon a question—one that very nearly came to me yesterday, one necessary for us to understand this event. Its answer may well change everything."

Mr. Bamber looked back and forth between the two of them, perhaps in amazement. "Whatever do you mean?"

"The poison was in the port," she said slowly. "The port had been decanted, then set out in two glasses before the butler ever entered the room."

Jonathan did not see her point. "We shall have to find out where precisely the port was at that time, of course, but how does that change matters?"

"The port had been let to breathe after pouring but before being drunk," she persisted.

He nodded. "And thus the poisoner had ample opportunity."

"Don't you see?" Miss Tilney asked. "*Two* glasses. There could be no guarantee that Mrs. Willoughby would pick up the glass with the poison in it."

The answer dawned in Jonathan's mind, its light putting every fact in new relief. "You mean that Mrs. Willoughby might not have been the target. The murderer might have meant to kill Willoughby himself."

Chapter Ten

All that need happen for the familiar to become unfamiliar is to look at it from a different vantage point. A painting hung on a different wall suddenly seems to contain more yellow. A vase moved from mantelpiece to shelf looks larger than it did before. Jonathan had always been keenly aware of this; as a boy, even the slightest tilting of pictures on the wall had sufficed to make them seem alien.

Never before had he comprehended that this phenomenon could be as true in the abstract as it was in the actual, for when he considered the poisoning at Barton Park in this light, entirely different motives—and suspects—came to mind.

As strangely as Follett had been acting, Jonathan had not been certain he was angry enough to kill a woman he had once loved. Far more plausible that he should feel murderous rage toward the man who had stolen her away.

Neither the colonel nor Mrs. Brandon had been fond of Mrs. Willoughby, nor she of them. Yet Jonathan could not imagine either of them deciding to kill her. Where Willoughby was concerned, however, their feelings ran deeper. Had not Colonel Brandon even challenged Willoughby to a duel once, been openly willing to take Willoughby's life? And the colonel's ward—Miss Williams, his cousin—she had been vastly wronged by Willoughby. Ruined, in fact.

Briefly he thought that the encounter he had witnessed between Willoughby and Miss Williams suggested her innocence, for surely she would not wish to meet with a man whom lately she had attempted to kill. However, it might have been Willoughby who had instigated the meeting.

Bamber, however, did not seem convinced. "Do you not see the problem? Why would the poisoner have poisoned only one glass? Would he not have poisoned both, to ensure he killed Mr. Willoughby?"

"That would require the poisoner to be willing to kill Mrs. Willoughby without any specific murderous intent toward her," Miss Tilney said. "Such coldness, such calculation—that is not even human. No, no, I cannot imagine it."

Bamber considered this, slowly nodding his head. "The poisoner might have thought that Mrs. Willoughby would not drink. It is unheard of for women to take port after dinner. The rational assumption would be that she would merely lift her glass."

"A fascinating point, Bamber." To Jonathan it appeared that his new friend had some instincts for investigation. "But as I think back upon the evening—was there not some small disturbance just as the tray with the port was being brought into the room?"

Miss Tilney nodded. "Yes, yes, you are quite correct. I could not see what happened—"

"I remember it now!" Bamber snapped his fingers. "Someone bumped into the tray, and one of the glasses was spilled! It had to be poured again at the last moment—"

"From the bottle, which was not poisoned," Jonathan continued. "The question is, who bumped the tray?"

Bamber's ruddy countenance had gone quite pale. He no doubt understood the significance of this answer. "I very much believe it was Willoughby. He loudly claimed that Follett had jostled him—but it was Willoughby."

"We cannot dismiss Follett from consideration," Miss Tilney said, too wise to leap to conclusions. "He may have found it more expedient to nudge Mr. Willoughby into the tray rather than to do so himself. Nor can we entirely exclude the possibility of a reckless poisoner who did dose both glasses, for the incident with the tray may have been merely an accident . . . one that preserved Mr. Willoughby's life."

"All possibilities must be considered—and, furthermore, shared," Jonathan said. "The constables must be made aware of this line of inquiry."

"Indeed we should inform them without delay," Miss Tilney agreed. "How will they ever find the right murderer if they do not even know the intended victim?"

Like nearly all other well-bred young ladies of her class, Juliet Tilney had never set foot inside a constabulary, much less a gaol. The village of Barton, small as it was, made do with one building for both purposes. Juliet shivered as she saw the bars on the windows. At least Mr. Darcy and Mr. Bamber were with her. What a terrible thing it would have been to go alone!

Yet the constabulary was not so intimidating inside as out. The cells were empty, and while the stone rooms were starkly furnished, they appeared reasonably clean and humane. The constables themselves had chairs and a small table, and a kettle had just been put on to boil for a pot of tea. Atop one of those chairs lay a volume of *Ivanhoe*—which Juliet had been wild to read but had not yet managed; had their errand been any less important, she would have immediately begun asking about its merits. The book apparently was in the possession of Constable Baxter, who was not amused at this interruption in his day. Constable Hubbard was not to be seen.

"What is this, then?" Baxter asked. "Do you know something about the poisoning you've not told us?"

"We have no more answers," Juliet replied, "but one more question. How can we be certain that Mrs. Willoughby was the intended victim?"

Baxter stared. "Seems clear enough, what with her being the one that's dead."

Juliet persisted, "Might not the poisoner have been attempting to kill Mr. Willoughby instead?" As curiosity dawned in the constable's face, she told him the rest, as straightforwardly as possible. In the end, she thought, Mr. Darcy and Mr. Bamber would have to explain in full; it was unlikely her thoughts would be taken seriously. Yet she could not contain the words; the idea, new and bright, burned within her mind and must be shared.

"'Tis a fair enough question," Baxter finally said. "No reason to assume that was the case, but no reason to assume otherwise, either."

"So you'll consider it?" Juliet felt a flush of pleasure and pride when the constable nodded. How wonderful to think that even a girl such as she could speak, and the law might listen.

Better yet, this might turn the constables' attention away from Marianne Brandon. If they believed her so in love with Willoughby that she would kill his wife, then how could they believe that she would take the risk of Willoughby dying instead?

She said as much to Mr. Darcy as they left the constabulary. He did not react with similar elation. "If they are determined to think the worst of Mrs. Brandon," he said, "then they will easily enough convince themselves that she was willing to kill either or both of the Willoughbys."

"Surely they are not so fixated upon her as that." Juliet did not know whether she truly believed as much, or whether she only wanted to.

"We will know soon enough," Mr. Darcy said. "The authorities will not let the matter go on much longer without appointing a new magistrate, and when that man takes up the role, his attitude toward Mrs. Brandon's guilt or innocence should be swiftly made plain."

Mr. Bamber cleared his throat. "If I might—"

Juliet turned to him. "Yes, Mr. Bamber?"

"I wish to beg a favor of you both." Bamber had a fair face, one which plainly showed his eagerness, and it struck her that he was most attractive in his person.

Mr. Darcy said, "I am sure we both are willing to oblige you."

"Wait and hear what I ask before you reply," Bamber said. "I was hoping that, perhaps, if you would be so kind, you might, ah . . . include me in your investigation? Properly, I mean. So far I have inserted myself, and you have been most gracious, but I wish to make sure that your wishes in this matter are the same as mine."

Her first thought was to refuse him. The investigation of murder was inevitably indelicate, in her limited but intimate experience. She and Mr. Darcy had been thrown together into their endeavor, or else she would never have dreamed of undertaking the task with a young man she had then known for not even one week. Mr. Darcy must have felt much the same, because he said, "We have done this before, you see—"

"Of course, you have more experience than I do in these things—which is to say, any experience at all. However, talking with Hitchcock, well, that was one of the most interesting conversations I have ever had. Long have I thought that the sciences might, in time, be able to assist in the enforcement of the law, but never did I anticipate having the chance to actually make it so." Bamber's cheeks had gone ruddy with excitement. "Consider, too, that this is a case of poison. You may have need for chemical analysis, and I could put together a sort of makeshift laboratory that might serve that purpose."

That was an excellent point. Juliet realized also that, had she and Mr. Darcy wished to ban Mr. Bamber from taking part in their efforts, they should not have let him begin. Having done so, courtesy suggested they should allow him to continue—and if he had much to offer the investigation, why should they not?

There were other reasons. Juliet said, "Mr. Bamber, you must understand—in many ways, our investigation into the first murder was neither gentlemanly nor ladylike. One must perpetrate certain rudenesses for the greater good."

"I comprehend you entirely," Bamber said, "and I promise there will be no averse judgment from me on that score. Should my own behavior at any time lead to misgivings, please say so at once, and I shall amend as required."

This seemed to decide the matter for Mr. Darcy. "I am willing, if Miss Tilney is."

So she smiled up at Mr. Bamber. "Welcome to the investigation, sir."

Jonathan was not without misgivings about Bamber's joining in with the work of determining Mrs. Willoughby's killer—but he could not articulate why, beyond a vague sense that spending time with Miss Tilney was valuable to him. But surely it did not follow that this time would be less valuable if shared. Besides, Miss Tilney had no objection, and Jonathan inherently trusted her judgment.

He might well have considered the matter at more length, however, had he not needed to excuse himself for his afternoon's errand. Already he was much preoccupied with the prospect of meeting Miss Williams.

Sufficient time had not elapsed for his first letters to his parents to be both read and answered. But so often had Jonathan's parents spoken of Miss Williams since learning of her at Donwell Abbey that he felt he did not need to read their letter to him in order to know what they would say, what they would wish.

Tell Miss Williams that she is always welcome to come to us, his mother, Elizabeth, would write. *That we should love to be introduced to her, and to tell her more of Susannah.*

There is no need to suggest more fondness for Mr. Wickham than actually existed, his father might add. *Yet there is also no need to speak more of his misdeeds than those which cannot be avoided in any truthful narrative of his life.*

This hit upon the problem precisely: Jonathan knew his parents did not have a truthful narrative of his own life, not in one important respect, one of which an introduction to Beth Williams must remind him. Few things could cause him as much pain as recalling Susannah's death.

How little reason there had been for fear before, and how much reason for hope! Jonathan, his parents, and his younger brothers had delighted in Susannah's company; and as her visits grew longer and longer, it seemed entirely likely that she would eventually come to live at Pemberley, adopted by his parents in spirit and perhaps even in law. After Aunt Lydia passed away, Susannah's future with the Darcy family had seemed all but certain. The only reason their parents had not raised the question with Wickham already was because they knew it would touch his pride.

Then, not quite one year prior, Susannah had contracted a very serious putrid fever. Mother had nursed her tenderly;

Father had brought in the best physicians. Susannah had seemed to be past the worst of the danger when her father, Wickham, had summoned her home. Had he wanted his daughter back so that he could care for her in her infirmity? Not at all—in fact, he seemed deaf to all protestations regarding her health.

No, Wickham had demanded that Susannah return home because he had learned that she was beginning to call Fitzwilliam Darcy "Papa." For this alone, he had demanded that Mother and Father return the delicate child to a place she scarcely knew; Wickham sent only a maidservant to fetch her home.

The journey had been too much for Susannah in her weakened state. Her condition had worsened even before she returned to Wickham's house, and very shortly thereafter, she had died.

"Mr. Darcy." Jonathan was startled from his memories by the approach of Colonel Brandon; he ought to have anticipated it, for Brandon had met him at precisely the time and place mentioned in his note of invitation. "Good afternoon to you. I hope you fare well?"

"I do, sir. I hope that you and Mrs. Brandon do also." It occurred to Jonathan that neither he nor Miss Tilney had spoken to their hosts of their plans to meet and discuss the investigation. Should he ask Colonel Brandon about her, as though he did not know her whereabouts? No, he decided—a lie of omission may yet be a lie, but it is still less damning than a lie of commission. Best to say nothing of Miss Tilney at all.

If Colonel Brandon noticed Jonathan's silence on the matter of Juliet Tilney, he gave no sign. His countenance was more somber than usual. "Miss Williams's home is not far from here. She consented to the meeting, but you must remember—these concerns have always pained her heart. It will not be an easy matter for you to discuss."

"I do not expect it to be."

Yet at first all went well. Miss Williams, a handsome young woman, greeted him civilly, and her child was in a happy mood, able to make himself winsome by playing with a toy horse on the floor at their feet. "Do you see any great resemblance," Miss Williams asked, "between him and your uncle? For that matter, do you see it between your uncle and me?"

"I had not yet considered the matter," Jonathan confessed. He could scarcely admit that he had seen her before—twice—and that both those occasions awakened curiosity about her role in Mrs. Willoughby's death. Despite the awkwardness he felt, he forced himself to study Miss Williams's face. "In truth, you do not much favor—though both you and your son have his coloring." Susannah had been more like Aunt Lydia than either Miss Williams or little George, and for this lack of resemblance, Jonathan was grateful.

Miss Williams considered his words for a moment. "All my life I have wondered what I might have inherited from my father, but now that I know, it does not seem to matter so much."

"It certainly must help to have inherited his money," Jonathan said.

Colonel Brandon blanched; Jonathan knew too well what this meant. Referring outright to money was sometimes acceptable, sometimes not, and he could never work out which was which. Apparently, in this case, he had erred.

Yet Miss Williams laughed out loud. "You are an honest soul, Mr. Darcy."

"Forgive me if I spoke out of turn."

"Not at all. The money *does* help—and from the stories I

have heard, I may have been better off with the money and without the acquaintance." There was a bright edge to her sunny mood—a sense, perhaps, that her smile and cheer were willed rather than felt—but this might be no more than a very kind wish to put Jonathan at ease. Her conduct might not always have been that which a lady's should be, but her manners were far better than those of many ladies he had known. "As a small child, I used to tell myself stories in which my father was a duke or an earl or even a prince. Someone very grand, very noble, who would come for me if only he knew I existed. Those foolish fancies I gave up long ago, but I must admit, it was very saddening to learn that his character was so disreputable."

Jonathan thought hard. "He was an excellent rider. Apparently a brave soldier, although he changed regiments often. He could be quick-witted, and very charming when he chose."

"That, Mr. Darcy, is the kind of praise that damns with its very sparseness," Miss Williams said. "I had already named my son before I knew the name of my father, and I almost wish that they had not the same one. But I may hope that little George will grant it more distinction."

"He could scarcely grant it less," Jonathan said. He meant no humor, but Miss Williams laughed once more.

"Again, you are an honest man. I am glad to have made your acquaintance."

Could a murderess so deeply value honesty? Was not her forthrightness an indication that her morals were generally more upstanding than her one great transgression might suggest? This seemed possible to Jonathan, but then it occurred to him: *If Miss Williams prizes honesty above all else, might she not consider Willoughby's lies a sin worthy of punishment?*

He could scarcely say this aloud, nor even ask about Willoughby in any politeness. So Jonathan confined his remarks to the purpose of their meeting. "My parents would very much like to meet you someday." He suspected they would be very disappointed that Miss Williams little resembled Susannah, but they would still honor the connection. He thought of inquiring whether Miss Williams would wish to know more about her half sister herself, but she had not asked. Perhaps it would be distressing to a young mother to hear of such a fate befalling a child. Regardless, he resolved to follow her example in this and remain silent upon that subject.

Miss Williams smiled—and again, Jonathan glimpsed that bright edge. "Please give my regards to your parents. But, I pray you, assure them that I ask nothing of them. We are well seen to, my George and I." She ran her fingers through her child's downy hair. "Have we now not everything we need?"

An odd way to put it, Jonathan thought. To judge by Colonel Brandon's puzzled expression, he found it strange, too.

Jonathan might have considered the peculiarity further, had he not been reminded of more urgent matters by glimpsing what hung on one of the hooks by the front door: a blue cloak.

When Colonel Brandon and Mr. Darcy left, Beth paid them every arrear of courtesy, as though they were any other callers, on any other day. Not one full minute after their departure, however, she ran upstairs to peer out her window to watch them going.

Mr. Darcy was definitely the young man she had glimpsed just after her talk with Willoughby. But did he recognize her? If so—if he knew she had so recently been with Willoughby—what must he think of her?

She told herself, *At least it was not one of the constables.*

∽

After a morning of such interest, Juliet could not but find her afternoon at Delaford somewhat dull. Marianne's duties as the lady of the house kept her busy with her housekeeper and other servants, so it seemed as good an opportunity as any for a guest to take advantage of the library. The Brandons did not yet own *Ivanhoe*, but among their volumes Juliet found *Rob Roy*, a great favorite. There were passages she very nearly knew by heart. This was just as well, for Sir Walter Scott's words on this occasion remained all but unread. Juliet's eyes traveled the lengths of each line over and over, but little of it penetrated her thoughts. Her mind would not set itself to Scottish adventure when a murder remained unsolved.

In no circumstances can I imagine the colonel or Mrs. Brandon to be guilty, she mused, staring at the page as blankly as though nothing were writ upon it at all. *Yet it is wisest to adopt the philosophy Mr. Darcy and I took at Donwell Abbey. We must investigate everyone—obtain and verify any proofs of either innocence or guilt—without influence from our personal feelings and conjectures.*

The butler came in, and Juliet straightened, willing herself to appear a proper lady, correctly interested in poetry or sermons or something more "suitable" than the adventure story she actually held—until the visitor was announced, "Mr. Follett, miss."

Juliet righted herself. Mrs. Brandon would not be long behind—she would not leave her young guest to welcome a visitor on her own, least of all an unmarried man. Yet Juliet's fears were less for her reputation, more for the fact that Mr. Laurence Follett might very well be a murderer.

Mr. Follett entered and gave her a quick bow. He had no time for more before Marianne bustled in, all smiles, though in her eyes could be glimpsed some confusion. "Mr. Follett—how lovely. To what do we owe the pleasure of your visit?"

"To the loveliness of your guest, Mrs. Brandon." Follett said this almost without warmth; clearly he had no thought of flattering Juliet. This, of course, rendered the comment even more flattering, and she tucked it away in her memory, to be mulled over at pleasing length sometime in the future. "I am an artist in need of a subject, and I wished to ask whether Miss Tilney would consent to sit for a portrait, and whether you as her hostess would permit the same. All sittings would of course take place here, under your watchful eye."

"A portrait!" Marianne's eyes sparkled. "That is an excellent notion. Would it please you, Miss Tilney?"

Juliet might have been more pleased had Follett's manner not been so cold and correct. She was an object he wished to use, no more to him than a bowl of grapes and pears might be to the painter of a still life. Yet sitting for a portrait would serve her purposes as well as his.

So she smiled. "It would, very much. Thank you for considering me, Mr. Follett."

Now she would have the chance to consider him in turn.

Jonathan walked away from Miss Williams's house with Colonel Brandon by his side. Fortunately the colonel was not one to speak for speaking's sake, for which Jonathan was grateful.

Miss Williams had asked about her father, very little about her sister. This he now realized to be entirely natural: Miss Williams would have spent her whole life curious about her paternity, whereas her sister had never been more to her than an idea—a child who died before Miss Williams even learned of her existence.

If she had asked about Susannah, Jonathan did not know whether he could have answered. Every time he thought about his cousin, the little girl who had been to him a sister in all but name, he had to remember: *Susannah died because Wickham learned that she called my father "Papa."*

And I am the one who told him.

Chapter Eleven

Shortly upon Hubbard's return to the constabulary, Baxter told him of the theory presented by Mr. Darcy, Miss Tilney, and Mr. Bamber—that the poison in the glass at Barton Park that fateful night had been intended not for Mrs. Willoughby but for her husband. Although good ideas often fail to find receptive ears, it was not so in this case, for Constable Hubbard's imagination (a stubborn, inactive thing at most times) was immediately captured.

"That would explain it all, would it not?" Hubbard asked. "Mrs. Brandon could not have killed the wife and expected to marry Mr. Willoughby herself, not without doing away with her husband, too, and she would have had to know *that* would raise suspicions. Yet if her sentiments toward the man bend more toward hate than love, she might well have struck at him."

These were Baxter's thoughts precisely, as he said both to Hubbard at the time and to his wife that night. Mrs. Baxter was by nature shy and rabbity, more likely to panic at the thought of trouble than to cause it. Yet such information as this could not but be shared, and so at the butcher's shop the next morning, she whispered as much to one special friend. This special friend was by nature not shy at all, and, for her, causing trouble was no deterrent but a positive encouragement. So *she* told everyone else she encountered that morning, on which she conducted several errands which took her to nearly every shop in Barton, where the story sprang anew from the lips of many. As is the way with such stories, it gained detail and nuance in the telling, none of which had much to do with the facts as originally presented.

The nursemaid in Miss Williams's house heard that the poison had been in both glasses, that both the Willoughbys were meant to die, but Mr. Willoughby was so strong and hale that he had not been overcome.

Mr. English, the farrier, had it that Mrs. Brandon had been seen buying up boxes of rat poison, great crates of the stuff, more poison than could be needed to kill ten thousand rats, and had been heard to swear vengeance upon Willoughby.

Mrs. Tyler, the wife of a local solicitor, was told that the only reason Mrs. Brandon had not yet been arrested was due to Colonel Brandon's standing in the parish, and that his brother-in-law, Mr. Tremblay, was to be the new magistrate, and so that woman would get away with it sure as anything, just like she had with the last fellow she murdered.

Mr. Matthews, a farmer come to Barton to sell his parsnips and radishes, was informed that Mrs. Brandon had meant to kill the man who had jilted her, but had changed her mind at the last moment due to her love for him, and so had switched the glasses so that Mrs. Willoughby would perish instead. The poison had been hidden in a ring Mrs. Brandon always wore, which had a cabochon gemstone that could be slid aside to release fatal powders. (He heard the story late in the day, after it had had time to develop extravagant new flourishes.)

There were those, of course, who did not believe a word of it; Mrs. Brandon had not been seen in Barton at all since the events in Surrey, and her presence would have been noticed and commented upon even without the purchase of undue amounts of rat poison. There were more, most in fact, who believed very little of what they had heard—but believed a little, which can be even more dangerous. The existence of the outlandish rumor allows those who hear it to scoff, and then to put their faith in other rumors that are more plausible yet no more true. So it was that all Barton had decided, before dusk, that Willoughby had certainly been the target all along, and that it was even more likely than before that Mrs. Brandon was guilty.

One of the rumors, almost accidentally, touched upon the truth.

And one of the listeners was a servant at Allenham.

The evenings at Allenham were both better and worse than Jonathan had feared they would be before his visit.

Better, in that Willoughby, in what must be assumed to be a state of shock, was much distracted for the majority of the time—either in calculating the size of his inheritance from his wife or in fearing the hangman's noose. Perhaps, even, by the memory of his wife . . . though Willoughby never so much as spoke her name. Worse, in that Jonathan could not forget Mrs. Willoughby's final distress even if her husband had, and that the grief that *ought* to have been felt haunted the house as surely as any ghost could have.

We did not pretend Susannah had not died, Jonathan thought as they sat through a mirthless dinner, during which both Willoughby and Follett drank far more than they ought. *Father controlled himself, but these men know little of such self-possession.* Indeed, the irritation both men felt toward each other was less and less veiled as the days ran on. As for Jonathan and Bamber, their new camaraderie had to remain concealed so far as was possible, in order to hide their investigation into the murder.

Thus dinner was utterly joyless, and conversation consisted mostly of Willoughby loudly recounting incidents at school where Jonathan had looked—or had been made to look—very foolish.

"Do you not remember the time that Thumps could not bear the singing of hymns?" Willoughby's lips were tinted a deeper red from the wine he had copiously drunk throughout the evening. "When he ran from chapel and was found in a hallway, hiding in a corner?"

"Rocking back and forth yet again," said Follett. "I saw it myself. Whatever was that, Thumps? Were you throwing a fit?"

The music and the brightly colored light through the stained glass windows had simply been too much for Jonathan to bear at that time, but he did not explain, as he knew these two men would not understand. Instead, he glanced over at Bamber, hoping for help.

Such aid was given, for Bamber immediately said, "Oh, what was that, compared to the time you tied Hodge to his bedpost and left his window open on the coldest night of the year?"

"We got someone every single term!" Willoughby said. "Here I thought you'd taken that turn, Bamber, but I suppose it was Hodge after all. The next year was you, wasn't it, Thumps?"

Jonathan could still remember the faint crusting of frost upon the bed frame, the snowflakes that had dusted the wooden floor. "Yes. It was me."

Willoughby and Follett both laughed again, though Jonathan could see that true mirth was far from their hearts. Disgruntling though it was to be ridiculed for someone else's amusement, he found it even worse to suffer such for only the pretense of fun.

After dinner the usual port and cigars would have been shared, most likely as the accompaniment to yet more objectionable memories, had not the butler drawn Willoughby aside for a private word. "I wonder whence the need for counsel arises," Bamber said as they milled about in Willoughby's study. "Some servant girl in trouble, perhaps."

"Does it matter?" Follett tapped his fingers on Willoughby's cigar case. "It spares us a few minutes with the man, so let us be grateful where we may."

Jonathan and Bamber exchanged a look. Follett was scarcely pretending to like Willoughby any longer. Had he attempted to kill Willoughby and failed in his effort, instead murdering a woman he had loved? If so, Jonathan thought, surely he would be more distraught. He would not bother to hide his grief without also hiding his hate . . . or, perhaps, this was yet another of the finer points of unspoken human behavior that Jonathan had never fully understood.

From the hallway, Willoughby cried out, "Good G-d!"

All three men startled, then hastened to see what had occurred. Willoughby stood in the hall, his face pale as paper, staring at the butler and a maidservant. "Whatever is the matter?" Follett said. "What has happened, Willoughby?"

"The servant girl has heard in Barton—" Willoughby had to stop and gather his breath. "She has heard that the constables no longer believe my wife was the intended target. They think that instead this murderer unknown intended to kill *me.*"

Jonathan felt only mild disappointment that the constables had spoken. The killer might have been less circumspect without their theory becoming common knowledge. A sideways glance from Bamber revealed that this feeling of chagrin was entirely mutual. Follett, however, was deeply shaken. He staggered to one side like a wounded man, turning his face from them all.

The shock of the gentlemen present must have emboldened the maidservant, newly important as the teller of the tale. "Everyone is saying it, and also the constables think it was rat poison used. They say—they say it was Mrs. Brandon, sir."

"That is a lie," Willoughby said with conviction. "Never would she hurt me. Her character is too fine, and her feelings . . . let us say only that I would feel safer in Marianne Brandon's presence than in that of any other upon this earth."

Here, at least, was opportunity, so Jonathan seized it. "Did you see anyone tamper with the port, Willoughby?"

"Had I seen anyone tamper with the port, I should by G-d have said so before now, shouldn't I?" Willoughby's contempt, though never pleasant, at least kept him from sensing any hidden meaning within Jonathan's question. "If by *tamper* you mean *spill*, then yes, I saw Follett blundering about, and he half shoved me into the tray."

"I barely touched you," Follett protested. "You knocked it over yourself."

Willoughby scowled—clearly angry—and for a moment Jonathan thought accusations would soon fly. But his response was no more than "Never take the blame for anything, do you, Follett?" Having apparently had enough of the topic, Willoughby stalked off.

Follett followed suit, but in the opposite direction, muttering, "The sooner I can put an ocean between myself and that man, the better it will be!" No response seemed desired, and none was given. His departure left Jonathan and Bamber alone.

"Willoughby reveals himself!" Bamber's fair face had

flushed with excitement. "Did you not think his reaction somewhat . . . theatrical? A show of fear, rather than true feeling?"

"I could not say," Jonathan replied. How he wished he better understood subtler displays of emotion! "Follett seemed very affected as well."

Bamber shook his head. "That is understandable, for we speak of the murder of a woman he loved."

Jonathan reviewed the past few minutes in his mind, considering. "If one of them is the culprit, then he was most adept at controlling his reactions when the port spill was mentioned."

"Indeed," Bamber said. "Willoughby brought it up himself. Perhaps he intended to introduce the subject at the time and place of his choosing."

"Entirely possible." Yet Jonathan felt as though he had more questions and fewer answers.

He waited for Bamber to retire for the evening before continuing his own efforts. Jonathan wondered at his delaying even as he did so and realized he wished to have something of significance to tell Miss Tilney that Bamber would not know. This was a curious impulse, one Jonathan did not fully understand. It would have to be considered at length at some point in the future, when the demands of the investigation did not weigh so heavily upon him. For the time being, his priorities must remain on the investigation.

Luck was with Jonathan, for he did not have to skulk in the area of the back stairs for very long before he found one of the servants going about her business; even better, it was the Allenham housekeeper, a stout woman called Mrs. Fargate. She stopped short at his approach, straightening immediately. "May I be of any assistance to you, sir?"

"Yes, ma'am." This next was dishonesty, which Jonathan

disliked in every possible way. After much consideration, however, he thought the lie harmless and potentially useful. "I am glad we are able to speak in confidence. This morning—just outside the house, I saw a scurrying—forgive the impertinence, but do you believe the house to have . . . rats?"

This startled the good woman almost beyond composure. "Good heavens. And here I thought Mr. Willoughby had got it all wrong, but maybe we need to keep a lookout at that!"

"What do you mean?"

Mrs. Fargate had regained some of her aplomb. "Forgive my mentioning it, sir. Two days ago, or thereabouts, Mr. Willoughby said vermin had been seen about in the garden. I thought he had mistaken some squirrel or rabbit for a rat, as we have no such problems at Allenham, I can tell you. I keep a clean house and see that my girls do their jobs proper. But if you have seen it also, then perhaps they are coming close to the house. Not in yet, mind you—we would have seen the signs of *that*—but we must be cautious."

Jonathan tried to sound neutral, almost disinterested. "So Mr. Willoughby came home with rat poison for the household just in time."

"Indeed not, sir. The master of a house doesn't trouble himself with the likes of that, does he? But I shall send a boy out for it tomorrow. Oh, what a pity Mr. Willoughby doesn't like cats. No poison so effective against mice or rats as a cat, mark my words." Her gaze had become careful and shrewd, that of a servant aware that they must speak above their station, but confident of their correctness. "The problem with poison is that oftentimes it kills more than the creature that was wanted dead. Bad work, if you ask me."

Willoughby bought rat poison, Jonathan thought, keenly aware of the importance of what he had just learned. *He told*

Bamber that he had done so. And yet the housekeeper knows nothing of it.

To Mrs. Fargate he said only, "I entirely agree."

That next day, Juliet's announcement that she wished to take another morning walk met with approval from Marianne, but surprise as well. "Yet again! I always thought myself passionately fond of walks, but my enthusiasm is nothing compared to yours."

"If you feel I am neglecting you—"

"Not at all." Marianne soothed her guest. "Besides, you have been fortunate enough to meet with friends on your walks. Mind you, we will soon invite these friends to dinner, so perhaps your morning walk will no longer seem as pressing."

She spoke, of course, of Juliet's time with Mr. Darcy, and Mr. Bamber, too. Colonel Brandon glanced from his wife to Juliet and back again, apparently considering whether to speak, but he said nothing. Juliet wondered at it, but unspoken words are easily forgot, and she did not dwell on them many moments after leaving Delaford.

When Juliet reached the orchard, Mr. Darcy and Mr. Bamber already stood beneath the tree, awaiting her.

"Have you heard?" Bamber said before she had even greeted them. "Our theory is known throughout the village, but they have blamed Mrs. Brandon for it again, and even more so than before."

Her heart sank. "Oh, no. How horrible for her. We must set to our work in earnest and delay no further, even if it spites hospitality."

"We must hope that Mrs. Brandon understands rumor is meaningless." Jonathan looked slightly past Juliet as he generally did, but she could sense his true sympathy. "What I consider more significant is Willoughby's reaction to receiving this information."

She listened to all that was then told to her of Willoughby's greater concern for his own life than for that of the woman he had married. One point stood out sharply. "He purchased rat poison when there were no rats? For the housekeeper would know that more surely than anyone else at Allenham," Juliet said.

"Looks dire for Willoughby, does it not?" Bamber said grimly.

"It does, but we cannot assume the worst explanation is necessarily the true one." Juliet had learned at Donwell Abbey that assumptions are the enemy of sound judgment. "Willoughby could have truly seen rats, and it is not impossible that he might have purchased the poison himself, without informing the housekeeper. We will need more information before we can see clear."

"Master of a house doing his own marketing, and then not even telling his housekeeper of it?" Mr. Bamber's tone first struck Juliet as rude, but then she saw how very kindly he smiled at her as he said it. "Unlikely, but, as you say, not impossible."

"There are others we must consider as well," Mr. Darcy said, "such as Miss Williams. We must not concentrate all our speculations upon those present as guests that night. We must consider that someone from without could have intruded upon the Middletons' home with the express purpose of poisoning either Mr. or Mrs. Willoughby."

"I am not sure I follow your reasoning." Bamber spoke

politely but firmly. "How could anyone not present at Barton Park that evening be aware of Sir John's plan to present them with glasses of port?"

"That is a valid point," Juliet said, "but in our short acquaintance, we have already learned that Sir John is a talkative man who might speak of his plans to anyone or everyone. His mother-in-law, Mrs. Jennings, is even more garrulous. Willoughby told us all of the toast in advance, did he not? The port tradition seems to have been known widely in Barton. So we cannot discount the possibility of an outside influence at work that night."

The frustrations inherent in investigating a murder seemed only now to become apparent to Mr. Bamber. "Must we entertain every speculation, no matter how . . . speculative? Only worthy hypotheses should be tested, or else much time will be wasted."

"We will gather more information," Juliet said. "Only in this way can we discover which hypotheses *are* worthy. Mr. Darcy has shown us the way, if we will but follow."

"Thank you," Mr. Darcy said, "but now I must confess that I am uncertain of your meaning."

"What I mean is that you had the good sense to speak to the Allenham housekeeper. If we are to learn the most pertinent details of what happened that night at Barton Park, we must continue speaking to all those on our list, most importantly to the Middletons' servants—this afternoon, if possible." The next day was to be Mrs. Willoughby's funeral; decorum would prevent them from doing much else on the morrow. "Servants always know far more than their masters wish to admit."

Marianne, who disliked speculation upon any matters of courtship, refused to let herself question Follett's motives in wishing to paint Juliet, or Juliet's suggestion that she might go out in the afternoon as well, to meet Mr. Bamber and Mr. Darcy in Barton. *Young people like to keep company with each other,* Marianne told herself, *and it need be no more than that.*

So, when told of the proposed afternoon outing, she said only, "It seems a pleasant day for it. This may be our last touch of warmth before autumn begins to hint at wintertime."

"Indeed—why, we will need cloaks every day, soon!" Juliet was more inspired by this idea than Marianne would have anticipated. "That day Miss Williams came to Delaford—she was wearing a cloak, was she not? I think I remember admiring it. A lovely light blue, was it not?"

Marianne frowned. "I cannot recall. It would not surprise me if she did."

"What do you mean?"

Smiling at the memory, Marianne replied, "A year ago, the local merchant stocked a wonderfully soft wool, dyed palest blue, absolutely perfect for a cloak, in the opinion of nearly every woman in Barton. Both my elder and younger sisters made cloaks of that material, Brandon obtained one for Miss Williams, Mrs. Jennings had a cape done up for her daughter Mrs. Palmer—why, I imagine every third woman in Barton has a cloak or pelisse made from that same wool. Sometimes they looked like flocks of birds flying together. Had I not just had a green one made, I might well have joined them."

"Oh." Juliet seemed disappointed, and could there be any wonder why?

Marianne petted her friend's arm. "Never fear. Your cloak is very handsome, but if you wish to brighten it up with a bit of trim, I am sure we can find something nice. Or might we see whether the merchant still has any of that blue woolen cloth in his stock."

"That will not be necessary," Juliet said, straightening and then smiling at her hostess. "I should not wish to join the flock."

To the good fortune of the investigative party, Lady Middleton had that morning left along with her children to visit her sister, Mrs. Palmer, in the next county. This left Barton Park occupied solely by Sir John, who was happy to have visitors, happy that they were young and handsome, and happy to indulge them in whatever fancies they might have. How strange that they should wish to speak to the servants! But what of it? Never let it be said that he would deny the young their fun. He himself was occupied with matters of business, but was in the next room, and the housekeeper could serve as silent chaperone. Thus it was that Juliet found herself seated in Sir John's drawing room, with Mr. Bamber to her left and Mr. Darcy to her right, the wordless housekeeper well behind, and the other servants being trooped in one by one.

The cook said she had nothing to do with the port whatsoever, drink was a butler's job, and they should all of them know it, and her girls were better trained than to go creeping about beyond the kitchen while the work of a large dinner was still ongoing. Juliet considered the cook's stern demeanor, decided her subordinates certainly obeyed her, and realized the kitchen maids did not have to be questioned.

The butler, Montgomery, did not appear pleased to have been presented for questioning, but he obeyed Sir John's instructions fully. He answered every question: The port had been purchased some weeks prior, but the bottle had remained sealed until a few hours before the guests' arrival. Montgomery himself had decanted the bottle, allowing sediment to sink to the bottom. Only then had he poured the first two glasses, that they might breathe and improve with exposure to air until dinner's end. Those two glasses had remained on a tray in an anteroom, rarely if ever unattended—the butler had assigned a footman to keep charge of them and make sure the glasses were not unexpectedly upset by one of the servants rushing in and out to complete dinner preparation.

The young footman appeared deeply grateful for the chance to talk. He had kept watch over the tray the whole time—almost the whole time—just except for a few moments when he had to step out—only moments, mind you—and while he went to ask for a bit of bread and cheese in the kitchen, as the servants' dinner would be late due to the party—and what with one thing and another, the tray had probably been left alone for a quarter of an hour altogether, here or there, between the guests' arrival and the fatal event.

Juliet and Mr. Darcy exchanged a glance. This absence might mean much, though how much remained to be seen. "The glasses were not distinguished from each other in any way?" Juliet asked. "They were not—differently etched, or one marked with a ribbon bow, or any such thing?"

"No, miss." The footman had gone almost limp with thankfulness that he was not being blamed. "Exactly the same, they were. At least, until they was upset."

Bamber shifted in his chair, as though stifling a reaction. Juliet feared she was not so circumspect. "There was a spill, was there not?"

"Just as Montgomery was walking the tray out, why, one of the glasses was spilled!" The footman shook his head in remembered dismay. "It was Mr. Willoughby—he knocked into the tray, though he said it was that other visitor of his, Mr. Follett, who knocked into him and caused the mess. Montgomery handled it quick as anything—wiped the tray, poured another glass, brought it out only a second delayed, and none the wiser unless they saw it as it happened."

As soon as the footman had left, Bamber said, "Well, now we have it. Willoughby must have taken advantage of the unattended tray to poison both glasses, then deliberately spilling one to ensure his own safety, while condemning his wife to death."

"This is possible," Mr. Darcy said, "though it may also be Follett caused Willoughby to make the error, meaning to save Mrs. Willoughby alone—but chance turned against him."

"Or the spill may have been purely an accident," Juliet added.

Mr. Bamber seemed unconvinced, but Mr. Darcy was of a more open mind. "We must determine who was capable of reaching the glasses during that time—the brief interval between our arrival and the toast. The woman with the blue cloak I saw earlier in the night, but if she had been lurking about, she would have had time to slip in with a dose of poison. Though, as Miss Tilney has informed us of the popularity of blue cloaks in this village, even if true that fact alone does not tell us much."

"It would tell us that the culprit is likely female," Juliet pointed out, "or a man willing to don women's attire if it affords him an opportunity for murder."

"Both of the men who had motive to harm Mrs. Willoughby were members of our party," said Mr. Bamber. "And I distinctly recall Willoughby having briefly left the room during dinner."

Juliet nodded—this much was true, she recalled. "So we

know he was where he ought not to have been. But did not Mr. Follett also step out in that time?"

Mr. Bamber snapped his fingers. "Of course. I went to look for him at one point, caught sight of him not very distant from me in the far hall. What he was doing, I could not say, but he was nowhere near the anteroom where the port was being kept. From there I could not have seen him."

"He was not there *at that moment*," Mr. Darcy said. "Follett could have had time to do more."

Juliet sighed. "What we must learn in order to find the killer is the very thing only the killer is likely to know—who was meant to die?"

Chapter Twelve

The next morning, the unseasonable warmth had vanished and autumn claimed the countryside entirely. Although the sun shone bright, the wind thrashed trees, clutched at cloaks and coattails, threatened to snatch hats from heads. In the few still moments, chimney smoke rose thicker from every house, and walkers moved more briskly, no longer idling in pleasant sunshine but hurrying toward their destinations.

I did not know Mrs. Willoughby beyond a few short moments, Juliet mused as she stood in the churchyard, *but she seemed as though she might be glad that the mourners would be uncomfortable at her funeral.*

How unchristian of her to think so. Unhappiness, Juliet knew, often manifests as pettiness, sometimes even cruelty; the most wretched souls cannot conceive of having fellowship with others in anything but equal misery, and so they attempt to create it. Mrs. Willoughby had died a very unhappy woman indeed. How terrible it would have been for her to know that, at her funeral, only one person seemed to grieve—and that person, the man she had chosen not to marry.

Laurence Follett maintained his composure manfully, but his countenance was gone white, and his eyes were rimmed with red. Mr. Willoughby, on the other hand, seemed to have dressed with especial flair rather than delicacy; he was not so crass as to eschew mourning, but the dark-colored clothing he wore nonetheless reflected his love of luxury and distinction more than any love he ought to have felt for his wife.

Everyone else stood quietly, performing the social duties attendant upon a death but without the sincere grief that elevates such from mere display to respect.

Mr. Edward Ferrars read at the graveside, though no one present paid much heed to the words. Juliet considered her distraction to be an honorable one, as she was studying the reactions and responses of those gathered near. One of these persons had to be responsible for Mrs. Willoughby's death.

Marianne stood quietly, staring at the grave without feeling. As sincerely as Juliet believed her friend to be innocent, she could easily imagine the constables interpreting Marianne's untroubled countenance as coldness.

Colonel Brandon, next to his wife, at least wore an expression of mourning. Juliet suspected that whatever sadness he felt was in the abstract: the loss of youth, the wrongness of murder, or other such general tragedies.

Mr. Ralph Bamber showed good manners by keeping his head bowed, and his lips moved along with the prayers. He had some pity for the fallen woman. Juliet was beginning to like this young man, not least because he appeared to be Mr. Darcy's true friend—and she knew he did not have many. As for Mr. Darcy himself, he was openly distracted, peering around the scene at first this and then that. His mind so often galloped away on one of his paths! Juliet had to stifle a fond smile.

Elinor Ferrars was in attendance despite what Juliet understood to be a lack of acquaintance with Mrs. Willoughby. Perhaps she had come merely to support her sister, though in this late stage of her confinement she could not have been faulted for failing to attend even the funeral of one very dear. It struck Juliet how protectively Elinor hovered near Marianne, how watchful she was. The cloak she wore had been made of that same pale blue woolen cloth. Mrs. Ferrars was not the sort to be carried away by passion, but to plan ahead—to rationally consider that the removal of a person might be the removal of a threat to those she loved—no. Surely not. Juliet could not let her imagination run so amok as *that*.

I take it as an axiom, from this moment on, she thought, *that if my suspicions are capable of including Mrs. Ferrars, a modest clergyman's wife great with child, then those suspicions have gone too far, and no longer provide true insight, only absurdity.*

Recognizing the sudden silence, Juliet righted herself. Mr. Ferrars's final words had been spoken. In accordance with custom, Mr. Willoughby stepped forward to throw the first clods of dirt upon her coffin. At the sound, Juliet shivered. Yet even that was not so fearful as the utter indifference of Willoughby's manner.

It did not matter that Mrs. Willoughby had been proud or cold. She had not deserved such an end as this.

"Of all the funerals I have performed," Edward said, "Mrs. Willoughby's may have been the most bleak."

Elinor nodded, not much heeding what he said. She found the path uphill much more difficult going than it would have been only a month prior.

Edward added, "True, I have not been a clergyman three full years yet. Worse funerals may come. But I must say, I do not anticipate them."

"It would be rather ghoulish were you to anticipate any funeral, dearest," Elinor said absently.

They walked together back to the parsonage. Elinor's cloak rippled around her, providing not near enough protection from the chill—and its pale blue shade made it inappropriate for a funeral—but none of her proper coats fit her any longer. She would have to make do with the cloak for some time yet.

"Mrs. Willoughby's service made me think," Edward said. The tenor of his voice had changed, which drew Elinor's full attention. "Will my mother's funeral be so very different? She, at least, has led a full life when measured in years. Yet in the gifts of love, mercy, charity—she is no less impoverished than Mrs. Willoughby appears to have been."

"You love your mother very much." Elinor had never doubted this, even when the elder Mrs. Ferrars behaved her worst. "As Fanny and Robert must, too."

"In their way. But they have lived in service to my mother's fortune more than to the woman herself. Such is the evil of money, Elinor. Greed can sully the finest human feelings, even the love that should exist between mother and child. Fanny and Robert will be grieved by my mother's loss, but how much can they honor that grief while they are also calculating how much they will gain by their inheritance?"

It was a harsh judgment, but Elinor could not deny its justice. "Does this influence your decision—not to forgive them?"

"Not to be forgiven by them, you mean," Edward scoffed, but she detected in him less firm resolve than he had before possessed. "I can never honor my mother completely, not so long as she demands to be honored in only those ways that are unworthy of us both. Still, I can feel for her most keenly. She demands obedience because it is the only form in which she recognizes affection, when in truth that form of obedience alienates affection more often than it brings it near."

Elinor realized that she had erred in urging Edward to reconcile with his family. Yes, the reconciliation would be most proper, best for their child, and ultimately restorative to

Edward himself, but she could not force him to it. Forgiveness blossoms when it will. We can no more demand it come early than we can demand springtime in December. She would do best to remain silent, allow Edward to continue thinking and praying upon the subject, and hear him when he wished to speak. Only then could change come.

Jonathan had not been oblivious to the tragic nature of Mrs. Willoughby's memorial service, but he had not been greatly occupied with it, either. He was impatient for it to be over, the better to resume their investigation.

As all departed, Mr. Bamber had fallen into step on Jonathan's left; Miss Tilney came up to his right. It was, Jonathan thought, as though they had all understood their places from the beginning. As unaccustomed as he was to finding friendship, he was wholly new to the pleasure of introducing persons to each other who then discovered a bond. Being part of a *group* of friends—this was something Jonathan had often witnessed but never experienced.

Bamber's mood was darker that morning than Jonathan had ever seen it. "It is a very grave sin," he said as the three of them walked with no particular direction, but in the general direction of Barton proper. "A grave sin indeed. Is forgiveness even possible, for such as this?"

"Our Savior can forgive us for any wrong of which we truly repent," said Miss Tilney. "I should rather ask, is true repentance possible within the soul of one who has committed such an act?"

"No one can ever know save for the guilty soul himself," said Jonathan. "Or herself. And in any case, I doubt we shall be told."

Their path took them past Miss Williams's home. Perhaps he should have thought first of her role as one of the main suspects in their investigation, but he did not. To him, Beth Williams was first and foremost the half sister of his late cousin. Once again, he thanked the merciful Lord that Miss Williams had not greatly resembled Susannah. If she had, the wretched guilt that tormented him would surely have become unbearable.

Would that we were Catholics, he mused, with a disregard for doctrine that would have horrified his parents. *Then I could go to confession. If I could admit it to one person, only one, and know my secret would be kept—perhaps my suffering would be lessened.*

Then again, I do not deserve to have it lessened. It remains my fault that Susannah is dead, and it always will.

Why had he not understood how Mr. Wickham would react? Jonathan would never have mentioned Susannah's fondness for his father had he had an inkling of the anger that would result. He had tried so hard to understand the rules and customs of society, so that he might feel moored and certain within them, but always there were exceptions, uncertainties, lacunae that felled Jonathan's efforts at comprehension. He had committed many social errors, knew it inevitable that he would commit many more, but surely none could be more lamentable, more shameful, than this.

"Are you well, Mr. Darcy?" Miss Tilney asked.

"I am. Forgive me, I became lost in thought." This was a stock response Jonathan had learned, which served his purposes very often. Miss Tilney did not seem entirely convinced, but when Bamber then made some comment upon the village, she replied to that rather than pressing further. Jonathan felt much relieved. He asked her, "Did you notice aught during the service that would aid our efforts?"

"Nothing so like, but I thought much upon the matter,

and I have come to think—" Miss Tilney took a deep breath before continuing: "I am newly convinced that Mr. Willoughby could not be the killer."

Jonathan was much surprised, though his astonishment was as nothing compared to Bamber's. "Upon my word, that is an extraordinary assertion. What can have convinced you, Miss Tilney?"

"Only think," she said, "he had the opportunity to do this at any time. He could even have poisoned her slowly and kept it a secret from everyone, even her physician. Why should he strike so suddenly, so precipitously, and in circumstances of such danger, where he might well be seen? There could be no reason in a man choosing to take such a risk of discovery when doing so was wholly unnecessary. Mr. Follett, however—he was visiting for a short time, and might have wanted the event to take place beyond Allenham's walls, the better to divert any suspicion."

All very logical—but as it happened, Bamber now believed Willoughby *must* be the killer.

"Since when has Willoughby ever asked anyone's advice on any subject whatsoever?" Bamber said, which was an excellent point. (The closest Willoughby had ever come to it, in Jonathan's knowledge, was demanding that other boys do his sums for him.) "He would not have known how much poison it took to kill, or even to begin to kill. So he struck rashly, foolishly, putting in far too much poison to ensure his wife's death."

"Why would he not do so at his own home?" Miss Tilney asked.

"You answered your own question. Would not Willoughby, too, wish the deadly event to 'take place beyond Allenham's walls'?" Bamber asked quite rationally.

Miss Tilney, however, remained unconvinced. "Clearly we

will not agree. What think you, Mr. Darcy? Your vote will decide it—for today's deductions, at least. Does the information we have learned incriminate Willoughby more, or Follett?"

"Neither," Jonathan said. "What we learned makes it clear that either man could strike in this manner. Or not strike, as the case may yet prove."

Under less grim circumstances, Bamber's befuddled expression might have been comical. "Neither of them the guilty party? Come now, Darcy, you cannot be ever looking so far afield when two such suspects stand before you."

"We do not even know whether Mrs. Willoughby was the true target," Jonathan reminded them both.

Miss Tilney nodded, saying, "We have yet properly to turn our attention to Miss Williams, as well."

Jonathan added, "And there are still others with reasons to dislike both Mr. and Mrs. Willoughby. There were others with the opportunity to poison the glass of port. It is just as Dr. Hitchcock said—anyone could have such an amount of poison on them at any time."

"But not everyone would kill," Miss Tilney said. "The *means* of Mrs. Willoughby's death may not tell us as much as we would wish. We shall have to look more closely at *motives*."

In the first few days after learning of Willoughby's engagement to Miss Sophia Grey and her fifty thousand pounds, Marianne had been half mad with grief. Her wildness of thought took many forms, some of them daydreams of a nature she would not have gladly admitted to anyone and could hardly bear to remember herself. She had imagined Miss Grey falling down a flight of stairs, drowning in the

Thames, even once being trampled to death by horses. These imaginings included Willoughby—now free of the engagement, and suddenly indifferent to fortune or the lack of it—returning to Marianne repentant. Sometimes the words she had put into his mouth rang stronger in her memory than anything he had ever actually said to her: *My actions may have been inconstant, Marianne, but my heart never. Can you doubt that? Do you not understand the truth of my heart, that it has always, ever, belonged only to you?*

How disbelieving she would have been in those fevered days to learn that within two years, the woman she had imagined dead would indeed be in her grave, and she would care not one whit what Willoughby thought about it!

With Miss Tilney out, Marianne and Colonel Brandon had the afternoon to themselves. He had but few affairs of business to occupy him, and she looked forward to some time in which they might read, talk, and while away the hours with the simple pleasures they both enjoyed.

One of those pleasures was music. Marianne went to the pianoforte to play, though she hesitated at the keyboard. Would something lively and cheerful come across as disrespectful so shortly after the funeral? Would something more mournful cast even darker shadows over the day?

In truth, her thoughts dwelled upon the speculation amid Barton that the poisoner's true target had been not the late Mrs. Willoughby, but Willoughby himself. Marianne found herself hoping that this was so, if only because it would mean that Willoughby was not the killer. How horrid, how shocking, to think that a man might do someone such a harm— much less a man once dearly loved.

Even worse was considering *why.*

Marianne had not replied to the letter Willoughby wrote her while she was in Surrey. This ought to have been understood as a refusal. But what if Willoughby had assumed the opposite? What if he had gained hope and, from that, a terrible determination to be free? The note he had clandestinely slipped to her the night of Mrs. Willoughby's death suggested this might be so.

Still, even now, Marianne could not believe him to be a wicked man. But he was a careless one, a reckless one, and capable of making in haste a decision that he would later regret . . .

"Oh, Willoughby," she whispered as she sank onto her piano bench. "Willoughby! When will I cease to repent of you?"

A small sound made her turn; at the doorway stood Colonel Brandon. The stricken expression on his face told Marianne that he had both overheard her words and misunderstood her meaning. "Colonel—"

"You need not apologize," he said, more gently than she would have thought, given the circumstance. "Your heart is your own, and I would not have you deny the truth of it."

This struck Marianne as not at all germane to her situation. "I have never so denied my feelings, nor would I. Willoughby is my greatest regret, for he was my instructor in folly and indulgence. I do repent of him. But while I may regret *him*, I do not regret the break between Willoughby and myself."

"Yet the break between you has not been complete," Brandon said. "Do not think I blame you. I understand how love can linger even when all hope, all expectation, has gone."

"Whatever can you mean? Be clear with me at once. If any word I have spoken, or act I have committed, has caused you to doubt me, then tell me what it is."

Brandon hesitated before saying, "I know that Mr. Willoughby has written to you. I saw the letter at Donwell Abbey."

Marianne's cheeks flushed hot. "You lowered yourself to snoop among my things?"

"I did not. The letter's discovery was accidental. Given all that had occurred, I could see no use in speaking of it at the time. I would not even have spoken of it now."

"You mean that you think me inconstant—unloving, untruthful—you think me capable of professing love to you while feeling it for another?" Marianne's temper could bear no such provocation. "If you thought me so false, I wonder that you married me at all!"

With that she departed the room, her desire for concord with her husband no longer so great as her indignation.

Juliet returned to Delaford with her mind full of arsenic and teaspoons. Marianne welcomed her back in a distracted, somewhat forlorn manner, perhaps more affected by the funeral than Juliet would have foreseen. Colonel Brandon had absented himself to look after matters in the orchard. This suited Juliet perfectly well, as she hoped to have some time to herself in which to consider the thorny question of motive.

Yet not a quarter of an hour after her return, the butler showed in Mr. Follett.

"Forgive my impertinence," he said, behaving not at all as someone who believes his actions require forgiveness. He wore his rumpled, stained painting clothes and carried with him canvas cases that held the tools of his profession.

"Mr. Follett!" She was caught entirely by surprise. He had sent a note to request a sitting for her portrait, but she had believed their engagement to be for the following day. Had she been mistaken? "Did I mistake the date, or—"

"You made no error, but this afternoon I find I require occupation. Have you any other commitments, Miss Tilney?"

"Indeed not," Juliet said. She must take advantage of opportunities as they presented themselves. "Choose our place, and I will rejoin you shortly."

Thus it was that she soon found herself wearing simple white muslin, near a sunny window in the Delaford morning room, sitting for her first portrait.

"Turn your head ever so slightly to the left." Follett made a quick motion with his paintbrush. Juliet could smell the fresh paint that gleamed upon his palette. "Tilt a bit this way—yes. That will do."

"How do you find yourself this day, Mr. Follett? Though, to be sure, it is a sad one." This, Juliet thought, would open the door to conversation that might reveal much about the man's feelings toward the late Mrs. Willoughby, not to mention her husband.

"In need of occupation, as I said." Mr. Follett continued blending paints upon his palette. "Desirous of other things to do, other places to be. A cousin of mine has set up shop in the wilds of America, a place called Pennsylvania, and I believe I should be better off there than here, even if I were to be surrounded by *Americans*."

Was this a joke, or a hint that Mr. Follett might soon flee the area, thus evading punishment for a crime? Juliet endeavored to make her next question sound innocent. "Are you truly going to America? It sounds rather primitive."

His reaction indeed revealed a great deal, though not what she would have intended. "Do not speak, Miss Tilney. When you speak, your mouth moves."

"But—we must have some conversation, if we are to be seated here many days—"

"Why must we, Miss Tilney?" Mr. Follett's gaze scrutinized her face without ever meeting her eyes. "You are my subject, just as a landscape might be, with no more speech necessary between us than would be necessary for me to have with a tree. Besides, you are a young lady, and the general conversation of young ladies dwells upon limited topics in a limited sense."

Juliet had to bite her tongue, though she felt sure his artistic eye would capture the angry flush in her cheeks.

"And what of truth do we find there?" At this point, Mr. Follett spoke more to himself than to her. "Very little. Only that which is convenient, or decorative, or serves the young lady's purpose. None that suggests true virtue, honor, or strength of will. *Your* only purpose here, Miss Tilney, is to have a fine portrait painted. That is best served by remaining quiet."

She could not resist saying, "You might learn much from Mr. Darcy, sir. His conduct is much more correct."

"Thumps? You make me laugh." But Follett did not laugh.

"Mr. Darcy is more than you think him." Juliet spoke without calculation—but if this was rashness, she was willing to be rash. "He is intelligent and thoughtful. He pays attention to those around him when it is most important to do so. And he keeps to his purpose even when it is difficult."

Mr. Follett stared at her. "I rarely think upon Mr. Darcy," he said, his phrasing curiously slow, "and when I do, it rarely improves my opinion of him. Your thinking upon him has created some sort of romantic creature. Do you hope he will spirit you off to Pemberley and all its riches someday? But no answer is necessary. Of course you do. Now, enough of your chatter."

Both prudence and courtesy commanded that Juliet cease

speaking. But what had those to do with investigation? Push she must, and push she would. "You will have difficulty finding a wife with such manners."

She half expected an explosion of temper, but that was not Follett's way. "Remain as still and silent as stone, Miss Tilney," he said. Juliet felt the implication was that, if she did not assume this state on her own, he would see to it that she did.

This is a man who could hide his wrath while mixing poisons, she thought.

Follett's expression grew darker and darker as he worked, and Juliet chose not to interrupt him again.

As the painting continued in future days—assuming that he did not discard this as a mere whim, or Juliet herself as too much trouble—Mr. Follett might ultimately speak more than he was willing to do today. Even this, however, had taught Juliet much: that he considered himself greatly wronged by a young woman. Her identity was not hard to guess. It was written on the newest gravestone in the Barton churchyard.

The afternoon at Allenham was as dismal as might have been expected. Perhaps the only event more unbearable than a household sincerely grieving is a household forced into the pretense of it. A few of the late Mrs. Willoughby's cousins had come, murmured various platitudes, asked leading questions intended to determine whether or not she had yet made her will, and if so, whether they were in it. Upon learning no will existed, they one and all found they were eager to begin their journeys elsewhere.

Willoughby received all these visitors politely but distantly. He showed great solemnity but little sign of grief, so far as Jonathan could discern it. (He knew he sometimes failed to pick up on subtleties, but Bamber's skeptical countenance suggested this impression was valid.) They both attended this visitation in the parlor for its duration, but Follett did not.

"He has left the house," Bamber murmured at one point, while Willoughby was otherwise occupied. "To paint Miss Tilney, I think. The man is desperate to be distracted from his grief. You cannot still suspect him!"

Jonathan could, and did. But it was not Follett alone he suspected.

He excused himself as soon as he decently could and went upstairs to his bedchamber, where he intended to wash his face with cool water from the basin, then sit in stillness and silence for a time. Spending so much time in unfamiliar company, with no relief to be had in the usual rhythms of the day, wearied him greatly. Even a quarter of an hour of silence and solitude would do much to restore him. However, after ascending the stairs, he saw a bustle of activity near a bedchamber that he realized must have been Mrs. Willoughby's.

They are packing away her things, he realized. No doubt Willoughby would sell her ostentatious jewelry—that or save it eventually to give to some other woman. Jonathan wondered what would become of her dress the color of moonlight.

One of the parlormaids came out carrying a bundle—and the object atop it caught Jonathan's attention. "I beg your pardon," he said. "Was this Mrs. Willoughby's newspaper?"

"Reckon so," replied the maid before remembering that she was speaking to a gentleman. "I mean, it must have been Mr. Willoughby's paper. What use she had for it, I surely cannot guess, and now we shall never know. We thought to throw it out, but such things cost a pretty penny, do they not? You may have it if you like, sir."

"Thank you." Jonathan took the paper.

Mrs. Willoughby had not at all seemed like the sort

of woman to trouble herself much about political affairs. Therefore, Jonathan felt sure that she had this paper in her possession for some very particular purpose.

And had not Mr. Follett made an especial point of purchasing a newspaper but days before? He had claimed that he needed to look into shipping matters for business, but perhaps he had concealed his true purpose.

After some consideration, Jonathan decided to take the newspaper into Allenham's long-neglected library. If any house servants reported that he had taken something from the late Mrs. Willoughby's room into his own—even so innocuous an object as a newspaper—it would raise questions and suspicions. If either Mr. Follett or Mr. Willoughby realized that Jonathan was working to determine the identity of the killer, they would guard their words and actions far more closely. A newspaper would draw no notice in the library.

The library was blessedly empty, and luckily Willoughby was the sort to order fires lit in every room whether or not the space was expected to be used. Jonathan settled himself into the chair nearest the blaze, impatiently flipped past the front page of advertisements, and began scouring the paper for some piece of news that could possibly link together Mrs. Willoughby and Mr. Follett. In short order, Jonathan had learned more about the ongoing Scottish insurgence, the Greek War of Independence, and the likelihood that the United States would swell to twenty-four in number come 1821. He even read an editorial decrying the Pains and Penalties Bill as a great injustice to the queen consort. But he saw not one item that he could imagine pertaining to either Follett or Mrs. Willoughby, much less both of them.

Then, to Jonathan's dismay, the library door swung open, and Follett walked in, past Jonathan, toward a window that showed the sunset.

Jonathan hesitated before speaking. Follett—stained with fresh paints, and even more haggard than he had been during the funeral—had not yet noticed Jonathan's presence. Instead, he stared out of the window, expression blank, as though he saw nothing.

People often take actions which they later regret, sometimes bitterly. The more harmful the action, the greater the regret. Might this not be what troubled Follett, if he had killed Mrs. Willoughby for spurning him? In the alternative, if Follett had intended to kill Willoughby but had erred, how much greater would the regret be!

Miss Tilney had said they must come to understand motives, and motives could be uncovered only through eavesdropping (defensible if ungentlemanly, but reliant upon fortunate timing), stealing letters (were the killer here so foolish as to write down their intentions), or conversation. While she would have gleaned what she could from Follett during her portrait sitting that day, that did not excuse Jonathan from the need to discover more himself if he could. He braced for the task, then began with a simple query: "Follett. Are you unwell?"

Follett turned toward him slowly, as if disbelieving. "Thumps?"

How Jonathan despised that nickname. "Yes. I was wondering whether—"

"I was told I had much to learn from you, and the more I think about you, the more I believe I have learned," Follett said. "Remove yourself from my sight, or I swear I shall remove you from this world."

This was wholly unexpected. Jonathan could but say, "I beg your pardon?"

"You are perhaps more than I have thought you to be. I am informed that you keep to your purpose. You are intelligent enough when it comes to facts and figures, but you think the rest of us dunces, and I, at least, am not." Follett rose from his stool and stalked toward Jonathan, menace in his bearing. "They say it was Willoughby at whom the murderer truly struck. Who among us would have better motive to kill him but you?"

Jonathan at first wondered if he had misheard. "I?"

"*Always* you have hated Willoughby. When I heard you had accepted his invitation, I was all astonishment, because why would you ever willingly put yourself in the presence of one who had bested you so often at school? Who had never liked you nor been liked by you?"

So that my parents might believe I had a friend, Jonathan thought but did not say.

Follett continued to rave as he got to his feet, his voice rising in pitch on every word. "Why would you come but for hate's sake? Always so silent, so secretive, so strange—no doubt brooding over your wounds, plotting your revenge!"

Footsteps in the hallway beyond proved to be Bamber, who must have heard the commotion. Jonathan was grateful to no longer be alone in such a situation.

By this point Follett was very near Jonathan's person, and his hands had clenched into fists. "You had your vengeance, didn't you? But you acted so foolishly an innocent woman was killed!"

Bamber tried to intercede. "I say, now, there is no call for this."

"No call?" Follett shouted. "No call? When Sophia lies dead in her grave?"

"I did no such thing," Jonathan said, and he could think of no better defense than the full truth. "I would never commit an act so wicked, nor would I ever endanger my freedom and my life on the account of John Willoughby."

Follett laughed, a terrible sound. He staggered backward, as though his outburst had taken the last of his strength. "Keep your distance from me, *Thumps*, or you'll get such a thump as will send you to your eternal punishment."

On the whole it seemed most prudent to leave. Bamber hurried out with Jonathan, murmuring, "You see the truth now, do you not? Follett's grief is so great, he even blames you! Is that the act of a murderer?"

"It is interesting that you use the word *act*," said Jonathan. "For *had* I committed a murder, and I wished to evade detection, I would very much like another person to be blamed instead."

"Do you truly believe that?"

"At this time I know not what to believe," Jonathan admitted.

Shaking his head, Bamber said, "You should think it through carefully, Darcy. If you convince all and sundry that Willoughby was the true target, it may well be *you* who dies on the gallows."

Chapter Thirteen

Dinner at Delaford that night was a largely silent affair. Juliet's strange experience sitting for Mr. Follett occupied her thoughts so much that she scarcely noticed the Brandons, beyond sensing a certain darkness in their moods. That she attributed to the aftermath of the funeral.

The next day, however, her suspicions were piqued. Colonel Brandon had left the house before Juliet rose for breakfast, though she had risen early, and Marianne came down as late as was decent, pale and tremulous, very much appearing not to have slept at all.

Juliet knew that her parents sometimes quarreled; it was impossible for even the most harmonious marriage to avoid all disagreement. Yet they resolutely kept any serious quarrels from their children's hearing, and both Mr. and Mrs. Tilney remained united as parents even when they did not possess unity as man and wife. So Juliet remained rather innocent as to exactly what the nature of any such disputes might be.

"Is—" What could Juliet say? "Is all well, Marianne? Is the colonel all right?"

Marianne opened her mouth, then closed it again. After a moment's consideration she said, "There is much that transpires between husband and wife that cannot be shared with the world. You need not concern yourself, dear Juliet—the trouble does not touch you or your presence in our home."

Although Juliet did not feel entirely satisfied with this answer, she knew better than to press. Talk over tea that morning dwelled on inconsequential topics—the very ones Marianne least valued—but such subjects were harbors in times of distress.

After Marianne had retired to her sitting room to write letters, Juliet lingered in the drawing room, wishing to give her hostess some moments of privacy, which seemed to be sorely needed. It was as well that she did, for almost as soon as a guest could in politeness arrive, the butler announced, "Mr. Bamber, miss."

Ralph Bamber came in, carrying a parcel that must have been purchased in the village, and a broad smile on his face. "Miss Tilney," he said without preamble. "What luck to find you alone!"

Anyone else would think he was on the precipice of some grand romantic statement. Amused, she said, "Mrs. Brandon will certainly join us shortly, once the butler informs her you are here."

"It must seem importunate, my coming to see you so early in the day, but I must make you aware of a turn that matters have taken within Allenham."

"Whatever do you mean, sir?"

Juliet listened in surprise and dismay as Mr. Bamber revealed the unlikely direction Mr. Follett's suspicions had taken the night prior. "Oh, no, no," she said. "That is not to be believed. Surely no one else will agree with such folly?"

"Odd as our dear friend Darcy can sometimes be, I tend to agree with you," Mr. Bamber said. "It is only Follett's grief that makes him speak so."

"Or his desire to cast suspicion on another is indeed desperate, and yet for some reason Follett blames Mr. Darcy instead of Mr. Willoughby, surely a more likely target." Juliet considered this. "Perhaps it has to do with the spilled glass we learned of. Follett may have assumed from this that Willoughby could not have planned the poisoning, for if he had, surely he would have taken care not to disturb the glasses any further."

Mr. Bamber seemed taken aback. Young men so often were, when young women showed quickness of mind. He at least recovered himself rapidly. "You are astute, Miss Tilney."

"Thank you, Mr. Bamber." Already Juliet could hear Mrs. Brandon's footsteps on the stair. In a lower voice, she added, "I hope Mr. Darcy did not fail to accompany you out of fear that Follett would read some malicious intent into his every action."

"Oh, no, not at all." Mr. Bamber cleared his throat. "I was perhaps too rash, leaving Allenham without speaking to Mr. Darcy first, but such was my eagerness to see you."

Then Mrs. Brandon came in to join them, and more trivial, more correct conversation took the place of any talk about the investigation. Such speech could almost be given by rote, which allowed Juliet's mind to wander. It did not take long for her thoughts to find Mr. Bamber.

Is it possible that Mr. Bamber wishes to court me?

Juliet did not think she had been misled by false pride; in truth, she had not seriously considered Mr. Bamber as a potential suitor before this moment. Yet she ought to have done—it was the role, nay the *duty*, of any young unmarried woman away from home. Part of the reason families so willingly allowed their daughters to take such journeys was the opportunities thus provided for making the acquaintance of eligible matches. Given the smallness both of Mr. Tilney's parish and Juliet's future dowry, the search for a potential husband of both property and good character held great importance.

Her parents were not avaricious. For herself, Juliet thought finery very nice but knew that the best and happiest moments of life have but little relation to riches. Yet many among the unhappiest moments can often be linked to poverty, and this state could only be avoided through a prudent marriage.

Ralph Bamber would be a vast deal more than merely "prudent" as a match. Mrs. Jennings had already informed half the county that he was to inherit a fine house in Dorset, that his great-uncle was a viscount, that one of his sisters had married into the smart set in London. As for other considerations . . . he was a handsome man, even if ginger. (Juliet had never entirely understood the prejudice against ginger hair, but it could not be denied that many held it. Mr. Bamber, she thought, provided a striking proof that the color could be most becoming.) He showed signs of intelligence and curiosity. Unlike the others at Allenham, Bamber treated Mr. Darcy with respect. Best of all, he did not find Juliet's independence shocking or improper; if anything, her desire to investigate Mrs. Willoughby's murder was considered by him as an inducement. Was this not, in all respects, precisely the sort of man she had hoped to find?

Juliet knew this to be true, but that knowledge revealed another, deep within: the only problem with Mr. Bamber was that he was not Mr. Darcy.

Jonathan came down to find the breakfast room empty save for Willoughby, who was sipping coffee. Most striking was the contrast between the black armband he wore and the smile playing upon his lips. This smile broadened when he glimpsed Jonathan. "Thumps! Looks like only you and I will breakfast together this morning."

Where was his one ally? "Bamber—is he not—"

"Ran off into Barton this morning practically at dawn, the

butler says. Some errand of his own." Willoughby shrugged. "Follett's up sulking in his room. I should not be surprised if we did not see him all day. He must be embarrassed, after carrying on like that last evening." This comment strongly suggested that Willoughby must have overheard some of the commotion in the library the previous night, but he made no further reference to Follett's accusations. That silence seemed ominous.

Jonathan saw no point in prevarication, so he went directly to the question that seemed to him most immediately significant: "I take it you do not believe what Follett said of me last night—that you do not think me the murderer of your wife."

Willoughby raised both eyebrows. "You have not the smallest degree of grace, have you?"

Mockery was to be expected, but worth enduring if his line of questioning bore results. "So I have often been told. Yet the way in which I phrase the question should not deny me an answer."

"Impertinence deserves no answers," said Willoughby, who was in a position to know. Yet he was not a man to refuse any chance to talk. "You know of my belief, that Sophia caused her own death. But even were that not to be true, you could not possibly be the killer. Even if you had the malice in you for such an act, you could not pretend innocence to save your life—which would quite literally be the case. If you cannot conceal even your small strange habits, how could you hide such a crime as murder?"

Jonathan knew the justice of this even as he felt demeaned by it. As long as Willoughby was speaking openly, he should press on. "Follett is angry with you for preventing his marriage to the late Mrs. Willoughby, is he not?"

"Follett never even proposed. Sophia's guardians would never have allowed her to accept him, were she so inclined, which neither he nor I will ever know. If he did not understand as much, he is a fool. In truth, I believe he *did* understand—but he chooses to remember it all differently in order to supply himself with a grievance."

This could be so, Jonathan realized. The supposed worth of a thing sometimes increases with its impossibility. None could know whether Follett's love of an unattainable Miss Grey would have survived had she become attainable once more.

Could Follett himself have realized this only after the poisoning? Was he horrified not by the death of a woman he loved but by the unspeakable crime he had committed for a feeling that had not possessed the virtue of love after all? If so, he would keep pointing the finger at Jonathan—who, in this hypothesis, must be Follett's chosen scapegoat—and the accusation would be heard by others who were not well acquainted with his character, and would thus be more credulous in the matter than Willoughby had been.

Footsteps on the gravel path outside made Jonathan look up to see Bamber striding back toward the house, a small parcel under one arm. Such a relief it was to see a friendly face!

"Good morning, all." Bamber's fair cheeks were rosy with the exercise of his stroll into Barton. "I am not too late for coffee?"

"You could scarcely be 'too late' for anything save hearing the cock crow," Willoughby said. This was an exaggeration—already it would be appropriate to pay morning calls—but Jonathan could believe this hour to be the earliest one in which Willoughby had much interest. "Whatever led you out at such an hour?"

"I had business in the village, which is no business of yours," Bamber retorted in apparent good cheer. He gave Jonathan a glance filled with meaning, which drew Jonathan's attention to the small parcel beneath one of Bamber's arms. Whatever was concealed within it was apparently not to be shown to Willoughby—but would be revealed to Jonathan very shortly.

Marianne, though still prone to sensibility, was no longer child enough to give way entirely to every tumult of the heart. After Mr. Bamber's departure, she attended to the tasks of the day. These were few and simple, largely those she had chosen for pleasure—but even arranging the flowers in each room touched her sensitive nerves. Thus she felt especially glad to see Mrs. Jennings's carriage arrive.

During the initial months of their acquaintance, Marianne had found Mrs. Jennings's company all but unbearable. Mrs. Jennings's loud cackle, her gossipy ways, and her lack of tact still sometimes rankled. However, Mrs. Jennings had resolutely stood by Marianne after Willoughby's abandonment and declared to all who would listen that John Willoughby was a good-for-nothing. When Marianne had shortly afterward fallen ill with the putrid fever that nearly claimed her life, Mrs. Jennings had helped nurse her with no less tenderness and dedication than Marianne's own mother would have given. Those weeks had taught the lesson that persons might appear vulgar without truly being so. Truth was not to be found in appearances, only in actions. All Mrs. Jennings's impolitic joviality did not diminish her worth as a faithful friend.

"Well, well!" Mrs. Jennings cried, upon being shown into the drawing room where Marianne and Juliet awaited. "How surprised I am to find you two here alone."

Marianne flushed. Was Brandon's absence so marked? Did others suspect difficulty? "I am sure I do not know what you mean, Mrs. Jennings. The colonel often has business with his tenantry in the mornings, particularly at harvesttime—"

"Hush, my child, how would I not know that? I who befriended him ere you were born? No, it is the absence of visitors I find most perplexing." Mrs. Jennings's merry eyes twinkled as she looked at Juliet. "I was certain there would be a gentleman caller for Miss Tilney. The only question, thought I, was whether 'twould be Mr. Darcy or Mr. Bamber."

Miss Tilney blushed with mortification as Mrs. Jennings chuckled. Though Marianne was rather interested in this question herself, she had grace enough to pretend she was not, and she knew better than to mention Mr. Bamber's most recent visit. To do so would subject Juliet to the full force of Mrs. Jennings's mirth. "I am sure both young men are staying close to Allenham at present. They will wish to support their friend during his mourning."

"Faugh! Such mourning as *he* is capable of requires no support, as it is no mourning at all." Mrs. Jennings had briefly tolerated Willoughby when it appeared that Marianne and the colonel were willing to do so, but this tolerance had not survived Mrs. Willoughby. "True, these are dark days for the rest of us until the poisoner is found. But I shall be very much surprised if he is found far from Allenham."

"You must not say so," Marianne pleaded. "It is very wrong to say such a thing where it may not be true!"

Mrs. Jennings was not one to heed exhortations to silence. "Say it I shall, for the gossip in the village has taken a false turn, and all blame will fall upon *you*, Mrs. Brandon. It is the duty of your friends to turn suspicion to the direction in which it should rightfully lie. That, I say to you, is Mr. Willoughby and none other."

To that, Marianne could say not one word.

∽

As soon as Jonathan could extract himself from Willoughby's company, he went to find Bamber, who had gone for "a stroll about the grounds." As Jonathan had expected, this meant that Bamber had gone to the old greenhouse, which had just become his new laboratory.

The greenhouse stood on the far edge of the small grove of trees to the east of Allenham, not particularly far from the house, but entirely shielded from its view. Long but narrow, the structure had indeed been long neglected. Its glass panes were somewhat clouded with age, but he could see the glow from a small oil lamp flickering within. As Jonathan came through the doorway, he saw a few discarded flowerpots stacked in a corner and a battered wooden table on which glass and ceramic containers lay—shabby items no doubt taken from a ragpicker's pile or a rubbish heap but scrubbed clean. The greenhouse contained no seating save for a wrought iron garden bench, but this little seemed to matter, for Bamber was so busily moving about, putting items in order, that he had no moment to sit.

"There you are, Darcy!" Bamber had clearly been impatient for Jonathan's presence, a sentiment rare enough that Jonathan could both note and enjoy it. "Come and take a look at this, will you?"

"Your laboratory is taking shape nicely," said Jonathan. "At least, I assume so, for I have never seen such a place before."

"Mark my words, one day shops will sell all sorts of beakers and bottles and scales and the like. For now, my fellow natural philosophers and I must be inventors before we are scholars. But come, come, see what I have brought!"

Jonathan startled when he realized what Bamber had

placed upon the table amid his instruments. "Is that one of the Middletons' drinking glasses?"

"The very one used by Mrs. Willoughby, the one which held the poison. I convinced that Hubbard fellow to let me have a look at it. Not as though *they* will learn anything from it—they kept it only to have an object to hold up at the trial and make the jury gape. We, however, may discover much."

"I do not entirely follow," said Jonathan. "We know that arsenic was in the glass. Hitchcock determined as such."

"Yes, yes, but we do not know the form of the arsenic, nor its source, for none of the existing tests are as precise as they should be. Nor is a judge likely to put faith in such evidence as Hitchcock found. I intend to see if I can do better." Bamber's grin was broad; nothing made him as happy, it seemed, as the chance for discovery. "Let us take a look, shall we?"

Bamber held the glass up to the oil lamp, capturing its light. Its cut-glass ornamentation turned prismatic, casting dazzling small glints of light of every color. Jonathan squinted to see that detritus was just barely visible in the bottom—both the expected purplish smudge of dried port and something else, something almost grainy as sand. He asked, "Is that the arsenic?"

"I believe so. But here is the pertinent point, Darcy—look how rough that is. As I thought. Mrs. Willoughby might not have been able to taste the arsenic, but she undoubtedly felt it."

"She would have thought it sediment from a poorly decanted bottle, no doubt." Jonathan could not but pity her, forcing herself to drink for politeness what would have been disagreeable—and then, horribly, fatal.

"When arsenic is extracted from paint," Bamber said, "the result would surely be sort of a paste, which might be expected to dissolve fully in a liquid, given time. However, were the arsenic simply rat poison, it would be grainy, like this."

"Are you certain these grains could not be extracted from paints? As I understand it, painters must mix many of their pigments, and work with turpentine and other chemicals, so it is possible that Follett has the necessary knowledge to do so. And until we have seen such an extraction, we know not what it would look like."

Bamber hesitated. "Perhaps you should be the natural philosopher instead of I, for you understand the first principle. Assumptions are not knowledge. Theories must be tested. So I shall steal a bit of Follett's paints and attempt to extract arsenic from them. I shall also mix some rat poison into port to see whether it resembles what we have here. Only then will we know for certain. But I have faith that the results of these experiments will bear out my previous conclusion, and we will be able to eliminate the paints as a source of arsenic."

This did not fully exculpate Follett, Jonathan knew. Nor did it explicitly incriminate Willoughby. Yet the tests might lead them in a certain direction, and they must welcome any chance for solid information where they otherwise possessed only suppositions.

After those at Delaford attended church that morning, Marianne had rather conspicuously taken herself off to the garden to collect herbs for drying. Uncertain what was afoot, Juliet asked the colonel the first question that came to her, which was whether he would invite Mr. Darcy and Mr. Bamber to call soon. "They do not wish to linger long in that house, I am sure," she said, "and I know that you consider young Mr. Darcy a friend as much as I do."

"Indeed. In fact, I believe we shall have Mr. Darcy to dinner, if Mrs. Brandon agrees—once on his own, that we may speak more freely, but Mr. Bamber can later be made a member of the party."

Juliet found herself nearly as pleased at the prospect of dining with Mr. Bamber as she was at the prospect of dining with Mr. Darcy. Well . . . almost nearly. "Thank you so much, Colonel."

His saturnine gaze could seem intimidatingly perceptive, at times. "Miss Tilney, it seems to me that you and Mr. Darcy have sought each other's company very often in these past few days."

Would even Colonel Brandon prove a matchmaker? Juliet prepared to assuage his concerns on that score.

Instead, he surprised her, adding, "If this companionship is in service of yet another murder investigation, I must warn you against it."

In her surprise, Juliet did not even attempt to deny the investigation. "But—last time, were it not for us—"

"Last time, Miss Tilney, the killer you sought proved to be but a young woman who had been made to fear for her virtue, who acted only to protect herself," the colonel said. "This crime is far different. Poisoning is calculating, planned, *chosen*. The person who committed this crime acted out of malice. That person was willing—perhaps eager—to kill. Such a person would have few compunctions against killing again."

His meaning struck Juliet forcefully, and she could not speak.

Colonel Brandon concluded, "Here, there is true danger. Do not allow Mrs. Willoughby's fate to befall *you*."

Chapter Fourteen

By the next day, Marianne could bear confinement at home no more.

Neither she nor Colonel Brandon had spoken again of what he had overheard, of the letter he had read, or aught else that pertained to the former connection between her and Willoughby. If her husband doubted her love and faithfulness—and it appeared he did—Marianne's spirit could know no peace.

Although she might have confided in her young friend, Marianne sensed that she would need the guidance of those more experienced than herself. Nor should a guest be so burdened. Instead, she forced herself to brighten and prepare for a walk to the parsonage.

Juliet offered to come with her, but Marianne kindly yet firmly refused. "No, no—this is not a true visit. I merely wish to make sure that my sister is well, as it is such a delicate time. Besides, so much has happened, so much event and tumult! You have need of some solitude to regain your tranquility. Our souls are much the same in that way, I think."

"Indeed they are." There was much in Juliet's answering smile that made Marianne suspect her friend might be carrying some unseen burden of her own. But as Juliet had good manners enough not to pry, her example should be followed. So Marianne then set out for Elinor's home, to share her burdens with her elder sister, whose counsel she trusted beyond any other.

Marianne found that her mother and younger sister, Margaret, were then in attendance upon Elinor, apparently now doing so on any day that Mr. Ferrars would be absent for any length of time. (Edward could nurse as tenderly as any woman, but that day he was visiting the sick of the parish, most of whom suffered from complaints that would resolve neither as soon or as decidedly as Elinor's condition.) Marianne would not have chosen to present her worries to all, but she wished very much to tell Elinor, so she erred on the side of speaking.

Erred she had, for Mrs. Dashwood was eager to advocate for the hurt feelings of Colonel Brandon.

"Why does Willoughby still trouble your thoughts?" Mrs. Dashwood scolded as she brought a cup of tea to Elinor. "What is he to any of us any longer?"

"He is still our friend," Margaret muttered. "At least he wishes to be."

Marianne elected to ignore the latter and challenge the former. "I hardly see how any of us can avoid thinking about Willoughby in the light of the terrible crime against his late wife. As he is to be our neighbor in perpetuity, we cannot forever avoid saying his name, however much we might wish to do so. My attention to Willoughby is only what it must be, given our circumstances. But the colonel has assumed so much more! And such an assumption as that—how can such doubt, such belief in my inconstancy, exist with the feelings that should bind together husband and wife?"

"Marianne. Dearest." Elinor took her sister's hand. "Colonel Brandon's affection for you is so plain to see. Surely his faith in you is equally as great. There is nothing for it but to trust."

"That would be true for you, dear Elinor, for your thoughts and feelings are ever yoked to discipline and principle," said

Marianne. "The rest of us are too apt to brood and weep where we should not, especially in matters most tender to our hearts."

Mrs. Dashwood's umbrage still flowered full. "To think that you should trouble such a devoted man! After he brought you the truth about wretched Willoughby's faithlessness, so that we might mourn him no longer—after he brought me to your side during your sickness! Is this gratitude? Did not we every one of us agree that your marriage should be his reward for all?"

"I am not anyone's *reward*," Marianne insisted. "I did not wed as a payment for his services to our family! I accepted Colonel Brandon because I felt I could truly love him, and indeed I have come to do so. I have told him this. But does he believe me? Can he truly put Willoughby in the past as I have done?"

"But you read Willoughby's letter," Margaret pointed out with far more glee than was proper. "You did read it! And you did not tell the colonel."

"That was only to save the colonel the indignity," said Mrs. Dashwood with more spirit than sense. "And why should he not be rewarded for his great goodness?"

Elinor sat up straighter on the divan. "Mama, Marianne is quite right. We wished Colonel Brandon to be rewarded for his kindnesses not merely with Marianne's hand but with her sincere love. My dear sister, do not doubt his faith in you. Remember, he is older and more experienced, but to matrimony you are equally new. The events of the past few months would test any bond, and yet the connection between you has flourished."

Marianne could see some truth to this, but it was poor balm for an aching heart. "Then how could he disbelieve me?"

"Did he truly disbelieve you?" Elinor questioned. "Consider that he had faith enough in you not to question you about Willoughby's letter. Few husbands would be so forbearing in similar circumstances."

Perhaps this, too, had merit. "I suppose. But I cannot bear much more misunderstanding between us."

"Then I will suggest to you the surest remedy for misunderstandings, one known to us all, and yet one we are all sometimes strangely unwilling to take." Elinor patted her hand. "Speak with your husband. Tell him what you truly meant, and everything that you have feared. If you speak to him with half so much feeling as you have shared with your family today, Brandon will rest more assured of your love than ever before."

Despite Marianne's hopes, Juliet's quiet day did not add much to her tranquility. She did her best to concentrate on *Rob Roy*, and at times was caught up in it, but mostly her thoughts turned toward the night to come. Then Mr. Darcy would come to dinner, which surely would afford them an opportunity to discuss the investigation. Juliet had taken Colonel Brandon's warning to heart, which made her most impatient to share it. Mr. Darcy's safety mattered as much as her own . . . and as he was staying in the same house as their two principal suspects, no doubt he needed to hear it even more than she. Her hope was that they would adopt greater caution without abandoning the investigation altogether.

(It was not that she did not see the danger of pursuing a murderer—she very much did—but to Juliet's mind, it was equally hazardous to allow such a murderer to remain at liberty.)

The afternoon was marked by Colonel Brandon's return

home with a letter for Juliet that had arrived from her parents. "Oh, dear," she said as she took it from him.

"I take it you informed your mother and father of the death of Mrs. Willoughby," he said. "Do you think they will wish for you to return home immediately?"

"If they did, my father would probably already have arrived on Delaford's doorstep. But I fear they will be greatly shocked and grieved."

Colonel Brandon, she saw, well understood this. "I have written to your parents myself, to assure them of your safety and our vigilance. It seemed best to send it after you had first written them, so that you might share the news with them yourself—but they have been reassured and we may hope are now more at ease than when this letter was sent."

"Let us hope so," Juliet said, before taking herself up to her room to read.

The handwriting on the outside was her mother's, which gave Juliet reason to hope. Henry Tilney was a wise, loving husband and father, but he could react poorly to a shock. Catherine Tilney, however, might have been quieter in the first moments of revelation but was more likely to have a nuanced response.

(This daughterly conclusion might have been somewhat unfair to Mr. Tilney. What Juliet considered "nuanced" would, by others, be called "prejudiced toward the interesting." What novelist could fail to be intrigued by news of a murder?)

The letter read:

> *Dearest Juliet,*
> *What extraordinarily poor luck you have had as a houseguest! A second murder not three full months after the first is quite the coincidence to behold. Your*

father is of course beside himself, but I have, with
some difficulty, prevented him from fetching you home
immediately. There is no risk to you, I realize, and
surely Mrs. Brandon must be much afflicted. Your
friendship is a great consolation to her, I know, and we
need not deprive her of it.

Juliet took heart from her mother's assumption that she
was in no danger herself. Perhaps Colonel Brandon worried overmuch. In doing so, she blithely overlooked the fact
that the colonel suspected her investigation, but her mother
apparently had not guessed at it.

It is far happier news that you are also reunited with
another friend. Mr. Darcy sounds like a most unusual
young man, but one with a respectable and honorable
character. I should welcome more news of him, and
I am happy that you both should have the chance to
further your acquaintance under somewhat more
pleasant circumstances.

From this the letter diverged from reacting to news to
giving it, sharing much about Juliet's sister, Theodosia; her
brother, Albion; and her aunt Eleanor. Although all of this
diverted Juliet very pleasantly, she found herself going back
to the paragraph about Mr. Darcy.

To a stranger, those lines would perhaps read as no more
than a polite acknowledgment of Mr. Darcy's presence.
Juliet, with a daughter's familiarity, could tell that her mother
wished to tacitly encourage the development of her friendship with Jonathan Darcy—and the only way in which such
a friendship could develop, in the eyes of polite society,
was toward a matrimonial end. Yet thus far. Mr. Darcy had

shown few signs of wishing to court her. Besides, had she not glimpsed the possibility of another prospect altogether?

Would she, ultimately, have need to write her parents of Mr. Bamber?

Jonathan took his carriage to Delaford that evening. Although the distance between that house and Allenham could be no more than three miles, the autumn chill had begun to settle over the countryside, and the warmest coat Jonathan had brought with him was one he disliked wearing. Sometimes certain textures against his skin proved troublesome, even maddening; the mere brush of his coat's cuffs against his wrists pained him. Jonathan could endure it when required, but he far preferred the carriage.

What difference a change of house brought! Where Allenham had been oppressive, Delaford felt more comforting and familiar to Jonathan from the beginning; it reminded him somewhat of Netherfield—the house where his aunt Jane and uncle Charles had first fallen in love and to which they had returned in recent years, the better to look after his aging grandparents. Naturally the greatest comfort came from the fact that he not only knew but also greatly liked all three of the persons he had come to visit.

"How good it is to see you without Willoughby present," Mrs. Brandon said, with unexpected candor, as they took their places at table. "For that matter, without any other persons present that we do not consider true friends."

"Hear, hear," said Miss Tilney, who looked uncommonly well that evening. Her lilac dress suited her exceedingly, as did the way she wore her hair.

Mrs. Brandon continued, "Mr. Bamber and Mr. Follett seem excellent young men—Mr. Bamber in particular, perhaps—but they were not at Donwell Abbey, and so they cannot share the bond that exists between *us*."

"They were, of course, your schoolfellows." Colonel Brandon appeared to be studying Jonathan more carefully than did his wife; his tone suggested he had glimpsed more of the truth. "Do you consider them your particular friends?"

"Not at all," Jonathan said. The others laughed—had he erred in telling the truth? But no. This was not the laughter of mockery, only of surprise. "Bamber is not a bad fellow, but Willoughby and Follett . . . I provided much humor for them, never deliberately."

Miss Tilney seemed almost angry on his behalf, which was strangely gratifying. "How unkind. I thought that when they . . . I mean, that they did not seem appropriately welcoming to you. But I had not guessed they were vicious in that way. Whyever did you accept the invitation? For that matter, why did Mr. Willoughby send it?"

"My parents wished for me to cultivate connections among my school friends," said Jonathan, "and I tried to oblige them. In Bamber's case, at least, they shall be satisfied. As for Willoughby—I have suspected that he meant to amuse himself at my expense, but that may be uncharitable of me."

"I have no doubt of it." Mrs. Brandon stabbed at her venison as though it were Willoughby's heart. "That is just his idea of 'fun.' Odious man!" Her eyes flickered over to her husband as she spoke.

Colonel Brandon's attention, however, was upon his dinner guest, and he spoke more temperately. "For the duration of your stay, Mr. Darcy, you are welcome at Delaford on any day, at any hour. If you wish, even, to spend part of your stay in this house rather than Allenham, the invitation shall be issued, and we will be only too happy to have you."

Blessed escape! Yet Jonathan caught himself. Surely, for the purposes of the investigation, it was better for him to remain near their two main suspects (though he reminded himself not to dismiss other persons of interest, such as Miss Williams). He could endure Allenham for a nobler purpose, and that endurance would be aided by the knowledge that as soon as he wished to leave, he could, and without disappointing his mother and father. "Thank you, Colonel. Although I am settled at present, I will think upon your kind invitation."

After dinner, the party moved to the parlor. With so few guests, the Brandons did not stand on false ceremony. Instead, Mrs. Brandon occupied herself with her embroidery, while the colonel took up a volume of history. Although she often glanced at her husband, he seemed wholly engrossed in his book. It struck Jonathan as somewhat peculiar that husband and wife should be so little engaged with each other, but perhaps they meant to allow him time to speak with Miss Tilney in relative privacy. They sat by the fire, some feet from either of the Brandons.

Miss Tilney whispered, "We have been warned."

"Whatever do you mean?"

"The colonel said that we must consider the different nature of the murderer in this case, as opposed to our first. Mrs. Brandon defended herself, no more, whereas this killer fully committed to murder another person. Colonel Brandon went so far as to say that such an individual would be willing to kill again in order to remain unknown."

Jonathan now glimpsed her meaning. "You mean, that this person might attempt to kill us."

"If we are indiscreet about our investigation," she said. "So please, Mr. Darcy, do take care."

"Of course," he said, greatly touched. "And I trust that you will as well."

Did he really think Willoughby, Follett, or Miss Williams capable of yet more murderous intent? On the balance, Jonathan thought not, if for no other reason than simple prudence would discourage homicidal acts while so much attention remained focused on Mrs. Willoughby's demise. Yet, while having little fear for his own safety, he resolved that if even greater discretion were necessary to protect Miss Tilney—or merely put her mind at ease—then it should be so.

For the moment, he felt, he could best reassure Miss Tilney by changing the subject. "I brought something for you to look at, something that was found in Mrs. Willoughby's room as the maids removed her belongings." He went and fetched the item from the hall, where he had bid a servant to leave it until such time as it could be perused at leisure.

"A newspaper?" Miss Tilney took it, frowning. "She might have wished it only to read."

"Perhaps. But Willoughby only buys the *Country Journal*, as a general rule, not the *Times*. Mrs. Willoughby could have bought it herself, but this strikes me as an unlikely action for her to take. Most importantly—on my second morning here, Follett mentioned that he wished to buy a copy of the *Times*. He claimed that it was to follow the shipping industry, for purposes of business, but—"

"But what does a painter need to know of shipping?"

Miss Tilney took the paper from Jonathan, flipping to the inner pages in search of enlightenment. Jonathan shook his head. "I have read and reread every story, and none of them seem to pertain to either Mr. Follett or Mrs. Willoughby. And yet one of them must."

"It is a puzzle," Miss Tilney said, folding the pages resolutely. "I shall read it as well, and perhaps I will see a link you did not. In such a case, the more eyes at the task, the better. Has Mr. Bamber seen this?"

"No, not yet."

Jonathan still did not feel entirely ready to share every element of the investigation, if only because he so valued Miss Tilney's friendship. The fellow feeling between himself and Bamber was still very new, for all the years they had known each other; he had met Miss Tilney only this past summer, and yet the accord between them ran much deeper.

From the corner, Mrs. Brandon cast a brief appraising glance in their direction. Time to speak upon another subject. "You said something earlier that I wondered at," he began. "It seemed that you thought ill of Willoughby and Follett when they did something—but then you did not explain."

"I thought it might embarrass you."

"You may be correct, but until I know what you would have said, I cannot be certain."

Miss Tilney lowered her voice. "The nickname 'Thumps'— I cannot divine its meaning, but if I understood its intent, then that was reason enough to think poorly of both men."

Jonathan had been able to meet her eyes earlier, at least for a few brief moments, but now he could not. "You understood its intent correctly."

"Humph. Will you tell me what it refers to, or is it best that I not know?"

Although he was in no hurry to retell the tale, Jonathan recalled that Juliet already knew it, in essence. "Do you remember what I said to you, about—about my rocking back and forth when I think deeply upon a subject?"

"Oh. Yes, I do. What of it?"

"I did this at school once where others could witness it, and as I did so, my chair made a thumping noise. Ergo my nickname came into being." Jonathan's cheeks were warm, and not from the fire.

"How vicious of them," she said with feeling. "What difference could it make if your chair thumped? That is no reason to mock someone years and years after the fact, much less to rename them."

The sting of that nickname had lessened already, and Jonathan wondered whether it might never bother him again, now that he had Miss Tilney's defense ringing in his ears. "Thank you, Miss Tilney."

Marianne would not have interrupted Miss Tilney's chat with Mr. Darcy for all the world, but the only other person to speak with was her husband, who—at least, so she imagined—had no interest in speaking with her at this time. So she dedicated herself to her embroidery with more than her usual zeal for the craft—which was to say, any zeal at all.

As she worked a fine corner, she recalled that Elinor had given her some green thread, which would be ideal for the flowery design's leaves. The coats hung near, which meant there was no need to summon a servant; Marianne rose herself and went to fetch the thread. When she did so, however, she found a sheet of fine paper folded neatly in her pocket. She unfolded it, and even before reading a word, she knew the handwriting to be Willoughby's.

> *Dearest Marianne—*
> *We must speak alone, and soon. Do not refuse me this*
> *small consolation. Send word through whatever means*
> *you can, whenever you can, and I will meet you in the*
> *place of your choosing.*
>
>   *W*

He must have slipped it into her pocket at the funeral, when she was giving him her condolences for his wife's death. Even as Willoughby put his bride in the grave, he had been scheming to meet with his former love.

And what would Brandon think if he found this message, too? Even the most devoted of husbands could scarcely be blamed for concern after reading such as *that*.

"Insufferable," she muttered, crumpling the note in her fist. As she passed the fireplace on her way back to her seat, she tossed the paper into the flames, into obliteration.

Jonathan returned to Allenham late in the evening, but not so late that he might not have the chance of speaking again with Bamber. He hoped that much experimentation had occurred that afternoon—who knew what other facts might have been discerned?

Indeed, his three former classmates were not yet abed when Jonathan arrived. However, speaking with Bamber proved unexpectedly difficult, as Willoughby apparently wished to spend the night playing billiards, a pursuit in which only Bamber would humor him. Follett had ensconced himself in the library, and no one dared disturb him. Jonathan was invited to join the game, but he declined. (He was exceedingly skilled at billiards, but he anticipated that the inevitable aftermath of a victory over Willoughby would be a challenge to a rematch, which given Jonathan's ability was likely to lead to yet another rematch, and then another, until Jonathan felt obliged to lose on purpose simply to escape the man's company . . . and that, he refused to do.)

It was almost midnight before Willoughby and Follett went upstairs, and Jonathan at last had his chance. He did not even need to seek Bamber, who found him right away. "There you are, Darcy," he said. "My word, but that man never tires of games! At least, for games he is very likely to win."

"Is Follett still in a temper?"

"Yes, indeed. He believes you guilty with all his heart. Luckily Willoughby does not agree."

"If Willoughby is, as you think, the murderer—would he not be eager to blame me, or anyone else, for Mrs. Willoughby's death?"

"Willoughby's clever in his own way," Bamber replied. "He knows you're an unlikely target. Mark my words, he will find another to blame, someone far more credible. My guess is he'll turn on Follett."

"How can Follett believe me guilty?" Jonathan still could not comprehend this. "How could any person in his right mind do so?"

"You *are* an odd duck, Darcy," Bamber said, not unkindly, "but consider that Follett is *not* in his right mind at present. The woman he loved has died horribly at the hand of another. Enough to drive any man half out of his wits, would not you agree?"

Jonathan had to admit the justice of this, but added, "I should think the guilt of having actually been her killer—whether intentionally or inadvertently—would also cause irrational statements. One such statement might be a foolish choice of an alternate suspect."

"You can counter any argument, can you not? Well, let us say that for now it is safest to assume that Follett genuinely believes you guilty, and you should avoid him as much as possible. If he accuses you falsely, he has every reason to wish you to remain alive, well, and eminently capable of being accused. If not—then who can say but that he might attempt to do you harm?"

Jonathan resolved to lock his bedroom door for the remainder of his nights at Allenham. "We must increase the pace of our investigations, and it is imperative to remain discreet. Let us call upon Miss Tilney tomorrow morning."

"Indeed, we shall." Bamber seemed very pleased by the suggestion. After a moment's pause, he added, "Listen, Darcy, were I to, ah, further my acquaintance with Miss Tilney, I should not be stepping upon your toes, should I?"

Jonathan stared down at his unmolested feet. "You have never treaded upon my toes."

Bamber laughed. "What I mean to say is, you are not courting Miss Tilney, are you? I have been looking for signs of it, and though you are clearly quite fond of her, you do not behave as a courting man would. Then again, you are not like other fellows, are you? So I could not be certain without asking you."

It took all this for Jonathan to understand that Mr. Bamber wished to court Miss Tilney himself.

Courtship had always struck Jonathan as among the most bizarre of human behaviors. He who often found it difficult to look a stranger in the eye, who disliked any touch that did not come announced by custom or ritual—the idea that he should wish to press his mouth against that of another person, to be bodily connected to a woman, seemed very foreign indeed. (At times, at night, he had amorphous dreams that suggested what the appeal might be, but upon waking, he invariably found the entire idea strange again.) Thus his first instinct was to say that no, he had no intention of courting Miss Tilney.

Yet . . . he liked Miss Tilney so. He knew that she liked him in return. The thought of her being with another was unpleasant to Jonathan in senses he could not easily define. Bamber was a mark above Willoughby or Follett, but despite the man's intelligence, Jonathan realized he did not consider Bamber truly her equal in the way that surely should matter most between a husband and wife.

Yet how could he say any such? The only way to prevent Bamber from courting Miss Tilney was to court her himself; and, feeling as he did, Jonathan did not think he could do so in good conscience.

So, despite the fact that it pained him, he could but say, "No. I am not courting Miss Tilney."

Bamber beamed. "She is such an excellent girl! You will put in a good word for me, will you not?" He clapped Jonathan on the back, not noting the resulting wince, and his laughter prevented any possible answer. For this, Jonathan felt unexpectedly grateful.

As Juliet lay abed that night, she stared out at the crescent moon high above the surrounding trees, in a more peaceful and poetical state of mind than might be anticipated in a young woman investigating a murder. That was not her *only* purpose or practice in Barton, and for this hour at least she felt at ease to mull upon other considerations.

How good it had been to speak with Mr. Darcy tonight! How open he had been, how meaningful their conversation! Yet . . . it now seemed all but certain to her that Mr. Darcy's sentiments were not those of a suitor. He rarely met her eyes. He did not pay compliments of the kind that indicated courtship. He stole none of the small, blameless touches that were acceptable—but telling—between unmarried men and women. When Juliet considered the matter, she felt rather sad, for she and Mr. Darcy shared true honesty of exactly the sort she would wish with her husband someday. Certainly he was eligible, and she found him extremely handsome. Sometimes she remembered the first night they had met—resting her hand on his muscled forearm—and felt a warm flush from her fingertips to her toes.

Still, if he did not feel the same, there was nothing for it. Juliet would have to look to another. She did not wish to be disappointed in "only" having Mr. Darcy's friendship, for friendship had its own value. Yet she could not wholly ignore the question of matrimony—even at age seventeen, well before the years of danger.

For a woman, the choice of whom to marry—assuming circumstance gave her that choice—was the greatest single decision she would ever make. On that choice, all happiness depended; from that choice, such misery could result! One generally knew the most pertinent facts about a man from the beginning: his family, his fortune, his expectations. Courtship allowed at least a glimpse of his character. However, the strictness that governed all conversation and company between young men and women ensured that no true intimacy of the spirit could be achieved before the promise had been irretrievably made. Sheltered though she was, Juliet knew that many came to regret their choice. Countless more found neither bliss nor misery in their marriages; many people in fact found very little in wedlock, if anything at all.

Juliet's parents showed that better was possible. She believed the colonel and Marianne did as well, regardless of whatever misunderstanding seemed to have come between them of late. Her own choice would come someday. Would she choose well?

Mr. Bamber—intelligent, helpful, attractive in his person, jovial in his manner—deserved consideration. Somehow the idea struck her as uncivil; no man wishes to be second choice to his friend. Yet it was that friendship that first made Juliet like him, Bamber's ability to see Mr. Darcy for the good man that he was, and to refuse to take part in any cruel mockery. And was it not true that many a second attachment had made for a happier match than the one first contemplated? Marianne and Colonel Brandon proved as much. Though Brandon and Willoughby were certainly not friends . . .

Her eyes opened wider. Sleep, which had been softly stealing upon her, loosening her thoughts, vanished in an instant.

Colonel Brandon would have had no reason to hurt Mrs. Willoughby, so naturally they had not considered him among the potential suspects. Now, however, they understood that the intended victim might have been Willoughby. Brandon and Willoughby had no love lost between them—the colonel had in fact once challenged Willoughby to a duel, and though on the day Brandon had thrown away his shot, he must have felt at least willing to kill the man at that time.

No, not merely willing. Ready. *Eager.*

If he believed, rightly or wrongly, that Willoughby might be a threat to his marriage . . .

As much as Juliet wished she could decide otherwise, she knew: to their list of suspects must be added Colonel Brandon.

Chapter Fifteen

As propriety would have it, gentlemen and gentlewomen of sufficient means would never intrude into the areas of the house designated for the servants. The kitchen is one such place. Hot stoves, pans to be scrubbed, pigs' heads for boiling: none of these are considered objects of duty or interest to the genteel. It is a point of pride that a woman has never had anything to do in the kitchen; for men, such ignorance is assumed.

However, this is but one of the many areas in which propriety and truth do not entirely match. A good number of households must practice more economy than they let on, and thus many wives and daughters are experienced makers of pickles, or they clandestinely trade recipes for spruce beer and seedcake. Even in homes so grand that servants bustle along every floor and corridor, smaller children sometimes find their way to the kitchen, for how could they not be curious about the place from which issue puddings and biscuits? It would be a strict cook indeed who had never once rewarded such exploration with a treat, which had the natural effect of encouraging further intrusions.

Through such means, Jonathan had become very familiar with the kitchen at Pemberley. Ralph Bamber knew less of kitchens—his nanny had been far stricter—so he proclaimed himself glad of a guide as they made their midmorning incursion. Bamber held the candlestick.

"They should be done with the morning washing up," Jonathan whispered as they made their way through a corridor, "but not yet slicing meats for luncheon."

"Goodness, Darcy. How much time did you spend in the kitchens?"

"As much as I could manage." Jonathan had sometimes hidden from louder houseguests there. His parents, once they realized how much comfort he took from the room's warmth and familiar actions, had allowed it from time to time. "If Willoughby did purchase rat poison, but for the actual purpose of killing rats, then I predict we will find it in the back stores here."

"So you said last night, and I tend to agree. But I question our own assumptions. Why should he not put the poison where it is meant to go, then take what is needed on the fateful night in question?"

"Willoughby's servants fill this room every day." Jonathan peered around a corner, saw no one, and led Bamber into the service corridor, a hall rather darker than the ones they were familiar with in Allenham. "I would wager he never comes here himself. Thus his presence would be noted, and remembered, and reported, if he came to procure a measure of arsenic."

"Yet if he had purchased rat poison for any legitimate reason, surely he would have told his housekeeper of it. According to you, Mrs. Fargate knew not a thing."

"True," Jonathan replied, "but it is just possible that the poison was given to a butler, a footman, or one of the maids. Correct habits would require them to report this to the housekeeper right away . . . but few of us at any station in life always follow entirely correct habits, and the staff will no doubt have been much distracted and agitated at the death of their mistress."

"You *have* thought this through," Bamber said in evident admiration. "All right, then, let us begin."

As Jonathan had anticipated, the kitchens were empty save for one young scullery maid, who was working hard on scrubbing pots—so much so that she did not even notice them at the far end of the long room. It did not require much searching to realize where the stores must be kept, and to hurry down the few steps that led to that windowless room. The door creaked as they opened it, which made Jonathan flinch, but the scullery maid was too far away to hear.

Bamber held the candle forward, its flickering light illuminating dozens of loaf sugars wrapped tight in paper and string, cakes of tea and jars of coffee, marmalades, and jams, and even long trays of sand with stems sticking up, the evidence of the citrus fruits thus preserved for many months. Alongside the foodstuffs could be found stacks of candles (wax for use through most of the house, a few of tallow for the servants), reams of writing paper, and many cakes of soap stacked high upon a dry shelf. Jonathan stepped forward, peering into the shadows. "If it is here, it will be in the very back, somewhat away from the food."

"Let's hope so," Bamber said. He had taken a very large breakfast.

He cast a look onto the floor, into the corners. If Allenham did have rats or mice, they might have left telltale signs—but he glimpsed none. He also saw no arsenic.

"Drugs are not always labeled, you know." Bamber drew out one of two packages he considered suspicious, but rattling sounds they made indicated that something besides arsenic powder rested inside. "There is talk in London of making a law that dangerous chemicals must be sold in packages that have a written or printed warning. Until it is passed, however, arsenic could . . . it could look like anything."

Jonathan, heartened, continued the search with this in mind, but absolutely none of the opened packages contained anything that remotely resembled arsenic powder. "It looks as if Willoughby bought no rat poison after all. That, or—"

"Or he bought it for his own purposes, not those of the house," Bamber concluded. "And I would wager those were dark purposes indeed."

By this time, Juliet's morning stroll had become habit, and she doubted that Marianne would ask any questions. However, over breakfast, Colonel Brandon surprised her. "I am walking into Barton this morning, Miss Tilney, and thought you might enjoy the outing, if you will join me?"

It would not have been impolite to refuse, if she could have thought of an adequate excuse in time. Juliet's reasons for wishing to avoid the colonel's company were threefold: First, that she wanted to speak openly with Mr. Darcy and Mr. Bamber about their efforts, and any meeting at all would be rendered impossible. Second, that she knew they had to now include Colonel Brandon among their suspects—not one she thought especially likely, but the question could not be completely disregarded. Finally, she wished her efforts to remain secret, and regardless of the colonel's guilt or innocence, he had already warned Juliet of the dangers inherent in this investigation. If he caught her at it, he might feel obliged as her host to inform her parents or even to send her back home.

But has the colonel already proven his innocence? Why warn me against a dangerous unknown killer if he were himself the killer? If he actually wished me harm, he would not warn me first. For a moment she brightened, but too soon she realized that Brandon's warning could not be considered exculpation. *He could have meant to discourage the investigation in order to avoid being found out.*

Her instincts still said that Brandon was innocent, but even at seventeen years of age, Juliet possessed sufficient wisdom to know that one and a half investigations had not given her an unerring eye for guilt.

Juliet's mother had urged her to pack for the colder weather that might come, and on this chilly morning, how glad Juliet was of it! She drew her warm cloak more closely about her. "What errand brings you into Barton, sir?" she asked the colonel, expecting to be told of some mundane household matter.

To her astonishment he replied, "I am bade to visit the constables."

"What? Surely they do not suspect you." Had Hubbard and Baxter been a step ahead of them? Juliet was chagrined at the very thought.

"Why should they not, if Willoughby was indeed the murderer's true target? It is known that we met on the dueling field before, so they will not credit me with any great wish to preserve his life now," Colonel Brandon pointed out, but Juliet took comfort from his manner of speaking, which was not so grave as his words would imply, and which lent itself more to the theory of his innocence than anything else yet said. "In truth, I suspect they wish to inform me of the appointment of the new magistrate, on whose identity and character much of our future happiness may depend."

Juliet saw the justice of this. "How can it take so long for a magistrate to be appointed?"

"Often it takes much longer. The position can be vacant for some months. I suspect Mrs. Willoughby's death has hastened matters."

"Would they mind greatly if I attend the meeting as well? I am very curious to know how such things are done."

Brandon seemed surprised by her request, but he considered for a moment before saying, "I will ask. Your presence will disconcert them to some degree and ensure that they keep to the matter at hand, without undue insinuations regarding Mrs. Brandon."

This, Juliet understood, would not actually relieve the constables' suspicions of Marianne, but it would at least keep the colonel from being forced to hear them. How lucky that her keen interest should also provide some small benefit to her host.

The constables greeted the colonel civilly, and although they were not overly familiar with Juliet, to her their words were genuinely cordial. However, their subject was not one to inspire ease of conversation. Although the appointment had not been made, Constables Hubbard and Baxter had been given to know which man would be named the next magistrate—and the gentleman in question could not be considered impartial, for it was Mr. Tremblay, master of Whitwell, brother-in-law to Colonel Brandon himself.

"Mr. Tremblay is in Avignon with my sister, visiting his relations," the colonel said. "Her health is delicate and may not permit their return for weeks yet, even months, if the frost comes early."

"He will no doubt be urged to return soon, without his wife if necessary." Baxter spoke politely but firmly. "Any undue delay might be seen as favoritism, if you understand me—as an impediment to justice."

"I trust that your investigation will have collected all vital evidence here before his return." Brandon's voice had become chilly. "That you will have searched widely and considered all alternatives."

Hubbard straightened up and gave Baxter a fleeting, almost panicked, look. "Searching! Yes, by all means, sir, we will have searched far and wide."

Colonel Brandon's face might have been carved in stone. "For instance, at Allenham."

"Right you are," Baxter said, his words coming rapidly. "Of course. We shall be searching Allenham soon. Very soon. Well before Mr. Tremblay's return."

Hubbard added, "Which naturally we are sure will be soon. As he is a man committed to justice."

Juliet knew the colonel understood the unspoken expectation as well as she did: Mr. Tremblay would be expected to arrive promptly in order to investigate and prosecute. If not, the public would believe that the killer had been allowed to walk free—and would assume that killer to be Marianne.

She is guilty if they prosecute her based on no more than a terrible incident in the past, Juliet realized, *and she is guilty if they do not prosecute her, for they will believe a relative sheltered her. The people of Barton will never believe Marianne innocent . . . not unless the true murderer is found, and soon.*

Colonel Brandon was much disquieted by the constables' information.

It might have been expected otherwise. He knew his brother-in-law to be a fair and temperate man. They had seen little of each other in recent years, given the Tremblay family's long visits to France following the peace brought by the Battle of Waterloo, but Brandon considered Mr. Tremblay a friend. In the abstract, there was no person more wise or trustworthy that could be wished to oversee the investigation into Mrs. Willoughby's death.

However, the Brandons did not live in the abstract. They lived in Barton, where gossip would turn Mr. Tremblay's kindness and justice into favoritism, blackening the names of both his family and Brandon's, possibly forever.

It had not been so very long since Brandon and Marianne were wed, on a day that he considered the brightest and best of his life—a day during which it had truly seemed that all sorrow might be left in the past. Such, he reflected, is the corrupting effect of happiness on the human mind. It could render one foolish, without perspective, without foresight.

He had all but forgotten Miss Tilney's presence at his side until they were several paces from the constabulary, when she asked, "Do you think your brother-in-law will return soon?"

"If asked, yes. He is not one to shirk his duty, no matter how onerous he might find it, and if my sister's health were to delay his departure long, she could remain in Avignon with his family." They loved her quite as one of their own.

(How strange it had been, to think of that family as members of an enemy nation! Brandon prayed war between England and France would not arise again soon, or ever.)

"Will he be just toward Marianne?" Miss Tilney asked.

"Yes, but in this case, justice will be seen as corruption, and persecution will be seen as justice." Colonel Brandon turned up the collar of his coat against the autumnal wind. "There is no good to be reckoned in it for any of us, and yet I cannot say that any other magistrate would serve us better."

Then he startled, for Mr. Willoughby was coming toward them, his cloak billowing in the breeze. Brandon's first thought was that Willoughby's purposeful stride was intended to spark a confrontation, but when Willoughby showed equal surprise at the encounter, he knew that could not be so.

Miss Tilney valiantly attempted to smooth the conversation between them. "Good morning, Mr. Willoughby. What brings you into Barton?"

"I mean to speak to the constables," Willoughby said, staring not at Miss Tilney but at Brandon. "Rumor has reached my ears that the poison was not meant for my late wife, but for me. If *some person* wishes me dead, I intend to know it, and to protect myself through whatever means prove necessary."

Understanding the implicit suggestion, Colonel Brandon decided that candor would serve better than courtesy. "When I wished you dead, Mr. Willoughby, I proclaimed as much and challenged you fairly. Upon the day, when I decided I would not shed your blood, I fired into the air. Is it likely I should do so, but later turn to poison?"

"I know not what turns your mind may take, cold-blooded creature that you are."

Colonel Brandon was not a man easily goaded, but he could not help sharpening his tone in response to this. "It is most remarkable, how much greater your interest in the matter has become now that it is a matter not of your wife's death but your own safety."

Willoughby's eyes widened. "Do you think no one should care what becomes of me? I believe I could name one lady who will."

This reference to Marianne could not be borne. "Given your past connection, it is astonishing to me how little you ever knew her."

"Perhaps. But I do know this, Brandon: I am at greater liberty than I was ever before. Nothing need stand in my way any longer."

By this he meant, nothing need stand in the way of his pursuit of Marianne.

Colonel Brandon did not doubt his wife's honor. Her heart,

however—was that still his own? Had he not heard her whispering Willoughby's name but days before?

Perhaps confused by the lack of response, Willoughby strode away from them, toward the constabulary. Miss Tilney watched him go; Brandon did not.

Once again, Constable Baxter told no one of the impending search of Allenham but his wife. Once again, she told no one but her most inquisitive friend. And once again, this friend told fully one-third of the population of Barton village. The only household that did not discuss the matter of Willoughby's possible guilt that evening was Willoughby's own.

The subject was raised at Barton Cottage, where the Brandons and Juliet had gone to dine. Mr. and Mrs. Ferrars were also in attendance; Juliet welcomed the chance to know Edward Ferrars better, as he was the only family member she had not yet spent much time with (unless one counted the funeral, which could not be considered an opportunity to converse). Mr. Ferrars's thoughts on the matter were succinct. "Although I know little good of John Willoughby, I cannot think him so wicked as *this*."

"Nor I," said Margaret, who then silenced under her mother's sharp gaze.

"I cannot be impartial on the subject," said the colonel, "and so I will not attempt to judge. It will be in the constables' hands soon enough."

Elinor said, "I am not impartial, either, but that is precisely why I do not think him guilty. Many of us at this table have been given cause to regret Willoughby's temper, his rash decisions, his tendency to act without due consideration. These are not the traits of a worthy man, but nor are they the those of a poisoner. A poisoning seems to me a most deliberate act, one that requires planning, caution, consideration. None of these are hallmarks of Willoughby's character."

"That is it precisely." Edward gave his wife a look of such tenderness as must endear him to Juliet, or to any young woman attempting to study the signs of true affection and respect. "You are better with words than I am, my dear."

"May we please speak of another subject?" Marianne asked, and thereafter the weather fulfilled its eternal function as a neutral topic.

Juliet, meanwhile, was struck dumb with admiration. Would that they could invite Mrs. Ferrars into the investigation, too! Her analysis of Mr. Willoughby's character and habits struck her most forcefully, and for a moment Juliet was ready to exonerate the man. She caught herself, however, remembering, *Willoughby paid a price for his past rashness. The experience could have taught him much . . . for instance, how to hold his tongue and act in secret when such action so demanded.*

It could also have encouraged his determination to undo his hasty actions, by whatever means possible.

The next morning, Marianne awoke not to sunshine or birdsong, nor to the gentle words of her husband, but to the thought that this was the day the constables would search Allenham. If poison was found there, then Willoughby might be arrested immediately. At the very least, he would be under sharper suspicion. She had begun to believe Willoughby's guilt possible, if not probable, but the love she had once felt for him did not allow her to think on such and remain unmoved.

Yet the idea did occur that suspicion of Willoughby meant freedom for her.

Appearing in public for the first time would not be easy—but it would never be easy, and at this point delay made the matter worse rather than better. Marianne had not had a bout of her strange flashes of memory in some days, despite the strain she had been under, and when should she be stronger and safer than on this day, when the village's distrust had focused almost wholly on another?

So, at breakfast, Marianne announced to Juliet, "I should like to walk into Barton this morning."

True friend that Juliet was, she understood what this meant and remained too tactful to speak of it directly. "You must have many errands you wish to run."

"It has been a season ere I went to the milliner's, or to the dressmaker's." Marianne could scarcely imagine caring about such things ever again, but they would be a pleasure to behold if only because they would signify her willingness to be seen by all and sundry. "Yes, yes, let us finish our meal and make haste. I am quite eager for our walk."

Belatedly, she recalled her guest's habit of taking a stroll in the mornings, but Juliet raised no objection. It then occurred to Marianne that Juliet had often been meeting with Mr. Darcy, Mr. Bamber, or both on these occasions—but both men would certainly remain at Allenham this morning, given what was to unfold there.

The day proved chilly but bright, without wind, and so Marianne could relish being out of doors. Already the autumnal leaves had begun changing color, becoming rich and warm, adopting an entirely new form of beauty. How Marianne wished she could sketch as well as Elinor, so that she might capture some element of this exquisite scene!

With such determined cheer did Marianne enter Barton,

Juliet by her side. However, she could not long maintain her spirits, not when faced with so many stares. Every person they passed seemed to be studying Marianne avidly, and unkindly. Whispers rustled behind her like the train of an evening dress.

More fool I, thought Marianne. *They may no longer blame me for Mrs. Willoughby, but what does that matter, when they know about Mr. Wickham?*

Her breaths quickened with her pulse. Everything seemed to be surrounding her and yet vanishing at the same time. The worst memories of her life once again swelled up and overtook her, all but blotting out her true surroundings. Marianne felt herself back where she had stood, tears in her eyes, trembling, before George Wickham. When his hands had reached out for her—when she had understood his wicked intentions, and outrage and terror had scalded away everything else in her heart—

"Marianne?" Juliet took her arm. The world seemed to be spinning, and Marianne could not catch her breath. She knew she must steady herself, but how could she do such a thing when she half believed Wickham still stood before her? "Marianne, you are quite overcome. Let me send someone to fetch Dr. Hitchcock."

"No, no, I do not need a physician. I need—quiet, warmth, a place to sit down." Those were the only remedies Marianne and her husband had yet discovered. Such moments had become rarer as time passed, but why had she been so foolish as to think they were ended forever? The horror of what had happened that night—of what she had done, what she had been forced to do—would never leave her. "Are we—how far are we from Barton Park?"

"At least half a mile," Juliet replied. Her concern was clear, for how could Marianne not know how far they were from any friendly place?

Then another woman's voice said, "You can rest in my sitting room."

"Oh, thank you so much!" Juliet said, "It is so kind of you, Miss Williams."

Beth, Marianne thought. *It is Beth come to save me.* She felt as if she had half lost her mind.

For her part, Beth did not look directly into Marianne's face, not even as she took her arm. Marianne remained too blinded with fear and memory to resist. Beth said only, "Both of you, come with me."

Chapter Sixteen

Juliet first believed that Marianne must have taken ill. Even having heard Marianne's references to "being overcome," she could not imagine any incapacity so great as this would be the result of memory alone. Could it even be poison at work—the murderer striking again?

However, Marianne remained able to walk, with Miss Williams and Juliet standing on either side of her, for the few minutes it took them to reach Miss Williams's home. The structure was not unlike Dr. Hitchcock's house, although rather than having a shop beneath her, Miss Williams occupied the entirety. They settled Marianne down upon a sofa as their hostess called to her servant, "Quick, a glass of wine."

"No, no," Marianne protested weakly. "I will be well now. All that is needed is time and quiet, and the memories will pass."

"Memories?" Miss Williams asked under her voice.

"Of Mr. Wickham's death." Juliet replied, before recalling that Mr. Wickham was Miss Williams's father. She felt her cheeks glow with heat at her appalling tactlessness.

Yet Miss Williams kept her composure. "He treated her abominably, did he not?"

"Yes, he did. Nothing less could have moved her to such an act."

"For so many years I longed to meet my father," said Miss Williams, "but the more I have heard of his true character, the more I comprehend that his absence from my life was not a loss but a gift."

The maidservant, who listened not to the guest but to the mistress who paid her wages, appeared with a glass of wine. Despite Marianne's earlier protestations, she took it. Between sips she breathed in deeply and slowly, visibly calming more and more—yet her state of agitation had been such that Juliet suspected they would need to remain in Miss Williams's home for at least half an hour. Thus emergency must give way to courtesy. "We have not been properly introduced. I am Miss Juliet Tilney of Gloucestershire, a friend of your guardian and his wife. I was with them at Donwell Abbey."

"I am Miss Elizabeth Williams of Devonshire," she said, then smiled. "As is evident, because this is my house."

"Yet it must be said! Introductions are most strange sometimes, are they not? We repeat information known to all and treat it as a discovery."

Beth nodded. "You put it very well."

Juliet had been prepared, by what she had heard of Beth's scandalous birth and even more scandalous behavior, to find her ill-mannered, brash, and in some way marked by all that she had done and all that had been done to her. Instead, she seemed a perfectly normal young woman—perhaps somewhat less genteel than most company Juliet kept, certainly marred by the loss of her virtue, but, for all that, not lacking in manners or sense. Hurrying to Marianne's aid showed quick thinking and a compassionate heart, and Juliet resolved to think well of Beth from now on . . .

Unless, of course, she proved to be Mrs. Willoughby's killer. For the pale blue cloak hung on a peg near the door.

⁓

If Juliet and Marianne were surprised to be in Beth's home, Beth was even more disbelieving. For more than a year she had resisted this meeting—had all but slammed the door in Colonel Brandon's face the first time he asked—but here she was, going to great pains to make sure Marianne was entirely comfortable and well.

In the first throes of her terror after Willoughby's abandonment, once she had known herself to be soon a mother, Beth had gone almost wild with fear and rage. The fear was long behind her; we cannot fear a thing once that very same thing has come to pass, and thus the shame of being an unwed mother, which might burden her life forever, had nonetheless ceased to be a source of fright. However, rage still burned and blazed within Beth's heart every day, very nearly every hour. Most of that anger belonged to Willoughby, who had certainly earned it. Some of that anger had belonged to the late Mrs. Willoughby, though that much at least was spent.

Very few, Beth thought, would have guessed that she had been angry with Marianne, too, but she had been—had continued to be—up until the moment Beth saw her overcome in the village square.

Marianne had, unwittingly, committed the sin Beth's bruised soul found most difficult to forgive: she had captured Willoughby's heart and earned his enduring love. These were the very prizes Beth had believed herself to be in possession of during that fateful trip to Bath, the ones for which she had staked her reputation and her future.

The memory of her last conversation with Willoughby burned in Beth's mind, rendering her restless and uncertain. Why had she been so willing? Why had she let him talk her into sin upon sin? And that time, he had not even the decency to come to her house. Perhaps he hated the very idea of seeing Georgie.

In truth, Beth knew, Willoughby would never have been hers. His affection had never been sincere, and what he had offered her had been, for him, no more than a means to obtain wicked pleasure. Yet how could she not feel the twin flames of envy and hatred when she saw the beautiful young girl Willoughby had evidently thought her superior in every way? Marianne had so thoroughly eclipsed all of Beth's dreams that it had been tempting to blame her for Willoughby's desertion; perhaps he would not have behaved so badly had his heart not been stolen away. Although Beth had realized the injustice of this, our feelings do not always comply to the rules of fairness. The heart blames where it will.

To have this young woman then marry Beth's beloved guardian instead—to become almost a kind of stepmother, if the relations between their households allowed—had felt like the final, most insulting blow from fate.

Yet she is just another young woman, not so different from myself, Beth thought, *save that she has been luckier, and heeded wiser counsel. To despise her for that is pettiness at best, wickedness at worst.*

Are you not done with wickedness?

Marianne Brandon and Juliet Tilney remained in Beth's home scarce more than the half an hour earlier predicted by Miss Tilney, yet to Beth it seemed a millennium. In time, she might be glad of the greater familiarity between herself and these two young ladies. But their visit would be sweeter to her in memory than it was in continuation.

Once Marianne had regained her color and her strength, she rose to her feet. "Thank you so very much, Miss Williams. I believe I am myself again."

"Then I am glad." Beth wondered whether she ought to offer tea. It was not the hour for it, but was failing to do so a lack of courtesy?

However, it seemed that both Marianne and her friend Miss Tilney wished nothing more than to return home as soon as it could be accomplished. Beth helped them to the door, where Marianne paused. "I hope—if I dare ask, would you be so kind as to call upon us at Delaford? The colonel and I have long desired your presence there."

As unthinkable as such a call had long been to Beth, on this day she replied, "I shall come very soon, I promise."

Allenham had not been in a state of such upheaval ever before—not even after its mistress's death—as it was on the morning that the constables came to search.

Willoughby himself stormed about, chastising servants for failures as trivial as the slightly asymmetrical placement of the breakfast dishes upon the sideboard or a threadbare tassel on a footman's livery. Follett had stalked past them all at breakfast, cast a venomous glance at Jonathan, and then gone to stand at the end of the drive, apparently waiting to have a talk with the constables himself. This malice, plus the general sense of disorder, left Jonathan disoriented, worried, and cross. Any one of these sensations is unpleasant on its own; the combination felt nigh overwhelming.

Alone of anyone in residence at Allenham, Bamber seemed at ease. "Follett must truly believe you guilty, which means he himself must be innocent," he said as they sat in the morning room to look out on the road, the better to see when the constables would come. Follett paced at the end of the drive as though he had half a mind to fetch them himself. "Would he be so desperate to speak to the lawmen if he were guilty?"

"If he wished to give them a new choice of suspect, he might." Jonathan felt somewhat ill.

The constables arrived, spoke only briefly to Follett, and went to work with their search. They were exceedingly thorough, going through every single room with a zeal beyond propriety. Although Jonathan had nothing in his room more incriminating than a volume of Tacitus, he nonetheless felt significant relief when they found nothing that excited their interest. Whatever Follett had said to Hubbard and Baxter about Jonathan did not appear to have registered strongly with them, if at all.

Jonathan began to believe that this search would be much ado about nothing, which meant he was very much surprised when Constable Hubbard called out, "Eh, and what is this, then?"

The constables were, at that time, in the carriage house— standing next to an elegant white phaeton. When Jonathan and the others hastened over, they saw that, underneath the phaeton's seat, Hubbard had found a small box wrapped in brown paper, unlabeled, which he had opened to reveal a white powder inside.

"The chemist will have to take a look," said Baxter, with a hard stare at Willoughby.

For his part, Willoughby was either very much astonished or excellently pretending to be so. (He was talented in the art of false protestations, as Jonathan had good reason to know.) "It is a parcel like any other. It could contain anything."

"We shall find out soon enough what it contains," Hubbard promised, "and I wager we shall find it contains rat poison. Have you purchased any such poison of late?"

Willoughby's great—perhaps exaggerated—astonishment only grew. "I bought some recently, but for its intended purpose. That, however, I left for the servants to put in its proper place. If one of them put it here, then I am to blame of nothing worse than hiring a housekeeper who does not know how to run a household."

To Jonathan this seemed a slander on the pleasant Mrs. Fargate. Bamber, who stood near, murmured, "We know it was not placed in the pantry stores, do we not? No one would have hidden the poison here for any legitimate purpose."

Jonathan had to admit that the phaeton had been a clever hiding place. As an open conveyance, a phaeton would be reserved for warmer weather than Devonshire currently enjoyed. Furthermore, such a light, elegant phaeton as this would usually be driven by a lady, rather than a gentleman, which likely meant that this one had been for the sole use of the late Mrs. Willoughby, and as such was in no danger of being disturbed anytime soon.

Hubbard, peering at the pale grainy substance within the box, squinted with suspicion. "Looks like rat poison to me."

"This is trickery," Willoughby exclaimed. "Trickery and malice. I did not harm my late wife, but someone wishes me thought guilty of it."

"Who would do that, then, hmm?" Baxter asked. "One of your friends?"

Jonathan nearly flinched, but Follett's theories had found no purchase in the minds of any other present. Willoughby shouted, "I do not know, but the villain will be found and punished, that I promise you!"

With that, Willoughby stormed off to his room. Bamber said to Follett, "You see the truth now, hmm?"

"I know Willoughby did not love her," Follett replied. "I

have known that since the beginning." With one more glare at Jonathan, he stalked away, too.

"It shall all end very swiftly now." Bamber looked triumphant. "Willoughby's days as a free man cannot be numbered high."

But Jonathan shook his head. "The presence of the arsenic at Allenham does not prove that Willoughby is the guilty party."

Bamber was unimpressed. "Tell that to a jury."

Word of the discovery of poison at Allenham spread through the village as swiftly as all other gossip. (If fire spread with equal speed and thoroughness, no town in possession of a single candle could long stand.) This could only incriminate Mr. Willoughby, and there were many persons receptive to his guilt; among their number were tradesmen whose bills had been paid slowly and begrudgingly, young women who had been called by sweet names both Beth and Marianne would have recognized, and tenants who had already been given reason to suspect their new landholder would prove neither generous nor even interested.

However, the perversity of public opinion as such that, even when it is proved wrong, it will come up with ways to appear correct. Some still thought Mrs. Brandon had done it; had she not acted like a madwoman in the village that morning for all to see? Others thought Willoughby's had been the hands that delivered the poison, but that it had been done at Mrs. Brandon's urging. Another camp held that Mrs. Brandon had known nothing of it, but that she was the reason for Willoughby's action, which meant she was nonetheless to blame.

Such theorizing foundered on the fact that the powder within the discovered tin had not yet been proved to be arsenic. (Baxter had wanted to test it straight away on a stray dog, but Hubbard, who was fond of dogs, had both forbidden this and then taken the animal home.) But when has gossip ever waited for facts?

By the evening, Marianne felt more herself again. Not for weeks had memories of that terrible night overtaken her with such force; she had allowed herself to hope that they never again would. *I ought to have known better,* she thought, *than to believe that one can so easily leave a murder behind. Justified or not, defending myself or not, I took a man's life, and that can never be forgotten. If the memories are painful, then that is no more than the price to be paid.*

She was drinking her third cup of tea—with extra sugar, that it might prove restorative—when Colonel Brandon returned home. Marianne overheard Juliet informing the colonel, in a low tone, of all that had transpired in Barton that day. As little as she liked being talked about, Marianne felt some measure of gratitude that she would not have to tell her husband any of this herself.

He appeared in her sitting room moments later, concern upon his countenance. "Marianne? I have heard you are unwell."

"Another of my bad dreams while waking. I had thought them ended, but it would seem not."

The colonel nodded, as understanding of her fearful episodes as he had ever been. "Was it difficult, meeting Miss Williams properly?"

"If such as that can be called proper!" Marianne considered.

"It might have been difficult, had the necessity of moment not preoccupied us both. As it was, she aided me with courtesy and grace, and she has agreed to call upon Delaford soon."

Brandon smiled—the first smile Marianne had seen on his face in days. "Such a connection between the two of you has long been among my dearest hopes."

The silence between them lasted a few moments longer than it should have. Elinor had urged Marianne to speak openly (a point on which she had rarely needed such encouragement), but it was so difficult to do so! When the colonel took a step back, suggesting he was soon to leave the room, Marianne hastily said, "Why—why did you not tell me that you had known of Willoughby's letter?"

He did not answer immediately. Marianne had the distinct sense that her husband was asking himself that same question. Finally Brandon said, "I feared your reaction."

"I was hasty to blame you for snooping among my things. Please forgive me."

"You are forgiven, but it was not that response I feared." Colonel Brandon could not meet her eyes. "I thought that if I spoke to you, I might detect some lingering partiality for Willoughby in your heart."

Marianne had struggled mightily with her temper before, but it threatened to unleash itself anew. "You cannot believe I would have accepted his invitations?"

"Never did I think so. Your virtue and forthrightness cannot be doubted by anyone who knows you, least of all one who loves you so dearly as I do," said the colonel. "But your heart could nonetheless have been stirred. Who knows better than I the power of first love? How long it lingers after all hope is gone?"

This response quieted Marianne's anger, but it did not restore her to serenity. Brandon took her silence for understanding and kissed her forehead with much relief. But his words echoed in her mind afterward for quite a long time.

If all in Barton thought no surprise could compare to the results of the constables' search of Allenham, they were informed otherwise the next day, when the most shocking action was taken by—of all persons—the staid Lady Middleton.

Unlike her husband, the jovial and boisterous Sir John, Lady Middleton did not keep company for its own sake; she did so for the sake of status, as well as the opportunity to see and be seen, to scorn and to be admired. (It did not occur to her that others' judgments might be equally as severe as her own.)

The death of Mrs. Willoughby had dealt Lady Middleton a severe blow. Barton Park, her elegant home, had become the site of a murder, one so scandalous it would be spoken of in the village for years, if not generations, to come. She feared that others might disdain her invitations, should the house become known only for the vilest act ever committed within its walls. Although she was not an especially intelligent or insightful woman, she had understanding enough to know the more time that elapsed between Mrs. Willoughby's demise and another event, the more strongly forbidding her home's reputation would become.

Given this, in addition to the fact that she had already got a handsome replacement for the ruined rug, she felt nothing would do but to have another party. Lady Middleton did not consider herself unfeeling in the matter, for she had tact enough to inform the invitees that no refreshments would be served.

Mr. Willoughby was not invited, as he was officially in mourning, which placed even stricter limits on behavior than the pain of honest grief. However, a note came to Allenham addressed to Mr. Darcy, Mr. Bamber, and Mr. Follett.

"Is this what the next year is to be?" Willoughby complained upon the reading of the invitation. "To hear of all the fun going on elsewhere, but never to be welcome at any of it?"

"That is how I understand mourning, yes," Jonathan replied. He thought mostly of the fact that, as Willoughby could not attend, the Brandons almost certainly would, which made it very likely they would bring Miss Tilney.

He was not the only one with such thoughts. Bamber said, "If it were not entirely crass to do so, I might even ask Lady Middleton to throw a ball. Is Miss Tilney a very fine dancer, Darcy? She has the spirit for it."

"I . . . why, yes, she is. Though I do not think such an opportunity will present itself at Barton Park."

"The lot of you are disgusting." Follett, who had never come closer to them than the margin of the drawing room, now stalked out in high dudgeon. When it came to it, Jonathan suspected, Follett would attend the party nonetheless—if only because it would allow him a chance to avoid Willoughby's company for a few hours.

It might prove too ghastly for him, Jonathan mused, *seeing the place where his former love was killed. Unless, perhaps, he did it himself, and he wishes for another opportunity to mourn her publicly.* Follett, after all, would have had nearly as much access to the kitchen stores and the carriage house as Willoughby did himself, and therefore could have been the one to hide, then move, the poison.

Jonathan looked out from the window into the gloaming, most particularly at the bowling green that had thus far gone unused. A flicker of movement caught his attention, then jolted him with astonishment. There, darting between the bushes, was a woman—her face could not be seen, but she was unmistakably wearing a pale blue cloak!

Jonathan dashed out of the room, little minding the two startled persons he left behind. He could take no time for explanations were he to have any chance of apprehending the woman.

As it happened, he would have done as well to inform them, for by the time Jonathan hurried onto the grounds, the woman in the blue cloak could no longer be seen. He ran the length of the bowling green, searching for her in the twilight, but not so much as a rustling shrub revealed which way she had gone.

Whatever business the mysterious woman in the blue cloak had had on the night of Mrs. Willoughby's death—that business had not concluded.

Chapter Seventeen

The invitation to the Middletons' home was received with as much, if not more, consternation at Delaford that it had been in Allenham. "I do not know whether I can bear it," Marianne said. "But I suppose we must go?"

"Sir John has been my friend these many years," Brandon said, "so indeed we must." He thought the event the worst possible shock for his wife, but he also knew that a refusal would cause grave offense—not with the amiable Sir John but with his wife, which might well have more force in limiting their friendship. Brandon understood some of Lady Middleton's motives; although he could not entirely condone the swiftness of her action, neither could he entirely condemn her reasons. He knew better than most: the sooner an unpleasantness is faced, the less opportunity it will have to grow.

Miss Tilney was far more sanguine about the prospect of returning to the scene of a murder than Brandon would have thought. "The young men should have a chance to leave Allenham for an evening," she said, "so that they are not unduly burdened by another's mourning, and as we find Mr. Darcy and Mr. Bamber so agreeable, why should we not be pleased to see them again?"

"But in such a place!" Marianne protested. "Under such conditions!"

Miss Tilney said, "It is, I admit, awful to think upon. However, I believe that visiting Barton Park again may be more awful in the dreading than in the doing. Once we are there, you and the colonel will no doubt recall other, happier days you have spent in that house, and the night of Mrs. Willoughby's demise will lose some of its power."

May it be so, Brandon hoped. Yet Miss Tilney's words awakened in him a suspicion. Not only did the girl sound undaunted by the prospect of returning to Barton Park, but her voice also carried a note he could only call enthusiasm. Only one reason could explain her wish to return there—and that would be the continuing investigation of Mrs. Willoughby's murder.

He had warned Miss Tilney, but had she heeded his warning? Was she still searching where she should not? Brandon resolved to keep a close watch upon her.

Juliet was indeed secretly pleased by the invitation, for precisely the reasons Brandon feared. (Her most particular desire was to practice moving from the drawing room to the place where the port had been and back, to determine precisely how much time the murderer would have had to have been absent.)

Other implications of the party at Barton Park did not occur to Juliet until Mrs. Jennings appeared at the very end of calling hours, flustered nearly out of her continual good cheer. "What a to-do. To think, a party to be held precisely where Mrs. Willoughby died! Of course, any house of any age has seen many deaths, though in my experience, genteel people have the good manners to die in their bedrooms. Alas, Mrs. Willoughby had no choice in the matter. I suppose there is nothing for it but to make the best of the evening without giving way to unseemly merriment."

Juliet privately suspected that one would have to be very merry indeed to reach a height of mirth Mrs. Jennings would consider unseemly. "I feel sure our hosts will set the appropriate tone."

Marianne seemed to doubt this but said only, "At the very least, our next evening at Barton Park must be more pleasant than the last evening we spent there."

"Aye, and Willoughby to be absent, but all the other young men to be present!" Mrs. Jennings's eyes twinkled. "Well, Miss Tilney, you have been leading them all a lively chase. It seems that your preference has alighted on each of the three men at different moments during your stay in Devonshire."

"Indeed it has not," Juliet said, stung.

That good lady was not to be so easily dissuaded. "Wait and see, once you have made your choice, it will seem as though that gentleman was the only one who could ever have won your heart." Mrs. Jennings chuckled, while Juliet tried not to perish from mortification.

Why, oh why, did Laurence Follett choose that moment to arrive at Delaford for another portrait sitting? They had of course prearranged the day, but the dramatic events that had marked Juliet's recent hours had entirely erased the engagement from her recollection until his knock sounded upon the door. As soon as the butler showed him in, Mrs. Jennings chuckled knowingly, and Juliet felt sure that her entire face glowed pink. Luckily for her composure, Mrs. Brandon quickly showed them into the morning room where Juliet had posed the first time. "Do I need to change into the dress I wore before?" Juliet asked, trying to settle her nerves.

Mr. Follett seemed to be insensible to Juliet's awkwardness. "There is no need for it today. Your face is my only object this afternoon."

As he set up his easel, Juliet stole a glance at the portrait in progress. What she saw unnerved her, for Follett had painted her dress and the background with some degree of detail, but her face was, thus far, nothing but a blank blur. Why should he leave the face for last? Had he been imagining someone else's features all the while? Then again, she knew nothing of art. Perhaps this was how all portrait-painters accomplished their work.

But he had commanded her not to speak, before—a wholly unnecessary direction, if he had not bothered to paint her mouth.

Does he dislike me so? Juliet wondered. *Or do I, perhaps, remind him of the former Sophia Grey?* She had discerned no great similarity in their features. Yet she had met the woman only once, and had beheld Mrs. Willoughby mostly during the moments when she lay dying. The agony on her features . . .

"Whatever are you doing?" Follett snapped. "Are you to begin weeping because you do not think the picture pretty enough yet to suit your vanity?"

Juliet had been disquieted rather than in tears, but all emotions save fury deserted her at that moment. "Perhaps you are capable of seeing a woman die and going on untroubled within mere days, but I am not."

"Do not speak of her." He stepped back from his canvas, as though he wished to put as much distance between himself and the picture—and his sitter—as possible. "Do not pretend yourself a victim after the death of a woman you did not even know."

"I am but a witness," Juliet said.

She had meant this only as a protestation against the charge of considering herself the person most afflicted after Mrs. Willoughby's death. As soon as Juliet had spoken, however, she realized her choice of words had been poor, for it further incensed Mr. Follett. "What did you see? Tell me, this moment, precisely what you beheld. Of what are you a witness?"

"I saw a woman's death. What else do you think I might have seen?"

Whatever he might have said, Juliet would never know, for he then caught sight of a newspaper folded on a nearby table—the very one Jonathan had brought from Allenham. Juliet saw him startle, followed his gaze, and braced herself. If he questioned her about it, what would she say?

Merely that many people read the Times, she decided.

Follett seemed to realize that for himself, as he resolutely turned away from the newspaper and got back to work. His anger with Juliet had either faded or simply been supplanted in his mind by other concerns.

Other concerns that had a great deal to do with that copy of the *Times*.

The three young men staying at Allenham took a carriage to Barton Park on that night. Jonathan found himself forced to sit opposite Follett, who resolutely ignored him the entire time. It was Bamber who said, "Come, come, Follett, you cannot be serious. Surely you cannot persist in your mad theories about Darcy here when evidence has been found that points to Willoughby's guilt."

Begrudgingly, Follett said, "Until the truth is proved beyond any doubt, I hold it a point of honor to suspect *everyone*. Darcy included."

"Me, too?" Bamber laughed. "If you can speak to me, then you can speak to Darcy."

Jonathan did not feel much deprived of Follett's company, but judged it best to leave the matter between the others.

Barton Park welcomed them much as it had before—though not entirely. Lady Middleton, after much consideration, had opted to spare her guests' more delicate feelings by not only acquiring the new rug but also rearranging her furnishings, so that none of the rooms to be seen by guests looked precisely as they had on the night of Mrs. Willoughby's death. The very spot on the floor where the poor woman had breathed her last was now tactfully covered by their grand piano. This did not put the guests at ease to quite the level Lady Middleton had hoped, and Jonathan found it disconcerting—almost like traveling to an entirely new house. Still, her effort was not entirely without effect.

When the carriage arrived from Delaford, Jonathan contained his eagerness to see Miss Tilney; his parents had impressed upon him that showing open favoritism in public could be unmannerly, particularly to the lengths Jonathan had sometimes gone when younger. He regretted this, however, when Bamber walked forward to greet her with especial warmth.

Why should it bother him that Mr. Bamber wished to court Miss Tilney? If Jonathan did not want to court her himself—or, more properly, did not know whether or not he wanted to do so—what business did he have forbidding another suitor's pursuit? He knew it was the duty of every young woman to make an eligible match if she could, and even if the Bamber family fortune did not equal that of the Darcys, most young women would be delighted at the prospect of marrying into their number. Did Jonathan not wish the best for her?

This subject required deeper thought. For tonight, it would be best to pretend to have noticed nothing.

However, Jonathan's plan suffered from one great flaw: he had been observed by one who wished him ill.

Bamber accompanied Miss Tilney farther into the house, a development that would have disquieted Jonathan further had he not swiftly realized their purpose. No doubt they were testing the time it took to walk to the antechamber that had held the poisoned glass of port. Indeed, it was not but a few minutes before Miss Tilney and Bamber had returned and come to his side.

"Anyone could have reached the port, I believe." Miss Tilney almost looked dejected. "It was kept so close that it would not have taken even a single minute to poison the glasses."

"Do keep your voice down, Miss Tilney," Bamber said, following his own counsel. "Lady Middleton has brought us together to forget."

"Before I do forget, something happened at my last sitting with Mr. Follett," she said, her eyes shifting sidelong to where Follett stood, pretending to listen to Sir John. "I know not the meaning of it yet—"

Then the bell was rung for dinner, and there could be no more conversation. Jonathan shared a conspiratorial look with Miss Tilney; whatever it was that had occurred, they would discuss soon.

As they all sat together to dinner, Jonathan said something he thought rather ordinary: "How very good it is to see you, Mrs. Brandon, and all your party."

It was then that Follett began. "The compliment to you is plain, Mrs. Brandon."

"The compliment is surely as much to my young guest." Mrs. Brandon smiled at Miss Tilney, then at Jonathan, clearly expecting him to join in the praise. In so doing, however, she played into Follett's hands.

He grinned widely. "How true. No wonder she is such a

favorite of yours, Thumps! You must have shared many stories of our schoolboy days together with Miss Tilney, have you not?"

"No." Jonathan could think of few topics he would rather discuss with anyone. "At Donwell Abbey, we were occupied with far more important concerns." Then he stopped, suddenly aware of his blunder. They could scarcely forget that they were in the location of one murder if he began discussing an earlier one.

Follett surprised him by changing the subject. "So many better things to discuss, aren't there, Thumps? Like good books—especially your favorite—"

Jonathan finished the statement for him: "Gibbon's *Decline and Fall of the Roman Empire*." And how strange it was to feel a flush of enthusiasm for his very, very favorite book of all time, and see the pleasure reflected in Follett's face.

Follett leaned forward, mischief on his face, and said, "Go on, then. *Tell us more*."

Juliet sensed a trick being played, and she could tell that Mr. Darcy sensed it, too. Yet his enthusiasm for the topic seemed to outweigh any hint of danger he had perceived. "There is so much to tell," he said. "You must be more specific."

That lout Follett grinned even wider, though Bamber, while evidently amused, had the good grace not to join in. "Of course!" Follett said. "Never have I met a man who took more pleasure in being specific than you, Thumps. Tell us more about, say—Caligula."

Juliet was no great scholar of the classics, but even she knew that little about Caligula was fit for discussion in mixed company. This pitfall was avoided, however, as Mr.

Darcy explained, "His rule took place in the earliest stages of the Roman Empire. Gibbon places the *true* beginning of the decline at the end of the rule of the Antonines nearly two centuries later."

"I beg your pardon." Follett's mock gravity set Juliet even more on edge. "The Antonines, then. I'm sure Miss Tilney is eager to hear all about them."

They mean to make him bore me, Juliet realized. *They wish to humiliate him in my presence, because they believe me to be a favorite of his.*

Whether or not she was favored by Jonathan Darcy in the way Mr. Follett believed, Juliet knew herself to be his friend. So she smiled warmly at Jonathan, forgot every other person in the room, and said, "Indeed, I yearn to hear more about the Antonines. Tell me, Mr. Darcy, when precisely did they rule?"

Thus began one of the more extraordinary half hours in Juliet's memory. There was no question she could ask about the downfall of the Roman Empire that Jonathan could not answer with a lengthy quotation of Gibbon. The topics became more arcane with every further query she posed, and all others in attendance had begun to stare. Yet Juliet kept a smile on her face throughout and persisted.

"I see. How very interesting! But precisely when were the payments to the Praetorian Guards changed, Mr. Darcy?" she once asked and was rewarded with a slack-jawed stare from the disbelieving Follett. Juliet saw this only out of the corner of her eye, because her attention remained on Jonathan Darcy. In this way alone could she prevent his humiliation.

At this moment, rescue came to them all in the form of the Middleton children rushing in to demand their mother's attention. This led Lady Middleton to tacitly suggest that her guests praise them as quite the handsomest, best-behaved children ever known, which was rather far from the truth.

Still, at least the subject was changed. Follett sighed with audible relief. Even Juliet could not help straightening. This, perhaps, led Mr. Darcy to at long last realize his error.

"I fear I have monopolized the conversation," he said. "Please forgive me."

"You require no forgiveness for answering Miss Tilney's questions," replied Mrs. Jennings, her eyes twinkling. It occurred to Juliet that what Mrs. Jennings had seen might have been observed by the others as well: her avid interest in an eligible young man.

Does everyone believe us to be courting? Juliet wondered. *Do they wonder about us? If only I knew the truth myself!*

For then, perhaps, I would know what to make of Mr. Bamber— who was, even then, smiling at her warmly.

The next morning, Jonathan did not feel entirely satisfied with the events of the night before. They had had little chance to investigate—Lady Middleton had planned the evening thoroughly, allowing for few unaccounted moments in which they might have explored Barton Park. Bamber and Juliet had given him despairing glances, before becoming engaged in conversation. Yet this was not the main source of dissatisfaction.

As ever, Jonathan had recognized the need not to speak at length about Gibbon only *after* speaking at length about Gibbon. Most of the company had no doubt been rather bored (which he found an inexplicable reaction to hearing more about the ancient Romans, although his parents had informed him was far from an unusual response). Yet had not Miss Tilney asked many questions? If she had not been genuinely intrigued, then she had kindly meant to give him an opportunity to speak on a topic he enjoyed.

Afterward, however, she had been unusually distant from him. She had turned her attentions more toward the Brandons, the Middleton children, and of course Bamber. Had Jonathan angered her in some way? How could it be wrong to respond to the questions she asked? Once again, he had found himself in one of the thorny, uncertain areas of interaction in which the rules were all unspoken and unfathomable.

Willoughby had determined that riding was not seen as a breach of mourning and now wished to spend all his time in the saddle, and urged his companions to join him as well. Follett and Bamber seemed willing; Jonathan was even eager, for riding involved little to no conversation.

It proved a relief to see that the horses in Willoughby's stables appeared to be carefully and humanely kept. Jonathan was given a white mare to ride, older and very steady; she was not a mount to dash up hills or gallop picturesquely toward the horizon, but this was precisely why he liked her. How pleasing it was simply to meander along the edge of Allenham's grounds in such uncomplaining company, while Follett and Bamber seemed determined to race each other from one edge to the next.

Somewhat surprisingly, Willoughby did not immediately join in the galloping about. He kept searching the horizon and the nearby roads, as though he hoped to see someone passing near. All the walkers of Barton must have been kept indoors by the low clouds that threatened the sky.

Bamber finally shouted, "Come on, Willoughby, what's got into you?" Which was in Jonathan's opinion a rather extraordinary thing to say to a man who had lost his wife not two weeks prior—but no one else seemed to object. Follett pulled his horse back, stilling, perhaps waiting to see what Willoughby would do.

Willoughby urged his horse forward, though still at no more than a steady walk. This was somewhat disappointing, for the stallion was a beautiful creature, and no doubt a swift one; it would have been a joy to see such an animal run. Jonathan might have admired the horse for more time had Willoughby not lurched to one side—then to the other—then fallen off his horse entirely, tumbling down into the grass.

Had he been poisoned also? Jonathan could not imagine it, but nor could he imagine Willoughby falling off his horse like a child. He urged his horse toward Willoughby, as did Follett and Bamber. All three arrived at the very moment that Willoughby sat up, brushed grass from his face, and winced. "My elbow—"

"Is it broken?" Bamber asked. Follett merely stared.

"No, but it will not be right for some time to come." Willoughby struggled to his feet as his horse trotted up. He limped slightly as he went to it and took its reins. "I cannot comprehend it. One moment I was riding, and the next it felt as though the saddle was slipping out from beneath me."

"It was," Jonathan said, pointing to the off-kilter placement of the saddle, which had slid almost completely to the horse's side.

"By G-d, so it has! The stable boy must have forgotten his task." Willoughby angrily examined the saddle, then went very still.

"Willoughby?" Bamber asked. "What is it?"

"The stable boy fastened everything properly," Willoughby said slowly, "the girth was buckled, but look." He pointed at the girth, which had almost torn in two. No—Jonathan caught himself—not torn. The line was too clean, too straight, for a tear.

He looked over at Bamber, whose eyes were wide. He, too, had drawn the obvious conclusion: Willoughby's saddle girth had been deliberately cut.

Which meant that someone had attempted to kill Willoughby.

Chapter Eighteen

All Allenham was in an uproar. Willoughby had commanded many of the servants to abandon their usual duties in favor of keeping watch over the stables, the kitchens, Willoughby's bedchamber, and any other room he might be expected to enter. The kitchen staff, the gardeners, and the handyman had to create a comprehensive list of every single knife on the estate, to determine which if any were missing, and to test them on a leather strap to see which might have been capable of making the cut in question. Jonathan realized this last was potentially useful in any investigation, and thus had for once to credit Willoughby with showing sense. The display did not allow him to credit much else.

"Compare this to his reaction to Sophia's death," Follett said in a low voice. The three guests at Allenham had gathered in the study, where they would shortly be questioned by the constables, who had only just arrived after Willoughby's summons. "He is desperate to know who would do him harm, but has not shown the slightest curiosity as to who murdered his wife."

Bamber nodded. "One wonders if that is because *he already knows* who murdered his wife."

"The difference is most marked," Jonathan said, "but the fact remains—someone *did* cut the girth on Willoughby's saddle, certainly with the intent of hurting him, if not killing him. If Willoughby poisoned his wife, then this latest attempt means that we have not one but two would-be murderers in the vicinity. If he did not, then the killer is still at work, either because this person meant to kill Willoughby all along or because both of the Willoughbys were meant to die."

This sobering statement quieted the others, which gave Jonathan an opportunity to consider.

If both of the Willoughbys were marked for death from the beginning, surely the arsenic would have been placed in both glasses so that they would die at once, without having first been put on guard. It could be that the spill saved Willoughby . . . but perhaps not for long. If only they knew whether Follett was responsible for the spill, or if it had been Willoughby himself!

In one hypothetical, Willoughby had murdered his wife and someone was now trying to kill him—perhaps to avenge her, perhaps for reasons of their own. In the other version of events, another party had meant to kill Willoughby, had failed, but still intended to succeed. In either situation, the same questions remained: Why had they done this so swiftly, when suspicions were still heightened? Why had they chosen such an unreliable and yet inarguably deliberate method for this second attack? If this were a case of one killer rather than two, a third question had to be raised—why had the poisoner not used poison again?

He studied Follett carefully. Follett had shown little concern for Willoughby's fall—an indifference toward his life—but at least until recently, he had also blamed Jonathan for Mrs. Willoughby's death. Had he blamed Jonathan only to conceal his true intentions toward Willoughby?

Should the other guest present be considered? Helpful though Bamber had been, Jonathan knew everyone must be considered in turn. Bamber thought Willoughby guilty of murder, but he had shown himself committed to investigating the event through science and deduction. He would hardly be encouraging Jonathan and Miss Tilney's efforts were he contemplating a crime of his own. Besides, even Jonathan, who occasionally found it difficult to read the emotions of others, could tell that Bamber was genuinely astonished by this turn of events.

Once again, Jonathan thought of the woman in the blue cloak. She would have had the opportunity to slip inside the stables. They would need to look far more closely at Miss Beth Williams . . .

The low clouds still held back rain the next morning, which allowed Juliet to take her "morning walk" to the orchard. As she had hoped, Mr. Darcy waited there for her, Mr. Bamber by his side. She had not dreamed, however, that they would have so much to reveal, and of such a shocking nature.

"The girth cut through?" Juliet exclaimed. "They are certain it was not simply worn, frayed, something of the sort?"

"We saw the cut for ourselves," Mr. Darcy said. "The line could not be mistaken for any natural wear. It was undeniably deliberate damage. Had Willoughby fallen on rougher ground, he might well have been killed."

"Who would have done it?" Mr. Bamber seemed almost dazed. Juliet pitied him; this was his first murder investigation, and no doubt he had not fully accustomed himself to the shocks. "Who would have dared so much?"

Mr. Darcy pointed out, "Whoever dared so much accomplished very little. A half-cut girth is not a reliable means of ending a rider's life. The girth might have held. In the alternative, we have what actually transpired—in which Mr. Willoughby suffered no more than stained riding breeches and a sore elbow."

"This does not seem like the act of the same person who

would put so much arsenic in a single glass of port," said Juliet. How many possibilities unfolded from this one change? It felt as though an image in two dimensions had suddenly acquired a third, with planes and angles that could not readily be seen.

Mr. Darcy shook his head. "Some essential element of this has escaped us. I sense it."

"As do I, Mr. Darcy. Yet there is nothing for it but to think deeply upon the matter and trust that more will in time be revealed." Juliet cast a glance up at the dark skies. The rain would not wait for them much longer. "As puzzling as this event may be, it gives us more information to consider. Even if that information is confusing at first, it must ultimately help us to clarify the situation."

"You are more optimistic on that point than I, Miss Tilney." Mr. Bamber smiled at her. "What an intrepid spirit you have!"

How kind he was toward her. How much he admired the very qualities she most wished for someone to admire. Juliet felt her cheeks flushing warm and hoped her blush was taken only as the effect of the chill in the air. "I can linger no longer. The rain is sure to come soon, and I wished to take my letter to the post personally."

"I should be very happy to walk you there!" Mr. Bamber said quickly, giving Mr. Darcy a glance that Juliet did not understand. "You don't mind if I do so, do you, Darcy?"

Mr. Darcy said, "No, of course not. If Miss Tilney will excuse me?"

She would have preferred for him to join them, but she found the prospect of spending more time with Mr. Bamber to be a pleasant one. "Of course, Mr. Darcy. But—I hope you will call at Delaford very soon? The Brandons have asked after you in particular."

(This was true only in the most general sense. Yet Juliet felt no guilt, as she knew the Brandons would welcome Mr. Darcy's visit equally as much as she.)

Happily, Mr. Darcy nodded. "I should be very glad to see the Brandons again."

Juliet thought, for a moment, of asking Mr. Darcy to accompany them into the village—but she did not. Mr. Bamber offered his arm, she took it and began on her way.

Jonathan felt certain it was impolite to simply stand in place and watch Mr. Bamber lead Miss Tilney away, but he knew not what else to do. He possessed a stronger aversion to Allenham than ever before, given Willoughby's wild mood and the suspicions held by everyone from the constables down to the scullery maid. So he stood where he was, watching Miss Tilney's white dress vanish around the bend of the road.

"For shame, Mr. Darcy!" cried a merry voice. He turned to see Mrs. Jennings, who despite her age and considerable size appeared to be an avid walker; she had come up the path behind him quickly enough that he had not had a chance to notice.

"Good morning, Mrs. Jennings," he began. "What do you mean by—"

"I mean, sir, that you young men have no spirit these days! I declare, what have they come to, when you stand there allowing the girl you prefer to be swept up by another, and not even trying to vie for her attentions yourself?" Mrs. Jennings waggled her finger at him. "That is no way to win the hand of a lady."

How was Jonathan to answer this? He did not know whether he could decently ask for Miss Tilney's hand, nor even whether he wanted to. He did prefer her company to that of nearly anyone else he had ever met—but surely that was an unworthy reason to interfere with her marital prospects, particularly when her marrying Mr. Bamber would mean keeping two friends instead of losing one.

Yet—if he *were* to go to Delaford later today—to call without Mr. Bamber present—that could scarcely be considered improper. Could it? Miss Tilney had expressly invited him, without including Bamber in the invitation. He considered the question so deeply that he forgot to answer Mrs. Jennings at all.

Luckily, that good lady was in the practice of conducting conversations with or without replies. "Whatever brings you out this way, if not to walk with Miss Tilney?"

"The constables are searching Allenham again," he said. "We were all questioned, and then we were told to put ourselves out of the way." Jonathan would have met Miss Tilney here regardless, weather permitting, but wished to conceal their investigation from the one person in Barton most likely to spread word of it.

"Questioned? Searching? Did not they find the poison in his stables?"

"This is not about Mrs. Willoughby's murder," Jonathan explained. "This is about yesterday's attempt to murder Willoughby himself."

In a lifetime of gossiping, Mrs. Jennings had rarely been as richly rewarded for her inquisitiveness as she was on that morning. An attempt on Mr. Willoughby's life, too? What was becoming of Barton, of England, of the world?

So she asked everyone else she met that day, and she met many. Every single person came up with a theory to explain it, and no two of these theories were precisely the same. Unlike any of the previous revelations, this news convinced some that Mrs. Brandon might not, in fact, be to blame; all but the most baroque imagination among them had difficulty envisioning her creeping about the countryside in the dead of night, sawing saddle girths in two. The suspicions of the townsfolk could now be more evenly distributed among the company present at Barton Park on that first fatal night.

Colonel Brandon was a military man—that meant he had killed—and had he not challenged Willoughby to a duel only two years before? *He* need not worry about walking alone in the night; he would be strong enough to saw through leather in a matter of minutes.

Mr. Willoughby's so-called friends—were they not a peculiar lot? Mr. Follett, the proud artist, skulking about; angry at all the world; and, word had it, once a suitor of Mrs. Willoughby's. He had motive enough to want revenge! That Mr. Darcy never looked anyone in the eye—was that not shifty and suspicious? And Mr. Bamber went about plucking plants from the marsh and talking about "tests" for poison, did he not? No decent man would have such morbid curiosity.

(Those who spoke this last conveniently ignored their own morbid curiosity, as is common in such situations.)

Miss Williams thought herself high and mighty since becoming rich, did she not? Her reasons for despising both Willoughby and his wife were all too well-known. Had there not been a strange altercation between the two of them in the village but days ago, one several had seen but none overheard, yet obviously to all a very tense meeting indeed? A few of the shopkeepers mentioned that she had been purchasing some strange items of late, though nobody knew precisely what. She bore watching.

One highly imaginative soul went so far as to speculate that the clergyman's wife, Mrs. Elinor Ferrars, was not really with child but went about with a padded sack strapped to her belly, this sack filled with the implements of murder with which she had been at work avenging her sister's jilting. Despite the curiosity throughout Barton, the public temper had not reached a high enough froth for this theory to gain purchase.

Yet not even the most intriguing theories had the sheer power of the one undenied fact: someone had tried to murder Mr. Willoughby, too.

Willoughby fell from his horse, but he yet lives.

When this gossip arrived via her nursemaid, Beth experienced such shock and disquiet that she felt she could not endure it. After some time spent in anguished reflection, she decided that, as her sentiments could not be escaped, they must be shared. Only one person in Barton could sympathize with her predicament. So Beth took up her blue cloak, glanced upward at the rain-dark clouds, and decided she might make it if she went with haste.

The first drops began to fall when Beth was within sight of Delaford. Though it was not ladylike to run, she began to go as fast as her legs would carry her. It was not likely that anyone should mistake her for a lady in any case. What did it answer, dressing in finer clothes, buying a fine house? Every person in Barton had always known, and always would know, exactly what she was: the daughter of an unmarried woman, the unmarried mother of a son, both born to disgrace and having borne it for herself and her child. Willoughby had made her forget that for a brief time; her riches had gone to her head for an even briefer period. The town always remembered the truth. Beth carried her history with her.

As she approached the door, she saw that she was not the only person hurrying to Delaford before the storm. A young man, tall, holding on to his hat—"Mr. Darcy?" Beth called, as they both rushed to the door together.

"Oh! Miss Williams. I hope you are well." He seemed uncertain what to do or say.

Beth took the opportunity to knock. "Let us hope they are welcoming visitors, or else you and I shall become very wet indeed."

However, the Delaford butler admitted them without delay. Colonel Brandon was out, again tending to the needs of the tenantry as the harvest drew to a close, but both Miss Tilney and Marianne Brandon were at home. This suited Beth's purposes very well. Raindrops pattered against the windowpanes, then hammered—no one would be leaving very soon. Together they were shown into the drawing room, but made an awkward party of four. Besides, what Beth had to say was reserved for one person alone. "I hear you have quite the library, Mrs. Brandon," she began.

"It is the colonel who has built the marvelous library at Delaford," Mrs. Brandon said, "though I have convinced him to read more novels. Would you believe he has only just begun *Evelina*?"

The hint had not been taken, so Beth pressed her point home. "I should very much like to see the room, if you would be so gracious as to show me."

Mrs. Brandon rose immediately. "Of course. Miss Tilney, Mr. Darcy, you will excuse us, will you not?" As she left the room, she whispered to Beth, "How good you are to give the young people a chance to speak!"

Let Marianne Brandon think Beth was motivated by goodwill. Untrue though it was, her assumption was a charitable one, which for Beth proved a welcome change.

How grateful Juliet was that Miss Williams had left, for this allowed her to speak more openly to Mr. Darcy. "Can you still imagine Miss Williams a murderer? Her kindness to Mrs. Brandon after that strange spell in the village square—it was most gracious, most good of her."

"There is no person among our potential suspects who has not shown *some* sign of goodness and cordiality," Mr. Darcy noted. "Even Willoughby can make himself hospitable when he chooses. If the murderer were an obvious villain, our investigation would already be ended, or would not have been necessary."

"Too true." Juliet rubbed her temples. "Why does thinking hard make one's head hurt? Our heads are meant for thinking, so I do not know why they are not better suited to the purpose."

He smiled at her joke but was not long distracted from their purpose. "At Barton Park, you had something else of import you wished to share, but you have not yet told me of it. The shock of the attempt on Willoughby's life distracted me, I fear."

"Oh—compared to that, my news will seem trivial and obscure indeed. Do you remember the newspaper you brought from Mrs. Willoughby's room, the one you thought might have been given to her by Mr. Follett? Well, Mr. Follett spied it lying near while painting me, and his countenance grew so strange!" Juliet had watched Follett carefully at the session's end, wondering whether he might not have attempted to take the paper with him, but he had not. "I believe he surmised it was simply another copy of the *Times*, but I would wager that he did give that to Mrs. Willoughby, for it has a very powerful meaning for him."

"I have reviewed every story within it," said Mr. Darcy, "and I cannot imagine what story contained there could have anything to do with Mr. Follett or Mrs. Willoughby."

"Nor I." Then Juliet straightened. "Perhaps what we seek is not within the paper. Perhaps it is on the front page."

"Among the advertisements?" Despite his surprise, Mr. Darcy did not reject her suggestion outright. Within moments she had fetched it into the room so that they could review the front page together.

The *Times*, like every other newspaper, put its most expensive advertisements on its front page. Juliet ran her fingers along the edge of the newsprint, taking in notices of new books to be sold and plays to be seen, unusually effective medicines to buy, horse auctions, open positions for servants on great estates, and more. Mr. Follett had apparently claimed that he wished to check shipping schedules, and indeed more than one shipping line had advertised on this page . . . but another bit of newsprint leaped out at her, demanding its due. "Mr. Darcy!"

"I see it." His finger pointed at an advertisement for arsenic wafers. Its headline: "A Woman's Face Is Her Fortune."

"It promises an end to all blotches, moles, pimples, and freckles," said Juliet. "But to take several together—or to grind them into a powder—might that provide enough arsenic to end another's life?"

"We shall have to ask Bamber, but this may well be a vital clue. Just because Mr. Follett *could* have taken arsenic from his paints does not mean that he *did*."

Juliet's mind was awhirl. "But then why give Mrs. Willoughby the paper? Unless . . . you do not think it was some kind of warning?"

Mr. Darcy did not reply. He had gone deep into thought, even more so than herself; she could practically see the ideas unfolding behind his dark eyes. "One person or two?" he murmured, which Juliet understood immediately to refer to the question of whether or not the person who had struck at Mr. Willoughby was the same one who had killed his wife. "One or two?"

He began to rock back and forth, which at first startled her. Then Juliet recollected what he had previously told her—sometimes, apparently, Jonathan Darcy found it difficult to think intently without moving his body in some way. Pacing would do, but rocking, he had said, was his true habit. Indeed, it was the habit that had led to his cruel nickname. Why could someone not stop Mr. Willoughby from saying it?

Just as Juliet laid this concern aside to turn to the matter of the attempt on Mr. Willoughby, Mr. Darcy abruptly stopped moving. "*Oh*. Miss Tilney, I beg your pardon, most sincerely."

"For what, Mr. Darcy?" She genuinely did not understand what he meant.

"For—the way that I was conducting myself—"

"Oh, do not worry about that." Juliet smiled at him. "Remember, you told me of your habit, that it helps you to think more deeply upon subjects. We are here to think deeply, are we not?"

He looked upon her almost in wonder. "You did not mind it?"

"Not in the slightest, sir. I told you I would not, if you recall."

"I had not believed you," Mr. Darcy admitted. "Forgive me."

His eyes met hers, only for a moment. Yet Juliet would think upon that moment frequently during the next many days.

Marianne never welcomed morning callers to the library—the room was not one traditionally used for that purpose—and at the moment wondered why it was not. This room was among the most pleasant at Delaford, smelling comfortably of leather, tobacco, and old books, and the mere presence of so many tomes suggested endless topics of conversation.

Yet Beth Williams already seemed to know of what she wished to speak. "What do you think of this business at Allenham?" she said.

"Most shocking," Marianne agreed. Juliet had shared the story when she returned home from her morning walk. "Can you believe that someone would attempt to murder Willoughby?"

Her question was a mere figure of speech, the sort of polite formality she despised when spoken by others. Yet Marianne did not blame herself for it when Beth did her the courtesy of answering honestly. "Yes, in truth, I can believe that."

They looked at each other for a long moment. It seemed to Marianne that Beth had come near laughing, a most unseemly response that nonetheless was entirely understandable. Marianne had loved Willoughby too recently to truly wish such ill fate upon him, but then, her sufferings accounted for little compared to Beth's.

Her honesty would not permit her to refute Beth's words as propriety demanded. "There is . . . some truth in what you say, Miss Williams."

"Oh, indeed." Beth's cheeks had pinked with the effort of maintaining decorum. "The difficulty will be in determining only one suspect."

Do not laugh, Marianne told herself. Broad, loud laughter was considered vulgar, particularly from a young lady, and if she began to laugh on this subject, she would not be able to contain her mirth within the bounds of decorum. "He would be very shocked to hear you say so."

"Aye, to be sure. Mr. Willoughby is very sure of his welcome, is he not?"

The impudence he had shown, writing to her, believing she would still wish to meet with him after marrying another! "Indeed he is, even when he should know better. Especially where he should know better, in my experience."

"As in mine." Beth covered her mouth with her hand. "I last spoke to him but days ago, just after Mrs. Willoughby's death. In my foolishness, when he asked to talk with me, I thought that—that perhaps his ill-tempered wife was the only reason he had taken no interest in little George. For myself, in my vanity, yes, I hoped he might have kind words for me, but that mattered little compared to what I wanted for my son."

"Of course," Marianne said gently. How wrong people were to think of Miss Williams as nothing but a giddy, sinful girl. Sin she may have done, but at heart she was first and foremost a mother like any other, who wanted the best for her child.

"Instead, all Willoughby wanted was to very nearly threaten me to leave town. He said he could have no more suspicion circling him about town after Mrs. Willoughby's death. That I must leave Barton behind forever, or else I should be sorry."

How Marianne wished she could not have imagined Willoughby saying these words! What a perfect gentleman she had once believed him to be! But he had ever possessed a cruel tongue, one he did not hesitate to use to insult anyone who had angered or irritated him. That was the opposite of true gentility. If only Marianne had known that sooner. "Willoughby often convinces himself that what is best for him is best for another, and then cannot understand the perversity of refusing his sensible wishes. If he ever scolds you so again, come and tell me, and then I will speak to Mr. Willoughby on such terms that I promise he will trouble you no more." Marianne had had little luck controlling Willoughby in the past, but her wretched experiences with the man had given her a weapon to wield: the power to shame him, deeply, forever. She did not doubt that a scolding from her on the subject would affect Willoughby greatly.

"Oh, Mrs. Brandon—I had not realized it would be so—how good it is to talk with one other person who knows what John Willoughby truly is!"

"The colonel knows," Marianne said. He had taken Willoughby's measure accurately from the beginning, nearly the only person who had.

Beth nodded, admitting the justice of this, but she added, "Not as you and I do."

"No, no. I believe we know better than any two other people on this earth."

How indelicate of her! How unkind! Yet Marianne's damaged heart—however healed by the colonel's kindness and love—still desired such balm. She could only resolve never to speak so again.

Let Miss Williams be the judge of her own words, Marianne thought, *and do not wonder overmuch at her glee in knowing Willoughby's life to be endangered.*

Chapter Nineteen

The next day, Marianne found that her courage was more than equal to another walk toward the village. Perhaps she would not go all the way into the square again, but she was willing to see and be seen. The worst, she felt, was over.

"You will not mind my joining you this morning?" she asked Juliet. "Mr. Darcy would of course be very welcome to walk with us as well. Or his friend, that Mr. Bamber?"

"I do not think either will be eager to go about in this mud," Juliet said. "We spoke at some length yesterday, so there is no need to—I mean, we shall see each other again very soon, regardless of whether we meet today."

Her friend's apparent disinterest in meeting either of the young men again anytime soon struck Marianne greatly—so much so that she suspected Juliet's sentiments were in fact highly interested regarding one gentleman or the other, but that she wished to remain discreet regarding the matter. Marianne, who had had cause to repent her previous indiscretions, admired Juliet's conduct and pressed no further.

As they set out, Marianne said, "I must admit, Miss Williams's kindness during my difficulty in the village has given me strength. Simply knowing that, were I to be overcome, assistance and shelter would be near . . . that helps me to feel that I shall not be overcome at all."

Juliet nodded, though her expression seemed wary. "It does seem that Miss Williams now wishes the acquaintance far more than she did previously."

"We are now brought together by precisely that which formerly separated us before," Marianne said, "our experiences with Mr. Willoughby. Those experiences differ, but the selfishness he displayed was the same. Do you know, even after his wife's death, he insisted upon meeting with Miss Williams in the street, there only to command her to leave town?"

How much more interested Juliet had become. "That is what they spoke of? I mean to say, he insisted upon meeting her in public for this?"

"I suppose he would not be seen entering her home so soon after Mrs. Willoughby's death." Marianne sighed as she thought of the dead woman whom she had once hated. Now her heart held nothing but pity for one who had died young and terribly, and who had never known true love. The latter seemed as terrible as the former.

The roads were indeed muddy from yesterday's showers, but far from impassable. More worrying was the pale gray sky overhead, one almost unbroken cloud stretched thin from horizon to horizon. More rain would come. Marianne saw this only as evidence that she had been correct to take her walk this morning, without further delay. Another happy result of her choice: they passed few persons along the way, as the state of the roads kept the less stalwart indoors.

Yet luck could be perverse, for as Marianne and Juliet rounded the curve of the hill that separated Delaford from the main road, whom should they find on his black horse but Willoughby?

There was nothing else for it but to speak to him. Marianne began with the same strict courtesy she would have given anyone else. "Good morning, Mr. Willoughby."

Before Juliet could even echo her, Willoughby said, "What

of good is there in it? You have been told, have you not, of the villainy at work? That someone has attempted to harm me, and no doubt means to try again?"

Marianne allowed Juliet to reply, "We have indeed heard of it, sir, and we condole with you in such a time of trial."

Willoughby never so much as glanced at Juliet. His thoughts, his attention, remained focused on Marianne alone. "Have *you* nothing to say to me? Are you truly gone so cold that you can hear word of an attempt on my life without any feeling?"

So well did he know how to sting her conscience! No word could pierce Marianne's heart more surely than the accusation that she might be "cold." She said, "It is terrible news indeed. Our thoughts are very much with you, Mr. Willoughby."

"'Our'?" His tone had gentled so that Marianne blushed—to think he would speak this way to her out of doors, on a public road, with Miss Tilney standing with them! Willoughby seemed not to notice her at all. "Do you only ever speak for your household any longer? Or have you anything to say for yourself?"

"Should we not all feel concern for the safety of our neighbors?" Marianne lifted her chin. Two could play this game of asking questions that seemed to have but one answer.

Willoughby seemed more encouraged by her reply than she would have liked. He smiled. "It is good to know you still possess true feeling. He has not taken that from you, at least. May we speak again?"

"As neighbors, we can scarcely avoid speaking on occasion, no matter how much we might wish it," Marianne replied. "Come, Miss Tilney. We may not have long before the rain begins once more."

As she and Juliet resumed walking toward Barton, Marianne could not help listening for hoofbeats behind them;

happily, when they came, they were headed in the other direction. They had escaped relatively unscathed.

Juliet said, "Mr. Willoughby seems most . . . presumptuous."

"He is that, indeed. He judges my husband for qualities anyone with sense would recognize as virtues. He speaks to me with undue familiarity, though it was he who created the breach between us." Marianne shook her head. "Worst of all is that he appears to believe that his wife's death should be an opportunity for some sort of—for relations between us of a nature that is distasteful, if not actually immoral."

"Do you believe that his presumption may have led to someone having evil designs upon his person?"

Marianne sighed. "I do not know that Willoughby has done anything to deserve such an ill as that. Yet however wrong it would be for someone to kill him for it, it cannot be denied that others have been killed for less."

Their walk into the village otherwise passed without incident. Although Marianne could not but be aware of the many eyes upon her, she was at no point overtaken by memory. This steadiness of mind was assisted by Juliet, who pretended to be very much interested in looking for complexion wafers—her, with her lovely skin! Juliet could scarce need anything less—but it kept them busy, going from shop to shop, finding nothing. How dear her friend was, to pretend such concerns, all for the purpose of steadying Marianne.

Willoughby's solitary morning ride surprised Jonathan, but pleasantly so. He would have thought Willoughby unlikely to desire much time on horseback for a long while after so nearly meeting calamity in that way; perhaps the assumption was that his would-be killer would not attempt the same method twice. When Jonathan said as much to Bamber, the reply was punctuated with a laugh. "Indeed, for it will be many a year before Willoughby mounts a horse without checking every single buckle and strap thrice over! The point is, we have a morning to ourselves, and I intend to spend it in my laboratory. Why not come with me?"

When they entered the lab, Bamber laughed out loud for pride. "Aha, Darcy, I told you—look at this!"

Jonathan accepted the small glass vase he was given, which contained a pinkish gray paste. "What is it?"

"Arsenic as extracted from paint." Bamber's enthusiasm was palpable. "Note that it is a paste—not grainy! Therefore the arsenic that killed Mrs. Willoughby did not come from Follett's paints."

"Well done, Bamber. This of course does not exculpate Follett—he could have derived the arsenic from elsewhere— but it is nonetheless good to know. Would that science would tell us even more."

Bamber hesitated. Jonathan could not be certain whether his countenance betrayed uncertainty or eagerness. "Darcy, I must take you into my confidence. I have been thinking upon the matter of arsenic—about whether there might be some way to determine whether the arsenic in Mrs. Willoughby's glass that night was definitely derived from the same package of poison found in Willoughby's stables."

"Most extraordinary," Jonathan said. Indeed he was much impressed with his friend's intelligence and enterprise. "You mean to say, you have created an entirely new method of testing arsenic, one with such precise results?"

Bamber chuckled. "Not yet. First I must run some trial tests and see whether the results prove true. Only then can

I run a test on this glass—and I will need a bit of the poison from that container, but I wager the constables will allow me a sample of the powder that was found in the stables."

"The Royal Academy will elect you yet, Bamber."

Although Bamber ducked his head, Jonathan could tell how much his comment had pleased his friend, who said only, "The sooner I begin, the sooner we will know if I have made a breakthrough or if I have been but woolgathering."

Willoughby assumes what is best for him is best for everyone, thought Beth, *but it is folly to assume that what is best for him could* never *be best for me.*

Her conversation with Marianne Brandon had been illuminating in this regard. Now that Beth considered the matter in this light, she knew that she needed to leave Barton, permanently, as soon as possible. She could scarce believe she had not seen this earlier; there was no more time to waste.

All she had done, the past several months, was accumulate more that must be packed away or sold. Why had she bought so many things? The cuckoo clock from Germany had made baby George laugh, so perhaps she did not regret that. Beth had chosen her new dresses wisely—fashionable, but not so much so that they would look strange in a few years' time, made with materials of quality—so those were worth the having, though she might have satisfied herself with two or three fewer. Yet why had she spent twenty pounds—more than a servant's yearly salary—on a bed? Why had she bought fine china? Above half of it would need to be sold, and though it might sell at good prices, Beth would still be the poorer for it.

When her inheritance was new, and the wounds of her

treatment by Willoughby had been even more painful, Beth spent—not with complete abandon but with all the rapture of new liberty. Even in the fever of it, she had known that she felt herself to be buying more than mere objects. She felt as if respectability itself was available to her again, and so soon after she had believed it lost forever. Beth had better reason than most to know that the trappings alone would win many of respectability's benefits. People might not remember her disgrace as acutely as they had before she owned a good house, fine furnishings, even a pale blue woolen cloak.

All of these items had now to be placed in one of two categories: those to be sold, and those to be packed. She must divest herself entirely of her worldly goods before she could flee.

Throughout her confinement, Elinor Ferrars had moderated her choices. She had neither eaten all she wished, nor refused to eat more than usual. She had made provision for everything necessary to tend to an infant without knitting booties and bonnets enough to outfit an entire regiment of babies. And she had limited her appearances in company so that she would neither overexert herself nor entirely forgo the companionship of her family.

Yet it appeared at last that the matter was no longer hers to decide. Walking felt even more ungainly than it had only a few days prior; the desire to remain near to home, to clean and arrange and rearrange all the child's things, had come upon her with great power. Elinor had never heard her mother mention these precise sensations, yet her reason told her this must mean that her lying-in was very near.

Thank goodness, she thought, looking out of the window that showed the path into Barton, *that I took care of all needful things well before. There is nothing to be done now but to wait.*

"When do you think it will be?" Margaret asked. The youngest of the Dashwood sisters was now of an age to walk from house to house by herself, and she had taken to dropping in of her own accord at the oddest of moments, ever eager, wishing to have the very first news of the baby's arrival. "Can it be very much longer, do you think?"

Elinor thought not but said only, "When my time is near, the entire family will know it, and asking will not make the day come sooner." Margaret scowled, as though her nephew- or niece-to-be were deliberately thwarting her, and Elinor had to smile.

Then Margaret asked a very different sort of question: "You say that the whole family will know it—do you mean the Ferrars, too?"

How sharply Elinor became aware of the small distance between the sitting room and Edward's study! He was preparing the next day's sermon, but she doubted him to be so deeply engrossed in that task that he would not be distracted by Margaret's curiosity. She answered with care. "We will send word once the baby has arrived."

"But will they even read the letter?" Margaret asked. "Uncle John has said that Aunt Fanny burns any correspondence she thinks beneath her to read, and you know how unpleasant she is about my uncle."

Privately Elinor thought that Mrs. Ferrars's curiosity about her grandchild would overcome Fanny Ferrars Dashwood's sense of hauteur, but she said only, "It is not ours to determine whether or not they read our news. We can but speak freely and truthfully, and let the Ferrars family do as they will."

"I think it shameful," Margaret said, "that they should be so mean when they know a baby is to come."

"Do not judge." Elinor stroked her sister's hair, which still hung loose down her back; within another year, it would need to be put up. Margaret would not be a child much longer.

"*They* judge."

"Is their poor behavior reason for us to copy it? No, Margaret. We must hold ourselves above that." Elinor could not help hoping that Edward not only heard her words but would also heed them.

That afternoon, much to Juliet's surprise, Mr. Bamber came to visit without Mr. Darcy by his side. Juliet had been wondering if such a moment could come soon; now it had. The colonel, their chaperone, sat at the far end of the long room, much engaged with his accounts, so they were able to speak freely as long as they kept their voices low. She listened with ever-rising admiration as Mr. Bamber told her of a test—one entirely new to science—that he had developed expressly to link the arsenic found in the Allenham stables to that in Mrs. Willoughby's drinking glass.

His cleverness struck her most forcibly. "To invent such a test as that—you will be the marvel of London, Mr. Bamber."

He attempted to demur, but his fair features could not conceal a flush of gratification. "My only aim is to prove to the world who is responsible for the death of Mrs. Willoughby."

"Nonetheless, should your test succeed, you will do good far beyond the confines of Barton. I cannot imagine any person in the world who would not honor such an accomplishment." Juliet paused. "Aside, that is, for poisoners, who will be much dismayed."

Bamber smiled broadly. "How clever you are, Miss Tilney. Not only are you capable of understanding the complexities of the matter, but you even respond with wit!"

Such a compliment would have delighted even one far more worldly than Juliet Tilney. "Have you not shared the news with Mr. Darcy yet?"

"I have done so," replied Bamber, "yet I found I wished to inform you myself, on our own. You will not think the less of me, I hope, for showing such partiality?"

He looked at her as he spoke with such genuine feeling that Juliet felt certain at last that Mr. Bamber truly meant to court her.

It was not as though she had not considered it before; Mrs. Jennings had teased Juliet on the subject too often for her not to wonder. Yet Juliet's thoughts had been more focused on the investigation—and upon Mr. Darcy—and had believed that Mr. Bamber's were as well. Instead, he appeared to have been thinking of her the entire time, and rather seriously, too.

Perhaps she should consider him with equal seriousness.

Yes, she wished for Mr. Darcy's attentions, but he showed no sign of paying them to her. Juliet did not wish to make herself unhappy by hoping for more than his friendship, especially given that his friendship meant so much. The heart may ache, but life must continue. Besides, Juliet knew her parents had not sent her to Devonshire in hopes that she would continue her efforts to identify murderers. No, the most important work of any young woman of her age and station was the search for a gentleman who would make a good husband, one who fully satisfied both necessity and sentiment.

Was it not possible that Ralph Bamber was precisely the person? He was handsome, intelligent, courteous, and ami-

able. His actions had showed him to be far more the gentleman than either Mr. Follett or Mr. Willoughby, and to be a
true friend to Mr. Darcy. Were she to wed Mr. Bamber, the
three of them would be able to continue their friendship,
with all its attendant pleasures of freethinking and excellent
conversation. His fortune would support a family in comfort,
even elegance. Most significantly, Bamber showed every sign
of appreciating Juliet for more than her features or the same
tired accomplishments every young woman of the gentry was
forced to acquire and display; he valued Juliet's cleverness, her
vitality, her humor, even her sense of justice.

Juliet was not immediately overcome by the throes of love,
for the heart does not turn so easily. The place Mr. Jonathan Darcy occupied in her affections would not be swiftly
usurped. Yet she resolved in that moment to consider Mr.
Bamber far more seriously than before. How should she study
him? How should she determine whether he was the correct
man to entrust with her hand? She was not at all certain, but
it seemed she must begin . . .

Blessedly, the colonel struck up a conversation with Mr.
Bamber, who seemingly welcomed the chance to visit in general company. Juliet was grateful for the delay. Such thoughts
as these must be collected before they are acted upon.

As the two men became much engaged in their conversation regarding Colonel Brandon's experiences in the West
Indies—stories that Juliet had by now heard—she felt free
to let her attention wander. The copy of the *Times* that Mr.
Darcy had brought had been neatly placed on a writing-desk;
it looked as though the pages had even been pressed. Juliet
took it up again with new determination. The advertisement
for arsenic wafers could not have been an inspiration to suicide for Mrs. Willoughby, nor to murder for Mr. Follett or

for anyone else, as none such were to be bought in Barton. What, then, had been so important about this issue of the newspaper?

Mr. Follett claimed he wished to look at shipping schedules, she decided. *Might he have been telling the truth?*

The first advertisement, for ships traveling to and from the Mediterranean, provided no enlightenment. The next, however, touted ships for both passengers and cargo traveling to and from America. One ship name leaped out at Juliet, and only with difficulty did she stifle a gasp as she read it.

The *Fox.*

Allenham's stables had proved a far more congenial place to spend the day than Allenham itself was, or so Jonathan had decided before midafternoon. The stable boys, although wary of Mr. Willoughby's whims and tempers, felt free enough to make conversation and to enjoy a few jokes and games among themselves. A handful of the hunting dogs came to sit amid the hay as the horses were brushed and fed their mash, another element that made the hours there so pleasant.

Jonathan found ample opportunity of inspecting the saddles, and of speaking at length to the lads about their duties, about Willoughby's habits, and about the days leading up to Willoughby's accident. The general sentiment among the stable boys was an almost unseemly relief that the cut was known to be deliberate, although this did not arise from any ill feeling toward Willoughby. They only expressed their happiness that none of their number were accused of negligence.

As each one of them spoke, Jonathan studied them as intently as he could manage. He found it difficult to assess the more subtle aspects of human behavior at times, but he could nonetheless judge the stable boys' tones of voice, their postures, their movements. None showed any sign of guilt or even hesitation; thus, Jonathan felt confident that none of them had been persuaded to create the damage themselves. Whomever had wished Willoughby ill had visited the stables personally.

One detail struck Jonathan with particular force. The lads informed him that Willoughby did not have one single favored horse, and thus no favored saddle. He would choose his mount on a particular day—or sometimes a day or two in advance. That did not mean he would choose the same one the next time, and some of his horses were well fit to more than one saddle. There was a total of eight saddles for gentlemen, kept at or near readiness at all times.

Given this: How could the guilty party have known which saddle would be chosen by Willoughby?

If that could not have been determined . . . was it possible that the cut girth was not meant to kill Willoughby but instead another member of the party, perhaps even Jonathan himself?

Chapter Twenty

What had been rumor became fact when word arrived that the new magistrate had at last been appointed—and was indeed Mr. Tremblay, the master of Whitwell, and brother-in-law to Colonel Brandon. Mr. Tremblay had written the pertinent authorities to confirm that, while his wife was not well enough to come with him, her health had improved sufficiently for her to remain contentedly in Avignon with his family. He would leave within the fortnight and be once again in Barton within the month.

This information was received with consternation in diverse quarters, for even more diverse reasons. Many believed that justice had been permanently thwarted; Brandon's brother-in-law would surely be in no rush to convict Brandon's wife, would he? Yet as the local tide had turned against blanket condemnation of Marianne Brandon, some also saw Tremblay's appointment as the best possible news, as he would be certain to protect this innocent woman, for her husband's sake if not for her own.

Brandon himself felt very different. He respected his brother-in-law for both his character and his judgment; however, he also knew Mr. Tremblay to be very sensitive to his honor, in particular any matter that might be considered a blemish upon it. After thinking more deeply upon this matter in the previous days, Brandon had realized how powerful the question of honor would prove in the case of Mrs. Willoughby. Tremblay would convict Marianne before he would ever allow it to be said that he had let her go out of partiality; he might well err on the side of condemnation.

Constables Hubbard and Baxter knew Mr. Tremblay also, though not so well as to be certain which way the man's sentiments would direct him. They agreed, however, that Tremblay's judgment on the matter of Mrs. Willoughby's death could not be unbiased. Better by far for them to make an arrest before Mr. Tremblay's arrival.

But the recent attempt on Mr. Willoughby raised an almost unsolvable question: Did they seek one murderer or two?

This very question much occupied all three of the young persons who had avowed themselves committed to the investigation. Their morning walk was later that day—a Sunday, and so time had to be made for church—but all were eager to express their points of view.

Jonathan said, "I think it can be but one murderer at work. How many persons could undertake such wickedness in such a small community, all within the space of weeks?"

Bamber would not be easily convinced of this. "I tell you now, Willoughby himself must have killed his wife; the business with the saddle was undoubtedly someone wishing to avenge her, and I would wager a hundred pounds that the perpetrator is Follett. What say you, Miss Tilney?"

She walked between the two of them, her bonnet and cloak much stirred by the autumn wind. "I see merits in both your positions. On one hand, these are two very different sorts of mischief. One crime is wholly unlike the other, and that tends to suggest two different minds conceived them. Yet consider: Why should Willoughby have been attacked *now*, when the entire community is already searching for a murderer?

Another attacker could, and in wisdom should, have waited some weeks or months before striking. I can fathom it only if the crimes are the work of a single killer—one who meant the poison for Willoughby, not his wife, and has become frustrated by that failure, frustrated entirely beyond patience."

"Or one soon to leave Devonshire, who must act upon his opportunity," Bamber pointed out. "Such as Mr. Follett."

"You suggest that Mr. Follett acted out of fondness for Mrs. Willoughby, yet our conversation during our portrait sittings suggests to me that he is angry with all women—myself included, but more importantly the late Mrs. Willoughby. He has much to say on the subject of women's fickleness. Nor have we adequately considered Miss Williams's potential guilt." Miss Tilney sighed in dismay. "Oh, we had just ceased running about in circles when the attempt on Willoughby was made and set us spinning once more."

Jonathan had wearied of the ambiguity, but he knew the pathway out. "Our discussions have been valuable, but we must investigate further. I suggest that each one of us direct efforts toward one of three main suspects—Mr. Willoughby, Mr. Follett, and Miss Williams. We search their homes, if possible; we engage them in conversation about the crimes. That which was concealed from the constables may be concealed no longer, and they will say things to us that they would never say to Hubbard or Baxter."

Bamber proved willing to take up the plan. "I shall speak with Willoughby, and you can speak to Follett—"

"I think not," Jonathan said. "Follett no longer appears to suspect me, but I do not think he is likely to converse at length with me, either."

"Let me try again to engage Mr. Follett in conversation during our next sitting," Miss Tilney suggested. "He has sent a note saying that he wishes me to pose again tomorrow. Although he has been unwelcoming to my questions before, eventually he must give way, and I have much to say to him about a certain *Fox*." Jonathan was most curious what Miss Tilney meant by this, but she continued on, "As for you, Mr. Darcy, your family's connection to Miss Williams allows you to call upon her, and as you said the two of you spoke very cordially, she may be more open with you."

It struck Jonathan then that, if Miss Williams were guilty, and he helped to prove it . . . he would be responsible for the deaths of not one but both of Wickham's children. Susannah, then Beth. He prayed his parents would never know the truth about Susannah's fate, but they had so hoped to meet Miss Williams—to glimpse some shadow of Susannah in her—and they would know Jonathan responsible for her death. In their inevitable sorrow, Jonathan would bear witness to the depths of the misery and anger that would overcome Mother and Father if ever they learned the truth about Susannah . . .

"Mr. Darcy?" Miss Tilney looked up at him in concern. "Are you unwell?"

"Not at all," he said. "Yes. Bamber will speak to Willoughby, you to Mr. Follett, and I to Miss Williams. We must hope that the shock of the attempt on Mr. Willoughby's life will have rattled the perpetrator near as much as the victim."

"If," added Mr. Bamber, "they do not prove to be one and the same."

Difficult conversations were being planned throughout Barton that day, for at the parsonage, Edward Ferrars had set about writing a letter and was grateful for his wife's help in doing so.

"Dear Mother—"

"Should you not speak more warmly?" Elinor suggested.

Edward had taken the settee from their parlor to his study, so that she might rest in relative comfort while they worked. "'Dearest Mama,' perhaps?"

"Had we been in the habit of such endearments before our estrangement, I might consider using them again. As we were not, however, it would seem most insincere to begin now."

Elinor could see the sense in this, nor did it surprise her that the proud Mrs. Ferrars had neither given warmth to her children nor expected much of it from them. "Very well, then. 'Dear Mother'—"

But already Edward had set down his pen. "I do not know whether I can write in sincerity, and if my words are not true and honest, then I do not know that this letter is more wicked than the continued estrangement."

No doubt he expected Elinor to urge him onward; only days before, she would have done precisely this. Yet she had been given time to consider the harm of false forgiveness, to both those pretending to give pardon and those who believed themselves pardoned. Yes, a renewed connection with the Ferrars family would likely benefit their child, who was so soon to be in this world . . . but Elinor also knew that advantage is not the same as necessity. Even the richest dowry could not benefit a daughter, nor an ample inheritance a son, whose father had sacrificed his integrity.

When at last she spoke, she said, "You will have many opportunities to write your mother once you feel you can speak to her honestly and truly. Yet if you send a letter that is not the truth of your heart, you will never have the opportunity to take it back."

How gently he smiled at her then. "That is a very rational conclusion—and a very deeply felt one, too. There are those who think practicality and an open heart cannot exist within the same soul, but you, my wife, are proof to the contrary."

"Marianne is rather more reasonable these days, my dearest." Elinor prepared to rise from the settee, then wondered if she still could. *Pray God my lying-in is very near,* she thought, *for I do not know how much longer I am to remain ambulatory.* Yet the next sound she heard was the scratch of a quill on paper.

When she looked over in surprise, Edward had begun his letter in earnest. Although he did not look up from his task, he had sensed her astonishment, for he said, "Your words have liberated me, Elinor. I shall write only what I can say in both honesty *and* kindness. If this be enough to heal the breach between my family and me, then let it be done. If it is not, then the breach remains their doing alone, and it will be theirs alone to set right should they ever choose."

Elinor praised his wisdom and determination, even as she privately wondered what the response to his letter would be. The elder Mrs. Ferrars would hold her son's honesty in as little regard as she ever had, and no doubt she still preferred obedience to openness. Yet from her own mother, Elinor had seen how avid the anticipation for a grandchild could be. Mrs. Ferrars had already been shown to be vulnerable to that sentiment.

The baby Elinor carried might ultimately create the bridge back to Edward's family, far more than anything he might write on this day. Yet she felt gladness that he had made his own decision, in justice and without malice, one that would sustain him no matter what else would come.

Word came to Delaford in the form of a note, which informed Marianne that the constables would arrive the following afternoon to speak with her further on the matter of Mrs. Willoughby's death. Although Marianne had dreaded such a communication since shortly after the murder, the certain knowledge of it shook her terribly. She lowered herself into a chair, dazedly grateful that Juliet was not in the house, because not even to such a friend as she could Marianne bear to reveal the depths of the terror she felt.

Perhaps this is justice, whispered a traitorous voice within. *You went unpunished for the murder you did commit, so now you must hang for one of which you are innocent.*

Marianne had worn a dress with a high neckline that day, and how she wished she had not, for the murmuring of the butler and steps in the hall told her that someone had returned to Delaford. She assumed it would be Juliet, as Colonel Brandon's business in Barton had been thought likely to take the whole of the day, but it was her husband who walked into the sitting room. At the sight of her, he exclaimed, "Good G-d, Marianne, are you unwell? What has happened?"

All the uncertainty and unease between them ceased to have any importance. She flung herself into Brandon's embrace, sobbing out her fear onto his shoulder.

"You will be here with me, will you not?" she cried. "For if I do not have you by my side, I do not know how I shall ever bear it."

"I will be with you," Brandon promised. *"Always."*

So deeply did his words strike her that Marianne almost thought it worth being blamed for a murder—this chance to know how powerful was her husband's love, and how sure she could be of him in all the days to come, regardless of anything that had transpired in the past, whether it regarded Mr. Willoughby; Brandon's first love, Eliza; or anyone else in all creation.

⁂

How best might she convince Mr. Follett to speak more openly with her? Juliet wondered whether, perhaps, provocation might prove instructive. Certainly amiability had not coaxed him into conversation. She must dare more.

So she mused, pondering the possibilities on her walk back to Delaford. Mr. Bamber had taken himself off promptly to begin his conversation with Mr. Willoughby; as for Miss Williams, Mr. Darcy had decided to wait until calling hours the next morning, which would indeed be the properest, and least suspicious, opportunity for him to pay such a visit. For the time being, they walked toward Delaford alone together.

Under other circumstances, this would have proved an excellent chance for conversation. Yet Mr. Darcy seemed so very troubled! Furthermore, if Juliet had interpreted his reactions correctly, the source of his concerns had something to do with Miss Williams.

Of course Mr. Darcy has a personal connection to Miss Williams, even if a rather oblique one. No doubt that would affect him. It may prick his conscience, using their acquaintance in such a way.

A brisk breeze sent autumn leaves dropping all around them, a waterfall of orange and gold, and yet Mr. Darcy paid no heed. Juliet stopped mid-walk, so forcibly did his inattention strike her.

This, at least, Darcy noted. "Miss Tilney? Is all well?"

"All is well with me," she said, "but I feared that it might not be so for you. If you will forgive my impertinence . . . it seems you were much concerned when we spoke of Miss Williams earlier. May I know why it troubles you so?"

Mr. Darcy stared at a spot somewhere to the left of her face. "It did not pertain to the investigation."

"Oh." Feeling the sting of the rebuke, Juliet took a step back. "Forgive me. I did not wish to presume."

Before she could turn to leave, he shook his head. "You did not. You wished to know whether I was well, and I am not."

"This relates to Miss Williams?" Juliet wondered first whether he had fallen in love with Beth, but surely not. Her own recent musings about romance must have been clouding her judgment.

"Long have I carried this secret," he began. "It is the most shameful of my life. In some ways you are the very last person I should ever wish to know it, and yet somehow you are the only person to whom I can imagine telling it."

She readied herself for what might prove a long hearing. "If it will help you to have a listener, then I am ready. If it would not, we may consider the whole matter forgotten."

"I know not where help is to be found, if indeed it can be. But silence has proved so wretched that I must speak."

Mr. Darcy told her, then, of his little cousin Susannah, how she had been nearly adopted by his family, and how the vile Mr. Wickham had insisted on her return while she remained unwell, resulting in the poor child's death. "All," Mr. Darcy said, "because he had learned that Susannah had begun calling my father 'Papa.' That wounded his pride, and for that reason alone, he risked—and lost—her life."

"How terrible for your family," Juliet said. "For you, for your parents, even in some sense for Mr. Wickham, for he was granted the gift of a child and did not possess soul enough to value her."

Although Mr. Darcy nodded, he still seemed greatly burdened. What else tormented him so? After several more moments, he spoke. "My parents know that Mr. Wickham learned of it—of Susannah calling my father 'Papa'—from one of her cousins. What they do not know is that . . . he learned the truth from me."

Juliet covered her mouth with her hand. Mr. Darcy's

remorse struck her as forcibly as any of her own ever had or could.

"I was traveling back from school, and I paid a visit along the way to my aunt Kitty's home. My aunts Kitty and Lydia were particularly close, you see, and so this aunt had far more patience and affection for Mr. Wickham than anyone else in the family, though even hers had been exhausted by the end. Suffice it to say that he was visiting as well, and when we spoke over brandy after dinner, I thought—I truly believed he would wish to know how Susannah recovered from her illness, but even more, how well and happy she usually was at Pemberley. He had so thoroughly neglected her that I foolishly concluded that he would find it a relief—the promise of her becoming a part of our family—and his responsibility no longer. Instead, he became angry. Resentful. He said my father had stolen everything else from him, but he'd be—" Mr. Darcy cut himself off before resuming, "That he should go to the devil before he would let Father have Susannah, too. Within two days he had written to Pemberley, demanding her return. They had to let her go. Within a fortnight, she was dead. None of this tragedy would have occurred had I not spoken so foolishly. If my parents ever knew of it—but no. As terrible as it would be for them to learn of it, I know my own guilt, and *that* is the knowledge that burdens me. I know it shall do so until the end of my days."

Mr. Darcy was almost overcome, and Juliet allowed him to regain some small measure of composure before she spoke. "What you have told me is grievous indeed. Yet you must understand, Mr. Darcy, none of this was your fault. You spoke honestly, and you said nothing that Mr. Wickham should have found shocking to hear."

She could, in truth, comprehend the sting of a father hearing another man called by that name, but that sting should surely arise out of love for the child, not mere pride. Had Wickham's unhappiness come from proper feeling, that same paternal emotion would have insisted upon Susannah remaining at Pemberley until she had been returned to health and strength.

"Yet he *did* find it shocking, and Susannah died as a result." Mr. Darcy's head hung low, as though it were heavy. "My parents would never forgive me, and I do not think I shall ever forgive myself."

Greatly daring, Miss Tilney took Mr. Darcy's hand. It was not improper to do so, if one were consoling another in great distress. "The wrong was all Mr. Wickham's, not your own. I do believe, truly, that your cousin in heaven looks down on you not with blame but with love."

"But if I were—were more like other people—" Mr. Darcy had to swallow hard before he could continue speaking. "If I understood more of the feelings and the resentments that go unspoken—then I would not have erred so."

"Do not wish yourself different, Mr. Darcy. You are a good, kindhearted man who is willing to do much, even to risk himself, for the well-being of others. You are honest and true. No other merits could ever compare to these."

He looked up at her then, meeting her eyes for longer than he ever had before. Juliet became very aware of his hand in her own. Quietly he said, "I thank you, Miss Tilney. I will think long upon what you have said. Yet none of this can release me from fearing for Miss Williams. How could I tell my parents that she has met a fate even worse than her sister's?"

"If harm comes to Miss Williams because of the fates of the Willoughbys, then that is her own doing." Juliet released his hand, bringing the conversation back to the conventional. As refreshing as she found the honesty between them, she sensed that, to both of them, a return to politeness would come as something of a relief. "My mother always says, do not mourn a tragedy before it happens, for then if it comes to pass, you must mourn twice—and if it does not, you have felt sorrow where it was not necessary. Take heart, and do your duty."

So it was that Jonathan set out on Monday morning to call upon Miss Williams. As it happened, he left Allenham at almost precisely the same moment as Mr. Follett, who was on his way to Delaford with his easel and paints. Follett ignored Jonathan so completely that his barbed inattention was more conspicuous than any attention might have been.

Just as well, then, thought Jonathan, *that I was not chosen to speak to him.* In truth, however, he would have preferred any task other than the one that awaited him in Barton village.

Upon his arrival at Miss Williams's house, the servant seemed most uncertain about how to welcome a visitor; it occurred to Jonathan that very few must arrive, aside from Colonel Brandon. The fact of his cousin's social isolation had never struck him as pointedly as it did that day, when the sheer improbability of an expected visitor seemed to set the house akilter. When at last he was shown into the parlor, Miss Williams sat there with all the propriety he would have expected from any gentlewoman—but her countenance revealed her disquiet.

"Miss Williams," Jonathan began, "if I have called at an inconvenient time—"

"Indeed you have not, sir. Rather, I am much in need of counsel from an impartial person."

Jonathan did not share her certainty of his impartiality, but that, he supposed, must depend on the matter at issue. "How may I help you?"

"Is it ever moral to sustain a deceit? Not merely a lack of candor but true dishonesty—not merely toward one unworthy person but to all who may be encountered?"

This struck him as potentially far more pertinent to the investigation than any conversation he had planned. Jonathan knew he would receive more information if he told her no, that deceit was ever unworthy, that truth must reign. Yet the distress in Miss Williams's countenance kept him from his own deceit; he must answer her honestly. "Not every truth must be shared. Indeed, in propriety, many can never be spoken save to one's intimates, or even spoken aloud at all. Where deceit will cause harm to others, yes, it must be revealed. But not every secret can be so considered." Once more Jonathan thought of his mistake with Mr. Wickham, the truth he had told that had caused such harm . . . but though the remembrance must ever pain him, Miss Tilney's words had proved a powerful balm. He could maintain his composure enough to consider the morality of his own deception, the certainty that, as much as his secret's revelation would hurt him, it would cause far more pain to Mother and Father. "Where justice and compassion are best served by silence, then, yes, the deceit may be maintained. If instead others are harmed by silence, then it is immoral not to speak."

Miss Williams's features betrayed the greatest relief. "Thank you most kindly, Mr. Darcy. You have set my thoughts right, of that I am certain. How may I help you, sir?"

Jonathan simply prattled on then about the weather and the goodness of Colonel Brandon, as any other visitor might, for he believed the question Miss Williams had posed had revealed more truth than any of those he had planned to ask himself.

Juliet sat for Mr. Follett with more impatience than usual. Partly this could be attributed to the inevitable boredom of the artist's model; also to be considered was Marianne's distress as the visit of the constables drew nigh, and Juliet's wish to relieve her hostess of this terrible burden. Above all, however, it was curiosity that worked at her. How badly she wished to know the truth! How much she wished to help reveal it!

Alarmingly, Mr. Follett could detect the shift in her mood. "You are as fidgety as a child today," he said. "It is easier to paint fine ladies' lapdogs than it is to paint you."

"It seems as though you would prefer lapdogs to any human model," she replied, "as you so dislike any show of desire, will, or even thought in those you paint."

He stared at her. In truth she felt the impudence of her remarks, but today she was resolved to shake him. He demanded, "What is the point of thought in a model?"

"I should think a truly skilled painter would welcome the chance to portray not mere features but also feeling and sense. Do not the best portraits reveal such?"

Mr. Follett's patience—never in great supply—had already been exhausted. "I cannot paint what is not there, Miss Tilney."

Juliet remained steadfast, never shifting from the pose he had set her in. "Have you considered that the flaw may not be in your model but in your perception? Are you so certain that you see true?"

This, she thought, would provoke him to speak on the faithlessness of women, the emptiness of their souls, and from that she could turn the conversation to Mrs. Willoughby. Follett might be angered past the point of caution.

Instead, he said, "Then come and look, and say to me how much you believe I have seen."

Mr. Follett gestured at his easel. After a moment's hesitation, Juliet rose from her chair and went to examine the painting in progress. Before, when she had seen it, her face had been blurred and indistinct, her features entirely absent. Now, however—now she felt as though she were looking in a mirror, one determined to compliment her and to erase all shortcomings. Was her complexion truly so porcelain? Her dark hair so abundant and soft? Almost, but not quite. Truth had neither been fully told nor greatly abused.

What struck her the most, however, was the ... *tenderness* of the image. In this painting Mr. Follett had captured not only Juliet's likeness but also her spirit: uncertainty, hope, freshness, all could be seen. She would never have believed him capable of such delicacy and perception. Indeed, his skill impressed her thoroughly. For the moment, Juliet could only think, *Could the eye capable of such insight be so unkind toward one he had once loved?*

Could such gentility and refinement of feeling belong to a murderer?

She glanced over at him and saw that his anger had been swept aside, like a curtain drawn so that a view through a window could be seen. Juliet would have wagered that much of Mr. Follett's haughty, ill-tempered talk during their sittings had been bluster, meant to distract her and to disguise the more tender man within.

Mr. Follett was vulnerable now, however, and Juliet seized

the chance to use her sharpest blade. "What can you tell me of the *Fox?*"

He started at her. "I beg your pardon?"

"The ship. The one whose sailing was lately advertised in the *Times*. The one you had spoken of to Mrs. Willoughby."

Mr. Follett took a halting sideways step; Juliet's question had quite literally staggered him. "How do you know of this?"

"What I know, others know. If you do not fear the truth, I urge you to tell it."

He sat heavily in the nearest chair. "I intend to resettle in the United States. Cousins of mine have prospered in a city called Philadelphia; I intend to join them there and forge a new life. It is a new nation, one eager to make its mark. Its people will want portraits, and they have not nearly so many artists—at least, I have heard so. Though I have not yet chosen a date of departure, I considered booking passage on the imminent sailing of the *Fox*. I thought—I thought Sophia should know that. But it did not matter to her. Not in the slightest." He swore an oath that turned Juliet's cheeks and ears quite red to hear it as he rose. "Enough of this. Enough of memory. Enough."

With this, Mr. Follett stalked out of the house, leaving Delaford behind without waiting to hear anything Miss Tilney might have said in return.

At the constabulary, both Hubbard and Baxter were readying themselves for the walk to Delaford. Their courage had been fortified through a luncheon of good ale, better bread, and excellent cheese, yet each found reasons to hesitate a moment longer, then another. Although both men were much impressed with their status as enforcers of the law, and had even felt the headiness of knowing themselves answerable to no authority for some time to come . . . they also understood the standing of Colonel Brandon. His family had owned Delaford for well more than a century, and fully half the families in Barton owed some part of their sustenance and prosperity to that estate. True, Brandon had as yet raised no objection to any of their efforts, but if ever that were to change, surely it would come when his wife was directly threatened. To challenge one of the leading landowners of Barton—to suggest that his wife might be dragged away to gaol or even to the gallows—required courage. Neither Hubbard nor Baxter lacked that virtue, but they required some time to summon it in sufficient quantity.

Then came deliverance in the form of Mr. Bamber, who arrived half out of breath despite his youth and strength. "Good sirs," said he, "I have a request to make of you, one that may help us identify Mrs. Willoughby's murderer for once and for all."

Hubbard and Baxter exchanged glances before Hubbard said, "A request? How are we to give you knowledge that we do not ourselves possess?"

"It is not knowledge I require, only a bit of arsenic." Bamber glowed with the pride of accomplishment. "Specifically the arsenic found in Mrs. Willoughby's glass. I have developed a new test that can prove that it was *precisely this* arsenic that killed her."

The constables were much impressed by this information. Baxter asked the question both men shared: "You mean that the arsenic would have come from this container and no other?"

"That is precisely my meaning, sir. And as we know that this was the poison sold to Mr. Willoughby—poison he attempted to hide from you—poison Mr. Follett is unlikely to have known about and to which Mrs. Brandon had no access whatsoever—then we shall know Willoughby is all but certainly the killer. If it is not the same, then we will have a stranger mystery to unweave." Bamber hesitated before saying, in the gravest tone, "But I think it will be the same. Do not you?"

Hubbard and Baxter were in total agreement with Mr. Bamber, and they were deeply gladdened by his news. For not only did they now seem closer than ever to solving Mrs. Willoughby's murder, but they had no more reason to search Delaford.

Chapter Twenty-One

To possess an extraordinary skill is to wish to display that skill. The grandiose find every possible excuse to do so, while the judicious make no great show of their talents, but instead simply use them as circumstance commands. Jonathan was highly judicious about his skills at cards and billiards, and this—plus Willoughby's distaste for losing any manner of competition or game—had kept him from engaging in either while at Allenham.

Yet Mr. Bamber, instead of questioning Willoughby as they had planned, confessed to Jonathan that he had instead been much engaged in his laboratory since receiving a portion of the arsenic found within the Allenham stables. His eagerness was entirely understandable, and indeed, it appeared likely that these test results alone would all but solve the case.

However, in the interests of fairness and completeness, Jonathan decided to tempt Willoughby into conversation that afternoon. He felt the best means of doing so would be a billiards match. If Willoughby became angered by losing, so be it.

Jonathan had previously noted that people sometimes spoke more freely when agitated, even unadvisedly so, so he had gone so far as to hope that his host's displeasure would work to his advantage. Thus far, however, he had succeeded only in making Willoughby exceedingly cross.

"You cannot be serious," Willoughby said as Jonathan lined up a shot, one which would require the ball to ricochet off two sides of the table before hitting his chosen target. "That is beyond your power."

"We shall see," Jonathan replied. He then sank the shot. Willoughby swore but said nothing further. What questions might best draw him out? "Have you heard nothing from the constables?"

"They have yet to identify the person responsible for sabotaging my saddle," Willoughby said. "Rest assured that neither they nor I will rest until the wrongdoer is found out."

"I meant, regarding what they found during their search of Allenham."

Willoughby's face flushed. "That must have been where Sophia hid her arsenic, so that none of the servants would find it. Like as not, it would have gone unfound until spring—or one of the servants might simply have tossed it out as refuse."

Jonathan plunged ahead. "You still believe her to have taken her own life?"

"I am sorry to say it, but I do." Willoughby paused then, cue in his hands, bent over the cloth surface of the billiard table. Only then did Jonathan realize that some of Willoughby's devil-may-care attitude was mere pretense. "I did not always despise her, you know. When we were in London, we had some fine times together. She loved me at first, truly."

"Before she knew you better."

"Your accidental insults sometimes cut deeper than most deliberate attempts to wound, Thumps." Willoughby gave Jonathan a dark look before taking his next shot in the game. "The truth is, my heart was elsewhere—as I believe you well know—and that is the sin no woman can forgive. Marrying her was a great wrong to Sophia as well as to myself."

Jonathan noted that Willoughby seemed to feel himself exceptionally thoughtful, having actually considered the effects of his marriage on his wife. But Willoughby did not dwell on it long, not while there was a game to be played. He took yet another shot, missed, and swore again before nodding at Jonathan to take his turn.

As he lined up his next shot, Jonathan considered Willoughby's theory. Could this be true? Could his wife have died by her own hand? Almost certainly not. Mrs. Willoughby had been angry, contemptuous, uninterested in her husband—but not despairing. Besides, if she had wanted to end her own life, she could have chosen a means less painful, and one that would have not caused such a humiliating loss of control in company.

Did Willoughby even believe his own theory? This was possible, but Jonathan had doubts.

Jonathan shot and sank yet another ball. "The game is mine, Willoughby."

"So it would appear." Willoughby seemed to think the best response to defeat was to choose a pursuit at which Jonathan would be less likely to excel. "I have a mind to go shooting. The entire party would benefit from a day out of doors, don't you think?"

Jonathan strongly disliked shooting, though not for any reason Willoughby was likely to respect. Fortunately, another and more serious objection presented itself as he edged toward his next shot. "The house is in mourning, sir. No shooting parties should be—"

"To blazes with mourning!" Willoughby gestured so violently with his cue that Jonathan half thought he might snap it in two. "Am I to sit in this house moldering a year of my life away, all for her sake? It may be *proper*, Thumps, but I tell you, mourning is a barbarity and already I am weary of it." He set the cue down and went toward the door, saying as he did so, "I shall go ask the groundskeeper how long it would take to arrange a shooting party. Like as not we can tromp upon the grounds this very afternoon."

Would the groundskeeper actually comply? Jonathan suspected the response would be neither compliance nor outright refusal, but many delays for reasons of varying validity, probably until Willoughby gave up the idea and reverted to the strictures of mourning. Willoughby had always made great pronouncements as to how little he cared for the opinions of others, which held true only so long as he remained certain that he was in fact greatly admired. He lacked the resolve to defy public opinion in such a matter as this, and probably even possessed the reason to understand that he should at minimum hold to the rituals of mourning at least until his wife's murderer had been caught.

So Jonathan mused as he put away his cue and idly glanced out the window—then startled. There, darting behind the hedge, was the woman in the blue cloak!

She was leaving the grounds. Wasting no time, Jonathan ran downstairs as quickly as he could. He reached the front door only to be confronted by Follett, who had just returned from a painting session upon the grounds, and the servant assisting him.

"The woman outside," Jonathan began. "Did you see her? Wearing a blue cloak, hurrying away from Allenham?"

"I saw no such," Follett said. "Is there a trespasser on the loose?"

"I do not know," Jonathan said, "nor do I know any harm of her. But I would have wished to speak with her, if possible."

A loud bang from deep within the house made them all jump; the servant nearly dropped Follett's items. Follett cried, "By G-d, that was a gunshot!"

The men hastened to the back area of the house, specifically to the gun room, where a smoking shotgun with a half-split barrel lay on the stone floor. Soot stained Willoughby's shirt and hands. He stared down at the weapon in shock. "It—it exploded," Willoughby said, stepping away from the gun. "I merely went to check it, and it should not have even been loaded, but somehow this has happened."

"There is no 'somehow' about it," Follett said darkly. "Guns can malfunction, even explode, but only when they are loaded. If this one was loaded secretly—packed with powder—"

Jonathan said, "You mean, someone has tampered with the gun, in the hopes of causing harm."

Follett nodded. Willoughby, though shaken, said, "Fetch the constables at once." The servant dashed off to fulfill his master's command.

Someone truly was attempting to kill Willoughby, and it appeared the attempts would not end until Willoughby was dead.

Juliet had prepared herself to brace Marianne for the questioning to come, as had Colonel Brandon. The feeling in Delaford was not so different, she suspected, from that in a medieval castle under siege.

Yet within an hour of the constables' anticipated arrival, another note came, which explained that Mrs. Brandon was not to be questioned today—with the suggestion that the entire idea of her questioning had been abandoned.

"What can be the meaning of it?" Marianne wondered as Juliet sat by her side, studying the letter. "Do they mean to torment me by extending the suspense? For as much as I dreaded their arrival, I cannot think of anything more horrid than more hours or days of such dread."

"Do not be uneasy," Colonel Brandon said. "This may mean that they have discovered the true murderer and henceforth will leave you in peace."

"Then why do they not say so?" Marianne closed her eyes. "This is unendurable."

Colonel Brandon sat on the other side of his wife and took her hand, which she grasped with great feeling. Juliet had already realized that the Brandons had mended their quarrel, but only in this moment did she glimpse some of the true strength of the bond between them. Marianne could turn to him in her moments of greatest need; Brandon would support her, regardless of what travail might come.

This is what marriage should be, Juliet thought, *and when it is my time, I shall not settle for anything less.*

The sound of a visitor arriving at the door made Marianne grimace, but as it happened, the butler showed in Mrs. Jennings. "It seems, Mrs. Brandon, that you have not heard, for we find you in such distress! Soon as I discovered the news, I said to myself, 'They must hear this at Delaford at once!'"

With what Juliet considered great patience, Marianne said, "Tell me what, Mrs. Jennings?"

"Why, the constables are not to come to Delaford at all, for someone has tried to kill Mr. Willoughby again but made a poor job of it once more, as Mr. Willoughby is by all reports well. But the constables will be so busy at Allenham that they will have no time to trouble you." Mrs. Jennings beamed down at Marianne, her cheer infectious. "Is that not the best of news?"

This might prove but a brief reprieve, and all present knew it. But Juliet could see that even this small mercy had much restored Marianne's spirit.

"Indeed it is," Colonel Brandon said. "You have given us much comfort, and we are grateful to you."

Marianne laughed softly. Although her face remained pale and her eyes red, Juliet could see strength returning to her. "There can be no true good in any of this, not when a young woman has been so cruelly killed, yet I shall ever be glad for the loyalty and kindness you have all shown me."

Juliet silently prayed, *May Mr. Bamber's test prove true, so that my friend can be spared and given some peace.*

The constables and Willoughby shared a determination to search Allenham anew for any evidence pertaining to the tampering with the shotgun. Jonathan excused himself as soon as he decently could.

"What do you mean by this, Darcy?" Bamber asked. His sheen of pride had dimmed in the confusion following this second attempt on Willoughby's life. "Do not you wish to resolve this matter?"

"I do," said Jonathan, "and that is why I must go, for the woman in the pale blue cloak was lately seen nearby."

He set out on the walk from Allenham with few hopes; the woman had left some minutes earlier, more than long enough to make an escape. Yet within but a short time, he caught sight of her ambling ahead—and this was the correct word, for there was no urgency in her manner, no sense of secrecy as he had detected before. Did Miss Williams think herself safe and thus free to take an afternoon stroll, ignorant of whether Willoughby lived or died?

Jonathan followed at too great a distance to observe her features. But as he observed her demeanor, he became more and more certain of one key fact: the woman in the pale blue cloak was not Miss Williams.

He had new suspicions of her identity; and if he was correct, he had no answers but more questions than ever before.

Oh glorious day, Marianne thought. *Let the skies be cloudy, let the cold wind blow, for in my spirit shines a summertime no frost can ever steal.*

What she felt was not unalloyed happiness; her mixed feelings regarding Willoughby's potential guilt weighed too heavily upon her for that. Yet Marianne had learned that happiness unmixed with sorrow was likely not happiness at all, merely illusion. Suspicion still threatened her, but she had insight enough to recognize that the further strange, threatening activities at Allenham would draw more of that suspicion away from her. It seemed very possible that the constables' attention had been diverted toward likelier persons.

Margaret arrived then, quite on her own, merely hoping for a visit. Brandon had the wisdom to tell the maids to bring some tea and biscuits, so that they might take the opportunity for some companionship and merriment on what they had thought would be a dark day indeed. Juliet spoke of Mr. Bamber's cleverness, and Marianne wondered whether she should invite him as well.

When yet another visitor arrived, Marianne said only, "It appears we are holding a party unawares—oh! How lucky it is you, Mr. Darcy!"

"The constables are no longer coming to search Delaford, so we are all happy together," Margaret explained.

Jonathan Darcy seemed to be surprised at the merry scene, as well he might be. Still, Marianne fully expected him to join them. Instead, after a brief pause, he said, "I am very glad for your deliverance, Mrs. Brandon. However, I am here on other business."

"Whatever do you mean?" Marianne said.

"I followed someone here," Mr. Darcy said. "When I departed Allenham, I saw her at a great distance—a young woman wearing a pale blue cloak, whom I believe to be the same one previously seen near both Barton Park and Allenham at significant times. Clearly she is not the killer, so I only wish to know what her true business has been."

No one in the room knew what to think—save Margaret, who blurted out, "I *knew* someone was following me!"

Following this, the conversation became rather muddled for a time. Margaret, greatly distressed at being found out, at first refused to explain, and then insisted that everyone must leave the room save her sister before she would speak a word. As the matter finally settled, Marianne kept both Miss Tilney and Mr. Darcy with her while the colonel distracted Mrs. Jennings as best he could in another room. Margaret's face remained flushed with embarrassment, even as Marianne said gently, "We will not be angry with you, I promise. But your presence at those houses, at those times! It must be explained. We must have the truth."

"I like my new brother very much," Margaret began, sniffling. "Please tell Colonel Brandon that I am very glad he has married you. I only thought—I wished for Willoughby to be our friend again, and Willoughby told me he wished that, too."

Juliet and Mr. Darcy shared a look as Marianne straightened. "Willoughby came to you?"

"We saw each other in Barton one morning—Mama was busy in the market, while I stood nearby—and he said how much he hoped we would all be friends together again someday," Margaret said. "He knew you would not forgive him unless he was able to ask you properly, so he asked if I would deliver his notes."

"So that is how they have turned up!" Marianne exclaimed. "I thought it some trickery of his."

"So it is," Mr. Darcy said, "though of a different sort."

"But that first night," Juliet said, "the night of Mrs. Willoughby's death . . . Whatever were you doing there upon that occasion?" Marianne realized the penetration of this question right away: it seemed unlikely that Willoughby would have asked Margaret to risk discovery on an evening when he would be perfectly capable of delivering his own notes to Marianne Brandon.

Margaret hung her head. "I only wished to see the pretty gowns that all the women would be wearing. You both looked very well indeed."

Very gently, Mr. Darcy said, "You went to Allenham this morning, so I suppose he has given you yet another note."

Shamefaced, Margaret reached into her tiny reticule and pulled out a folded sheet of paper. Marianne took it—some part of her longed to know what might be written there—but the other, better, part of her triumphed. She crumpled the paper and threw it into the fireplace, which made Margaret gasp.

Marianne took her little sister's hands. "Listen to me, Margaret, and mark my words: we cannot be friends as we were with Mr. Willoughby, not ever again. You have heard us say so, but you must accept that it is true. Nothing can ever change that, least of all trickery and deceit."

"But I do not think he has killed his wife, and I know that he is very sorry for how he acted before!" Margaret protested.

"I know that, too," Marianne said. "His regret may someday amend his behavior, but it has not done so yet. Consider, Margaret. If Willoughby had truly changed, if he were committed to doing right henceforth, would he ask this of you? Would he urge you to lie to your mother and sisters? Would he ask you to hide his letters where I would find them if he thought that any open, respectable correspondence was possible?"

Juliet added, "He has put you at some risk, Miss Dashwood. It is unsafe for a young woman to go running about alone after dark, and he even brought you very near a murderer! Willoughby could not ask a girl of your age to take such risks, not if he had learned from his past mistakes."

This made more of an impression on Margaret than anything her family had said so far. "Oh, I had not thought of that."

"You are not to go to Allenham again," Marianne said, "and if Willoughby approaches you, tell him good day and walk away."

"Will you tell Mama?" Margaret looked even younger than her years in that moment, and so Marianne took pity.

"No, there is no need for that, as long as you do not undertake any more of Mr. Willoughby's errands ever again." Marianne sighed as she turned to Mr. Darcy. "So you set out to follow the intruder across the countryside? How intrepid of you! It might have been a far more dangerous character, for all that you knew."

"I began to pursue her," Mr. Darcy said, "but then a far more alarming event occurred. Only after that was settled was I able to follow in earnest."

"Wait," said Juliet, "you must say: What was this alarming event at Allenham?"

Marianne was prepared for almost anything Mr. Darcy might have said other than what emerged: "There has been another attempt on Mr. Willoughby's life."

Before the afternoon was through, a few other callers had come to share their happiness and relief with the Brandons ... including, Juliet noted, many who had been sparse with their support during the time of greatest doubt. The public mood had clearly turned. These guests were all received with civility, yet she did not doubt that the Brandons would forever remember who had and had not shown true loyalty.

Others of the callers, however, were those whom they could welcome with all their heart, such as Sir John Middleton, Mrs. Dashwood, and Mr. Edward Ferrars (though the latter was obliged to promise that the maids were watching Elinor every moment, before any of the Dashwood women could entirely enjoy his company). Mr. Darcy did not stay very long; Juliet did not need to be told that this was because he wished to learn more about Willoughby's would-be murderer.

Given the importance of the inquiries at Allenham, Juliet was somewhat surprised to see Mr. Bamber arrive at Delaford not three quarters of an hour after Mr. Darcy's departure. Her surprise was not unpleasant, however, and certainly his warm words to Marianne demonstrated his good nature. "You cannot know, Mrs. Brandon, how greatly concerned we have all been for your sake! The mere idea that you could have done this—why, it was laughable, or ought to have been. These doings at Allenham will entirely exonerate you, of this I am certain."

"Thank you, Mr. Bamber. I will always remember your kindness and friendship throughout this time of trial." Marianne smiled toward Juliet. "If you would entertain our guest? I should speak further to Mama." With that she glided away. Juliet knew full well that Marianne and Mrs. Dashwood had already talked at length. She had intended only to give Mr. Bamber a chance to speak.

Speak he did. "Our investigations are less complicated now, are they not, Miss Tilney?"

"They are changed," she said, "but far from over. We have certainly lost one of our key suspects in Mrs. Willoughby's death, for the true identity of the woman in the pale blue cloak has been revealed."

Mr. Bamber listened in astonishment as Juliet—finally out of earshot of those who did not need to know of Willoughby's notes—explained how young Margaret Dashwood's errands had confused their efforts. When all had been told, he said, "Truth be told, I never considered Miss Williams to be very likely. Motive she had, I grant you, but she could scarce have expected Mrs. Willoughby's death to change her situation. So she had no reason to take such a risk."

"Regardless, it appears she did not," said Juliet. "Given the attempts on Willoughby's life, must we assume that Follett is guilty of all?"

"It is shocking indeed." Mr. Bamber shook his head, his emotion clearly genuine and great. "But if Willoughby is guilty, and Follett strongly suspects this, might he not be striking about at Willoughby, hoping to enact vengeance for Mrs. Willoughby's sake? We must hope to prove the truth before Follett makes himself a murderer, too."

Mr. Bamber's mind seemed quite made up, but Juliet trusted he was proud enough of his newly invented test for arsenic to fully trust its result, even if it tended to exonerate Willoughby. She said only, "We shall see."

"Regardless, it seems unlikely that Willoughby should invite me to Devonshire in the near future," Bamber said, "nor should I accept if he did. It is hard to think that I may never again encounter the friends I have made here." He hesitated a long moment before daring to add, "Most particularly you, Miss Tilney."

Mr. Bamber had not declared himself, but he intended to do so. Juliet saw that now, without any doubt. She knew his heart, and in that instant, she also knew her own.

She said only, "I do not expect I shall visit Devonshire again soon, either. We must enjoy our time in Barton while we possess it."

He seemed unsure what to make of this, but for the moment, that would do. Juliet very much hoped for his sake that he would not put her in a position to refuse him outright—what a blow to his pride it would be! The clever, good-natured Mr. Bamber deserved better than that. He deserved a wife who might love him with her whole heart, and that would never be Juliet Tilney.

Many weeks would pass, she felt sure, before she would entirely be able to set aside her thoughts of Mr. Darcy. Alas, it appeared he did not care for her in that way, and Juliet was determined to appreciate his friendship on its own merits. If that friendship had awakened in her a desire for more—if that desire was to be forever thwarted—at least it had showed her the trust and openness that was possible between man and woman, and she would settle for no less in a husband.

Nor had Mr. Darcy been her only teacher. Across the room, Colonel Brandon and Marianne stood side by side, speaking with Edward Ferrars. They were in many senses an unlikely pair, and their union was not without disagreement—but Juliet did not doubt the great love between them. She would never settle for a merely suitable match now that she had learned what was truly possible.

ري

At Allenham, Willoughby had sequestered himself in his room. Jonathan half wondered if he had pushed heavy furniture against the door to keep himself safe, then realized this could not be so. *That would keep out the servants,* he thought, *and not even peril to his life would induce John Willoughby to empty his own chamber pot.*

Bamber had gone to the Brandons and apparently intended to stay a good while. This left Jonathan isolated at Allenham with only Follett for company, a situation displeasing to both men.

"Do you think we can leave next week?" Follett asked. He sat on a low sofa, his hand cradling a snifter of brandy. "The weather has turned abominable—I cannot paint—and Mr. Willoughby requires no comfort." More quietly he continued, "Mrs. Willoughby will be more decently mourned elsewhere."

"I have written to my parents for guidance," Jonathan said. His father generally knew what was and was not to be done. Follett did not seem much impressed with this answer, however, and thus sank deeper into both the sofa and the brandy.

Jonathan did not regret the lack of conversation, as his own thoughts tended in a different direction. As soon as opportunity presented itself, he left the room as though to return to his own bedchamber. Instead, he quietly went to the gun room.

The sun was low in the sky, and no lamps had been lit here, so Jonathan had to peer through shadow. The air still smelled thickly of gunpowder. Apparently the constables had determined that the gun had been interfered with through the packing of far too much gunpowder into the cartridge, which might ignite with any sudden movement. Hubbard had said, "Lucky thing they did not use too much, for that could have taken your hands off, Mr. Willoughby—if not your head."

Ample stores of gunpowder surrounded them. The assailant could have used as much as was necessary, or even more. Maybe they had meant to avoid harm to another person who might have been near Willoughby . . . but they could have been no more certain that Willoughby would be the next person to hold that gun than they could have known which saddle Willoughby would use.

Which meant there was only one person this attacker could possibly be.

Chapter Twenty-Two

Spring is often considered the most fickle and changeable season, but autumn possesses trickery enough to be its equal. The colder days that had settled over Barton of late gave way to easier temperatures, and in the bright morning, Jonathan felt emboldened to ask the others whether they might not walk into Barton. He pointed out, "Even the strictures of mourning do not prevent a man from conducting necessary business," and that suggestion of freedom proved sufficient to move Willoughby. Although Follett declined, as had become his wont, Jonathan, Willoughby, and Bamber set out for the village before noon.

Willoughby seemed more engaged in the journey that in the destination. Jonathan noted how he studied the roads, particularly the path that would lead most directly to Delaford. Many were out and about, either taking care of errands or simply enjoying the fine morning, but none of those proved to be Marianne Brandon. This, Jonathan felt sure, was the only person Willoughby sought.

He has done much for her attention, Jonathan thought, *but pays little attention to her in return. If he did, he would notice that she does not wish for his company, no matter how much he wishes for hers.*

Follett's refusal to leave the house also demanded Jonathan's consideration. Was it natural for him to wish to remain in a house he so despised? Or did Follett want to avoid observation—particularly by the constables? Little aside from his desire to paint Miss Tilney would move him from the confines of Allenham. No doubt this was due to his professional ambitions . . .

Or was the truth possibly darker? Had Follett's fascination with, and contempt of, the late Mrs. Willoughby been transferred to Miss Tilney? Jonathan knew this to be unlikely, yet the thought disquieted him all the same.

In Barton, Jonathan made sure that their steps took them toward the constabulary. Only after it was within sight did he say, "We should speak to Hubbard and Baxter. No doubt they have further questions about the incidents at Allenham."

"Why should I plead for their attention?" Willoughby said. "I can see no need for it. Should they not be working to find the person who wishes to harm me, without my having to *request* their efforts?"

Jonathan replied, "There is often a very great gap between what *should be* and what *is*."

Bamber gave Jonathan a curious look—he had discerned how careful Jonathan's words were, even if Willoughby had not—but said nothing himself. Willoughby, meanwhile, had warmed to the idea. "Yes, let them ask their questions. Let me be seen to present myself to them. The community no doubt wonders greatly at it."

"What other topic could ever interest them as much as you?" Mr. Bamber said in a low tone, though not so low that Willoughby failed to hear it and shoot Bamber a dark look.

"Your impudence does you no credit," Willoughby said. "You have been finding fault with Allenham and with me since your arrival. You see rats in the kitchens, you excuse yourself at every opportunity, and you pester me about a greenhouse requiring repair."

Although Bamber had learned to defend himself and others from Willoughby when needed, he seemed to understand the necessity of placating his host from time to time. "I myself have done the work in the greenhouse, so do not take that as a slight."

These soothing words had their effect, for Willoughby's temper improved. He even smiled as he said, "I suppose I cannot blame you for leaving Allenham, considering the inducement of the lovely Miss Tilney."

Bamber's expression shifted in a manner Jonathan could not read. "Very lovely indeed."

Jonathan wondered greatly what might have transpired between Bamber and Miss Tilney, but it did not appear that more information would be forthcoming at present. Jonathan did not wish to ask further questions on the matter, yet he could scarce think of any other subject, and therefore was much relieved to note that they had at last reached the constabulary.

Only Hubbard was present. "How can I help you gentlemen?"

"We are here to help you, sir," Jonathan said. "I believe we know the identity of the person who has been targeting Mr. Willoughby."

Both Willoughby and Bamber stared, and Hubbard did not seem convinced. "Who is it, then?"

Jonathan knew this next to be a risk, but he knew his man well enough to feel encouraged about his chances. "It is Mr. Willoughby himself."

Both Hubbard and Bamber seemed shocked into silence by his words, but it was Willoughby's reaction Jonathan sought—and Willoughby did not react at all. This confirmed Jonathan's suspicions; Willoughby was an accomplished liar, but he would make much of the truth when it served him. Had Willoughby been innocent, he would have responded to the accusation loudly and angrily. The way he drew himself upright, pressed his lips into a thin line: those were the telltale signs of guilt.

Such would not suffice for the constable, however, so Jonathan continued: "Neither of the attempts to murder Mr. Willoughby were effective—and, indeed, they *could not* have been effective. The small amount of gunpowder in the shotgun that exploded was scarcely more than it would take to get off a shot. Nobody familiar with shotguns could expect that to kill anyone; the worst that was risked was a slight injury to the hand. Also, the saddle could only have been tampered with by someone who knew which saddle Willoughby would choose, and only Willoughby knew that. The girth gave way while Willoughby was riding slowly; I had noted how he did not join in a good gallop with the rest of us. But he rode slowly because he knew the girth would break, and by moderating his speed, he ensured that he would suffer no worse than a tumble."

"I say," Bamber murmured, "that struck me, too, how slowly he was riding."

Jonathan said, "I put it to you that any person who had the freedom to do these things also had the freedom to do much worse—and, had they actually wished to kill Willoughby, would have done so. Such half-hearted and harmless efforts can only be attributed to Willoughby himself."

Hubbard might not have known Willoughby as well as Jonathan did, but he had sensed that Willoughby's response was not that of an innocent man. "Well, Mr. Willoughby? What say you to this?"

"Absurd." Willoughby's tone gave the lie to his words, for he could scarcely utter them. "Why should I do such a thing?"

"For two reasons," Jonathan said. "First, to create the impression that you were as much the target of a killer as your wife—and, therefore, that you could not be her killer yourself.

Second, to engage the interest and sympathy of those around you, most particularly Mrs. Brandon."

Her name awakened Willoughby's anger. "How dare you, sir? How dare you speculate upon my—my—"

"It is not speculation. It is fact." Jonathan glanced at Hubbard, who as a local man probably knew the story. "As a result of the events at Donwell Abbey, I came to know more about the history of Colonel and Mrs. Brandon." He saw no need to mention Miss Tilney's part in the transmission of this information, for he had no doubt she had spoken truly. "You loved her and would have married her, but for the money. Having acquired the money upon losing your wife, you wished to reclaim Mrs. Brandon's affections. But I believe you very much mistake her if you think she is likely to be impressed by such as this."

"Here is what *I* think," Hubbard interjected. "I think none of this can be proved, but from this day on, it is very unlikely there will be any further such incidents at Allenham. I daresay the guilty party—whomever he may be—has learned his lesson and will cease from these theatrical efforts in future."

"I believe you are correct," Willoughby said. With that he turned and strode out of the constabulary, not waiting for Jonathan or Bamber. This suited Jonathan very well.

The bustling Barton village square on that brisk autumn day could not fail to notice Willoughby approaching the constabulary, nor Willoughby storming out again in high dudgeon, leaving his two friends behind. Gossips, perhaps wearied by so many days of excellent speculation, had barely begun their guesses when Baxter informed his wife of all. Once she had told her friend, the information flowed freely through the streets.

Willoughby had feigned attempts upon his own life? Although no one had guessed as much, none were astonished, and a few claimed to have had the suspicion all along.

A few said they pitied him—that he had acted out of fear, and after his wife's death, who could blame him? But they were a distinct minority among the population. Most had darker explanations for Willoughby's conduct.

"Could it be doubted why he had lied?" these would say. He had wanted the constables to search for an unknown assailant, someone who wished for the death of both husband and wife. Why do this except to direct attention away from himself?

Gossip is happiest where it is most familiar, and so the tales comfortably wound themselves around the village's prior doubts regarding Mrs. Brandon. She appeared to be innocent after all, but she had been the cause of it—Willoughby's motivation for both murder and deceit. They had known she was mixed up with the matter somehow, had they not? It went to show how wise they were after all, how this much at least had always been known.

Juliet was heartily glad to see both Mr. Darcy and Mr. Bamber when they came to call at Delaford. However, she little expected how much they would have to say, or how astonishing the news would be.

"Willoughby did this himself?" Marianne's disbelief faded swiftly. "He did try to speak to me after his fall, and he especially wanted to know what I thought of the danger to his person. He is forever wanting sympathy, and as he does not feel the loss of his wife himself, he would search for another means of obtaining it."

"If he further wanted to divert suspicion from himself," Juliet added, "it suggests that he may know precisely where such suspicion belongs."

Marianne became very thoughtful then, and she found reasons to speak to the staff. Juliet privately thought that her hostess strongly suspected Willoughby but found the idea of his guilt to be distressing. How terrible, to think that one had once loved a murderer! How much worse to suspect that the murderer might have killed *for her* . . .

Mr. Bamber shook his head. "You have an eye for such things, Darcy. All my work did not reveal any telltale mark he had left behind."

"Willoughby left a trail," Mr. Darcy said, "but the clues were in his behavior, not visible to the eye."

An idea came to Juliet then, and she sat bolt upright. "Yet he might have left a mark visible to the eye."

"What do you mean?" asked Mr. Darcy.

She began, "The glasses of port, that night at Barton Park—Mrs. Willoughby's glass was not marked. We thought it a sign of Willoughby's innocence, that the glass with the poison was not marked. But what if he marked the *other* glass? He could have poisoned both glasses, contrived to spill one, and then swiftly made a mark upon the glass that was poured anew and therefore safe to drink. Instead of distinguishing the glass *with* the poison, he could as easily have marked the one *without*. Thus he would know which was safe to drink."

"Miss Tilney, you are brilliant." Mr. Bamber glowed like an oil lamp. "Why did we not think of it before? For if that is true—and my test definitely proves that the arsenic found at

Allenham was the same used to poison her—then Willoughby will be proven guilty, absolutely!"

By this point, Mr. Darcy, too, was nodding. "Willoughby would have expected the glass with the poison to be examined in great detail, whereas the other glass could be—and was—ignored. And a marked glass would be of no use to anyone but Willoughby himself."

"I shall go to Barton Park this instant." Already Mr. Bamber had risen to his feet. "I shall ask the servants for that other glass. If there is a mark, then we shall soon know with certainty that Willoughby is indeed guilty of his wife's murder. Darcy, you should hurry back to Allenham, to see whether Willoughby is planning to make an escape to London. He spoke of wishing to go to London this very morning, remember?"

Mr. Darcy frowned in dismay. "I came down late to breakfast. If he is planning to leave Barton . . . it means nothing good."

"He could get to London and, thither, anywhere else," said Mr. Bamber. "Who knows but that he might travel even farther away?"

"Yes, yes, hurry. How good of you to think of it!" Juliet showed him to the door, before noting with some surprise that Darcy had not yet begun preparing to leave. "What delays you, Mr. Darcy?"

"Upon reflection, I realize that Willoughby would not flee on horseback. He would take much with him, if he were leaving Allenham never to return, and so I think he cannot depart quickly." Mr. Darcy shook his head. "Nor am I eager to be again in Willoughby's company. I reported his misdeeds to the police, and at the very least he is humiliated and angry. At worst—"

"Oh, no!" Juliet cried. "You do not think yourself in danger, do you?"

Mr. Darcy seemed much surprised. "I do not fear for my life. However, I would say that I am greatly in danger of some very ugly scenes." His smile was crooked, and she noted that his eyes had again met hers. "Do you think me very cowardly, for wishing to delay them?"

"Not in the slightest," she said. "Stay here as long as you like, Mr. Darcy. We are always glad of your company."

Edward's letter to his family had been sent but two days prior, and no reply was anticipated for some time. So it was with great astonishment that Edward and Elinor greeted an express rider who appeared that afternoon, dusty, weary, and on a horse that badly wanted water, bearing the reply from his mother in Bath.

As Edward saw to both rider and horse, Elinor exercised her wifely right to begin reading immediately. She knew Edward would not mind her doing so; more importantly, if Mrs. Ferrars's words proved especially unkind or unfeeling, Elinor would wish to prepare him for them. As she read, she was shocked indeed, though not at all in the manner she would have anticipated.

"The good man is exhausted," Edward said. "Was my mother's message worth the trouble he took?" His joke did not conceal his uncertainty.

"Oh, Edward." Elinor felt light-headed and did not know whether to blame her condition or the letter, though she considered the latter more probable. "Her reply is worse than we ever thought it could be, far worse indeed."

He stiffened. "She remains angry, then?"

"No, no, it is not that." Elinor put one hand out to comfort her husband, as well as to steady him against the news she bore. "Your mother forgives you entirely, and welcomes you back to the family, and—and intends to visit us immediately."

"Visit? Now?" Edward's relief had hardly existed before being obliterated by indignation. "With you so close to—she cannot mean it. She knows of your condition. She would not."

"She would, and she will, and that is not even the worst of it." Elinor closed her eyes in dismay. "She does not come alone."

Jonathan dreaded his next confrontation with Willoughby, and genuinely thought him unlikely to flee on such short notice, but these were not the only reasons he tarried at Delaford. He wished to be in Miss Tilney's presence, without Mr. Bamber. Mrs. Brandon's distractions about the house made the present opportunity all the more pleasing.

"Has it been a great source of unhappiness, staying at Allenham?" Miss Tilney asked, with sincere feeling. "Willoughby is not very kind to you, I know."

"He has not been especially unkind," Jonathan said, "particularly when compared to his behavior while at school. Nor do I feel so much at his mercy as once I did. My parents swore I would carry fond memories of school all my life, but I feel only relief that they are ended."

"Boys' schools sound terrible," Miss Tilney said, "for my brother is always complaining of his. My own school, I quite enjoyed, though I only went for a year. Had I been obliged to stay longer, its pleasures might have waned."

"Tell me more of your school." Jonathan would have asked

her to speak on about that subject or any other, so long as they might be together in this pleasant way.

"Mostly I learned at home from my parents, who were as strict with me as any schoolmaster could ever be!" When she laughed, Jonathan smiled, though inwardly he thought of the times he had been caned for his peculiar habits. The masters could be cruel; they thought nothing of raising welts or even drawing blood. He doubted Miss Tilney had ever endured such from her loving mother and father. "However, they sent me to a school for one year so that I might learn deportment, and perfect my French, and have proper drawing and dancing instructors."

"I might have liked school better, had we had more opportunity to dance."

"You do enjoy dancing, don't you?" Miss Tilney said. "Even though it involves many things you dislike—strangers, sometimes, and touches."

She knew him so well! "The touches are sudden, while dancing, but they are not unexpected. Dances have patterns and rules; everyone in the dance follows the steps, and as such, it is a pursuit at which I generally feel myself at ease." The noise and bustle of dances—that was another matter—but dancing itself, Jonathan felt, was generally a pleasure.

"I wonder whether anyone will hold a ball while we are in Devonshire, though I suppose Mrs. Willoughby's death would make it rather impolitic to do so." She sighed. "How I hope Mr. Bamber finds something of use at Barton Park!"

Already she eagerly awaited Mr. Bamber's return. Jonathan felt a twinge of sadness before reminding himself that he could not properly court Miss Tilney himself. Yes, he could look into her eyes easily enough—he knew and liked her enough for that—but the thought of touching her arm, of kissing her mouth . . .

. . . which had always seemed strange to him before . . .

. . . did not seem so strange any longer.

Jonathan had never understood the appeal of the kissing, embracing, and other physical contact involved in marriage. Yet as he watched Miss Tilney, and remembered the warmth of her hand in his when they had spoken of Susannah, he began to get the sense of it. Were he to kiss Miss Tilney, to press his mouth against hers—

His pulse leaped inside him, and it took all his discipline not to gasp.

This, he thought as he gazed at her, more astonished by the second, *this is what they speak of, the desire to be near a woman.* Never had Jonathan experienced anything like this sensation. Then again, he had never before been close enough to any woman—either in body or in spirit—to welcome her touch or to look deeply into her eyes. They had all been strangers to him. Miss Tilney he knew, trusted, liked. For her, such feelings were possible. More than that, they were imperative.

I cannot abandon her to Mr. Bamber, Jonathan thought, though for all he knew, she had lost her heart to Mr. Bamber already.

Marianne's happiness at Colonel Brandon's return to Delaford was shadowed only slightly by her disappointment that Miss Tilney and Mr. Darcy should lose their opportunity of speaking alone. The joy of knowing herself absolved from guilt shone within him as it did with Marianne herself, the surest proof of love.

Her delight redoubled when he presented her with a bouquet of flowers. "Peonies?" she said. "At this time of year? Wherever did you get them?"

"The Whitwell hothouse. My brother-in-law's gardener has never ceased his labors there, seldom as the Tremblays have been home to enjoy its benefits in recent years. It seemed likely he would have peonies to spare." Brandon's small smile warmed Marianne through. "I strongly doubt Mr. Tremblay will ever miss them."

"They are so beautiful." How Marianne loved their pale drooping petals! She glanced over to see that Mr. Darcy and Juliet were much in conversation, and so felt free to say in a soft voice, "May I ask you a question, one you will answer honestly, from your heart? Do not hide anything from me, regardless of how much pain you fear your words could cause."

Colonel Brandon appeared wary, as well he might. "Ask me anything you wish. From you I will conceal nothing."

Marianne took a deep breath. "Your belief in first love is so strong that you thought it would prejudice me toward Willoughby, despite all that had occurred between us."

"You deserved better. Please, forgive me," Brandon said.

"It is forgiven already. But—knowing your own fears about Willoughby—do you understand why I have fears regarding your late Eliza?" Even saying that name felt dangerous, but Marianne plunged forward. "I do not blame you for loving her, even for *still* loving her, but I would be no true wife if I did not want my husband's heart to belong only to me."

"Is this what has tormented you so?" Brandon clasped her hand. "For there was never any need for you to fear, Marianne. I *am yours*, only and ever."

Marianne felt the last of the heaviness drop away from her. How wonderful, to discover that love could continue to grow and deepen over time, that it was no mere mirage of courtship, but a journey two took together, never ceasing.

The moment was interrupted when a messenger arrived

with a note for them. Brandon said, "I wonder if perhaps it is from Beth."

"Beth? Why?"

"As I went through Barton today, I noted much activity at her home," he said. "I had no opportunity to call and inquire into the matter, but I feel certain something of import is being done."

As the butler approached, Marianne held out her hand for the note, which proved to be from her sister Elinor. She stared at the words, little believing them. "Oh, no, we are to be visited by the Ferrars. The awful ones!"

Brandon looked pained, as well he might. Edward's family approved very much of *him*, as he was a prosperous landowner with an ancient estate, but the reverse was not true, for Brandon valued character beyond circumstance. "Edward's family? Who among them is coming?"

"Edward's mother, who has consented to forgive him, if you can imagine the cheek. And she brings with her Edward's brother, Robert—and his wife, the former Lucy Steele."

Although the Brandons could not but dread the arrival of Edward's former fiancée or the coxcomb brother she had married instead, both knew their discomfort could not equal that Edward and Elinor must feel. Brandon asked, "They will be staying at the parsonage?"

"So they plan, but I fear we must invite them to stay with us. The parsonage will scarcely house them, and Elinor needs peace and quiet, not—and what is this?" Marianne stared, hearing yet another knock at the door.

Rather than another messenger, however, it proved to be Mr. Bamber back again, and somewhat out of breath. Marianne could not say why, but she suspected he wished to speak to Juliet and Mr. Darcy without their hosts in the room;

regardless, she and Brandon needed to leave them to their own devices, for she must instruct the servants to ready Delaford, while the colonel wrote a letter of invitation he would much prefer not to send.

Juliet could tell by Mr. Bamber's eagerness that he had found evidence of note, yet still she could not but gasp when— moments after the Brandons had left the parlor—Mr. Bamber withdrew from his pocket a glass wrapped in a handkerchief. She recognized the glass immediately as one belonging to Sir John Middleton, the match of the one that had held Mrs. Willoughby's arsenic-laced port.

What took her breath away was the sight of a distinct smudge on the base of the glass. The servants at Barton Park would never send out a drinking glass in such a state. Such a smudge would have to have been placed there by someone else, and deliberately so.

"You were correct, Miss Tilney," said Mr. Darcy. "The safe glass of port *was* marked."

"From that we must conclude that Mr. Willoughby himself marked it." Bamber shook his head. "A sad thing, to learn such an ugly truth about an old friend!"

Mr. Darcy said, "Others must learn it as well, and soon."

Juliet asked, "Shall we go to the constabulary directly?"

Mr. Darcy seemed on the verge of getting to his feet when Bamber said, "I ought to have left the glass at Barton Park, not taken it. Now—now the constables could say that I myself dirtied the glass accidentally upon picking it up. How foolish of me! Yet it seems to me there must be some means of using this evidence, regardless."

"A test," Mr. Darcy said. "If Willoughby is shown the glass—"

"Wait! Even better. Not a test, but a trap." Bamber snapped his fingers. "I am almost ready to test the arsenic from the stables, to see if it is the match of the arsenic found in Mrs. Willoughby's glass. Thus far, we have kept the knowledge of this test from Willoughby. But if we were to let him know of it, let him think that I should perform it alone, in the greenhouse, late at night—and you, Darcy, tell him of the marked glass being in the constables' keeping—"

"But that would be dangerous for you, Mr. Bamber!" Juliet did not know whether Mr. Willoughby, having once killed for his freedom, would have any scruples about doing so again.

"Not if I have a friend with me, someone Mr. Willoughby will not be expecting." Bamber grinned at Mr. Darcy. "You will be there, ready to witness all!"

Slowly Mr. Darcy began to nod. "Yes, it could work. It very well might draw Willoughby out and force him to behave in a way that will incriminate him beyond all doubt. When shall we do this?"

"Tonight is too soon, and I will need time to plant the ideas in Willoughby's mind. That can be done tomorrow, so . . . Saturday night, perhaps?"

Juliet felt a shiver of both fear and exhilaration. The truth was near at hand. She said, "Saturday night, all will be revealed."

Chapter Twenty-Three

When guests are joyfully anticipated, they cannot arrive too soon, and sometimes it seems as though a thousand delays keep glad friends apart. However, when guests are awaited with trepidation, they arrive with irksome punctuality. So it was to be with the Ferrars and their arrival at Delaford.

The Ferrars had been staying in Bath, where Edward's mother had taken up residence in hopes of easing her gout. As her fortune and social standing shone more impressively there than in London, she complained of her ailment long after it had ceased to trouble her. Mrs. Ferrars had been accompanied to Bath by her daughter, Fanny, and her husband, John Dashwood, the elder half brother of Elinor and Marianne. Then, after some weeks, the party had been joined by her younger son, Robert, to whom she had irrevocably transferred all family property when Edward had refused to break his engagement to one Miss Lucy Steele—and Robert's wife, none other than the former Lucy Steele, whose affection for the Ferrars' fortune proved more enduring than any feeling for Edward.

Robert and Lucy's marriage had appalled Mrs. Ferrars even more than the threat of Lucy and Edward's had, primarily because—having irrevocably given Robert the money—she had nothing with which to threaten them. The past year and a half, however, relations had thawed. Robert had always been his mother's favorite, with priorities so very like her own, so Mrs. Ferrars's heart would warm more readily to him.

As for Lucy, her talents as a flatterer, tested and refined by her pursuit of both the Ferrars sons, were deployed at their full power in the hopes of winning over her mother-in-law. To a great extent, this had come to pass. Mrs. Ferrars would ever wish her sons had married more ambitiously, but she found it most pleasant to hear the endless, fatuous compliments Robert and Lucy paid her on every meeting.

One member of the family, however, would not be so easily resigned to the match. Fanny had looked forward to her brothers' marriages, believing one if not both would guarantee her connections to other, more illustrious families. Instead, Edward had married into the Dashwood clan—to which Fanny was already connected, and the wealth of which were settled entirely upon her husband and son—and Robert had married Lucy, a vulgar girl of no breeding and less fortune. When Fanny first learned of Lucy's intention to marry into the Ferrars family, she had given her a scolding the likes of which no scullery maid had ever heard from a cook, or even a criminal in the dock from a judge. From that day on, a deep enmity endured between Fanny and Lucy.

Both women wished to maintain Mrs. Ferrars's good favor, which meant each strove to outdo the other in their endless praise and obedience. This contest being very much to Mrs. Ferrars's liking, she made sure to switch her preference between them on a regular basis.

Thus when Mrs. Ferrars read Edward's letter and declared her intention of traveling to Barton, Fanny quickly said, "But you cannot undertake such a journey alone. John and I shall go with you, to see to your every need."

"It will be too much for you, surely, at your age!" Lucy was more than ten years younger than Fanny, a fact she often mentioned in conversation. "Robert and I will accompany Mrs. Ferrars, the better to help her to and fro."

"The servants will see to *that*," Fanny said, "and you must realize how inappropriate it would be for you to visit Edward. Whereas John so longs to see his dear sisters, do you not, John?"

Roused from his stupor by the fire, John Dashwood began, "Oh, yes, Elinor and Marianne are always—"

"Edward is my brother now," Lucy said, "no more and no less, and as we parted on the best of terms ever to be friends, I do not see what is so wrong in visiting him. I daresay he shall be pleased to see me." *She* would be pleased to see *him*—his wife all swelled up and probably ill-tempered, himself trapped as a poor country parson in some run-down cottage or other. How Edward would regret his loss of one so young and fashionable as Lucy!

Robert, equally eager for a share of his brother's envy, added, "If Edward is so common as to take offense, then let him bear the burden of it. Neither Lucy nor I have any hard feelings, however, so we see no reason not to visit." Precisely why he or his wife should have hard feelings toward Edward, Robert did not go so far as to explain.

"And think of your little boy!" Lucy said to Fanny. "He has had a terrible cold. Surely you would not leave him at such a time?"

Indeed, Fanny's son had been ill the prior week, but by now only suffered the worst effects when it was suggested that he had regained strength enough not to require cake and other treats to amuse him. Fanny had made nearly as much of his illness as her son did, in hopes of drawing on the elder Mrs. Ferrars's sympathy; thus she was now trapped by her own falsehood, unable to deny the necessity of staying behind.

"Lucy, Robert, and I shall go to Barton, then," Mrs. Ferrars declared.

Fanny showed her approval of this plan later in the evening by treading upon the hem of Lucy's dress, tearing the ruffle.

The next day, just as the carriage was arriving for the three chosen travelers, they received Colonel Brandon's letter urging them to come to Delaford rather than the parsonage. All were relieved to be traveling to a larger and more comfortable home, not least because each believed and, in fact, *hoped* that Edward's parsonage must be exceedingly humble. Although it was a long day's journey, they did arrive on Saturday just before sundown.

Greetings were shared by all—the Delaford carriage had fetched Elinor and Edward—and Miss Tilney was happy to be introduced to everyone, as well as serve as the stranger before whom Mrs. Ferrars would feel obliged to be polite.

Very nearly the only person of the Ferrars' acquaintance not present was Mr. Willoughby, for whom a trap was at that moment being set.

Jonathan did not believe in ghosts, but he could not help but think that Allenham had begun to feel haunted.

It was said that ghosts were restless spirits, those who could not feel at peace. Who should be more restless than a young woman who went unmourned by nearly all, and whom should she wish to vex more than the husband who had welcomed her death—and, as they now knew, had caused it?

Given the strictures of mourning, Allenham had fallen almost completely quiet in the evenings. The pianoforte would not be played (as much as Jonathan enjoyed doing so); guests would not arrive; some of the rooms went unlit at night by either candle or fire. A chill was settling into the very bones of the house, where it would lurk until summer came. Willoughby had settled himself into a chair with a bottle of brandy, one in which no one had yet been invited to share.

"You two are going out?" Willoughby said roughly, as he saw Jonathan and Bamber in their coats. One lone candle cast its flickering light on half of his face; the rest was cast in shadow. "Making merry with the Brandons again, I expect."

How could he forget Bamber's plans for the evening, especially knowing that the results might incriminate him? Jonathan thought, before realizing that Willoughby was most likely lying.

It was Bamber who replied, "I have my experiment upon the poison, remember? The one that will tell us its source? Darcy comes with me to the greenhouse to assist in my endeavors."

"Of course," Willoughby said. "Experiments." His expression could not be read in the uneven light. He had shown so little reaction to Jonathan's conversation about the smudged glass from Barton Park. It would have been enough to convince Jonathan of his innocence, were it not for many memories of school in which Willoughby had steadfastly, convincingly sworn he had not committed the very pranks for which he was responsible.

Upstairs, Jonathan heard footfalls and some other activity, which seemed to come from Follett's bedchamber. Follett had secluded himself within it nearly all day; they would have to hope that he did not descend just when they needed Mr. Willoughby to be free—to come to the laboratory and attempt to ruin the experiment—because they required this final proof before they could go to the constables and declare Willoughby's guilt.

"Darcy comes to help me with my work in the greenhouse. We shall not be very long." Bamber began toward the door, obliging Jonathan to follow. "After that, we shall join you!"

As soon as they were out of doors, walking across the Allenham grounds, Jonathan murmured, "Why did you tell him it would not be long?"

"Well, we could spend all night in a dark, chilly greenhouse, waiting for Willoughby to interfere," Bamber said, "or we could finish the matter and have done with it. We may as well encourage him to act swiftly." This, Jonathan realized, was a sensible approach. Bamber continued, "They are having a party at Delaford tonight, are they not?"

"For the Ferrars family, yes. I do not believe they consider it much of a celebration—more of an obligation." Jonathan had been made to understand the give-and-take of social niceties, including the need to be hospitable to even the most difficult family guests; Lady Catherine de Bourgh, who considered Pemberley "polluted" by the very presence of his mother, nonetheless arrived for a fortnight every year. (His mother sometimes said Lady Catherine visited only to search for signs of decay and ruin, which was when his father would generally look disapproving and change the subject.)

"All the better, for Miss Tilney's observations of the event will no doubt prove entertaining!" Bamber cleared his throat. "Speaking of whom—I have attempted to speak to her of my intentions, but I believe she is somewhat shy in much matters. I shall have to plead my case at length if I am to succeed. Would you mind terribly if I called on Miss Tilney at Delaford alone tomorrow?"

Jonathan would mind exceedingly, though he sensed he should not say so. But then how could he deny Bamber the opportunity? And if it were already too late—if Miss Tilney's heart already belonged to Ralph Bamber—then Jonathan would not deny her joy. "I suppose not. Or I could call later, perhaps, after an hour or so."

"Jolly good."

An hour or so . . . that could be as little as half an hour, after which Jonathan intended to outstay Mr. Bamber, no matter how long it might take.

Unless, by then, Bamber and Miss Tilney were already engaged . . .

"Well, it looks as though you have done well for yourself, Mrs. Brandon." Lucy smiled insincerely at Marianne as she took the best place by the fire. Juliet, in a spirit of self-sacrifice, took the seat next to her, the better to spare either Marianne or Elinor the experience. "Quite the lovely house you have here. I can but imagine what that mantelpiece cost!"

"Thank you," Marianne said evenly, declining the uncouth invitation to put a price on every element of the room. "The colonel had already made it both comfortable and beautiful before our marriage; I really had very little to do to make it my home."

"Humph." Mrs. Ferrars would not be so easily pleased. "The fireplace is not nearly so grand as would be hoped."

"I myself adore a good blaze." Robert Ferrars ceased even pretending to pay attention to his newspaper as he stretched his arms lazily, with no more self-consciousness than a sleepy cat.

In so doing, he nearly upset the candle being used by Sir John Middleton, who—as one eager for any and all social intercourse—had invited himself over to welcome the visitors. He laughed good-naturedly, saying only, "It is all well and good to like a blaze in a fireplace, Mr. Ferrars, but you come near to starting one with the newspaper!"

Robert paid this no mind. "Soon I intend to have our current hearth removed and replaced with one twice the size."

Edward asked, "Your house is very cold, then?"

"Indeed not," Robert said with a sniff. "I should hope we can afford to keep ourselves warm, even if *others* cannot. But I cannot abide making do with carved wood when Coade stone is to be had. Coade stone is the thing, you know, to be seen in all the smartest houses."

Edward replied only, "I cannot imagine worrying more about the wood surrounding a fire than the wood within it." To this Juliet had to stifle a laugh, and Robert did not bother to suppress an expression of disdain.

His wife, meanwhile, sought additional proofs of her and her husband's superiority. "Such a dear village you live in, Mrs. Brandon. So tiny! So rustic! Very cozy, I am sure. But will not your onetime beau live very near?" Lucy's show of innocence was so patently false that Juliet wondered at her having the cheek even to dare it. "Mr. Willoughby? I recall Mrs. Jennings saying he was to inherit an establishment close to Barton Park, very close indeed, and you are not so far away from that house, are you?"

Marianne maintained her composure, even exchanging a brief, amused look with Colonel Brandon. "I would have thought you had heard—Mrs. Smith died, and so he has inherited Allenham."

Lucy's eyes flashed. "So you must see him every day, or close to it. Do you find it horrible strange? I could scarcely imagine."

"It is not so peculiar," Marianne said, "as you must know, since you have come here to see Edward."

"Oh! That is a very different matter, for it was I who broke with Edward, whereas you—but I do run on. How are you, dear Elinor? You look most uncomfortable. Should you not be nearer the fire?"

"I am quite well, thank you, Lucy." Elinor wore a shawl

draped over her shoulders, which helped to partly disguise her condition, as propriety demanded. The room felt almost overheated by the fire, which meant Elinor would be obliged to abandon her shawl if she came any closer, exposing her state most indelicately. Juliet first wondered that Lucy did not understand that, then realized she understood it quite well. *However did Mr. Ferrars come to believe himself in love with someone so mean-spirited?* Juliet wondered—but as it was impossible to voice such a question, she would never know the answer.

The conversational strain already being evident, Juliet decided that she must draw Lucy's attention insofar as possible. "You have come from Bath, have you not? I have always longed to visit Bath. That is the city where my parents met, and so it should be agreeable to them, but they both insist it is not to their taste. I am sure I should find it to mine."

This played to Lucy's worldliness and thus proved an excellent distraction. "A very sociable, lively place it is, indeed! Mrs. Ferrars has taken a place in the eastern part of Bath—that is the best part, of course, where the smartest stay. You should not catch me west of the Westgate Buildings, I assure you!"

"I shall remember that," Juliet promised.

A stirring at the front door made her wonder who else could possibly be arriving. To her astonishment, Mr. Follett entered. As he was greeted by Colonel Brandon, Marianne said, by way of explanation, "Mr. Follett is visiting in Barton." (She did not mention precisely who was being visited.) "We were asked especially to invite him, and thought you would be glad to meet more company."

"La! You do not fool me," Lucy simpered. "To be sure, he has been invited for Miss Tilney!"

Could that be true? Juliet was confused until she realized that Mr. Darcy and Mr. Bamber must have made the request of the Brandons. They would want as little interference as possible as they laid their trap for Mr. Willoughby.

How Juliet wished she could be there! It seemed cruel that she should be a part of the entire investigation but be obliged to remain elsewhere as all was resolved. Besides, even a confirmed murderer made easier company than Lucy.

Elinor had endured the slights of Edward's family time and again; she had borne Lucy's exaltation even when it seemed the end of all her hopes. She knew her capacity for patience and forbearance to be greater than that of many, and often she had been grateful for that fact.

At that moment, however, she wondered whether that capacity had vanished, because the very thought of remaining in the Ferrars' presence seemed wholly unendurable.

"Well!" Mrs. Ferrars finally arranged herself in her chosen chair, motioning for wine to be brought. "I am most surprised to see you in public, Elinor. In my day, it would not have been done."

"I have kept much to my home of late," Elinor answered, refusing to even acknowledge the condition that had inspired the renewed connection of the families, "but I made an exception for you, Mrs. Ferrars. As we cannot host you in our parsonage, I could not very well refuse to greet you elsewhere, especially given that we are in my sister's home so very near my own."

"I suppose the parsonage is quite humble," Mrs. Ferrars said with a sniff. "No more than a cottage, I daresay."

"It is a warm and comfortable house, very much to our liking." Elinor wished she had brought some embroidery or knitting—highly inappropriate for a party such as this, yet she might have been excused due to the need to prepare for her lying-in—anything to look at besides Mrs. Ferrars's smug face! So soon to be a mother herself, Elinor could little imagine the hardness of heart necessary to wish that the dwelling of one's own child should be small and unpleasant.

She might even have said as much, had Marianne then not caught her eye. Her comforting glance stilled Elinor's spirit, then made her smile at the sheer novelty of it: Marianne counseling her toward patience!

To judge by the twitching of Marianne's lips, she, too, was amused that, for this once, the sisters had to play each other's roles.

Juliet, meanwhile, began to wish Mr. Follett were there to court her, as dealing with a suitor would have been infinitely more engaging than listening to Lucy describe her own wealth.

"Of course it is such a bother, trying to find good servants," she said, blithely ignoring the bored looks on Elinor's and Marianne's faces. "They will lie and cheat you out of house and home, if you do not watch them constantly."

"No one has any standards any longer." Mrs. Ferrars sighed. "I caught my lady's maid steaming the lace instead of pressing it properly, and indeed I set her straight! If I find more proof of her laziness, she will have to go, though she is the third I have had in five years."

"Do not you find it difficult, Elinor?" Lucy's eyes were wide, hoping to drink in humiliation. "Managing a staff? Though maybe you do not need so many at a parsonage."

"One servant came with me from my mother's home," Elinor said, "and she in turn had come with us from Norland. Her daughter and son-in-law have joined her in our employ. I am very fortunate in them, and in their great loyalty."

Juliet bit her lower lip rather than smile. Loyal servants worked for generous, fair, reasonable employers. Mrs. Ferrars's and Lucy's difficulties with their staff indicated that they did not share those virtues.

However, Lucy seemed oblivious to this fact. "Is it not burdensome, telling them what to do and when to do it? Why, our kitchen maids were not even beginning the washing up until the entire meal was ended! Everyone knows they should begin the first moment a dish returns to the kitchen!"

"How did you learn this?" Marianne asked, all politeness. "I confess, I have no idea when ours are washed, as I trust Cook to manage the kitchen staff as she sees best."

Lucy seemed agog at such liberty. "You cannot do that! If you leave them to their own devices, why, they will not clean a thing. They will merely wipe dishes instead of washing them!"

Although Juliet's family employed relatively few servants, she knew better than Lucy did. People who were paid good wages and treated with respect tended to do their jobs very well indeed. Their maids would never leave dishes unwashed.

Dishes or glasses.

Barton Park was a well-run home, even though Sir John was too jovial and easygoing to be a severe taskmaster. The servants Juliet had spoken to had for the most part done their duty admirably, with the footman's small slip the only exception.

Dr. Hitchcock had instructed the Barton Park household not to wash any of the glasses or dishes after Mrs. Willoughby's death. Yet shortly afterward, when she had gone with

Mr. Darcy and Mr. Bamber to speak with him, Dr. Hitchcock had said that he had sent word to Barton Park that the poison was in that glass alone. Upon receiving this message, everything else remaining unclean after that terrible night would have been washed up immediately—including the other glass.

The mark they had seen on the rim of Mr. Willoughby's glass therefore could not have been there on the night of the murder. Which in turn meant . . .

"Make haste!" Juliet cried, jumping to her feet. All and sundry stared at her, even the gentlemen huddled around their newspaper in the corner. "We must to Allenham this instant!"

The greenhouse at Allenham would've been tropically hot on a summer's day, and comfortable even on a bright afternoon in wintertime. At night, at autumn, it chilled Jonathan nearly to the bone.

Bamber had set up his jars and glasses and was currently fiddling with the oil lamp he had brought. "Someone, somewhere, should invent a sort of small portable fire, for experiments such as mine," he said. "I daresay the man who does will earn a fortune."

"Why do not you invent it?" Jonathan suggested.

"I mean to make bolder discoveries than *that*."

"Like your test upon the arsenic, for instance."

"Oh, yes." Bamber seemed curiously dismissive of his tremendous accomplishment. "Of course."

How modest his friend must be, to so easily disregard an act of true genius. Proving the link between the poison found at Allenham and that found in Mrs. Willoughby's glass would make a powerful impact upon any judge or jury. No, it was not definitive proof—that could only be gained from Willoughby's reaction to their test on this night—but it would be incriminating indeed. Add to this the knowledge that Willoughby had purchased arsenic before his wife's death, supposedly for rats, though none had seen them, but household poison would not have been hidden away . . .

No one had seen rats at Allenham, except for the one person who had complained.

Right before their visit to the constables, Willoughby himself had made it clear that this person was Bamber himself. Yet it was Bamber who had consistently held that Willoughby's claim of rats was nothing but a dodge, meant to conceal his true purposes.

But Willoughby had not been lying about his reasons. It was Bamber who had concealed the truth.

Jonathan's consternation must have been evident upon his features, for Bamber looked at him with pointed curiosity. "Whatever is it, Darcy?"

"Should not Mr. Willoughby have come right away? He ought to be in considerable suspense."

"You worry too much." Bamber seemed to consider the matter, though Jonathan could now perceive that his actions were in fact well planned. "Let me go and fetch him, then. Say that I have found something he must see. When he comes here, he will endeavor to destroy my supposed results, and you will be here to help me suppress him."

The chill had crept into Jonathan's bones. Even his thoughts seemed to have frozen, his tongue gone clumsy. He managed to say, "Would he not be more likely to act when the two of you are alone?"

Bamber chuckled. "Oh, I doubt it. He will believe that you have seen the results, too, and so will be eager to overcome you as well. In fact, Darcy, I know precisely how it will go. Willoughby will accompany me. Once he is in here, then, it is a small matter to tip over the Argand lamp."

Tipping over an oil lamp spilled oil everywhere, which given the presence of flame, made that a very dangerous circumstance indeed. Jonathan said, "Then the greenhouse will burn."

"Yes, it will," said Bamber, "with Willoughby inside."

Chapter Twenty-Four

The smallest changes of perception are sometimes the most jolting, because they reveal more sharply that which *might* have been previously noticed but was not. So it was with Jonathan that night, as he saw Bamber truly for the first time.

"You wish to kill Mr. Willoughby," Jonathan said. "And you wish me to lie, and say his death was but an accident."

"Ah, Thumps, you are too pure of heart for your own good." The strangest thing about Bamber's expression was the true affection within it, coexisting with chagrin. "Forgive me for putting you in such a spot. My first thought was to claim that Willoughby had attempted to overpower me on the way to the greenhouse, that I had been forced to protect myself by wrestling the blade from his hand." Bamber patted a pocket of his coat, in which he had no doubt concealed a knife. "But then you glimpsed my purpose—indeed, you cannot lie, you cannot prevaricate, for your features betray you at every turn. When the time comes, let me do most of the talking to the constables, will you? We shall say that Willoughby came here to stop us from our experiment by violent means. As we fought him, the oil lamp was upset, and Willoughby met the end any wife-murderer deserves."

"Mr. Willoughby did not kill his wife, however." How could Jonathan have seen this only too late? "You did that."

"It was an accident!" Bamber protested, sincere pain on his face. "Women do not drink port after dinner. It is scarcely ever done! I thought, 'I will poison the glasses, he will drink his, she will ignore hers, he will die the humiliating death he deserves.' Then the spill occurred, one glass was poured anew. Still I thought, 'What of it? Either he will drink from the poisoned glass, and all will be done, or his wife will take it, but not touch it, and I shall have to find another opportunity.' A month at his house promised many chances. I ought to have chosen my time more carefully." He shook his head at the thought. "The poor woman. She may not have been warm and tender of heart, but she did not deserve such an end."

This regret—genuinely felt, yet but a fraction of the agonizing remorse that ought to have accompanied any such action—shook Jonathan more than Bamber's admission of guilt had done. He had learned at Donwell Abbey that even such a terrible act as murder could be committed by a decent person, were that person sufficiently threatened; he had seen then and since the toll that this act had taken on Mrs. Brandon. She had suffered and would ever suffer for having killed a man even in the most defensible circumstances.

Ralph Bamber was not only a murderer; he was also a person almost completely devoid of conscience. He retained just enough of that vital quality to pass as a normal man, but the truth had been revealed too late.

Most of the party at Delaford had merely stared at Juliet when she made her outburst, and as she ran for the door, she wondered for a wild moment whether she would have to go to Allenham by herself. Mr. Follett had come on horseback—she had never ridden upon a man's saddle, but she imagined she could do so if necessary—she felt fear such as she had never known, but no power would hold her back from what she knew to be her duty.

However, Juliet was fortunate in that two of the company, Colonel Brandon and Sir John, had long served in the army. They recognized instantly the tenor of voice, the state of alarm, that tells of great and genuine danger. Both hastened outdoors after her, and within two minutes' time, the three of them were in Sir John's carriage, horses galloping toward Allenham.

"Let me understand you clearly," said Sir John as Juliet braced herself within the carriage—they were moving at such a speed that every unevenness in the road jolted them sharply from side to side. "I do not think I heard rightly. Surely it is Mr. Bamber who is in danger from Mr. Willoughby."

"No, it is Mr. Willoughby who is in danger from Mr. Bamber, and Mr. Darcy may also be at risk." She could not be absolutely certain that Mr. Bamber meant to do either of the other men a harm—but she could think of no other reason for Mr. Bamber to prevaricate and maneuver all of them into their positions this night. "It is Mr. Bamber who is guilty of Mrs. Willoughby's murder, but he wishes to see her husband blamed instead."

Colonel Brandon did not seem convinced, and she was not able, in the rocking carriage, to give as succinct an account of her surmising as she would have liked. However, he said only, "We will account for their whereabouts and safety. Better to go and not be needed, than to be needed and not to go."

"Yes, yes, thank you, Colonel!" Juliet shivered—she had run outdoors with no wrap or cloak—but the cold did not chill her as deeply as her fear.

"I shall now fetch Willoughby," Bamber said. "If I claim we need his help . . . no. That has never moved him before, why should it now? I shall tell him you have got yourself locked in. He will arrive to mock you, and then all shall be seen to."

Jonathan had no intention of lying for Bamber's sake, but he thought it unwise to say so at this juncture. He asked the only question that came to his mind: "Bamber, why? Why should you murder Willoughby?"

Bamber stared in evident confusion. "Because I hate him. I hate him as much as you do, and I have done since I was a boy—since the first time he tied me to my bedpost on a cold winter night by the open window of my room at school."

Willoughby had done that to Jonathan, too, once. He had been so distressed by the belts that fixed him to his bedpost that he had scarcely noticed the chill.

"I hated him the first time he lied to a schoolmaster so that I should be caned in his place," Bamber continued. "I hated him when he spat in my food. I hated him every time he mocked me, tripped me, cajoled the other boys into humiliating me. For all this I hate Willoughby, and as you suffered much the same, I know that you hate him, too. When he dared to invite me here . . . to pretend, after all he had done, that I was his friend who would happily overlook every one of his sins . . . that was when I knew I could no longer suffer him to live." Bamber scowled then, perhaps the first true expression of anger Darcy had yet seen with him. "Do you not remember a few days ago, when they spoke of tying you to your bedpost? I claimed that they had done that to Hodge in my year—not to me. And Willoughby believed it entirely. One of the most painful and humiliating moments of my life . . . to Willoughby, it was not even worth the remembering."

None of what Bamber said about the past was incorrect, except that Jonathan did not think he hated Willoughby. Hating someone meant thinking about them, and Jonathan much preferred not to think about Willoughby at all. After

Willoughby had left school, Jonathan had put him out of mind, rarely recalling the man until his invitation to Allenham had arrived. Bamber had instead dwelled on those old injuries and insults, cultivating them within so that they grew larger, thornier, more wicked . . . until they had turned Bamber into a creature even worse than Willoughby had ever been.

"You have developed no test for arsenic, have you?" Jonathan said. "Nothing that would definitively link the arsenic found to that which was used on Mrs. Willoughby. You pretended to have done so, as it suited your purposes."

"If only I were capable of such genius! No, no, you are quite correct, Darcy. The test was but a ruse. I apologize for the deception," Bamber said, "but you can perceive that I thought it best not to burden you with the knowledge. It adds a note of uncertainty to my plans."

Jonathan knew he had to be very careful with his next words. "What I have realized, others might realize, in time."

"They will not do so after I tell them of Willoughby's violence, and Willoughby will not be here to inform them differently," Bamber said as he walked to the door, and through it. Jonathan realized his intention an instant too late to stop Bamber from locking the door, trapping Jonathan inside.

"Again, I apologize for inconveniencing you," Bamber said. His voice sounded strangely distorted through the glass. "Though you hate him as I do, I could not be sure you would join with me in my plan. As much as I hope you will support my story for my sake . . . let us say, I feel more confident of the matter in a situation in which you, too, could be blamed for Mr. Willoughby's death. It is but us in this greenhouse, after all. We and we alone can say what transpired here. Should the two of us disagree, I believe we both know who will be believed."

The constables would believe gregarious, amiable Bamber before anyone so peculiar as Jonathan, which Bamber knew as well as Jonathan did himself.

"But I have faith that we will agree, when the time comes." Bamber actually smiled. "Willoughby and I will return soon, and fear not, I shall open the door before starting the fire. Otherwise, how could I make sure Willoughby is inside?"

Jonathan could not but note that Bamber had promised to open the door . . . not to set Jonathan free.

With that, Bamber darted into the dark. Jonathan found himself alone, cold, trapped, and staring at a flickering flame that would soon be loosed into a conflagration.

Could he not break the glass and free himself? The wrought iron bench, while not so heavy as to be entirely immobile, was beyond his power to lift high enough to shatter any of the greenhouse windows. Although the wooden tables were lighter, they were also larger, thus proving too unwieldy for Jonathan to heft through the glass. Tossing the Argand lamp would start a fire, potentially without creating any means of escape. Jonathan tried chucking a couple of Bamber's pilfered vessels at the windows, but they were so flimsy that they broke into pieces on contact while only slightly cracking the panes.

Two options lay before Jonathan. In the first, he accepted Bamber's power over the situation and Willoughby's fate. Bamber would—*probably* would set Jonathan free as he had sworn, and expect any version of events later told to reconcile with his own. Jonathan would of course then tell the truth and hope to be believed, though he had no great confidence this would be the case.

In the second option, Jonathan had to put his trust in Willoughby. That path did not strike him as any safer than the first.

Yet, unlike Mr. Bamber, Jonathan understood the difference between wickedness and evil.

He heard footsteps outside, rustling and crunching in the fallen autumn leaves. Both Willoughby and Bamber were laughing—Willoughby at Jonathan's misfortune, Bamber at the thought that Willoughby should soon be dead. As soon as they stood at the door, Jonathan shouted, "Willoughby, come no further! Mr. Bamber means you harm!"

"What the devil?" Willoughby, still laughing, stood before the door, but he did not open it. "Has Thumps gone half mad?"

"All the way 'round the bend, I should say." Bamber's smile faded. There would be no release now, no matter what happened with Willoughby and the fire. Could Jonathan make Willoughby believe him?

Then in the distance he heard a carriage, one coming closer very quickly, and hope rekindled.

"Mr. Bamber put his laboratory in the greenhouse, behind the house itself," Juliet said as the carriage finally turned onto the gravel path that led to Allenham, small stones spraying and clattering from the horses' swift hoofbeats. "Look, there!"

In the murky distance, one tiny light flickered. Even a candle could make its presence known on such a dark night.

"We shall go and talk with them right away," Sir John said. Clearly he felt Juliet was being very silly, but did not wish to embarrass her. Never had she *hoped* to be silly, but she now wished for nothing more fervently.

The Allenham servants emerged to help them from the carriage, but Juliet leaped out straightaway; this was no occasion for gentility. She began running toward the back of the house, calling, "Follow me, without delay!" To her relief, Colonel Brandon and Sir John did so, and perhaps one or two of the servants as well.

Ladies' slippers are not made for running across uneven ground studded with stones and twigs, yet Juliet dashed forward as quickly as she could, without the slightest fear that she would fall. Her fear for Mr. Darcy was too great to admit any lesser terrors.

Despite the given wisdom that two strong men of the military should be faster afoot than a young girl, it had been some years since either Brandon or Sir John had been obliged to move at such speed; it had been but weeks since Juliet last played chase with her younger siblings. So she had gained many paces on them by the time she came close enough to see two men at the greenhouse door, silhouetted by the flickering of an oil lamp. "Mr. Darcy!" Juliet cried. "We have come!"

"The devil—" It was Mr. Bamber who spoke, who turned to her in shock. Next to him stood Mr. Willoughby, alive and well, though even by the dim light she could see he was much confused.

"Where is Mr. Darcy?" Juliet pushed past them both only to see Darcy inside, unharmed. How grateful she felt!

"I am well," he called, though he appeared much distressed. "Beware Mr. Bamber—"

"I know it was he who killed Mrs. Willoughby." Juliet turned to face Bamber. "I cannot say what he intended tonight, but I realized it could lead to no good."

"What is this?" Willoughby's patience, never a rich resource, had worn through entirely. "Bamber? Why should he kill my wife?"

"He meant to kill you," said Jonathan, "and he meant to try again tonight."

Colonel Brandon reached the greenhouse then. Sir John, puffing a bit, came up behind. "What is happening?" Brandon asked. "What is the meaning of this?"

Juliet realized she would have to explain more thoroughly. "As you deduced, Colonel, Mr. Darcy and I set about investigating Mrs. Willoughby's murder, just as we did Mr. Wickham's. Mr. Bamber has been pretending to help us, but all along, he has been attempting to shift the guilt to Mr. Willoughby, while it belongs to Mr. Bamber alone."

"You have become confused," Mr. Bamber said, so earnestly she might have doubted herself, were she any less sure. "This business has been too much for you. Any young woman would—"

"Any young woman who *thought the matter through* would realize," Juliet interjected, "that you supported Mr. Follett's position far from the poison at the time when it must have been put into the port—but only because doing so put *you* near that position as well, and thus free from suspicion. Then you brought us what was purported to be Willoughby's glass from the night in question, marked as though to show him which was the safe one to drink from, but days after the Barton Park servants would have washed and polished it to shining. You were the one who fetched the glass, and thus you were the one who marked it, and the only reason you would do so is to point all suspicion at Willoughby. Once I realized that, I knew that your supposed 'trap' tonight could not be intended for the purpose you claimed, and no good could come of it."

Darcy spoke next. "Furthermore, I have learned that Willoughby only purchased the rat poison because Bamber himself urged him to it."

"What has the greenhouse to do with all this?" Sir John's thoughts, more accustomed to timeworn paths, had difficulty adjusting to this unfamiliar terrain. "Why the devil are we out here?"

"Bamber intended to kill Mr. Willoughby tonight," Mr. Darcy said. "The plan was to upset the oil lamp, upon which Willoughby would have been swiftly engulfed in flames. Bamber asked me to lie about it, to say Willoughby came after us, that an accident occurred. Once he knew I would not do so, I—I suspect I would have been left to the flames also. As we are upon the topic, may I ask someone to retrieve the greenhouse key from Mr. Bamber? I am very ready to leave this place."

"But why would Bamber want to kill me?" Willoughby stared at Bamber, who had gone very still. "He has always looked up to me so."

"'Looked up to'—!" Mr. Bamber attempted to strike Willoughby then, but Sir John caught his arm. "Who has ever looked up to you, you vain, selfish, cruel, bullying jackanapes? Who has ever known you without learning to despise you? Is there anyone? Anyone in all the world?"

As Mr. Darcy breathed his relief, Sir John held out his hand for the greenhouse key; Mr. Bamber handed it over almost as an afterthought, so compelled was he by his anger toward Willoughby. Colonel Brandon, meanwhile, took up a nearby cord to bind Mr. Bamber's wrists. "Sir John, you must take the carriage into Barton and find the constables. Inform them that their killer has been found, only minutes before he would have struck again."

Sir John opened the greenhouse door, and Mr. Darcy—finally free—came to Juliet's side. She whispered, "Were you harmed, Mr. Darcy?"

"I am quite well, Miss Tilney," he said with a smile. "Well done."

❦

The shocking events of the evening would have been enough to exhaust Jonathan completely, and yet the night was but young.

After the constables came to remove Bamber, Colonel Brandon and Miss Tilney urged Jonathan to return with them to Delaford, at least for the remainder of the evening. "Mrs. Brandon would insist," said the colonel. "The women will wish to look after you."

"Really, it is not necessary."

Colonel Brandon's eyes held a rare glint of humor. "It is necessary to save me from my wife, Mr. Darcy, for if I return without you, her ire will be great. I have helped rescue you once tonight; I ask only that you return the favor."

"Go," said Willoughby, whose voice sounded hollow. "Go. I—I am in no fit state to be your host."

Thus Jonathan consented to be taken by carriage to Delaford, where the entire tale was retold to Jonathan's friends and acquaintances, as well as to some rather ill-mannered relations of Mr. Edward Ferrars, who kept interrupting to ask who every named personage might be. Mrs. Brandon did indeed insist upon Jonathan taking a restorative glass of brandy, although the greatest comforts came from the warm fireside and the presence of friends, most particularly Miss Tilney.

Follett took all this in with ever-increasing astonishment. "I can scarce believe it of Bamber. To have done her such a harm—and her death an accident!—to not even feel remorse enough not to laugh and smile afterward!"

Jonathan felt emboldened to ask, "What was in the newspaper that you gave to Mrs. Willoughby?" To Follett's surprised look, Jonathan continued, "It was found among her things. At first we thought it might incriminate you, but we have been unable to discern its meaning at all."

"I sought passage on a packet ship to America," Follett said, "and I asked the late Mrs. Willoughby to join me, to leave her husband and come with me. I have family in the city of Philadelphia, and with the money from her trust, we could have built a life there, far from scandal."

That, then, is what I overheard when I believed them to be speaking of the Oracle of Delphi, Jonathan realized, but he said nothing.

Follett continued, "Wickedness you may call it, but I submit to you that my desire to be with a woman I loved—to give her the happy life she could not enjoy with her unfeeling husband—that it is nothing compared to the evil we have witnessed from Mr. Bamber. She lived not long enough to even give me an answer, so do not judge her by my desires."

"She would have gone with you," said Miss Tilney, at which Jonathan was nearly as surprised as Follett. "My apologies, Mr. Darcy, for not telling you before, but so much has been afoot! Mr. Follett, I was with Mrs. Willoughby in her final moments. One of the last things she said was that she must 'catch the fox'—and the *Fox* is the name of the packet ship next sailing from Falmouth to America."

"These were her final words?" Upon that, Follett could say no more. Nor could anyone else, for several very long moments.

Yet silence stood no chance against Mrs. Jennings. "Mr. Bamber seemed such a pleasant young fellow," she cried. "Who would ever have thought him capable of this?"

"Resentment is, I believe, a more insidious poison than even arsenic," Jonathan said. "Willoughby could be unkind, but his sins were not so different from those of any other self-ish person: disregard for the feelings of others, acquisitive-ness, a certain crudity of manner at times. Bamber hated Willoughby for those traits, so much so that he developed instincts infinitely worse than any of which Willoughby has ever been capable."

Mrs. Lucy Ferrars interjected, "It was me that gave Miss Tilney the clue. But for what I said, who knows what murders might have happened this night?" She clearly saw herself as the center of this drama, a notion of which Jonathan did not bother to disabuse her.

Mrs. Brandon took one of Jonathan's hands in hers while also reaching out to Miss Tilney. "Both of you have undertaken to discover the truth of murders to which I was connected. You proved me guilty once, then proved me innocent. Let us pray that is an end of it!"

Juliet, half in a daze, answered questions as put to her even though her mind was almost entirely occupied by the question of how she could possibly explain this to her parents. The next letter she wrote would require very careful composition to be fully accurate without bringing her mother and father to a state of apoplexy. It seemed unlikely she would ever be allowed to go visiting from home again.

She rose from her place near Mr. Darcy by the fire to accept a glass of wine from the solicitous Mrs. Jennings. However, that good lady's concern proved to be situated very far from Juliet's own thoughts. "You poor soul!" Mrs. Jennings said, shaking her head. "How brave you are, my dear, to stand here as though your very heart weren't broke in two."

"I am sure I do not know what you mean, Mrs. Jennings." Juliet's heart had been in great distress tonight, but it was in no sense broken.

Although Mrs. Jennings appeared uncertain for a moment, she then smiled and patted Juliet's shoulder. "Yes, yes, you make the best of it, and a good girl you are to do so. You will not regret Mr. Bamber long, I daresay! Not with your pretty face."

"Oh, Mrs. Jennings, I assure you, I had not thought twice about Mr. Bamber." This was not strictly true, but Juliet felt explaining in more detail would lead to more confusion than clarity.

Mrs. Jennings chuckled. "*That* is the proper spirit, my dear. Would that more young ladies had your resolve."

Amid the confusion and conversation, Marianne did not forget her sister's condition. For all Mrs. Ferrars's proclaimed concern for her grandchild, she had yet to pay Elinor any but the slightest acknowledgment, much less devote herself to any comfort Elinor might require. Determined to right this wrong, Marianne made her way to where her sister sat in the corner.

"Often I have wished I had you with me at Donwell Abbey," Marianne confided, "to comfort and console me. Little did I realize Providence would place us together when the next trial came. Are you very much shocked, Elinor? May I fetch you a glass of wine?"

"I am not shocked," Elinor said almost absently. "I mean— of course it is all quite astonishing, but at the moment, I find, I can pay it very little mind."

"What do you mean?" Marianne asked. Then, as her sister's

face tightened, resisting a grimace, understanding dawned. "Oh! Oh, we must get you home to the parsonage at once."

"Do not make a fuss," Elinor said, though it was too late. All eyes had turned toward her as Marianne helped her from her chair, and Edward's eyes had gone very wide as he hurried to his wife's side. In a tone of greater strain, Elinor continued, "If you could send a servant to tell Mama—"

"We will send our carriage to bring her from Barton Cottage to the parsonage right away," Marianne promised, flush with concern. "Come, let us hurry."

No one else in the room could openly acknowledge what was happening; such things were not spoken of in mixed company, not unless exigency was far more acute than it appeared to be. Yet all attention was on Elinor as Marianne led her to her husband, to the door, toward the carriage that would bear her toward motherhood. The murder of Mrs. Willoughby, and the would-be murder that might have occurred that night, were already all but forgotten, for fascinating as death is, it will never capture our attention so completely as life.

Chapter Twenty-Five

Though a child may be eagerly awaited, no woman can anticipate its birth without some measure of fear.

Everyone in attendance on Elinor Ferrars that day—her mother, Marianne, Mrs. Jennings, the local midwife, and sometimes Juliet Tilney—had known many women who had died attempting to bring their children into the world; those young enough to still anticipate becoming mothers knew they, too, would someday face this greatest trial. No other event in a woman's life was marked with such hope or such peril.

Elinor proved admirably prepared: she had set household accounts in meticulous order a few weeks prior, and she had prayed fervently and humbly for the protection of her child and the salvation of her soul. As Providence would have it, her person was as well readied for the task as her spirit had been—matters progressed at a good pace, and although the pain could not be diminished, Elinor found it easier to bear knowing that all went well.

Standing at her sister's side, Marianne could not but marvel at Elinor's self-control. She neither wept nor screamed, though the agonies she endured would surely have excused either. As much as Marianne admired her sister, she did not think she would be equal to such restraint herself. Yet her sister's courage, she *could* emulate—and she resolved to do precisely that when the day came.

Mrs. Dashwood showed all the fearfulness her daughters

lacked, fluttering about hither and yon, sometimes of use as a distraction but not much else. Although no one else in the room would learn it, her worries came from her memories of Margaret's birth, which had been far more dangerous than her children ever realized. Mrs. Dashwood eagerly shared many of her woes, but that event was one that she held close, in the hopes that if she never spoke of it again, she might forget. She very nearly *had* forgot, until the hours when Elinor passed through the same valley of shadow.

Mrs. Jennings proved by far the most capable help, as she had not only her own experiences but also those of her daughters and sisters to call upon; she had attended near as many mothers in childbed as had the midwife. Her indomitable spirit shone best in such circumstances. (Inwardly she did wonder why Elinor, like so many women, dawdled so— Mrs. Jennings had never been more than four hours at the task, which she attributed entirely to her own considerable will. Yet on this subject she kept her peace.)

As an unmarried woman not related to the family, Juliet would not generally have been expected to attend, and indeed she spent most of that time drowsing in the parlor, except when interrupted by the few cries Elinor could not stifle. Yet as night gave way to morning, both Mrs. Dashwood and Mrs. Jennings required a few moments' rest, and so Juliet came to hold Elinor's hand while Marianne and the midwife were busier with other tasks. Though she remained in the room only for minutes, Juliet was greatly struck—in some ways, reminded of the deaths of Mr. Wickham and Mrs. Willoughby. These were events that propriety could not define or dictate, events in which the weakness of the flesh overcame even the strength of the spirit. *We are creatures made of earth,* Juliet thought, *ever and always, and we are never closer to it than at the beginning of our lives and at the end.*

She had returned to her place in the parlor near an hour when the baby's wail first sounded. Elinor was of course not yet out of danger; already the midwife was pinning the window curtains shut, and the servants were sent to stoke the fire high, so that the new mother would be kept warm and safe from noxious vapors. Yet it was the end of the most terrible pain, and the beginning of happiness.

Juliet embraced Marianne as Edward went in to meet his new son and namesake. Marianne whispered to her, "You are one of the family now, I think."

"Then I am lucky to have two such families." Juliet, despite her weariness, could not repress her smile.

Colonel Brandon welcomed his exhausted wife and guest home that morning with an early yet ample breakfast, then sent them both to bed before the Ferrars had even stirred. Marianne and Miss Tilney had, he judged, been through quite enough without being forced to contend with that family unrested. Properly he ought to have awakened one of the Ferrars with the news, or at the very least remained behind to greet them with the information when they descended. (He thought it rather telling that, for all Mrs. Ferrars's proclaimed concern for her grandchild, she could sleep so soundly without knowing of the safe delivery. Her concern, Brandon suspected, was more for what others would think of her if she was known to have neglected a blameless infant, particularly when many in society had already harshly judged her treatment of Edward.)

Instead, he left a note to be read, should they arise before his return, and walked into Barton to see Beth. The resolution of the matter of Mrs. Willoughby's death would be known all over Barton erelong if it were not so already, yet he knew it would give Beth some relief to talk of it openly. He hoped that the disquiet she had shown of late would be settled now that the murder was also.

His hopes were not entirely sanguine. Beth's longing for Mr. Willoughby's attention—for his love—had never entirely abated. Although Colonel Brandon believed she understood the deficiencies of Willoughby's character, he could not say whether that knowledge could entirely overcome the effect of his charm.

We spend much of our lives fretting about problems that may never arise, and yet we so rarely anticipate the ones that do occur. Brandon's train of thought was entirely lost when he approached Beth's house to find all in a bustle, with furnishings being loaded onto a cart. He hastened inside to find her holding little George, as she gave instructions for the packing of the china. When Beth saw Brandon, her smile was sad.

"I meant," she said, "to write you afterward, when all was accomplished."

"'Accomplished'—you mean to leave Barton?"

"Forever. Here, both my life and my son's will be forever tainted by my mother's mistakes and my own. Let the Lord in his wisdom determine what punishment I deserve, but George deserves none. His future will shine the brighter if we step out of shadows cast upon our past. It is not immoral to maintain a deception that harms no one but acts so profoundly for the good of another." She smiled slightly. "So Mr. Darcy has informed me."

This surprised Colonel Brandon even further. "You discussed this with him?"

"Only the general principle. Not the particulars."

The colonel saw the sense of her words, of her decision, yet remained shocked by the thought. Could he not persuade her to delay, to consider? "But you will not go so soon."

"I have chosen my next destination, and so I see no purpose in waiting any longer. This very day, we leave for Scotland. Already I am sending some possessions ahead."

"Scotland?" So distant, so wild: What could she be thinking? "Beth, consider this carefully. You have a child and cannot give in to every whim."

"I have considered it carefully. It is not a whim; it is my firm, decided choice, and I know it will be best for me and for George. In Scotland, no one will know our histories. One trip to a jeweler will provide me with a ring, and then I am a widow of property. I think that I shall also change my last name. 'Brandon' would lead to misunderstandings, perhaps, but would you be dismayed if I chose 'Christopher'? You have always been so kind to me, and I should like to honor you in this way."

He could scarcely fathom her gone from him forever . . . and yet, he could almost wonder that this idea had not been countenanced before. "There are risks in such a misrepresentation."

"They are not so very many," she said, "unless I attract the attention of a man with an overly grasping mother, and those I shall take care to avoid. I have decided that my late husband was a sailor of no particular family who came into some prize money in the wars. When my husband died, I shall say, he left me with little George and a substantial fortune. No one will expect even a lord of the admiralty to know *every* sailor in the Royal Navy. If I require a letter of introduction at some point, however, I thought you might consent to write one."

Beth's countenance faltered, and for an instant Brandon glimpsed the fear she felt about this step into the unknown, the unspoken plea behind all her brave words. He did not wish to lose her—though not a daughter to him, Beth remained very dear, and she and her child were the last links he had to his lost Eliza.

Yet perhaps he should consider it differently. Brandon had taken a wife he dearly loved; the second half of his life promised far greater happiness than the first, if he could leave that past behind as courageously as Beth did. By supporting Beth in this endeavor—by letting her go—he would fulfill his final obligation to Eliza. Their relationship was at last completed.

"I would be honored to do so," Brandon said, then trying the name, "Mrs. Christopher." His reward was Beth's smile.

Although no etiquette book precisely said so, there was a strong sense at Allenham that the resolution of the hostess's murder would be the appropriate time for guests to leave. Jonathan arose with the plan to make his intentions known at breakfast, instruct his valet to pack that very day, and leave the following morning. As strong as his desire was to depart, Jonathan wished very much to speak to Miss Tilney before he left; that evening should provide him with the chance to do so.

He descended the stairs to find Follett's trunk and valise already in the hall, his carriage being readied for the journey. "You are going already, Follett?" Jonathan said. He did not see Willoughby anywhere; he generally did not descend for breakfast so early, though different habits might have been expected after such a night. "You have said your farewells?"

"Willoughby requires no farewell from me," replied Follett. "I accepted his invitation only that I might see Sophia once more—and I am glad that I did so, even though it meant

I must see her die. Every day since then has been a torment. Her in her grave, Willoughby without a care: it is not to be borne. And now bookish Ralph Bamber is proved a killer! No, I cannot see the last of Allenham too soon."

"Will you go to America after all?"

"I know not yet what I should do," Mr. Follett said. "I believe I shall paint the baroness before I make my decision. But a new country, a new sort of life—its appeal for me is as strong as before, though for different reasons."

Jonathan could not put himself in Mr. Follett's place, to imagine what his sentiments must be. But he did not have to; he had only to accept that Follett was following the path he must. "I shall be leaving tomorrow and will give your regards to Willoughby when he awakes."

"No need for that. Simply tell him I am gone." Follett appeared abashed. "Please accept my apology for accusing you falsely. After her death, I was half out of my head. That is no excuse, but it is the only explanation I can offer."

"Your apology is accepted," Jonathan replied. In truth, Follett had offended him more by calling him Thumps, laughing at him, and in other ways reverting to the spiteful schoolboy he had once been. However, Jonathan neither expected nor desired Follett to repent of that; the acquaintance was ended, for which he was grateful, and nothing else was required.

"Look at you, Neddy." Edward held his son with such pride that Elinor could not but smile. Weary though she was, despite every ache and pain lingering in her body, she would not have rested through this moment for all the world. "I believe you are to have your mother's eyes. Good fortune indeed."

"But your hair, I think." Elinor touched one of the fair wispy curls atop her son's soft head. "My mother has already discerned traits of every one of his ancestors on our side; even his ears and toes are accounted for. The Ferrars family will be hard-pressed to find any trace of resemblance remaining. I suppose they will come today to behold him?"

"Not today," Edward said with firmness. "Mother will demand it, but she has been told no once and survived the experience, contrary to her own expectations. She requires more practice, I think."

Elinor felt relief and concern in equal measure. "We have only just mended the bonds with your family. I would not have them strained again so soon."

"Nor would I. Yet more than that, I will not have my wife and my son"—Edward paused, flushed with pleasure at speaking this word for one of the first times—"bothered when they require warmth and rest. And tea, of course. Would you like more tea?"

Most new mothers took only a liquid diet in the days immediately following their lying-in, a common practice Elinor had planned to follow. She had not reckoned that after such a trial as this, she would be ravenous. For once, let convention be for naught. "I should like the biggest breakfast Cook can make on such short notice. Do not tell Mama—she will think I am abandoning all caution—but I feel that it will not harm me."

"Cook already made scones," Edward confided, "and I shall return with a plateful."

Beth had spoken with her solicitor the day prior, and already he had paid her landlord a sum that would compensate him for her abrupt departure. Colonel Brandon was entrusted with a list of other tasks to be accomplished after her departure. The selling of her remaining property was perhaps the most onerous of these; she regretted burdening the good colonel yet again, but having made the decision, Beth knew she must act upon it before petty fears could mislead her and erase her convictions.

As the carriage was loaded with the last of her things on that fateful day, she said to Brandon, "If I am found out in Scotland—or if George and I decide Edinburgh is not to our taste—we might always set out for the United States of America."

"You need not stoop to barbarity," Brandon replied. This was a joke, mostly. "One matter you may not have considered is your connection with the Darcy family. Mr. Jonathan Darcy was very pleased to make your acquaintance, and his parents would still welcome a chance to know you. If you wished to visit Pemberley on your way to Edinburgh, their son could write them, and all would be swiftly arranged."

Beth had thought about this before, and though the idea of visiting the famed house of Pemberley intrigued her, she knew she must not deviate from her path. "No, I think not. If they wish to correspond—with 'Mrs. Christopher,' of course—I will happily do so, and what future meetings might arise from such, I would welcome. But our acquaintance must begin after I am established, not before. You have been very good to me, Colonel Brandon, but all my life I have felt the lack of my own family, my own home. I have always been weighed down with my mother's sins, and then with my own. That knowledge shall *always* be with me, but I intend to see that George is not so burdened. He will have no limitations upon him because of his mother's or grandmother's indiscretions. For him, nothing will be impossible."

Brandon did not reply, and Beth wondered if speaking

so had caused him offense. Then he reached out to touch George's wispy hair, and she saw he was very greatly moved.

She ventured, "We *will* see each other again." So Beth believed, though even as she spoke the words, she realized neither he nor she could promise that beyond any doubt. How she hated the idea of parting from Colonel Brandon forever!

Yet if that—even that—were the price of George's freedom, then it must be paid, and Beth knew the colonel, no less than herself, was willing to pay it.

"May it someday be so," said the colonel. He embraced Beth tenderly, his arms encircling mother and son both, and for that moment they were more truly family than perhaps they had ever been before.

Sometimes, when we are most hesitant, fortune provides us with that which will most strengthen our resolve. So it was with Beth at that moment, as, over Brandon's shoulder, she spied Willoughby on his horse. Willoughby looked directly at her, and Beth knew instantly that he was in fact coming to see her. That he had something to say to her, something of importance, surely—

Something she had no need ever to hear.

Beth handed George to the nursemaid already waiting in the carriage, kissed Brandon on the cheek, and allowed him to help her up the carriage step. She cast one final look at the life in Barton she would leave behind, then called to the driver, "We are ready."

As the carriage rolled away, she waved at Brandon, who stood watching until they could see each other no more.

Marianne had arisen with every intention of amusing and entertaining the Ferrars family as needed, only to find them fully occupied in entertaining themselves. The matter under discussion was whether baby Edward's name was in honor of his late great-grandfather, in which case his name was a laudable choice and a sign of proper repentance by Elinor and Edward, or whether it was intended solely to honor his father, in which case this was but more impudence. Marianne gave no opinion but was privately amused when Lucy declared that she should indeed name her first son Edward to honor the ancestor she had never met, which her husband, Robert, did not like the sound of at all.

This diversion Marianne was obliged to abandon when Brandon returned home. She excused herself to speak with him for what she thought would be but a few moments, until she received the news of Miss Williams's permanent departure from Barton.

"I am sorry that she is gone, just after we had come to know each other," Marianne said, holding her husband's hand, "yet her choice is, I think, a wise one, and must prove beneficial for her son. She, too, will improve when no longer tried by Willoughby and the memory of his misdeeds. But oh! What heartache in leaving one's home and the people most loved."

"Her greatest love is for her child, as it should be." Brandon embraced her.

Marianne whispered, "Would that we could say the same for Mrs. Ferrars." His laughter was the silent shake of his chest against hers.

How much I was willing to surrender for love's sake, she thought, *when I knew so little of what love truly is.* Marianne wondered if Willoughby had ever known it, or ever would, but only for a moment, as this was no longer a subject of great curiosity for her. What mattered was that she and her husband were learning more of it all the time, and she hoped they always would.

Jonathan set out for a solitary walk in the early afternoon. He planned to go to Delaford at some point, both to inquire after Elinor Ferrars and to provide the Brandons with some relief from the more odious members of the Ferrars family. However, his main motive was to speak with Juliet Tilney.

His discovery of his changed feelings toward her was, truly, one of the most momentous of his life. Nothing short of solving one murder and preventing another could have shaken this from Jonathan's mind, and even that had only stymied his resolve for a few hours. Today, his greatest object was to ensure that his departure from Barton would not be the last time he and Miss Tilney kept company.

I could ask Mother and Father to invite her to Pemberley, he thought. That would be very bold—a suggestion that he and Miss Tilney were courting and that a proposal would be imminent. Jonathan knew he was rather young for marriage; society would have had him wait at least another four or five years before taking a bride. Yet women his age were often married, and were even mothers, without anyone thinking this at all inappropriate. If they could marry at twenty-one, could not he? (He had some doubts that his parents would accept this line of reasoning, and his father did not entirely approve of Miss Tilney. But Jonathan's mother was very fond of her, and might perhaps be persuaded to plead her son's case.)

As he walked up the hill that brought him within sight of Delaford, he again came upon the lively Mrs. Jennings bustling along the road, no doubt carrying news to and fro. At the sight of him, she brightened. "Mr. Darcy! You will be pleased to know that the Ferrars—our Ferrars, I mean—they are the parents of a fine strong son. Mrs. Ferrars, too, is in good health and spirits."

"I am very pleased to hear it," Jonathan said. "It is strange to consider that a night so turbulent as the last could be followed by such an auspicious day."

"Aye, aye, though I am sure Miss Tilney's heart remains very sore. For her, I think, it is not such a bright morning."

This did not sound promising. "Whatever is the matter? Is she unwell?"

"She is brokenhearted about that wretched Mr. Bamber. To toy with her so, while going about his wicked business! I should wish to box his ears, were the constables not likely to hang him first."

Jonathan's spirits sank. He had not spotted any signs in Miss Tilney of particular affection toward Mr. Bamber . . . but he did not always understand that which went unspoken. Mrs. Jennings had the superior knowledge in this area, and no doubt her insights were sound.

His sentiments must have been obvious, for Mrs. Jennings clucked at him comfortingly. "There, there, Mr. Darcy. You can have your chance yet, I reckon. Give her heart some time to heal, and erelong, you can press your suit far more honorably. And successfully, if you have but the spirit to prevail!"

Juliet's visit to Delaford was to continue some weeks, though after only one day with the Ferrars, she hoped theirs would not endure half that measure. Much of the pleasure of the house was diminished when filled with company with whom neither she nor her hosts shared common interests or feeling, not even true joy in the newest member of the family.

So, in midafternoon, Juliet decided to take a walk about the Delaford grounds. To her relief, no one asked to join her—a walk with Lucy Ferrars would have been onerous indeed—and Marianne gave her a sympathetic, perhaps wistful look as Juliet departed the house. After such a tumultuous day, she longed for nothing so much as the quiet and beauty of nature. Wrapped in a warm cloak, she wandered through the trees, their leaves resplendent in gold and scarlet. She was so rapt in this sight that she startled to realize a figure was approaching her, and that it was none other than Mr. Darcy.

"Miss Tilney," he said as he came near. "What luck to find you. I hear that Mrs. Ferrars is well, and delivered of a son."

"She is indeed. Colonel and Mrs. Brandon are delighted."

"And—and you, Miss Tilney? How are you today?"

"After such a night as the one we all endured, I hardly know what to say." Juliet sighed. "It is very hard, learning what Mr. Bamber truly is. How easily he deceived us both! It is both humiliating and tragic, that one so blessed with a fine mind and a good position should be completely undone by hate."

"It is very hard indeed," said Mr. Darcy, and how forlorn he looked as he said it! The one friend he had believed himself to have at Allenham had turned out to be no friend at all. Little wonder he should feel it keenly. He continued, "I hope you do not take it much to heart, Miss Tilney. It is not your fault that you did not see through his deceptions."

"Nor yours. We were both quite taken in." Juliet had thought herself so clever throughout their investigation, only for its conclusion to show her that she could still be easy prey for a clever manipulator. She added, "Henceforth I shall be more careful in assessing the character of others."

She would have thought that her dismay would be shared by Mr. Darcy, that it was a subject they could, and should, discuss at length. Instead, he took a step back. "I shall return to Derbyshire on the morrow."

Juliet hardly knew what to say. There was no way for their

acquaintance to continue, absent another happy circumstance bringing them both together. But how many such
coincidences could there be? Certainly Mr. Darcy had no suggestion or invitation to offer. Perhaps . . . perhaps he had not
greatly wanted one.

She tried to smile, though she suspected she made a poor
show of it. "Then I wish you all the best, Mr. Darcy."

"And I you, Miss Tilney."

So they parted—Mr. Darcy convinced that Miss Tilney
suffered greatly from the loss of Mr. Bamber, who would have
been her choice; and Miss Tilney bewildered by Mr. Darcy's
apparent lack of interest. Even such a small misunderstanding has the power to bend the course of a life. The courses
of Mr. Darcy and Miss Tilney might well have parted there
forever, had it not been for the extraordinary circumstance
that would, in the fullness of time, reunite them.

But they could not know this yet.

Jonathan remained at Delaford for some hours, though never
afterward could he recall much that came after his private
conversation with Miss Tilney. The rest was a muddle of
unpleasant relations of the Ferrars and Dashwood families,
of Colonel Brandon's interest in more of the details of their
investigation, and the warm farewell he received from Marianne Brandon. However confused his recollection was, contemplating it remained a pleasure, one he enjoyed in front of
the hearth at Allenham until, not long before the hour of the
evening meal, Willoughby returned home.

"You at least are still here, Thumps," Willoughby said.
"The others have abandoned me, or have been carted away to
gaol. That Bamber—of all the cheek!"

"*Cheek* is not the term I would have used to describe his murder of your wife," Jonathan replied, "though no doubt great impudence was involved. I fear I will not remain at Allenham much longer. My plan is to set out for Pemberley tomorrow morning."

Willoughby scowled. "Why should you do so? When suspicion is at last cleared from this house, and we may resume something resembling a pleasant existence?"

"Without an audience for your mockery, I believe your interest in me will soon diminish to nothing, and I have no greater inclination for your company for its own sake than you do for mine." This honesty was uncivil, Jonathan realized, but he had told, and been told, many lies in the past several days. He could bear only the truth, however coarse.

Apparently, Willoughby, too, was in a temper for plain speaking. "You despise me, do you not? You always have, only because I was all that you were not—popular with the others, liked by everyone."

"I disliked you when you mistreated me," Jonathan said, "but beyond that, I have not given much thought to you, and I doubt I shall do so at all in the future."

Willoughby's face fell. It was, perhaps, the first time he had ever encountered his own insignificance. "You can be most unkind, Thumps."

"I intended no unkindness, which is more than you can say toward me." Jonathan rose to leave the room; he would ask for dinner on a tray in his room. "One other matter, Willoughby—"

"Yes?"

"My name is Darcy." With that, Jonathan went upstairs, never to speak to Willoughby again.

✌

Elinor and her son grew stronger every day, and within due course she was able to welcome callers to admire the infant, who was of course incomparable to every other that had come before in the eyes of his doting parents and family. Even Mrs. Ferrars pronounced him to have her eyebrows—which showed remarkable discernment, in that the child scarcely possessed eyebrows at such an early stage—and gave every indication of helping him in his future.

Colonel Brandon wrote a letter of introduction that would explain the background of "Mrs. William Christopher," which enabled Beth to find a home in an excellent neighborhood of Edinburgh. Although she found the accent surpassing strange, she otherwise admired the Scots character and was welcomed into their society. One younger widower showed great favoritism toward her very soon, but Beth proclaimed herself in mourning for some months yet to come. She would not undertake another romance until she felt very sure of the character and honor of the man in question, nor until she felt that she could trust such a man with the truth of her past. That time would be slow to arrive, if ever it did, but she had come to believe it possible.

Marianne and Colonel Brandon wished Beth well in her endeavors but were happy to have no obligations outside their own family and closest friends. Being an aunt proved one of Marianne's purest delights, though this worked a greater magic on her younger sister. Finally becoming older and wiser than someone, even baby Ned, was the making of Margaret, who wished to set a good example. Within weeks, she had ceased some of her childish ways and begun maturing into the excellent young woman she would become.

As for John Willoughby of Allenham, he had an inheritance and no one of note to share it with. When propriety allowed him to find another wife, he would indeed seek one, but mourning would claim its due upon him for a long time yet. He had what friendships he had always possessed, which were highly reliant on shared shooting trips and the consumption of spirits. Those friendships were not enough to keep Allenham from feeling very empty. Willoughby attempted to say as much to Marianne Brandon once, not long after his guests' departure, but she had no time for him then, nor on any other occasion that was ever to arise.

Acknowledgments

As ever, my first gratitude goes to the wonderful Anna Kaufman, whose editorial eye has made these books so much better, brighter, and sharper than they would have been otherwise. I can't sing enough praises of the Vintage Books team who have helped through every stage of the process: Kayla Overbey, Julie Ertl, Annie Locke, Steve Walker, Martha Schwartz, Nancy Inglis, and Erica Ferguson. Of course, Perry De La Vega's cover design work continues to be a delight; Kimberley VanderHorst's sensitivity read helped make this story more authentic. Thanks as well to the Canadian publisher for this series, especially Lara Hinchberger, whose enthusiasm has made this entire process a joy.

Every single day, I'm deeply thankful for my agent, Laura Rennert, her team at Andrea Brown, and my assistant, Sarah Simpson Weiss, each of whom combine sharp professionalism with both compassion and wit. Thanks for keeping me anchored, guys. Much gratitude also goes out to my Patrons Virginia Davila and Elizabeth Stretz.

Thanks of course go to my friends and my family, even to Chief Household Morale Officer, i.e., Peaches. Above all, my husband, Paul, is always there with support, faith, and a sense of humor.

THE MURDER OF MR. WICKHAM

The happily married Mr. Knightley and Emma are throwing a party at their country estate, bringing together distant relatives and new acquaintances—characters beloved by Jane Austen fans. Definitely not invited is Mr. Wickham, whose latest financial scheme has netted him an even broader array of enemies. As tempers flare and secrets are revealed, it's clear that everyone would be happier if Mr. Wickham got his comeuppance. Yet they're all shocked when Wickham turns up murdered—except, of course, for the killer hidden in their midst. Nearly everyone at the house party is a suspect, so it falls to the party's two youngest guests to solve the mystery: Juliet Tilney, the smart and resourceful daughter of Catherine and Henry, eager for adventure beyond Northanger Abbey; and Jonathan Darcy, the Darcys' eldest son, whose adherence to propriety makes his father seem almost relaxed. In this tantalizing fusion of Austen and Christie, the unlikely pair must put aside their own poor first impressions and uncover the guilty party—before an innocent person is sentenced to hang.

Fiction